DARK RIFT

THE GRAY TOWER TRILOGY #2

Alesha L. Escobar

ISBN-13: 978-1481043991   ISBN-10: 1481043994

TABLE OF CONTENTS

DEDICATION
To my mother. I love you, and now
you know how the Story ends...

CHAPTER ONE

I carved the alchemical symbol for Fire in the waiting room's doorframe--a triangle. My head swam from the protective seal Nena had placed on my mind, but I managed to swat her hand away when she reached for the doorknob. I raised my trembling index finger to my lips in a gesture for her to remain quiet, and I charged my Fire symbol with magical energy, feeding it with mental concentration.

I unlocked the door and swung it open. The Cruenti warlock was gone. He may have worn an expensive black suit and appeared innocuous with his slight frame, but my senses had gone off and screamed for me to run. I breathed a low sigh and decided to obey my instincts. I rushed into the waiting room, my eyes on the exit just across from me, when something wet splashed onto my forehead. I immediately looked up to see the warlock plastered to the ceiling, salivating and watching me with his electric blue eyes. I swung my knife just in time to slice his chest as he landed on me. I fell into a roll with him and ended up on top. As I drove the blade toward his heart, he sent me flying backward with an invisible force. I crashed against a few folding chairs lined up against the wall and dropped my golden knife. I cursed at Nena in my head for having

1

invited the warlock in.

My head still throbbed from the mind seal, and I hardly had time to react when he rushed me and bared his elongated canines. I threw my arms up in a defensive position when he reached me, and he bit into my right forearm. I growled in pain.

"Morgan, don't eat her!" Nena shrieked.

I swung a left hook and nailed him right in the face. When he locked onto my arm like a pit bull, I howled and threw all my weight into a pivot, and we both hit the floor. He drew back when Nena screamed and smashed his head with a potted plant. He snarled at her, and she fell back. I rolled over toward my knife on the floor, grabbing it just as Morgan caught me by the ankle and twisted the bone. I heard a crack and screamed at the searing pain that shot through my leg. I used my good foot to kick at his face, which now resembled a rabid animal's.

The Cruenti crawled onto me and went for my neck. I held him at bay with my injured arm, and his swollen tongue, full of purple splotches, darted toward my face. I gripped my knife and made a few deep cuts into his torso. He shrieked and backed off to allow the wounds to regenerate. I jumped to my feet and nearly collapsed on my broken ankle. I eyed the doorframe where I had laid my Fire symbol and limped toward it. Nena stood in the little adjacent room, gripping another folding chair and using it as a shield once I made it inside. When he glided toward us, I released the Fire symbol, and his head lit up like a torch.

The putrid smell of burnt flesh filled the room, and he ran and jumped out of the waiting room's window. I cast a Circle of Protection around the little house and leaned against the doorframe for support. I still felt light-headed from Nena's mind seal, and tears stung my eyes from the pain in my arm and broken ankle.

"I'm sorry, Isabella," Nena cried. "He's been my client for four weeks and has never done that before."

"Are you sure?" I motioned toward my purse with a

weak hand. "Grab my satchel with the jade powder."

The gypsy woman did as instructed--and took a few crisp bills while she was at it. "He told me he's been a Cruenti for five years, but wanted treatment. He said that he was starting to change into a Black Wolf, and if Octavian can be a powerful Cruenti without being transformed into a Wolf, then why can't he."

"Well, he should've worried about the side effects *before* becoming a Cruenti." I opened my satchel and sprinkled the jade powder on my arm. I lowered myself to the floor and rubbed it into my ankle. The jade stone had healing properties, and I would purchase it in small quantities from time to time. It was expensive as hell, but well worth it in my line of work.

"He paid me good money to help treat him," Nena said, adjusting her ugly plaid dress. "He said he wasn't eating wizards anymore."

Cruenti warlocks made pacts with demons to obtain special powers, and they satisfied the bond through Blood Magic, where they'd feed on other wizards and drain them of their powers. The worst part was that in order to be initiated, you had to use an innocent person as a sacrifice. Some normal people were crazy enough to become initiates, or sycophants, because they wanted to gain magical abilities, even though they weren't born with any.

I closed my satchel and waited for the agony in my limbs to subside. "Nena, you can't treat or cure a Cruenti. I'm surprised he hasn't ripped your throat out and stolen your powers."

"I swear to you, I wouldn't have let Morgan in if I knew he would react that way to you." Nena half-heartedly offered me ten dollars from the stack of bills she had swiped.

We both jumped when the Cruenti banged on the window of the little room we were in. He called out to Nena. "I didn't mean to scare you. It's your friend. She's...different."

3

"Go away." Nena ran and shut her curtain.

"Send her out to me, Nena." We heard a crash against the wall, but he couldn't break my Circle of Protection.

Nena scrambled to her closet and pulled out a staff. It stood at four feet tall--the same height as Nena--and looked like a gnarled wooden arm. She slid her hands palm down and gripped the staff, and she raised it and struck the floor. "Leave my property, or I will lay a curse on you such as you have never seen."

He crashed against the wall once more and let out a strangled cry. Nena pounded her staff again, and what looked like lightening shot across the floor. It moved toward the window where he stood. This time I felt his magic, and his presence, pull away and leave.

I drew in a deep breath, and my heart thumped painfully in my chest. I rose to my feet and went for my purse, all the while glaring at Nena. Not only did she almost get me killed, but she was also going to make me miss my ride. Word had come that the Nazis were sending in tanks to Odessa today, and if I didn't meet my contact who could give me a ride out of the territory, then I'd have to scramble down to the port and ride across the Black Sea.

"I feel bad about Morgan." She mumbled something under her breath and took out a cigarette. She snapped her fingers and produced a flame. "Let me make it up to you."

"Are you going to give me back the last half hour of my life?"

"Well, in case you're interested, Delana made it to Baltimore. She has Agate stone."

Hmm, I probably would pay the other woman a visit. I would be on my way to the United States next week to be with my family. "Bye, Nena. And don't let Morgan come back. He'll probably try to eat you."

"So...what is it?" she asked.

"What do you mean?"

"What is it that makes you different?"

I shrugged my shoulders. "Maybe it's because I'm a

4

Tower Slave." I had always hated that epithet. People hurled it as an insult toward wizards trained by the Gray Tower.

"I think that's why you asked me to seal your mind. Because you're different."

"Nope."

She was correct, but she didn't have to know that. She shouldn't know that. I had her seal my mind because I couldn't let a Tower-trained mentalist go rummaging through my thoughts and memories. I couldn't let anyone know that far from being a "Tower Slave," I was actually the one person that the Order of Wizards had vowed to kill--the Drifter. They believed I was a threat, so I had to show them otherwise; I refused to spend my life hiding and running.

I said goodbye once more to Nena. I headed into the waiting room and out the door, mindful of a possible ambush by the Cruenti. When I reached out with my senses and didn't feel him, I smoothed my wrinkled chocolate brown dress and walked down the street toward the café near the opera house. I could already see a group of men with guns drawn, barreling down the street in a jeep. The Resistance fighters might put up a fight, but the city would fall quickly if the Nazis were already sending in warlocks like Morgan.

I made it to the café and ordered a coffee. Only a few patrons sat inside enjoying meals and drinks. The owner looked nervous because of the commotion in the streets and talked about closing for the day, but I paid him a little extra for his trouble. I also told him that I was a member of the Order of Wizards, and I would kill any warlock who dared set foot in the café while I ate. He added a free dessert.

I made sure to fold my table napkin in a French fold as a signal to my contact. In order to deflect any unwanted conversation, I slipped on the diamond ring Kenneth Aspen had given me. If my friends saw me right now with it on, I would just die. Ken had tried to propose to me in Paris, but I thought he was going to confess to being a traitor--and I

5

had used a spell that almost stopped his heart from beating.

Needless to say, it didn't work out. Sometimes I wondered what my life would've been like if I had accepted his proposal, quit spying for the Allies, and settled down. I kept the ring on me because a small part of myself hoped that I'd see him again; perhaps we'd reconcile with each other. I almost laughed to myself when I thought of the time he had invited me to dinner at a bar in Cairo, Egypt, and an angry crime lord barged in looking for retribution against us. Our date had ended in a gunfight and an explosion, and when we got away, he handed me a single rose, still smoking hot from the fire, and said "Baby, next time, you pick the restaurant."

He was probably on assignment helping the French Resistance leaders, or blowing up Nazi weapons factories-- but hopefully alone and not with a cute girl at his side. I swore I'd track him down and give him a piece of my mind if that were the case. Suddenly, the reality of my circumstance hit me, and I felt like I held on to a dream that would never come true. Ken had probably moved on, and I didn't know if I'd be dead or alive by the end of the month. Aside from Cruenti warlocks, I had to watch out for a special group of Tower-trained trackers sent out to hunt the Drifter.

I slipped the ring back off and glanced around the area. Other shop owners were closing up, and a few more men ran down the street with weapons in their hands. I didn't see anyone else across the street or near the café, but I could've sworn a pair of eyes watched me.

I shivered, and hoped that my contact would arrive soon.

CHAPTER TWO

I second-guessed myself for just a moment when the old woman's eyes glared red. It was as quick as a flash, but I saw it, and it made me wonder exactly what type of spirits she communed with. Anyhow, I wasn't here to ask about a dead relative or to receive a message from The Beyond--I wanted a pair of earrings.

"There's still some hot tea in the kettle, if you want any." Delana gestured toward the stove and then took up her mortar and pestle. She ground in her herbal mixture and muttered to herself.

"Your kettle's painted with Cadmium." I could taste the bitter tinge of the toxic metal even from my seat.

"Suit yourself." She shrugged. "It's good tea."

The folding chair creaked beneath me, and I decided to stand. "Listen, I just want the earrings. You can keep your herbs."

"It comes free with the earrings." She said it as if I'd be an idiot to pass up such a bargain.

"Fine." I stretched and sat back down. "By the way, I saw your cousin a few days ago."

"Nena? How is she?"

"She almost got me killed." I shuddered at the image of the Cruenti, Morgan, with his electric blue eyes and glaring

7

teeth. He had almost torn me to shreds. Why would Nena ever think someone like that could be treated or cured?

Delana could be just as disturbing as her cousin, which was why I made it a rule to never ask her about her work. Still, it was difficult to ignore whenever someone like her was "touched" by the spirit world. That eerie gleam in her eye, the bluish tint to her face, and her erratic mutterings all gave her away. When I had first met her and saw it, I nearly jumped out of my seat and ran. My head had been filled with all kinds of warnings about wizards like her, and when I had asked her to make my Agate stone ring, I felt awkward and dirty.

"The money," she drawled as she held out her open hand. She needed a manicure--badly.

I reached into my pocket and took out a few crisp bills. "And the earrings will work just as well as my ring did?"

She snatched the money from me and chuckled. "If you don't think so, then why did you come? Arrogant Tower Slave..."

I wanted to yank the crackpot's white braid and tell her to never call me that again. I swore this was the last time I'd come to her for something, but crazy or not, she was good at making charms--and she actually had Agate stone.

"How long do you exactly plan on staying here in Baltimore?" I glanced around the cramped kitchen and wrinkled my nose at the musty odor wafting from her living room.

She poured the herbs into a satchel and handed it to me. "As long as I need. In case you haven't heard, they're sending gypsies to places like Dachau."

I placed the satchel in my purse. My hand brushed against my golden knife, and I wondered if I would ever have to use it against her. Just because I bought things from her didn't mean I trusted her.

"Don't worry," I said as I watched her pull out a cigarette and light it. "We'll win in the end."

She coughed out a puff of smoke and muttered again.

"So, the Gray Tower finally cares about the world. They're going to kill Hitler?"

"I'm not with the Order. I'm with the Allies."

She pursed her lips and took her time with her cigarette, staring into dead space. "They train you...they own you, alchemist."

"Just give me the damned earrings," I growled. She had better not think she was keeping my money if she didn't have the goods.

"Here. See if you like them." She reached into her ample bosom and pulled out two perfectly carved Agate stone earrings. She set them in front of me and stared into dead space again, probably listening to another spirit's chattering. I examined the earrings to my satisfaction and put them on. Anyone with a gun would have a hell of a time trying to hit me with a bullet.

"Thank you, Delana."

I didn't think she heard me, but she snapped out of her trance and put out her cigarette. "Ammon wants to know where you're going today."

I felt a knot in my stomach. She spoke with Ammon the most. "I have an appointment today, so I need to head out."

"He says you're pretty."

I closed my purse and pulled the strap over my shoulder. "Tell him I said thanks."

"What was that?" She cocked her head to the side and strained to listen.

I stood and glanced toward the exit. Was she talking to me? "I said..."

"Hmmm...how?" Her stare went blank.

"Er...yeah...I'm leaving now." I stepped away. God, this woman was cracked.

She let out a frustrated breath. "I'm not blind, I see her...What?"

I turned to walk toward the door, but felt something brush my cheek. My entire body stiffened with fear and my legs grew weak. "Tell him not to touch me!"

9

She still addressed Ammon. "Mmm, tell me plain, or I'll banish you!"

Though no windows or doors were open, a swift breeze ran through the kitchen and the dishes shook. The kettle fell to the floor and the table made a screeching sound as it slid a few inches toward me. I opened my purse and pulled out my knife, glancing in every direction and then backing away a few paces as I saw her regain awareness.

She wore an expression of horror mixed with remorse. "Please, Isabella, take your money." She got up and approached me, balling the cash in her right hand.

My hands trembled, and the back of my neck burned. "Just keep it, I'm going." I unlocked the door, a little uneasy about turning my back to her.

"I'm sorry," I heard her say.

I turned the knob and flung the door open. I wasted no time in sprinting toward the backyard fence and hopping the gate, which was particularly difficult to accomplish in a pencil skirt. I headed down an alley toward the main street and flagged down the first cab I saw. I jumped inside and would've gladly instructed the driver to drop me off at the nearest bar, but I still had my appointment to keep.

I could already tell this wasn't going to be a normal day.

***

"So...you gonna eat that?"

I glared at the taxi driver in response to his round eyes watching me from the rear-view mirror. I reluctantly unwrapped the other half of my chocolate bar and handed it to him. "Five cents off my fare?"

"Sure!" The candy was already gone, and he was licking his fingertips.

"Can't you drive any faster?" I smoothed my skirt and tried to ease the irritation in my voice.

"Relax, darling. We'll be there in no time. Hey, there's the White House. Nice, eh?"

"I've seen it before." I turned my wrist and saw that it was five minutes till nine o' clock.

"So what's a doll like you doing around here?" The cab skidded as we turned down Constitution Avenue.

"I'm paying you to drive me down to the Munitions building, not interrogate me."

He shrugged. "Sorry I asked...just makin' conversation." Then he muttered, "And I thought the broads up in Baltimore were snappy."

"Yes, that's us. Snappy broads." What a heel this guy was.

"See! We got something in common."

I wish I would've slipped on the diamond ring again. I had no time for flirtatious banter. "So are you trying to ask me out on a date or something?"

"If you're available, baby doll. My name's Ralph."

I looked at my watch again. I was supposed to be at the Munitions building at nine. I saw it just ahead, and decided to just run for it instead of waiting for Ralph to find a parking spot. "Hey, Ralph, can you just let me out here? I'm late."

"But--"

"Just do it."

I handed him his money and grabbed my purse. I rushed out of the cab and wiped my brow with the back of my hand. I wished I had worn a short sleeve dress instead of a blouse and skirt, because August mornings could be brutally hot here. As I smiled in response to a few men greeting me in passing, I walked in through the front entrance of the building and inquired at the reception desk about my meeting.

"Miss George," the young woman said as she clasped her hands together. "I think you're supposed to be in the building next to us. This is the Main Navy building."

A couple of uniformed naval officers who walked by to ogle us confirmed it. "Well, I suppose that's what happens when you're in a rush." I shook my head and felt my cheeks redden.

"It's all right." She brushed aside wisps of her dark brown hair. "Would you like me to call and let General Donovan know you're running late?"

My face tightened. "That won't be necessary. Thank you."

"Then good day, Miss George."

I turned and walked briskly toward the front entrance, thinking of all the glares and snide remarks I'd have to endure. When you had the head of the Office of Strategic Services and three FBI officials waiting for you, it was a good idea to at least be on time.

"Miss George?"

I turned toward the unfamiliar male voice. "Yes?"

"Do you mind if I walk with you?"

I noted the naval officer's rank, and I said to the general in the most apologetic tone I could muster, "I'm a bit in a rush. I'm sorry."

"Don't worry, I promise I'll keep up." The burly man's freckled face broke into a smile, and he offered me his arm.

"Do I know you?" We began walking toward the Munitions building.

"I'm Frederick Raye. You might know my daughter." We stepped outside into the sunlight and headed to the adjacent building.

I smiled. "I might."

General Raye's daughter, Bianca, was my officemate back in London. We were operatives for the Special Operations Executive, one of the few agencies that really took a chance on female spies joining the Ally cause. When I had first met Bianca, I thought she'd run back home to her father after a week with SOE, but she had proved me wrong, and became damned good at her job.

He laughed when he saw my expression. "How's Bianca doing?"

"Very well so far. I promise we'll take good care of her, General Raye. She's a very capable young woman."

"Please, call me Fred." We entered the Munitions building, and he walked me all the way up to my meeting room. Either he was a very classy gentleman, or he really had something else to say.

"Thank you, Fred."

"My pleasure, and if you don't mind me saying, I'm sure Major George would have been very pleased to see how his daughter has turned out."

For a moment my mouth moved, but no words came forth. My father had been well liked and respected when he served in the military, up until he disappeared sixteen years ago. "You knew my dad?"

"I might have." He winked at me and knocked on the door. A short balding man answered and gave him a mildly shocked look--while saving a scathing one for me.

"You're late, Miss George."

"My apologies," Fred stepped in and held the door for me. "I was speaking with Miss George and I guess I held her up a little too long." He said this loud enough for the men inside to hear.

"Thank you, sir." I gave him a quick nod of acknowledgement and slipped inside.

General William Donovan, the head of OSS, sat at the conference table at the end of the room. His wide forehead and square face made him look sterner than he actually was. Two other men in the room, probably agents, were in one of the corners enjoying drinks with their backs turned to me.

"All right, gentlemen," Donovan motioned for me to sit at the table across from him. "Agent George from the Special Operations Executive is here."

The balding man grunted as he walked alongside me and rolled his eyes as he took a seat at Donovan's right. He faced me. "*Miss* George, I'm Special Agent Andrew Lainey...FBI."

One of the men who had been enjoying drinks came over. He had fair hair and a lanky build. "I'm Luke

Jameson." He shook my hand and took a seat next to Lainey.

"And I believe there are no introductions needed between us, Isabella?" Neal Warren came over and claimed the seat next to me. His dark hair was brushed into a side part, and as usual, his hazel eyes observed everything and everyone in the immediate environment.

"Hello, Neal. It's good to see you again." It was a pleasant surprise to see him here. Agent Neal Warren was my British counterpart at MI6 and had also trained at the Gray Tower.

"Agent Warren," General Donovan began, "thank you for the report regarding the progress of our friends in England. We're taking the attacks on our naval forces in the Pacific very seriously. I think it's safe to tell your superiors in London that they can expect OSS to continue supporting your efforts in Europe."

"Thank you, sir," Neal said in his British accent.

Lainey drew in a deep breath and ran his fingers through his receding hairline. "You do know that unless we officially declare war, we can only offer a certain level of support at this time."

Neal nodded. "Of course."

Lainey turned to me and added, "And Agent George, we've received your report on behalf of SOE. You've done well considering your obvious disadvantage, darling."

I bit my lip at the backhanded compliment. "Thank you."

General Donovan glanced at Neal. "Agent Warren, a rather...delicate situation has come to our attention. About three weeks ago an OSS safe house in the south of France was destroyed. Two OSS operatives and the host were killed, as well as a member of the U.S. Army who was stranded there. Only one person survived, and he's in protective custody."

Neal showed no visible reaction. "And you're telling me this because...?"

"Because the culprit was a wizard," General Donovan said, eyeing us both intently, "a member of the Order."

That knot in my stomach suddenly returned. "How do you know it wasn't a warlock masquerading as one of us?"

"The survivor insists this was no warlock. I don't know whether he's paranoid or just scared out of his wits, but he's not even giving us the details. All we know is that he said the attacker was from the Gray Tower."

"Sir," Neal straightened his posture, "I am here to represent MI6, not the Gray Tower. Perhaps this matter should be brought up with the Tower's emissary here in Washington."

What a load of crap. Neal Warren worked for the Gray Tower first and foremost, no matter who his employer was. I gave Neal a sidelong glance, and gauging the other men's expressions it seemed I wasn't the only one thinking this. I cleared my throat and spoke up. "General Donovan, with all due respect, I'm here on leave and would appreciate it if I were left out of this. If Neal...I mean, Agent Warren is willing to investigate this, then you'll have this solved in no time."

"Or, perhaps you can tell us what exactly the Gray Tower has been up to these days," Lainey said, leaning back in his chair. I was waiting for him to rub his balding head again.

I gazed in Neal's direction to see if he would answer, and then I faced Lainey. "I can only speak of my own experience. SOE has taken in several wizards trained by the Gray Tower to help counteract the Black Wolves. They...I would never do anything to betray the Allies, or my country." What the hell was this? It went from a debriefing to the Inquisition in ten seconds flat.

Jameson set his empty glass down and stared at Neal and me. With Jameson's lean frame and youthful face, his attempt to look intimidating didn't quite work. "Can you tell us what the Gray Tower's--"

"I'm sorry, Agent Jameson." I stood. "I thought I was

15

here to help you convince the president that we needed to join the Allies and help finish this war." I may have hated many things about the Order, but I wasn't here to be turned into a pawn against it.

"Take a seat, Miss George." Lainey's voice grew tense and he gestured toward me to sit back down. "You're walking a fine line, girl. Are you loyal to America? Or to the Gray Tower?"

"Are you saying I can't be trusted?" Did these men even read my report? Did they know all the hell I went through and all the friends I had lost?

"Gentlemen," Neal said, "even if what you say is true, it doesn't mean this murderer's actions were sanctioned by the Gray Tower. And unless either of us has a direct tie to this mysterious wizard, then it makes no sense to lure us here and compel us to investigate."

They all exchanged glances, and then Lainey shot back, "Make no mistake that I could have you arrested if I wanted."

General Donovan held up his hand to signal silence from Lainey. "Agents Warren and George, you're free to leave. I simply believed that things would go more smoothly if members of the Order were to investigate this matter. This war...it's got people questioning their alliances, their friends...even themselves. The world isn't what it used to be."

"I understand, sir," I said.

The Master Wizards may have sometimes come off as cold or disdainful toward the world, but they at least prided themselves on a reputation of being champions of justice. It also wouldn't be helpful to breed tension between a country and the Gray Tower, especially when the world hung on such a delicate balance.

Neal shifted in his seat. I could tell that he had figured out at least half the case already, but needed to hold back in order to spoon-feed it to the rest of us. Sometimes I hated Philosophers. "You think the murderer is here," Neal said,

16

"or is at least en route to the U.S. You've decided that it would be much more judicious for members of the Order to catch the culprit here in America and turn him in so that the Gray Tower would be forced to recognize the crime and prosecute the murderer under Tower law. You want to avoid open conflict with the Order--that is a wise decision."

Lainey said in a low voice to General Donovan, "Watch it, now. This Brit here is one of those wizards who likes to mess with your mind."

Neal wasn't a mentalist, but I doubted the distinction mattered to Lainey who probably disliked anyone with a head full of hair. As a Philosopher, Neal could prognosticate or project others' actions based on mathematics, logic, and an understanding of human nature. He also dabbled in enchantments.

In any case, I've had enough and was too irritated to listen to the men's solicitations any further. I wanted to go home. "Well, I'm sure Agent Warren will take care of your rogue wizard. I apologize, but I don't think this investigation is for me."

General Donovan sighed. "Are you sure, Agent George?"

"Why do you want us specifically?" I glanced at Neal and wondered why he even entertained the idea of us hunting for a crazy wizard.

The general gazed straight into my eyes from across the table. "I think you can help...Neal too. I've known him for a while now, and based on your SOE file, you've proven yourself very capable. I respect what you do."

"Yeah, despite my *obvious* disadvantage." I crossed my arms.

"I told you they wouldn't help," Lainey said to General Donovan.

"On the contrary," Neal said, "I'll start today."

"Well, I'm not." I shook my head and rose from my seat. I headed toward the door.

"Your father would've helped..." The general caught my

17

attention and gave me that piercing gaze again.

"And where is my father now?" I opened the door and gave them all one last indignant look when that jerk Lainey addressed me.

"If you won't do it for us, then at least do it for Kenneth Aspen."

I paused, though I knew I'd hate myself later for doing so. "What are you talking about?"

Lainey waited until I had come back in and stood next to my seat. He answered, "One of the OSS operatives killed in that safe house was Kenneth Aspen. We figured you two must've been pretty close...he willed half of his possessions to you."

My stomach tightened and I sucked in a painful breath. It took all my strength not to crumble in front of these men. I tried to process what Lainey just told me, and it felt unreal; I told myself this must be a mistake. Though Ken and I had parted under less than desirable circumstances, it wouldn't have stopped us from caring about one another. And now? I'd never be able to make anything right with him. How was I supposed to be able to pick the next restaurant if he weren't even here in the world with me?

I heard Neal's familiar British accent, though it seemed far away. "I'm sorry, Isabella."

I grew cold, and faced Lainey with his balding head and imagined a target right on it. "Don't you think you should've told me this sooner?"

Lainey sat in his chair looking uneasy, while Jameson stood and towered over us, offering an apology. General Donovan cleared his throat and spoke. "You have our condolences, Miss George."

I really didn't care whether or not the general was sincere. "When can I talk to the survivor?"

"I'll send Jameson and Lainey around this time tomorrow morning to pick you up from your hotel room. They're the lead agents on this investigation, and I thought it would be helpful for you to get acquainted with them."

Oh, I was acquainted with them all right. There was no way I was going to work with these FBI agents. I turned to face Neal. "Are you at the Henley hotel too?"

He shook his head. "But I'll meet you there in the morning. Please, let me walk you out."

As soon as we stepped out of the room and walked down the hall a few paces, my eyes burned with tears, but I still wouldn't let them fall. My body was hurting all over. "They could've told me about Ken at the beginning."

"They should have," Neal said. The last time Neal and I were in each other's company, I had told him about Ken and the whole botched marriage proposal. He said it was fascinating.

I thought about the men in the meeting and directed all my resentment toward them--especially Lainey. While they probably didn't know about my romance with Ken, they were at least aware that we had crossed paths in Europe and had gone on a couple of missions together. They were probably saving the news of Ken's death for last, to ensure that I'd agree to help investigate. But why me? And what would make them think I'd help after how they've treated me?

"Whoever did this," I said to Neal, "I'm going to find him." I couldn't say whether or not I'd bring him to justice or kill him, though to be honest in that moment I felt like they were one and the same.

Neal pulled out a handkerchief and handed it to me. "All by yourself? I think not."

I shuddered as I dabbed my cheeks and wiped my nose. "They can all go to hell. They knew what happened to Ken and they brought me in there--"

"You'll need the FBI agents' cooperation if you want access to the survivor, and their resources."

"I can do this on my own..."

He pulled my Agate stone ring from his pocket, the one I had given Brande. I was surprised to see that he had it. I had told Brande that if he ever needed to send a message to

19

me, that he should send the ring. I left it with Brande in France when I convinced him to return to the Gray Tower and work on helping me from the inside. He was one of the seven trackers commissioned to hunt the Drifter--which everyone believed was my father. The Agate stone ring represented the pact Brande and I made, and I could taste the essence of the silver the stone was set in, and even detect a faint trace of Brande's scent.

"Brande told me everything," Neal said, "and asked that I look after you for a while." He pressed the ring into my hand. "Is that acceptable?"

I nodded. "All right."

"I'll see you in the morning." He gave a soft smile.

"Bye, Neal."

He left in the opposite direction, and as I walked down the hallway, I instinctively grasped the diamond ring Ken had left me, bitterly telling myself that he would've been alive if I hadn't botched his proposal. This morning I had hung it on a thin silver chain around my neck. I would have to take it off once I returned to London for assignment, but at least for now I'd keep it on me. I slipped the Agate stone ring onto my finger, and was almost to the door that led to the stairwell when I noticed one of the name placards on an office door: ROBERT CAMBRIA. He knew my father, and maybe even still kept in contact with him. I calmed myself and went for the door, and gave a timid knock. I heard a muffled voice on the other side telling me to enter.

I opened the door and stepped halfway in when I saw a man no older than me sitting behind the desk. He had cropped jet-black hair and a muscular build. "I'm sorry," I said, expecting to find a man who would be older and grayer. "I was looking for the general."

"Isabella?" He smiled. "Is that you?"

I closed the door behind me and stood in shock as he came around to embrace me. "Rob?"

He gave me a hug and then took a step back to look me up and down. "Every now and then someone wanders in here looking for Robert Sr. I'm guessing you were too."

"I saw the name placard and just remembered him. How is your father?"

"He's well," he said, reaching into his desk. "He retired a few years back and lives up in Boston."

He pulled out a pen and sheet of paper, and began scribbling. I noticed a framed picture of him and his wife and young son on his desk. I felt ill to my stomach and wanted to weep. I didn't want to cry in front of Rob and have to start explaining everything, so I kept telling myself that if I could just make it back to my hotel room, then I'd be okay.

"So...you have a family?" I accepted the note from him. It had his father's phone number and address.

"Yes, and another addition arriving soon. How about you?"

"No such luck as of yet." I gave a weak smile. "They're beautiful...congratulations."

"Thanks," he came around and sat on the edge of his desk. "How's Johnnie and your mother?"

"They're well. I'll actually be going home to them tomorrow or Wednesday. There were just some things I had to take care of with OSS."

"That sounds swell. Hey, I heard you went to the Gray Tower...so is that like the Freemasons but with magic?"

I smiled and shook my head. "No, but I was only there for a few years. They trained me as an alchemist."

When an awkward silence fell between us, he said, "Well, I'll have to call on you sometime and invite you to dinner with us."

"That...sounds nice." I slipped the note into my purse.

"It's good to see you again." He smiled with that same cheerful expression I remembered from long ago.

"You too, Rob. Take care." I gave him a peck on the cheek and turned toward the door. I paused when he called out to me.

"Just a second," he said, reaching into his desk again. He

pulled out a small key and handed it to me. "I know this may sound crazy, but my father left this with me the day he retired. He said you'd come for it."

"What does it--"

"I've tried everything around the old house, the garage...everything. I don't know what it unlocks. And the odd thing is, he said your father asked him to do this, but didn't Carson pass away when we were kids?"

He looked like he wanted to ask me to explain all this, but I didn't even know myself. I wasn't sure what to say about it, so I just told him, "Johnnie and my mom are up in Cambridge, so I'll pay your father a visit this week. Maybe he can tell me what this is about."

"Well, let me know what he says, and if you need anything--"

"No, Rob...you've done enough. Thank you."

I didn't want him to ask more questions, and I especially didn't want him getting involved. The last thing I needed was to worry about whether or not Robert would get himself killed trying to help me. I left his office and headed downstairs, picking up my pace when I looked through the front windows and spotted that guy Ralph in his taxi. I rushed outside and caught his attention; I slid into the back seat with a low groan. I wanted to leave Constitution Avenue as fast as I could.

"Where do you want to go now, baby doll?"

"The Henley Park hotel. I'll pay extra if you get me there quickly."

"You got it."

I felt ill again and hid my face in the handkerchief and softly sobbed. I guess I couldn't hold out until I made it to my hotel room. Even though I kept telling myself that there was no way I could've known, and there was nothing I could've done, the same gut-wrenching accusation kept burning in my mind--I was responsible for Ken's death...he needlessly died because of me.

CHAPTER THREE

After a lonely night of dinner and drinks at the hotel bar, I stumbled into my room and went to bed. I didn't dream, thank goodness, but during my sleep I'd have vague images and flashes of memories of Ken and me. I missed him, and I knew that the only way I'd find closure was to catch the wizard who had killed him and deliver him up to punishment by the Gray Tower. But what if it was someone high-ranking, like Leto Priya, the Master Mentalist? I remembered what Brande had once said, that Master Priya did terrible things to get what he wanted. But Priya knew nothing of my personal life, though he did pry into my mind once when I had finally reunited with my father in France. Priya wouldn't have known about my relationship with Ken and I didn't think Priya would go out of his way to do him harm...or would he? General Donovan said the murderer wiped out the entire safe house, and so far I still didn't see any connection to me except that one of the people in that house was Ken Aspen.

Sunlight hit my face to alert me to the start of a new day. I opened my eyes and slid across the bed to take a look at the clock on the nightstand. Lainey and Jameson would be here at nine, and Neal probably a little earlier than that. I had about an hour to get ready, and used the time to bathe and change clothes. I wasn't hungry, so I just drank a cup of tea.

The phone ringing had startled me, but I quickly ran over to it and answered. The tightness in my facial features eased at the sound of Ian's voice after the operator connected us. "It's good to hear from you," I said in response to his greeting.

"Likewise," he said. "How is your five-month leave so far?"

I sighed. "It just started, and already it's going horribly."

"I knew it. Your mother's too overbearing and Jonathan simply does not make a suitable older brother." Ian was the one responsible for recruiting me to SOE, and was also my handler. He encouraged me when I stumbled, set me straight when I needed it, and put up with all my faults. If my real brother, Johnnie, knew what I really did for a living, I always imagined our relationship would be like the one I had with Ian.

I snorted a laugh at his comment. "I'm going to tell Johnnie one day about you trying to steal me away."

He chuckled. "Now what's gotten you into such a sour mood?"

I fidgeted as if we were standing face to face and I had to explain all this in person. "We have...an issue with the Gray Tower."

"That's nothing new."

"This time it's very personal, Ian." The back of my mouth felt dry and ached as I held back a sob.

He seemed to pause, and I heard his breath. "Whatever it is, be safe about it. Be smart about it."

Ian knew enough about the Gray Tower to know that it wasn't to be trifled with, and I appreciated that he knew enough about me to understand that I would only hold back details to either protect someone or because I was still sorting through them myself. Sometimes I secretly wished that he really were my brother. Then at least I would have someone from the family I could talk to about all these things without lying or being evasive.

"Thank you," I said.

"Let me know if I can help, Isabella."

"I will. I'll speak with you later." I hung up and went for another cup of tea. The exhaustion pinched my shoulders and made my back ache.

At around 8:30 a.m. I heard a knock on the door. I had just finished pinning my hair back into a low chignon style in front of the full-length mirror. I wore low-heeled shoes, a black skirt and white button-down shirt; it would be another hot and humid day, and I decided to forego wearing a jacket. Today the diamond ring and Agate stone ring hung on the chain, tucked away beneath my high collar, and I wore the Agate stone earrings I had bought from Delana yesterday. The only ring I wore on my finger was the gold talisman ring with the engraved image of an owl. I had unofficially inherited it from my father's friend, Veit Heilwig. It protected against any body magic another wizard would attempt on me.

I went over and answered the door--it was Neal, as expected. He wore a dark gray suit. "Come in," I said, my throat feeling scratchy.

"Good morning," he said. He went over to the carafe sitting on a small table in the room and poured some water and drank it down. "How do you feel this morning?"

"I'm functioning."

"Are you going to want a weapon issued to you?"

"No," I said, thinking of how I wouldn't want to get caught doing anything stupid with a government-issued gun--not that I would do anything stupid.

He approached me and placed the palm of his hand against my cheek. It wasn't an affectionate gesture, but it felt more like something your mom would do when trying to assess if you had a fever and needed to head back to bed. He sent a tendril of energy through me, searching for any signs of distress or plain lunacy. "Truthfully...how are you?"

"I'm fine." I pulled his hand away before he could read

25

me any further.

Since the day we met, he kept insisting I had a powerful enchantment placed on me--which I did, but no one else seemed to pick up on it except him. I really wished he would just shut up about it. He could never pinpoint the spell or what it did, and when I had unlocked my memories and found out I was the Drifter, something changed in me. I confused him, and he couldn't read me as easily as other people. So, naturally I became an interesting riddle to solve--which was dangerous, because Philosophers loved solving riddles.

Lainey opened the door and poked his balding head in. He didn't even bother to knock. "Rise and shine, sweetheart. Are we ready to go, or do you need another hour to get dolled up?"

"I'm ready," I said in a stiff voice as I grabbed my purse.

Jameson entered. His shirt hung a little loose on his lanky frame. "Good morning, Warren...George." Jameson regarded me with a smile. I could tell he was trying to make up for yesterday.

"Hi, Jameson. You can just call me Isabella." I may have wanted to be treated fairly and as an equal member of the team, but I'd be damned if I went around being referred to as "George" all the time.

"So, you're Carson's daughter?" Lainey looked at me as if I were an odd spectacle before throwing on a pair of aviators. Maybe it really was a good idea I didn't ask for a gun.

I shouldered my way past him. "Let's go."

I wondered how well Lainey knew my father, and whether or not my dad had been just as annoyed with the man as I was. In any case, the sooner we resolved this matter, the sooner I could head off to Cambridge and see my family. And, I hadn't forgotten about visiting Robert Cambria, Sr. and asking him about that key. What if it led me to something that could help with interpreting the Turkish writing in Veit Heilwig's diary? Or the "map" in

26

there that I couldn't make sense of? I've already started reading and memorizing some of the meditations written in English in there, but I didn't dare try them since I didn't have all the information I needed.

I put my nagging questions aside as we exited the hotel and got into the car parked out front. Since Lainey was driving, I urged Neal to take the passenger seat and spare me from having to sit next to the man. As we took off, I fondled the rings hanging on my silver chain and thought of Ken. My sadness had now been tainted with anger, both at myself and at the culprit. I hoped that the survivor would be willing to speak with Neal and me so that we could catch the murderer, so that I could bring him down--one way or another.

***

No one really spoke during the car ride, which was what I wanted, but Jameson finally decided to make another attempt at being cordial and engaged me in conversation. I really wanted to be left alone to my own thoughts, but since he at least attempted to be kind to me, I forced myself to be patient with him.

"General Donovan said that once the war is over, that they're going to restructure OSS."

"Really?" I asked, feigning interest.

"It's going to be called the Central Intelligence Agency--C.I.A. What do you think?"

"Sounds all right," I said, turning to face the window and watch us drive down a stretch of road where rows of trees stood sentinel. We were in Fairfax County, Virginia. "Are they going to allow female agents in the CIA?"

"I think so," he said. "I'm sure they'd be glad to have you whenever you're done with SOE in London."

"I'll have to think about it." I almost reached for the diamond ring hanging on the chain around my neck. What would I do once the war was over and spies were no longer

27

needed? I supposed there was always teaching, but I had already immersed myself in this world and this was all I knew.

"Well don't think about it too hard, Miss George." Lainey slowed the car and turned into a parking lot. A single story administration building stood at the other end. "If you ask me, it would be a waste of time."

"Why?" I asked.

"We've had a few ladies come and go in the FBI, but what happened to them? That Jentzer woman--got married and quit the next day. That Houston lady? Same thing. It's like college to these women--all they're looking for is their MRS degree."

Neal faced Lainey. "And what are you looking for?"

"The bad guys." Lainey got out of the car and came over to my side and opened the door. He offered me his hand, but I rebuffed him.

Neal and Jameson flanked me as we walked ahead to the building entrance.

When we got inside, we saw a young man at the front desk shuffling paperwork and sipping from a hot cup of coffee. He looked up and greeted us. "Good morning."

Lainey took off his aviators and slipped them into his suit pocket. He produced his badge. "Special Agents Lainey and Jameson," he said, gesturing toward his partner. "This is Agent Neal Warren from MI6, and Miss George from the Special Operations Executive."

The young man picked up the phone receiver on his desk and began dialing. "Yes, Patterson is waiting for you. I'll let him know you're coming down."

Nate, an OSS operative, had come up to meet us and took us in the elevator down to the basement floor. We walked down the dimly lit hallway, greeting a few other FBI agents in passing, until we arrived at a set of double doors. Nate opened them and led us into a large room furnished much like a bigwig's office. It had a mahogany desk and leather chair, soft carpet, a couch, and even a liquor cabinet. A solitary door stood to our right, which probably led to a private bathroom. Agent Patterson, with his soft round belly and protruding nose, sat on the couch next to a man of herculean size. Patterson poured the man a whiskey while puffing away on a cigar. Nate took the men's coats and my purse and hung them on the coat rack.

When Patterson saw us, he gestured for Nate to come and take the whiskey bottle. He came forward and shook our hands. "Good morning, everyone." He turned toward the man on the couch. "Henry, these special agents are here to speak with you. They're working on catching the wizard who destroyed the safe house."

Henry sported a military buzz cut and still looked big and tall, despite sitting hunched forward on the couch. Henry sipped his drink and said nothing, and Patterson faced us again and explained, "He's been through a lot, you understand. He's not very...cooperative. We assured him that he's safe with us, but he keeps insisting on talking with just Miss George."

"Is that so?" I raised an eyebrow, finally realizing why General Donovan wanted me involved. They weren't going to get a word out of Henry unless he spoke directly to me. However, this man was a stranger. I had never met or heard of him until today. What did he want to tell me that he couldn't tell the FBI or OSS?

"We can move him to interrogation," Jameson suggested. It would be interesting to see Jameson with his thin build try to grab Henry and walk him over there.

Neal shook his head. "The last thing we'd want is for him to feel he's being harassed, especially if he's done nothing wrong. Let's keep him here."

"Let's get this over with." Lainey gestured to his partner.

He and Jameson walked over to Henry and introduced themselves, but the man pointed toward me with his giant hand and said, "I want to talk to her--and only her."

Lainey's forehead wrinkled, and I swore it went all the

29

way up to the rest of his balding head. "Listen, we're here to help. You can talk to us too, Henry. What's your last name?"

"Smith."

"All right, Henry Smith. I know you're nervous...maybe even afraid, but can we start with what happened at the safe house?"

Henry shook his head. "I want to talk to Isabella. She's the only one I'll trust."

Lainey glared in my direction as if I had orchestrated all this. "Well, Miss George, have at it."

Jameson shrugged and actually looked somewhat relieved. Maybe he rethought his suggestion to move Henry to interrogation. "If you need us, then we'll be outside."

All the men exited the room, leaving Henry and me alone. I tentatively sat on the couch next to him and noted the odd look in his dark eyes. "How do you know who I am?"

"I know your father, Carson."

"How are you acquainted with my father?"

He glanced around the room as if he were being watched. "We were in the military together. I'm a pilot. I run messages between Carson and General Cambria, and whoever else your father needs to communicate with. I was the courier who delivered that note in Paris back in June."

I gasped. My father had managed to send me a cryptic message hidden in an Emily Dickinson poem in order to let me know he was alive and would reunite with me. The note had arrived at an acquaintance's house although it was addressed to me. I always wondered who delivered the message.

"I got the note, Henry. Thank you. Please, continue."

"In late July, I was shot down while running backup for a covert mission and had to hide at an OSS safe house in the south of France."

"Okay, so you made it to the safe house, then what?"

He clenched his teeth and slapped his forehead as if

trying to force the memory to surface from his mind. I grabbed his hands, almost twice the size of mine, and held them down firmly. I gently released a tendril of calming energy, a little body magic I had learned while at the Gray Tower. It imparted minor physical healing and mental clarity. For a moment he looked like he would sick up, but he managed to clear his throat and speak.

"Thank you. I was there for a week, and there were three other men there: Claude Remi, the host, and two OSS operatives--Kenneth Aspen and Samuel Wilkins. I remember their names because Kenneth helped bandage my arm, and Samuel...we were taking care of Samuel because his left leg had to be amputated."

I squirmed at the image of the scenario playing out in my mind. "Go on..."

"Carson had shown up and stayed with us just a day. He needed me to deliver a message to General Cambria. There are a couple of us guys helping out."

"Why?"

He shrugged. "It's Carson. We all looked up to him. I don't know why he's doing what he's doing, but...he always seems to have a plan."

I wanted to tell him that my father didn't have much of a plan for his family besides making us all believe he was dead. "How long was it between the time my father left and the wizard showed up?"

He shuddered and glanced around again. "Less than an hour. The wizard forced his way in, and when Claude tried to fight, the wizard just lit him up like a ball of fire. Samuel couldn't do anything because of his leg, but he reached for a gun and tried to shoot...but the wizard did something to his mind and made him turn the gun on himself. Kenneth and I ran to the back room and barricaded the door. He pushed me toward the window and told me to go, but something made me panic and I just stood there and couldn't move..." He shook his head. "A big guy like me, scared."

"I think anyone would be. It's okay."

31

His forehead beaded with sweat. "I saw the wizard break through, and he had asked for Carson. When Kenneth told him that Carson had left, the wizard asked if we knew where Carson had gone, but we wouldn't tell him anything. The wizard said that if we didn't lead him to your father, that he'd come after his family."

My chest tightened and my heart fluttered. "This wasn't a warlock, this was a tracker from the Gray Tower."

His lips trembled. "I know, that's what I told the FBI."

"What happened next, Henry?"

"After the wizard threatened to go after you and the others, Kenneth just got this look on his face, like it was something personal. He just pulled out his gun and started shooting. He knew he didn't stand a chance, but he did it so that I'd have enough time to make it out of there and come find you. I jumped through the window and ran. I heard a scream and saw Kenneth fall out the window. He was--"

"I understand," I said in a hoarse voice as my eyes burned. "I knew Kenneth."

"I'm...sorry."

I cleared my throat. "Is that why you think the wizard is here in the U.S.? Because of what he said about coming after the family?"

"Yes."

"Who was this wizard?"

"I don't know...he wore all black and had his face covered. I couldn't say what his true voice was like, because he didn't use his mouth when he spoke to us. He communicated to us in our minds."

It sounded like it could've very well been a mentalist. Such a wizard could pry into others' thoughts, control minds, erase memories, or seal them the way Nena had sealed mine. The wizard who attacked the safe house probably couldn't probe Henry's mind because my father would've made sure to protect Henry with a powerful seal. Ken didn't even know my father was alive until that day, and so would have nothing of value to divulge. "Were there other wizards with the attacker?"

"He was alone."

It sounded like one of the trackers had gone rogue. They had never before touched our family or threatened it. The Tower had recruited and admitted me to the Order of Wizards without hesitation, even though it didn't have to. The Head of the Order could've easily detained me on Tower grounds, but he didn't. Yet, I knew they watched us, and they waited to see if my father would show up. That's why they pushed Brande, an Elite wizard, toward me. He was one of the seven trackers. However Brande's affection for me wasn't a mere ruse, and when he vowed to aid me back in France, I gave him my Agate stone ring and accepted his help.

"Henry, is there anything else you can remember about the wizard who attacked the safe house?"

"No," he said, rubbing his neck. When he kept rubbing vigorously and looked to be in pain, I pulled his hand down to look at the back of his neck.

I saw the phrase *In Mente*, meaning "In Mind," etched into his skin as if placed with a branding tool. My heart beat frantically in my chest as I jumped up from the couch and bolted for the door, but it was too late. Henry caught hold of me and crashed against me so that we both landed on the floor. He started retching...or crying...I didn't know which. I quickly turned on my side and made a move to stand, but he cried again and fell on me.

"Neal!" I screeched in the direction of the double doors.

"Help...me!" Henry shrieked as his pupils turned completely white, and his mouth widened an unnatural width. "Help...me!"

I screamed for Neal once more as I fended Henry off. In his desperation and frantic state of mind, he grabbed my shoulders and shook me, soiling my pristine shirt with tears of blood and grimy hands. Although my hair had come loose and fell into my eyes as I flailed about, it couldn't completely shield me from seeing a congealed black substance protruding from his mouth and dripping down his chin. "Henry...Henry! Fight it!"

"No!" he screamed as his huge strong hands reached for my neck. Suddenly he jerked his hands upward, and his arms shook as if he were physically struggling with someone.

I saw my chance and kicked Henry in the stomach while at the same time sliding myself backward. He lunged toward me, but I kicked again and made him lose his balance and fall backward. He started shrieking and writhing on the floor. I got up and ran for my purse hanging on one of the coat rack hooks and grabbed my golden knife. I immediately laid a Circle of Protection. A faint light shot up from the floor and enveloped me, and I watched in horror as Henry crawled toward me with tears of blood still flowing, asking me to help him. I didn't know what commands had been forced onto his mind, but whatever happened, he needed to remain in this room, or else he'd have an entire building of people to tear through. However, as long as he resisted the spell, it would torture him. He would either give in to whatever command had been latent in the spell--which probably was to rip my throat out--or die.

"Neal!" I screamed at the top of my lungs. This time he heard, and rushed in with Patterson, Lainey, and Jameson.

Neal quickly assessed the situation and immediately went into action. Patterson nearly fainted and fell back while Lainey and Jameson pulled their guns and kept their distance as if confronting a dangerous animal. They probably would've pulled their triggers if Neal weren't in the way. Since Henry seemed to ignore Neal's presence, it was safe to assume the spell was forcing Henry to only come after me. But that didn't mean he'd destroy anything or anyone blocking his path.

Henry coughed up more of the congealed black substance and Neal came up behind him and put him in a lock hold. "Is there a doctor in the building?"

34

"No!" Lainey said. "Just let go of him! We'll shoot."

"Stand down, Warren!" Jameson shouted.

"I can help him," Neal said, jerking his head in the direction of the bookcase. "Patterson, would you be so kind as to grab that medical handbook for me?"

Patterson held on to his potbelly as if he'd be sick. He looked at Neal as if he were insane, but with shaky legs he stumbled toward the shelves and grabbed the book. Lainey and Jameson shouted in fright when Henry, with his inhuman strength, flipped Neal over. He had anticipated that Henry would make this move and shifted his weight and hold on Henry so that he'd fall down with him. Neal immediately returned to a locking hold on Henry and now had his legs intertwined with the other man's so that he couldn't break free and rush toward me.

"Here!" Patterson's large nose flared, and he tossed the book toward Neal and backed away.

Neal muttered a curse word and shouted for Lainey to come and open the book. Lainey grimaced, but he shoved his gun into his holster and complied. He opened the book and held it at eye level for Neal. "What the hell is this supposed to do? Are you going to lecture him to death?"

"Turn to page eighty-four, please." He punched Henry to distract him. The man just kept shrieking and writhing like an animal.

"Flip through the next five pages at three-second intervals."

Lainey did as he was told. "Okay, it's your funeral..."

Neal nearly lost his grip on Henry. "This man's altered state of mind prevents me from using magic to make him fall unconscious, and any attempt to do it physically may inadvertently kill him."

"What do you need me to do?" I was already preparing another spell in my mind.

"Stay where you are," Neal said.

I nodded in understanding and began feeding more energy into my Circle of Protection. As it expanded throughout the room and enveloped the other men, I tossed my knife to Lainey. "If Henry gets loose," I told him, "use it. The knife's enchanted."

Lainey eyed me with mild shock, but then asked, "Don't you need this?"

"I'll just have to be Henry's distraction. If Neal needs me to stay put..."

"If he breaks free, I'm shooting." Jameson warned, as his skinny arms held his gun steady. He threw Patterson an annoyed glance, probably criticizing the man in his mind for having less courage than me, a woman.

When Neal finished the five pages, he reached into his pants pocket and pulled out a yellow, flaky substance. He shoved it into Henry's mouth and closed his hand over the bottom half of his face. Henry's body went into a spasm, and he choked until he swallowed whatever it was Neal had fed him. When Henry went limp and passed out, Neal finally released him and got to his feet, drenching with sweat and breathing heavily.

"What did you give him?" Patterson asked, finally approaching now that Henry lay prone.

"Just the right amount of opium. It's one of the few things that could incapacitate him while under the influence of an *In Mente* spell." Neal took out his knife. With tiny flicks of the magical blade, he erased the words etched into Henry's neck. I remembered how Neal once used that same knife to break an enchantment for me.

"You know possessing opium is illegal, right?" Lainey asked, though his tone clearly indicated that he was impressed.

"You're talking to a guy who deals in the black market," I said. When Neal gave me a critical eye, I added, "It's true. Sometimes I'm tempted to follow you around just to see what kinds of things you get into, Neal."

I finally broke my Circle of Protection and limped over. I supposed the shock and an adrenaline rush kept me from feeling any pain where I had landed on the floor.

"Are you okay, Isabella?" Jameson asked.

"Yes." I waved it off and gave a brave face.

"So what happened to Henry?" Lainey asked.

I eyed him with pity. "He had a nasty spell placed on him...one that tried to take over his mind and force him to carry out a command. He said the wizard that did this had his face concealed, so he couldn't identify him. From Henry's description, we're probably looking at a mentalist."

Neal stared at me, though he still hovered over Henry. "Did he say why the wizard attacked?"

I knew I had to choose my words carefully. My father faked his death for a reason, and if only a few trusted people knew the truth, then it was best that I help keep it that way--at least for now. "We didn't quite get around to that. The *In Mente* spell broke him."

Nate had come in with a medic, and they used a stretcher to place Henry on and took him away. Patterson ordered them to transfer the man to the nearest hospital with an armed escort.

"When he wakes up, will he be all right?" Patterson shot a painful glance in the direction of the soiled area of his carpet. He rubbed his large belly.

"It's uncertain," Neal said. "I unraveled the spell, but it has done a great deal of damage to him. Have him remain under protective custody and continue giving him medical attention. If Henry is able to share more information, have him contact Isabella."

Patterson nodded then turned to me and gave me his calling card. "Do you live out this way, Miss George?"

"Well, one thing I did get out of Henry was that my family may be targeted. I think that was his reason for wanting to speak with me privately. I won't be in D.C., I'm going to Cambridge, and I'll leave the address and number if you need to contact me."

"All right," Patterson said. "Excuse me while I go find someone to help me with my office." He grimaced at his carpet again and then headed down the hall.

37

"Isabella, we should assign a security detail to your family," Jameson said.

Lainey shook his head. "The wizard won't show or make a move with us hanging around."

I nodded, and for a second couldn't believe I was agreeing with the man. "Lainey's right. I'll go home as planned and watch over them. If the wizard does come around..."

"I'll be there with you to catch him," Neal said. He gave me a mysterious look as if he suspected there was more to the story and that he needed to stick around to find out what it was.

"Yeah," Lainey said, "you do that. Jameson and I will take care of Henry and try to gather more information from our end. We'll keep in touch."

"Then good luck, gentlemen." Neal shook their hands.

"Miss George," Lainey returned my alchemist's knife, "you did pretty well back there."

"Better than Patterson for sure," I quipped.

Jameson smiled. "Speaking of, we have to run some things by him before leaving. We'll meet you at the car."

I grabbed my purse and headed back into the hallway with Neal. We walked in silence over to the elevator. As we waited for its doors to open, he faced me. "Brande told me about Carson. The wizard was searching for your father, wasn't he?"

"Yes." I took in a sharp breath and could barely look him in the eye.

"You're thinking it was Master Priya who did this, aren't you?" He stepped aside and let me go into the elevator first.

"Are there any other mentalists hunting my father?" For a moment I thought of the woman Mehara, an Elite mentalist from Morocco. Concealed by her clothing in the right manner and using telepathic communication, she could've very well disguised her sex and committed the crime.

Neal followed me into the elevator. "It's not necessary to

38

be a full-fledged mentalist to do what that wizard did."

"Well whoever it was, he or she was pretty damned proficient at using and manipulating mental powers."

"If this person is one of the seven trackers, exposure will come easily. I will help you in this."

The elevator doors opened and we stepped out into the lobby. We began walking toward the exit. "You mean you're willing to expose one of your own confreres?"

"You may not like what they do, but for hundreds of years the position of a tracker has been one of prestige and honor--to capture and slay the Drifter. However if one has gone rogue..."

If only he knew I was the true Drifter and my dad the decoy. Would he still say this to me? Would he still believe that? "My father's a good man. I mean, he's flawed like any other human being, but I don't believe having the ability to travel through time should be an automatic death sentence."

He opened the door for me and continued walking along with me. "Exactly, Isabella. He's flawed, like all humans, and we are all subject to temptation and depravity. If Adolf Hitler can wreak havoc on the world with military power and his alliance with warlocks, can you imagine what someone would do with the powers of a Drifter?"

My eyes narrowed. I hadn't done *anything* with my powers, and I certainly wouldn't use them to harm innocent people. "Neal, I just think there are good people in the world, and bad people."

"Absolute power corrupts absolutely."

"So you're going to lump him into the same category as the wizard who murdered everyone in that safe house?" My jaw tightened, and I began to wonder why Brande even sent him to me.

Brande didn't know I was the Drifter, and like everyone else he believed it was my father. He used to talk the same way about the Drifter just as Neal did...but things were different now. Perhaps I just needed to be a little more patient with Neal for him to completely leave behind the indoctrination of the Gray Tower when it came to this matter. No wonder people called us *Tower Slaves*.

We made it to the car and then stood staring at each other. I wondered how he felt about not being able to accurately read me like he did most other people. He said, "If your father is a good man, let him sacrifice himself for the good of this world. If not, then we've protected humanity from a potential monster."

I resisted the urge to slap him. I told myself to continue being patient, for Brande's sake. He wouldn't have sent Neal if he thought the guy was useless to us. I looked straight into Neal's eyes and spoke. "You have to understand that my mother and brother don't know about all this. They don't even know I've been working as a spy for SOE."

"Very well, I have the perfect cover."

"Which is...?"

"You and I met in the U.S. ambassador's office in London. We work on the same floor."

"All right genius, and when they wonder why I'm bringing you home?"

"We're betrothed."

"You're not my type." He was nice to look at though, but I wasn't going to inflate his ego by telling him that.

"I assure you, I'm every woman's type."

"You're staying in the guesthouse, Romeo. Got it?"

"Understood."

"And don't do anything that would let them know you're a wizard, especially a Philosopher. Pretend you're a normal guy."

He gave me a sidelong glance. "The enchantment...something's changed."

"What enchantment?" My chest tightened, but I made sure my expression remained neutral.

"You know what I'm talking about."

"Like I always said...you're the only one who thinks

that."

He held my gaze, and for a moment I thought he'd try to reach into my mind. However probing someone's mind without her permission would be considered invasive, an attack even. Instead, he brushed his thumb against my cheek, a cursory move that allowed him to read me. Reading another wizard through heightened smell or sight, and especially by touch, could inform you if you were dealing with an alchemist or elemental, a strong wizard or a mediocre one, a healthy one or a cursed one, a tainted warlock, or a Cruenti.

"Most curious..." he said.

"Hey, here comes Lainey and Jameson." I turned and waved at the two men as they approached. Out of the corner of my eye I could still see Neal staring at me, and when he wouldn't relent, I faced him again.

"What is it?" My stomach clenched, and I wanted to tell him to stop looking at me in that way.

"It's nothing."

I shook my head. "With you, it's always something."

CHAPTER FOUR

Johnnie already stood in the front yard. He wore such a huge grin that I almost overlooked the fact that he donned a full suit and tie. I smiled back at him and got out of the cab, rushing into a tight embrace with him. I framed his face with my hands and stared into his brown eyes, which reminded me of our father's, and thought about how much I longed for this moment--I was finally home.

"I'm so glad to see you," I said as I brushed back his thick dark hair with my fingers. He stood just a bit taller than me, and had the same thick expressive brows as my dad.

"Go ahead, Mom and Rachel are inside." He pulled away and approached Neal, who was helping the cab driver unload my bags. When he stopped to greet my brother with a handshake, Johnnie nailed him with a bear hug. I smiled to myself and walked inside.

I stiffened a little as I headed up the front steps, unsure of what to expect. This would be my first time meeting my sister-in-law, and then there was my mother. She had never been the same since my father went missing sixteen years ago, and she had become sullen when I accepted the Gray Tower's invitation to join the Order. It seemed she took little joy in anything nowadays, which pained me because she used to be the type of person everyone would come to for advice or for a smile; her home was always open to friends, and her rich laughter would fill the house like a song.

I opened the door and went inside, navigating my way to the living room. For a moment I thought of our old house back in Baltimore and all my childhood memories associated with it; this new place would take some getting used to, but this large Victorian home did have its charm.

"Isabella?" Rachel quickly put away her feather duster and walked over to me. Her blonde hair was neatly coiffed in a waved pomp style and she wore pearl earrings and a stylish green day dress. She looked like the perfect housewife, and I wondered if I could ever pull it off.

"Rachel...hello," I awkwardly hugged her and self-consciously adjusted the diamond ring on my finger. I had the Agate stone and talisman rings on my chain.

"I'm so glad to finally meet you!" She beamed. "I've seen all your pictures, and Johnnie's told me everything about you."

"I'm glad to meet you as well...you look wonderful."

"Thank you," she answered with a smile. "Mother! Isabella's here." She gestured for me to sit on the sofa and went into the kitchen.

As soon as I sat down, my mother came into the room. She smiled at me with her eyes. I was very glad I inherited her beautiful green eye color and none of her pear-shaped body.

"Mom, how are you?"

She approached and gave me a kiss on the top of my head, probably the only extent to which she'd show me affection. "I'm well, dear."

"I hope you like iced tea, Isabella." Rachel set a tray on the coffee table and began pouring drinks.

"How do you like it here in Cambridge?" I accepted a glass of tea from Rachel and thanked her.

"It's quiet...too quiet."

Mom waved Rachel off when she offered her a drink,

and instead pulled out a Julep cigarette and lit it.

"Why, I think it's swell here." Rachel forced a smile. "Probably not as exciting as the ambassador's office, I imagine."

I felt like such a fraud walking in here with an engagement ring that wouldn't have a wedding attached to it and a career that didn't exist. I wondered what it would feel like to just tell them the truth. "Well, I'm mainly in the office doing...office work. It's not as exciting as one would think."

Johnnie stumbled through the doorway with my bags and Neal carried another two under each arm. "Izzy, which ones should we put into the guesthouse for Neal?"

I cringed. I wished he'd stop calling me that. At least Johnnie was a suitable nickname for Jonathan--but to call me Izzy? No. It was just as bad as FBI agents running around calling me "George" in gruff voices.

"Actually," Neal said, "all of these bags are hers."

When Johnnie gestured for Neal to set his bags down, my mother rose from her seat and beckoned him to her. "Hello, Neal. I'm Mary."

Neal approached and very graciously held her hands as he kissed both sides of her cheeks. "It's a pleasure to meet you, Mrs. George."

She had him sit next to her. "Believe me, I'm just as interested in meeting you. Do forgive me, but I don't recall ever hearing about you until...well, earlier today."

"That's because I proposed to her this morning. It was quite romantic if I do say so myself."

"Really?" My mother took a puff of her Julep and eyed him critically. I felt an urge to remind Neal about not saying or doing anything that would give him away, but Rachel grabbed my hand.

"Come on, Isabella. Let's go set the table."

I followed her into the kitchen and helped her grab some dishes and utensils. "The house is beautiful, Rachel." Why did this small talk feel more painful than an enemy interrogation?

"Thank you." After we set the table, she rushed over to me and nearly squealed. "Are you going to live out here? I think there's a house for sale nearby. What does Neal think?"

"We haven't decided yet. We still have several obligations in Europe." I followed her back into the kitchen and took the large bowl of salad. She grabbed the hors d'oeuvres, a modest platter of raw vegetables with stuffed dates in the center, and a meat loaf too. We set everything on the dining room table.

"I really hope you both can stay. Jonathan is ecstatic over you being home."

"I have to admit that I feel a bit out of place, having been away for so long." I glanced in the direction of the living room, wondering what my mother and Neal were discussing.

"Oh, don't worry about it, Isabella. I feel like I already know you, and...you just feel free to ask me anything because I want you to know me too." She guided me toward my seat, and when I sat where she wanted, she pushed my chair in and smiled.

"Um, thanks..." I scooted back just a little to alleviate the feeling of sitting in a high chair.

Johnnie glided into the room and wrapped one arm around me in a half-hug. "Now that you're back, have you given any thought to coming to Harvard?"

I smiled at him. "What did I tell you the last time you asked?"

"Jonathan's name is on everyone's lips." Rachel steered Johnnie to his designated seat across from me and made him sit the same way she had done me. "He's been partnering with Dr. Grey, working on some interesting historical texts. They even talked about it in the newspaper."

"Well," Johnnie blushed, "I'm more of an assistant than a partner."

"Jonathan's been working for hours on end," Rachel insisted. "He's presenting a paper next week."

"That sounds wonderful, Johnnie." I looked in the direction of the living room once more and began to grow worried. Was Neal subtly getting information out of my mother? I hoped she wouldn't discuss anything from my childhood back in Baltimore. She knew about that frightful day, when I was ten years old, and I burned with an inexplicable fire that did not consume me. My father knew then what I was. He understood. My mother didn't, and she was afraid. I think part of her hated my father because of that. I put on a false smile when Neal came walking in from the other side with my mother.

Rachel had Neal sit next to me, and my mother sat at the head of the table. She finally took her place next to Johnnie. We bowed our heads as Rachel said a short prayer, and we began eating. I glanced at my mom, who had traded her cigarette for a glass of chilled champagne. I wondered what she and Neal had been discussing.

At Rachel's prompting, Johnnie continued describing his current project. "I've been fortunate enough to help Dr. Grey translate and catalogue some recently discovered Persian and Arabic texts dating from the time of Suleiman the Magnificent. Can you imagine the impact this would have on our knowledge of history, culture, and medicine? I've even found references to the Gray Tower in there. Suleiman had a very progressive system when it came to integrating wizards into society."

"I've read about Suleiman when I studied at the Tower," I said as I held out my glass and let Neal pour me some champagne. "I thought those texts were in Turkish."

"Some were," Johnnie admitted. "The Turkish texts are being translated by Dr. Grey, and I'm handling the others."

"Maybe I will come down to the university for a visit, Johnnie." If I could speak with Dr. Grey and have him take a look at that Turkish text in Veit Heilwig's diary, then I could finally decode those cryptic pages.

Neal studied my brother for a moment and then asked, "Your Suleiman project sounds brilliant, to be sure. May I ask what led you to take on such a task? Isabella told me you teach western European history."

Johnnie gave a thoughtful look. "It's fascinated me for these past few years, and so when the opportunity came along, I went ahead and acted on it."

"And Johnnie wouldn't want to pass up such an exclusive project." I eyed my brother as I said this, knowing that he had also been preoccupied with my father's last mission in the Ottoman Empire, and his subsequent disappearance. How deep did his sorrow still run after all these years? Did he think he could find something out about our father by pursuing this project? I was once in the same place, and that's why I knew I'd have to find the right time to tell Johnnie that our father was alive. But how would I do this? When?

"This meatloaf's too bland," my mother said. "You usually make it much more flavorful, Rachel."

Poor girl, her stressed smile came back. "Well, you see, I wasn't sure if my seasoning would agree with Neal. Do you like spicy food in England?"

Neal smirked, and I reached beneath the table and pinched his thigh as a warning. "I most certainly do, Rachel. This meatloaf is delicious. I only wish Isabella would cook for me, then I would be much happier."

My mom snorted a laugh and Rachel gasped. Johnnie stayed out of it and gulped down some champagne. I wanted to tell Neal that he was a lousy fake fiancé.

"He's joking, Rachel." I glared at Neal. I was actually a decent cook, even though I've only cooked for myself.

I supposed the turn of topic from Medieval texts to the artistry of cooking suited Rachel well, because she spoke with Neal another ten minutes about it before finally offering to clear the table. I got up and helped her, but not before giving Neal a final glare. After we cleaned everything up, Rachel invited us into the living room where

47

they had a baby grand piano with a smooth walnut finish. Once she found out that Neal played, she begged him to serenade them with a song.

She hopped on the couch with Johnnie and curled up against him. I stood watching them from the kitchen doorway, gazing at them with both admiration and envy. I forced myself not to think about Ken, and what it would've been like for him to meet my family. I would've definitely liked to curl up with him and be romantic as well. My mom stood next to me, as if decidedly not won over by Neal and keeping her distance. Neal began playing Hungarian Rhapsody No. 2 while exchanging a few words with Johnnie and Rachel.

My mom faced me. "When were you planning on telling me your fiancé was a wizard?"

The question took me by surprise. I swore my mother could put Sherlock Holmes to shame. "I wasn't sure if you'd like the idea. You...don't even like me being one."

She frowned. "Or maybe I don't like secrets and lies. Maybe I don't like my daughter being halfway around the world and me not knowing what's happening with her."

"Did he say something to you when I left you two alone?" I swore that if he revealed anything he shouldn't have that I'd sneak into the guesthouse and smother him with a pillow.

"I asked him a few questions." She smiled. "He's sharp, contemplative...and he's playing Liszt's most difficult piece while casually chatting with two other people."

She gave me a triumphant look as if that had settled it. I crossed my arms. "And?"

"Even my brightest prodigies would stumble over Hungarian Rhapsody if someone so much as walked into the room while they were playing. He's playing it perfectly while being distracted, and he doesn't even have sheet music to go off of. He's so much like your father."

"So why don't you like him?" I asked more out of curiosity than anything else. Heck, it wasn't like I was really marrying the guy.

"Like I said...he's so much like your father."

Neal's piano serenade had ended, and Rachel and Johnnie cheered him. Neal then began regaling them with fictional stories starring him in the ambassador's office and how we supposedly met. He even got me to laugh--I had to admit, he could be entertaining when he wanted. The irony though was that most Philosophers I've known were so wrapped up in their calculations and projections that they tended to lose touch with flesh and blood. People were no longer freethinking beings with individual desires and dreams; to the Philosopher, they were possibilities, projects, and experiments.

My jaw tightened at the thought of my father and some of his own manipulative actions. He had been so concerned with out-maneuvering his enemies in order to protect us, that he forgot why he was doing it to begin with. Even he should be tired after running and fighting all these years. Didn't he want to come home to us? Or was I just a pawn in this critical match between him and the Gray Tower?

"Mom," I said, watching Johnnie attempt to tell a joke he had recently heard to Neal and Rachel, "do you miss dad?"

She gave a sad smile. "Every day. Sometimes I'm still angry over some of the things he did. If the Gray Tower called him in the dead of night, he would go. If the Masters wanted him to bring them our little girl...he did it. But, he's gone now, and that's all in the past. Isn't it?"

Rachel called out to us. "Please, come and have a seat!"

Johnnie beckoned to us. "I told Neal you used to teach piano, Mom. Could you play us something?"

She squeezed my hand and acquiesced. Neal made way for her as she approached and sat at the piano. She began flawlessly playing Moonlight Sonata. When Rachel signaled for me to come sit on the couch with her and Johnnie, I gestured to her to let her know that I had to make a phone call. I went upstairs into my bedroom and opened my purse, pulling out the elder Robert Cambria's phone

49

number. I didn't want anyone to overhear my conversation, so I decided to use the phone in the study a few doors down instead of downstairs in the kitchen.

I went inside the large study room, with its hardwood floor and matching mahogany bookcases. I went over to the corner where a typewriter stood on a small desk, and shut the curtains nearby. I walked over to the large desk and turned on the lamp since the sun was setting and the room was nearly dark. I eased into Johnnie's leather chair, glancing at a stack of books on his desk and carefully pushing aside a pile of papers. I reached for the phone and dialed Cambria's number, and after about four rings he picked up the phone.

"This is the Cambria residence."

"Hello, General Cambria...it's Isabella George."

"Isabella? Yes, yes, how are you?"

"I'm well. I just got back from Washington and ran into Rob. He gave me your number and address, and I was hoping to pay you a visit."

"Of course. Where are you?"

"I'm in Cambridge."

"How soon can you come?"

"Tomorrow morning."

"Bring the key when you come."

"Okay."

"And make sure you come alone, Isabella. Carson made me promise that only you would see it."

I heard footsteps in the hallway and I said in a hurried voice, "Thank you, sir. I will. I've got to go now, goodbye."

I hung up the phone and folded the note, placing it into my pocket. I slouched in Johnnie's chair and casually grabbed one of the books on the desk. When Neal came into view, I smiled at him. "How's it going?"

"Quite well. I'll be making bread pudding tomorrow morning with Rachel, and later in the afternoon I'll be playing poker with Jonathan and his friends. Now, as for your mother, I must say that she is a formidable woman...a little scary, actually."

"Agreed." I put the book away and stood. "Have you sensed anything so far? I haven't felt anyone else's presence yet."

He shook his head. "I'll be making a few phone calls tonight. My contacts will be able to tell me if anyone of interest has recently checked into any hotels in the area."

"You have contacts out here?"

Maybe it wasn't a good idea for my father to meet with me here in the U.S. He had promised to see me again before the end of this year, and I thought if I were with the rest of the family, that I could convince Dad to reveal himself to them and at least let Johnnie and Mom know he was alive. However if Neal had contacts around here and was still playing fiancé when my father showed up, I'd have a world of trouble on my hands.

"Does that surprise you?" he asked.

I gave a neutral expression and hoped he didn't sense my unease. "Nothing you do surprises me anymore. You carry around opium the same way other people carry around Aspirin. I'm just wondering what your role in all this is."

He approached and stood right in front of me. He reached for the silver chain around my neck and raised the Agate stone ring attached as a reminder. "A friend...I'm a friend."

I thought about yesterday when I felt like falling apart outside of General Donovan's meeting room, when they told me about Ken's death. I couldn't even shed a tear over him in front of them, because no one at OSS or SOE knew we were even together. I would always be grateful to Neal for his support, because he was probably the only person on earth who I could talk to about it.

"I know, it's just that lately it's been hard not to second-guess people. Brande's one of the few people I trust. I guess what I'm trying to say is thank you, and I'm glad he sent you."

51

"I think he would've preferred to come himself."

"I'm sure I'll see him sooner or later."

My mother walked in. "Neal, let me help you get acquainted with the guesthouse."

"He'll be right there, Mom." His back was to her, and I pressed my face against his right shoulder to stifle my laugh. She probably thought we had planned to sneak up here to be together.

Neal turned to face her. "Of course, Mrs. George. I apologize for any appearances of... impropriety."

She waved her hand through the air. "Oh, please. When I was your age, Carson and I were all over each other--"

"Ew. Mom. No."

"To the guesthouse, then." Neal wore an amused expression as he headed out the study and down the hallway.

"Do you need anything?" she asked, crossing her arms and leaning on the doorframe.

"No, I'm fine. I need to go to my room and unpack." I went over and gave her a kiss on the cheek. She smiled at me and followed Neal out.

As I exited the study and went toward my room, which was the one nearest to the stairs, I spotted Johnnie and Rachel coming up. I apologized to them for running off, but they graciously shrugged it off. It felt embarrassing, and a little weird to say the least, that they were having more fun with my faux fiancé than with me. I readily accepted Rachel's invitation to visit her book club tomorrow evening when the guys would be together playing poker. I hoped that at least to a small extent it would make up for me giving them the impression I was disinterested in being at home.

After hanging up some sweaters and dresses in the closet and tossing my undergarments into the dresser, I grew bored and pulled out Veit's diary. I grabbed a notebook and pen lying on the nightstand next to my bed and started copying the first few pages written in Turkish. It looked like Johnnie was going to get his wish of having me come down to the university after all. I hoped Dr. Grey would be available to meet with me and take a look at the text, but first I'd have to size him up to determine if he was the right person to do it. Whatever the writing in Turkish explained, it had to do with the Drifter, the Time Wizard who could predict the future, see the past, and manipulate the present--and God knew what else.

And here she was, sitting on a bed, not knowing how to do all this, or if it would even be worth it.

CHAPTER FIVE

After a quick shower and running downstairs to polish off my eggs and toast, I stole Neal away so that I could tell him I was going to meet a contact in East Cambridge. Since we had agreed that if one of us had to leave the house that the other would stay, he didn't insist on joining me. Besides, he had that bread pudding to bake with Rachel. My mother had woken up in a sullen mood and retired to the garden out back with her Mint Julep and the latest issue of McCall's magazine. Johnnie headed off for work.

I borrowed my mother's Saratoga and drove down Broadway, taking in the view of morning traffic, kids walking to school, and the gleaming sunlight and warmth that permeated the environment. All I had to do was take this street straight down to the Longfellow Bridge so I could cross the Charles River and make it into Boston. It felt odd at first driving around town during the day, because I had gotten used to being in the streets of Europe at night. For now, at least I could say it was quiet and peaceful--no bombs, no Gestapo or SS Officers, and no hiding. This was a very welcome change from the chaos of Nazi-occupied territory. However, it didn't ease my fear of the danger that the tracker-wizard posed to my family. Would he try to hold them hostage until my father showed? Or would he come with threats of violence, seeking information and clues as to my father's whereabouts?

I had no choice being thrust into this world, but at least Johnnie, Rachel, and my mom could have one, and a chance at a normal life. Whatever it took, I would keep them safe, and protect them from whoever would try to hurt them or use them to get to my father. I realized in that moment that my father probably felt the same way, but I hated the way he did things because it left too many doubts, and too many people confused and hurt.

I set my ponderings aside as I parked in front of General Cambria's house. I grabbed my purse and Veit's diary that I had hidden in a large handbag I found stuffed in the back of my closet. I walked past the gate and down the brick walkway with a meticulously manicured lawn on either side. The pale yellow house was medium-sized, and on the front porch I noticed a toy box. I smiled to myself and thought of Rob and his family, and hoped that they'd continue in their happiness. I was glad that I had refused his help, and hoped that he would just forget about the key.

I rang the doorbell twice and heard feet shuffling and General Cambria's voice. He opened the door and smiled at me. His face had aged, but he gazed at me with those same cheerful brown eyes I remember seeing when I was a girl. His hair had grown all white and his belly was full and round, and his manner of dress made him look like the quintessential grandfather. Of course, this grandpa was also a retired Army general and a staunch friend of my father's. I wondered if he ever looked back on that night my father disappeared and asked himself if it was worth the risk. I supposed Robert Cambria was one of the lucky ones--he didn't end up like Veit Heilwig.

"Isabella," he said, giving me a hug before ushering me inside, "come in and have a seat."

I went and sat on the couch, and grabbed the cup of coffee he gestured for me to take. "Thank you."

He sat across from me and gazed at an iron strong box

sitting on the coffee table. "The night your father left, he dropped off this box, and the key that went with it. He said only you would be able to open it."

I set the cup of coffee back down and reached into my purse. I pulled out the key and slid it into the keyhole. An invisible force pulled at the key like a magnet, and I heard a click. A soft flow of energy reached out and covered my hand. It felt like I was sticking my hand through a spider's web. I flipped the top open and peered inside, all the while holding in an anxious breath that waited to be exhaled. There were no magic potions or bright lights inside, but merely two things: a bundle of papers which were (to my chagrin) written in Turkish, and a plain gold ring...a wedding ring. Why did everyone like to leave me rings?

"I'm not sure I understand," I said, unhooking my silver chain and adding the ring to my growing collection.

"It belonged to your father," he confirmed, as if reading my thoughts.

"Why did he enchant it?" I could feel his magical essence mixed in with the gold.

"He said that with whatever he put into that box, he can use it to link with you and find you anywhere in the world...and you, him."

I nodded. "Please tell me you know about the Turkish texts."

He shook his head. "I'm afraid I don't know how to translate them."

Johnnie would probably be able to authenticate these for me, but these looked like the texts from Mehmed VI's collection that had been handed over to the Gray Tower years ago. I remembered tedious nights in the Tower's library with my cohorts reading about them when training as an alchemist. Mehmed VI was the last ruler of the Ottoman Empire before the Caliphate was dismantled and the nation became known as Turkey. My father had gone there to watch and lend aid, and probably had the chance to speak with and befriend Mehmed. My father ended up securing ancient texts from wizards in the East that spanned centuries. Master Erin said Veit had stolen something from the Tower, what if he had been expelled from the Order because he stole these texts for my father?

"Well, I think I know someone who can help me interpret these. Thank you for holding on to them."

"You're welcome. Make sure no one else knows about it." He looked a little worried.

"Henry Smith is with the FBI in protective custody. He said he was a messenger."

He nodded. "Is he all right?"

"He escaped being killed in a safe house in France, but had a dangerous spell placed on him."

"I'll call Donovan and find a way to check on him. Well, now that you've opened the box, I think you won't need Henry or me as go-betweens."

"You still need to be careful, general. It isn't over."

"Throughout the years I've had a few unsavory visitors come around asking about your father. I think I can handle it."

I wanted to point out the fact that he had also been a decade younger, but instead placed the bundled texts into the black handbag that held Veit's diary. "Thank you. I promise I won't trouble you any further."

"You haven't troubled me at all, Isabella." He rose from his seat at the same time I did, and came over and placed his hands on my shoulders. "Be safe."

"The same to you. And if Rob calls asking about any of this, tell him the key opened up an old box with family photos and letters."

He gave me a knowing look. "You've got it."

Suddenly I felt a shiver run down my spine, and I sensed the presence of another wizard. An odd noise engulfed the house, which sounded like the rumble of a jet engine when passing over a building. Whoever it was, the wizard had been listening to our conversation.

"Someone's here," I said.

57

Cambria held his index finger to his lips, signaling me to be quiet. He stepped cautiously toward a lamp stand where he pulled out a revolver. I reached for my golden knife in my purse and carved into the hardwood floor a Circle of Protection. I fed energy into it, spreading it out across the perimeter of the house, but then it broke like shattering glass. When I felt the power of my Circle fade and extinguish with such ease, I knew that the wizard who broke it was either an Elite or a Master.

The general mouthed the word, "Wizard?"

I nodded. He reached into the same drawer and exchanged the revolver for a sleek and shiny pistol that seemed to shimmer slightly when held to light. I could taste the mixture of silver and alloys in the gun. The bullets were tipped with iron. More than anyone, an alchemist like me understood what happened when one harvested the magical qualities of iron. I've used it before to corrode doors and human flesh.

I made a low warning noise when he started toward the dining room. He flung his right hand down, gesturing for me to stay in the living room, but I wasn't going to let him face this wizard alone--especially if it was the one who had killed Ken. I started following the general and he let out an exasperated breath, probably thinking what a horribly insubordinate soldier I'd make. I imitated his every step, careful not to make any noise or accidentally bump into anything.

When we made it into the wide hallway that led to the bedrooms and bathroom, I felt the presence of the other wizard grow even stronger. It washed over me like a cold wave, and I carved an Air symbol into the wall--a triangle with a vertical line across the top. I added a second triangle symbol for Fire. I slowly began infusing the symbols with magical energy and held my knife ready to use as a conduit. The general signaled to me and skipped the first door, but went to the second. He held up three fingers to mark his count, and on the count of three we simultaneously opened our respective doors.

Nothing.

We both turned toward each other in confirmation. He went to the last door at the end of the hall. I went to the next one on the opposite side, just a few feet away.

One. Two. Three.

"Run!" He shouted as he took a shot with his gun and staggered. Instead of falling to the floor, his limbs began to jerk like a marionette, and he stumbled into the last room.

"No!" I dashed after him. When the door slammed shut in my face, I activated the Air Symbol from down the hall and a howling gust of wind came flying my way. I held my knife upright and swung it toward the door just as the wind came crashing against me. I redirected the force of the air and threw the door open. I saw the wizard, dressed in all black and wearing a masked cowl, standing over the general who lay unconscious on the floor--at least I hoped he was unconscious.

I released the Fire symbol from down the hall and reactivated the Air symbol. Just as the wizard moved toward me, I fell onto Cambria to shield him, and a blaze of fire came flying into the room. It flew high above my head and crashed into the wizard with a roar, sending him flying backward over the bed and to the other side of the room. When the flames subsided, I stood up and saw the wizard slouched against the wall, unmoving. A charcoal black halo surrounded him where the fire had hit, but when I noticed that neither his clothing nor skin had been scorched, I quickly laid a Putrefaction symbol.

Before I could activate the spell, the wizard rose to his feet and moved with a deadly speed toward me before I could even stand. I dove sideways toward the bed to avoid him, but he caught hold of my left ankle. I shifted my body and pulled my right leg back and kicked him square in the face; he grunted and held onto me. When I felt him trying to use body magic to weaken my limbs and subdue me, I thanked the stars that I had Veit's talisman ring on my chain and lying against my chest.

I resisted his spell and I delivered another hard kick to his face. With the palms of my hands against the floor, I pushed myself backward and crouched so I could jump to my feet, but he lunged forward and struck me across the face. My jaw exploded in pain, and I saw stars as I went crashing to the floor. I was right next to the bed, and beneath it on the floor I could see the faint shimmer of Cambria's gun.

Unfortunately, I couldn't reach for it just then. The wizard jumped on me and had his hands around my throat. I gasped for air, placing my hands over his and trying to work my own body magic spell, sending tendrils of energy through his hands and up his arms. I directed the energy toward his heart, but I wasn't going to simply stop it--I was going to make it explode.

When he sensed what I was doing, he swung his hands outward and released me, but quickly reciprocated with another strike. As if that weren't enough, he grabbed fistfuls of my hair and slammed the back of my head against the floor. I saw red and black before I even felt the pain, and I lost hold of my concentration and relinquished the spell.

I let my arms fall out to the side, my right hand just inches away from Cambria's gun. I coughed and sputtered again, squinting my eyes and looking into the half-concealed face of the wizard. I took note of every little detail, from the complexion of his skin to his nose and clean-shaven face. The fact that he had absorbed the fire confirmed that he was not a mentalist, but an elemental. He could control and manipulate Earth, Air, Water and Fire--and he apparently had a secondary talent for mental magic, though to a lesser extent. A cold, quiet rage grew inside me and made me tremble, as it became clear who he was.

He must've interpreted this long pause as an act of submission, because he didn't try to strike me again. Straddling me, he bent down and tilted my chin, so I could stare into the darkness where his eyes peered back out at me. *Where's Carson?*

He asked the question telepathically like Henry Smith had described, and the voice sounded like a whisper inside my head. "Go find him yourself, you murderous bastard. You're no different than a warlock."

He sneered at my insult. *What was in the box? What did he give you?*

When I said nothing, he reached down and grabbed the three enchanted rings strung on the silver chain. He could tell they were all infused with magic, but since he couldn't taste metals like an alchemist could, he didn't know which one my father had enchanted. Of course, he wasn't going to let that be a problem because he yanked the chain off. My heart jumped, and I felt a lump in my throat, but if I made any sudden moves, he'd probably kill me.

"You'll never find my father," I told him. "I'm the only one who can activate it."

I didn't know if that was true, but hell, neither did he.

Take me to him, and I will not touch your family. The whispery voice in my head sounded cold.

"All right, but remember this is between you and me. This has nothing to do with them."

Very well. He opened his hand and spread out the three rings on the floor next to my head.

I turned and glanced at them, and his gaze followed-- and my right hand slid closer to the gun under the bed. "It's the plain gold ring."

He grabbed it and flung it across the room. *Don't lie to me.*

I guessed honesty really was the best policy. "Okay...it's the other gold one, the talisman ring."

He reached for it while keeping his gaze fixed on me. I slowly raised my left hand and offered it, so that he wouldn't notice what I was doing with my right. He took the diamond ring off and slid on the talisman ring.

Activate it, and lead me to him.

"Okay." As soon as he made a move to stand, I pulled

out the gun and aimed straight for his head. He made a blocking motion with his hands and turned his head just as I fired, and the bullet pierced his hands and missed his nose by a centimeter. He groaned in pain, using his true voice for the first time. He jumped back and dodged the second bullet, but I shot at him once more and hit him in the shoulder.

"Hotaru, you son of a bitch! It was you!" I pulled the trigger again and he dove for the window, crashing through the glass. My arms and legs quivered as I went over to the window and peered out. He had vanished.

I rushed back over by the bed and knelt over General Cambria. I lightly touched his forehead, scanning his body for any signs for life. He still breathed, but I could detect that Hotaru had injured his heart by literally causing some of the muscle tissue to die. By the minute, he received less oxygen-rich blood to his heart.

"Come on, general," I said as I clasped my fingers together, intertwining them and placing my hands palm down on his chest. I pressed down gently and sent a jolt of energy to his heart. His body trembled and then lay still once more. I sent a slow steady stream of healing energy to his heart tissue, hoping that I could reverse the damage.

I paused for a second and delivered another jolt. He trembled once more, and I felt his chest rise and fall. Then, there was nothing. Even though I felt dizzy and the back of my head still felt like it had been used as a punching bag, I detected some injuries still in his heart that I needed to heal in order to give him a better chance of revival. I fed more energy into the spell as I added more pressure through my hands. When my arms started shaking and the flow of energy had diminished, I knew that my body was telling me that it couldn't be pushed any further.

"Come on, Robert. Wake up." How could I ever face Rob and tell him what happened to his father? No, I needed to save this man. I choked on dread as my body collapsed and my vision dimmed from gray to black. An unwelcome unconsciousness crept upon me.

I hoped that Hotaru didn't decide to come back after me anytime soon.

CHAPTER SIX

"Drink, dear..." a vaguely familiar voice commanded me. A damp towel had been folded and spread across my forehead, and a cushion had been placed behind my head.

"Where am I?" I slowly opened my eyes and still saw hazy images around me.

"You're in my living room," Cambria said. "This woman said she knew you."

"What?" I squinted and raised my right arm so I could rub my eyes, but my limbs still felt weak, so I just let my hand drop back down.

"It's me, Delana." The gypsy turned my face toward her and tipped a glass of water toward my mouth. I took in a small sip and stared at her until she came into focus.

"Delana...what are you doing here?"

"Ammon told me a wizard was stalking you, and he led me here."

"And you came all the way from Baltimore?" I wanted to shudder. There were just too many creepy aspects to her statement. I didn't like the idea of a gypsy medium's "spirit" following me, especially a spirit bold enough to make physical contact. She set the glass of water on the coffee table while Cambria sat at the foot of the couch watching me, and probably feeling just as disturbed.

"Well, thanks for the help." I reached for my blouse and realized that it wasn't the one I wore when I came in.

"I found an old shirt that belonged to Helen," the general explained. "Your friend here changed you," he quickly added.

"Those herbs I gave you did the trick. I also healed the bruising. I see you haven't even opened the satchel." She flipped her long white braid over her shoulder.

"You went into my purse?" I sat up so fast that she jumped back in response.

"Don't worry, I wouldn't steal from you. I even put your rings inside."

"Do you need me to take you to the hospital, Isabella?" Cambria made a furtive glance in Delana's direction.

"No, can I use your phone?" I needed to warn Neal, just in case Hotaru was heading their way.

"It's in the kitchen." He helped me to my feet, and I stood on wobbly legs. We made it over to the kitchen and I grabbed the phone.

"I placed a Circle of Protection around the house!" Delana shouted from the living room.

I shivered and said in reply, "Okay, thanks! But don't do any more spells for me."

"Who is that woman?" Cambria asked.

"I buy enchanted jewelry from her." I dialed home and gripped the receiver in my hand. Each second felt like a millennium as I waited for someone to answer.

"Is Ammon a wizard?"

I shook my head, growing frustrated over the fact that no one had yet picked up the phone. "No, it's a spirit she speaks with, but I don't really get into that sort of thing with her. I just stick with buying the enchanted items."

"Ammon's a ghost?" He gave me an incredulous look.

"No, I said spirit--assuming that's what it really is. Don't talk to her about it."

He gave me a look as if assuring me that it wasn't going to be a problem for him. "No one's answering at the house?"

I shook my head and hung up. "I have to get back

there..."

He must've seen the indecision on my face. He had just recovered from the equivalent of a heart attack, and who knew if Hotaru would come back? However, if he stalked me like Delana said, then maybe he'd come directly for me and leave the general alone. I lightly reached out with my senses and touched Delana's Circle of Protection, gauging its strength. It should hold throughout the night. I'd definitely call General Cambria and check on him.

"Go to them," he said.

"You could come with me for a while."

"Go check on your family. I'll still be here."

"All right, but I'm calling the FBI so they can at least send someone over to watch the house."

"I'll do it. Now go."

"I'll call you tonight."

I ran into the living room and grabbed my belongings. Delana started asking me all kinds of questions, but I ignored her and headed toward the door. When she saw me rush out, she followed.

"Where are you going, Isabella?"

"Home."

"Can I come with you?"

"No." I jumped into the driver seat and fumbled for my keys while Delana poked her head in from the passenger side window.

"I know what you are. Ammon told me."

I cursed under my breath. "Just...get into the car, old woman."

She smiled and got inside. I started the car and took off, hoping that Neal and my family were okay.

***

I almost hit the hedges that lined the driveway when I swerved in and pulled up. I turned the ignition off and ran into the house, not even bothering to see if Delana followed.

The clock struck noon, and though the summer weather was cheery and mild, the turmoil inside me blazed like a storm.

"Neal! Mom!" I called for them as soon as I stepped into the living room. No one answered.

I ran into the kitchen, then the den, and finally went out to the veranda out back. I let out a sigh of relief when I saw Neal sitting at the table outside, enjoying lunch on the back porch with Rachel and my mom. I walked out and went to greet them with a hug and kiss.

"There you are," my mother said, apparently in a better mood than she had been in earlier this morning. "Did you see the bed of petunias?"

"They're beautiful," I said. I glanced back and noticed a single flower trampled underfoot near the narrow walkway. "Sorry about that. Is Johnnie home?"

"He's still at work," Rachel said, pouring me a glass of lemonade. "He should be here soon."

"Neal, may I speak with you for a second?"

"Of course," he said, standing and following me back inside. I led him to the kitchen so that we'd be out of earshot from my mother and Rachel.

"The safe house wizard is Hotaru. He confronted me today."

"Where?"

I frowned. "I was at Robert Cambria's house. I'm sorry, I should've told you."

"Are you hurt?"

"I'm all right, but I had a hell of a fight with him. Is there a way we could bring charges against him at the Tower? I'm not going to let him get away with what he did."

"Yes, but that means you'll have to be at the Gray Tower to do that. Are you prepared for it?"

I didn't think I was. I left the Tower an Apprentice, disillusioned by some of the people there, and put off by the way the Master Wizards demanded everyone's hearts and minds. More important, going there would be walking into

67

the lion's den. I would be walking in there knowing I was the Drifter and knowing they would turn on me. However the enchantment that masked me, that protected me since I was a child...it slipped a little back in France, and I also uncovered hidden memories. One of the Master Wizards, Serafino Pedraic, helped my father protect me long ago. He would be the one I could go to so I could reinforce the mask. Not only that, but if he and a group of other high-ranking wizards had allied themselves with my father, this meant that not all wizards agreed with the Tower's law regarding the Drifter. If I could show them who I was, and that I was willing to work with them to help the world in these dark times, then maybe they would change or even abolish their centuries old decree.

I faced Neal and nodded. "If that's what it takes, then I'll do it. Besides, if Hotaru wants to try and keep a leash on me because of my father, then he'll follow me to the Tower and leave my mother and brother alone."

"I'll go look for him," he said.

"Are you sure about that?"

Any wizards found aiding the Drifter would be subject to punishment, if not execution by the Gray Tower. No one had any proof I had yet reunited with my father and was working to help him, and as far as I knew, no one knew about Brande, or Serafino Pedraic, or the mysterious wizard who went by the name of Jerome. Veit Heilwig, a German alchemist, had been the only wizard expelled from the Order in connection with my father. If The Black Wolves hadn't kidnapped him and his wife, the Order probably would've gotten to Veit first.

Neal placed his right hand on my shoulder in a comforting gesture. "I won't mention anything about your father. Hotaru must be held accountable for what he did, especially since the safe house victims were non-wizards and under the jurisdiction of your government."

And because of Hotaru's brazenly immoral act, it made me all the more frightened of what else he was capable of.

"Please, be careful."

"I will be. When I return, will you tell me why you were with General Cambria?"

"I'll tell you everything you need to know." I decided it was fair enough to explain why I visited Cambria. If he risked his life helping us and chasing after roguish wizards, then the least I could do was fill him in on why. However, announcing to him that I was the Drifter was out of the question.

Delana wandered into the kitchen. "Excuse me, Isabella, where's the bathroom?"

"There's one by the study," I replied with a grimace. "Just make a left at the staircase."

She looked Neal up and down and frowned at him before turning around and heading toward the bathroom. Neal raised an eyebrow. "Who is that?"

"She's...an acquaintance. I'll explain later."

"Tell Rachel and Mary..."

"It's my turn to hold down the fort. Just don't get yourself hurt chasing after Hotaru."

You could get in a good punch with a Philosopher if he or she was having an off day, but they were extremely difficult to harm and kill in battle. He exited the kitchen and left through the front door. I waited there to intercept Delana, not even knowing what I was going to do with her. It probably wouldn't be worth intimidating her through magic. Even though the Gray Tower didn't train her, she had an impressive amount of magical strength. She knew things that even some Apprentices and Elites didn't know-- and of course I hadn't forgotten about those spirits she communed with. The Tower always taught us to avoid the temptation of theurgy, which was magic through invocation and cooperation with the spirit world.

I didn't know if Delana was a theurgist or something close to it, but messing around with the spirit world could grab the attention of things other than spirits. Delana definitely wouldn't have been someone I would share my

69

secret with under any circumstances, so the fact that she discovered it unnerved me. However, the day I last saw her, she actually seemed frightened of me. Was it because the Drifter was someone to be reckoned with? I wondered if she knew anything about my powers and how to control them. Well, as long as she feared me because of this, and if she wanted to be an ally, then at least it would be easier to keep control of the situation.

"Mmm," she said, coming back into the kitchen, "I like this house. Are we going out back to eat?" She peered through the window over the sink and spied the meal set out on the table.

"Yes, but first, there are a few rules I have for you."

She placed her hands on her hips and waited. Great, she wanted to be sassy as well. "What is it?"

"No one knows what I am." For some reason I hated the idea of saying "Drifter" aloud to her. It would be admitting some type of defeat. "So don't tell a living soul. Also, you are not to perform any magic without my permission. The only exception is self-defense or in defense of the members of this household. Don't speak with Ammon or any of your spirits while in this house, and don't offer your services to anyone as a medium."

She let out a low sigh, as if I were her teacher reprimanding her for a childish prank. "Fine, I'll agree to it."

"All right, let's go eat." I led her out to the back porch, ignoring her mumbling about me being an arrogant Tower Slave. I smiled at Rachel and my mother, who were now more notably subdued, and guided Delana to the seat next to mine. I made up an excuse about Neal having to step away for a work-related matter and took my place at the table.

Rachel was the only one to at least try to be jovial. "Isabella, I'm glad you're back, and I see you've brought a friend."

Delana reached for Rachel's hand. "A pleasure to meet

you, I'm Delana Balanescu."

"I'm Rachel, Isabella's sister-in-law," she said, regaining more of her cheerfulness, "and this is our mother...Mary."

My mom shook Delana's hand. "So what brings you from Europe?"

I tensed at her line of questioning and thought of how I could deflect her prying. "Well, Mom, Delana--"

"Your daughter will try to make up something surely as an attempt at modesty," she smirked at me when I gave her a warning look, "but the truth is that she welcomed me into her home when I fled Prague due to the persecutions."

"She stayed with you in London?" Rachel's eyes grew wide.

I nodded and went along. "Really, it's nothing."

"I hadn't a penny in the world," Delana continued, "and she took care of me while I was there. I eventually found work and made it to America, to be with family, and when I found out she was nearby, I felt it would've been an insult not to visit."

Rachel smiled at me. "Wouldn't it be swell to write a book about that? What a story it would make!"

I grabbed my knife and fork and dug into my pot roast and cabbage. "Do you write, Rachel?"

For a moment she paused to stare at Delana wrapping a piece of corn bread in a rag. "Well, I'm no professional, but I have sent in a story or two to McCall's."

"For the homemaking section?" I asked.

"Fiction," she answered in a soft voice.

"Rachel is very talented." My mother smiled at her before taking a sip of lemonade.

"Well, why don't you write professionally?" I asked.

"Oh, I wouldn't want to overwhelm myself." She stood and began rearranging plates and platters, and then grabbed Neal's empty wares. "I'm here with Mother, and I've got the house to take care of, and Johnnie..."

"What does Johnnie think?"

"He's very encouraging, bless him, but--"

71

"Rachel's side of the family is irritatingly strict and traditional," my mother explained.

"Excuse me." She grabbed most of the dirty dishes and snatched up a spare silver knife and fork from Delana's reach before the old woman could get any ideas. She quickly hauled everything into the kitchen.

I glared at my mother. "That was a little rude, don't you think?"

"I just needed her out of the way so I could tell you something," she said matter-of-factly.

"What is it?"

"I may overlook the fact that you left in the morning in a navy blue blouse and returned this afternoon in a black one, or that you're wearing the ring I've seen your father's friend, Veit Heilwig, wear for eighteen years because these may be unimportant in the grand scheme of things. But, I'm not going to sit here and pretend you're not hiding bigger things from me--more important things. I've put up with it for years with Carson, and I think maybe if I had been prying into his dealings more often, somehow he would still be here. I'm not going to make that mistake twice, and I want you to know that whatever it is...I'll do anything to help you. Understand?"

Delana let out a low laugh. Well, at least someone was amused. "I'll excuse myself and let you two talk."

When she had walked off and gone back into the house, I stared at my mother and spoke. "It's complicated. One of the reasons I came back, besides wanting to see you all, was that I had learned a dangerous wizard has targeted you and Johnnie."

"Why?"

"He believes you have information that he needs about Dad."

"And why would he believe that?"

"Because you're...we're his family, and probably the last people to have seen him alive."

"Why does this wizard need to know about Carson?"

"That's what I'm trying to figure out," I said, my cheeks stinging from the lie.

I just couldn't tell her that her husband was number one on the Gray Tower's wanted list, and to try to reach him or be with him would mean death for everyone. And, if I told her about Dad, I'd probably have to tell her about myself-- which I absolutely could not do. If the trackers got hold of her and pried into her mind and read her thoughts and memories, their fury would turn toward me, and my father's self-sacrificial act would be in vain.

"Are you even engaged to Neal?"

I didn't know why, but I laughed, and then I almost cried. "No, the wizard I told you about killed the man who gave me that engagement ring. Do you see why I was afraid to say anything? Why I felt I needed to protect you from all this?"

She nodded, and then got up and came over to wrap me in her arms. "I'm sorry you had to go through that. Needless to say, I know what it feels like to lose the man you love."

All these years I viewed my mother as an oppositional force, someone who tried to hold me back from exploring my abilities and studying at the Gray Tower because of her lack of strength or inability to understand that world. That was the main reason why I had eagerly taken off for London. I now realized that I've underestimated her, though I shouldn't have. She had spent years with my father, one of the brightest Philosophers the Tower has ever trained, and to be with someone like that could be intimidating and would force you to adapt. She could pick up on things that would bypass most other people, and worked through her inferences and conclusions quickly and accurately. I imagined she would have to do that just to keep up with my father.

My mother released me and gazed toward the house. "Johnnie, is everything all right?"

My brother approached with a nervous expression.

73

"There are two FBI agents in the living room asking for you, Isabella...and who's that strange woman in our kitchen?"

"I'll...be right there." Maybe I should've started wearing an "I'll Explain Everything In Due Time" sign around my neck.

My mom threw me a sympathetic glance. "Come and have lunch, Johnnie. And for goodness sake, watch my petunias. She'll fill you in on the details later."

He tried to protest, and was probably of a mind to accompany me back inside. However one stern look from my mother squelched it all rather quickly.

"Go ahead, Isabella. Have a seat, Johnnie."

He obeyed her, all with a look of confusion on his face. I headed in through the kitchen and saw Rachel sitting at the table speaking with Delana. I tugged at the old woman's white braid in passing, just in case she conveniently forgot about our arrangement.

I went down the hallway, past the staircase and into the living room. I felt somewhat relieved to see Jameson and Lainey standing there, but then I thought of two people for whom I had much to be worried about--Henry Smith and Robert Cambria.

"What's going on?" I asked.

"Henry Smith died last night," Jameson said, his expression a mix of anger and disappointment. "We headed this way as soon as it happened, and earlier today we got wind of Cambria's phone call."

"How is he?" I crossed my arms in a gesture of anxiety.

Lainey spoke up. "He's fine. We've got a few special agents watching his house."

"I hope you and Neal have good news for us." Jameson began pacing back and forth.

"The murderer is Hotaru Kimura, and he's a member of the Order."

"Shit," Lainey said. "How high up is he?"

I shuddered as our last encounter flashed through my mind. "He's an Elite. In fact, he's slated to be installed soon

74

as a Master."

Elites were responsible for training Apprentices and Practitioners, while the Masters instructed only Elites and molded them to become the next generation of leaders. I had met Hotaru when I first arrived at the Gray Tower, and ironically I even sparred with him a few times at the training grounds. He was strong, cunning, and one of the most arrogant men I'd ever met.

"And what are our chances of bringing him in for prosecution?" Jameson stopped pacing and faced me with a hopeful expression.

I raised an eyebrow. "Assuming you're even able to capture and arrest him? The Council would send Master Priya to swoop in and use lawyers to bail him out, and if that didn't work, they'd find a way to just take him away."

"And if we press the matter," Lainey said, "it would create a rift between U.S. and Gray Tower relations, which we don't need right now."

"That's why Neal and I believe we'll have a better chance seeking justice on Tower grounds. We're bringing this to the Council ourselves."

"Speaking of, where is he?" Lainey asked.

"He went after Hotaru. He promised he'd be back."

Jameson and Lainey exchanged doubtful looks. Jameson handed me his calling card with an address and number written on the back. "We'll be in town for the rest of the week. Call us at this hotel if you need us."

"I'll let you two know if I find out anything else." I slipped the card into my pocket.

"Take care, Isabella." Lainey smiled ruefully, and Jameson followed him out.

I closed the door behind them, and then remembered I had left my belongings in the car. I ran outside and over to the driveway, where I had parked my mother's car in haste. I grabbed my purse and handbag and brought them inside, careful to make it upstairs without being detected. I made sure Veit's diary was there, and sandwiched the bundled papers in between Veit's pages before stashing everything under my bed. I paused to switch Veit's ring over to my right hand and put the engagement ring back on my left ring finger. I had a feeling that my mother would at least withhold from Johnnie the part about me not really being engaged.

I went back downstairs and through the kitchen, halting in my steps when I saw my mother, brother, and Rachel sitting outside at the table conversing and eating. Delana still sat at the kitchen table, her expression stiff and her eyes oddly seeing something that wasn't there.

"Delana...are you all right?"

"Yes," she said to me absentmindedly in Romanian. "I'm trying to ignore what's coming my way."

"Is it tough?"

She faced me with a scowl. "Have you ever sat near a roaring ocean and pretended nothing was there?"

"My Romanian isn't so good. Can you please speak in English?"

"Something's scratching at my door. Something important needs to get in."

"No." I walked out, not wanting to hear any pleads, warnings, or threats.

I joined my family at the table, reminding myself that before the night ended that I'd ask Johnnie to take a look at the texts and to arrange that meeting between Dr. Grey and me. For now at least, I just wanted to sit and enjoy a meal with the people who mattered to me most, instead of worrying about all the horrible ways I could lose them.

CHAPTER SEVEN

It was six o' clock, and Neal hadn't shown up yet. I felt ill to my stomach and tried to block out images of Hotaru engulfing him in fire or burying him in an earthquake. Rachel sensed my unease and coaxed me into helping her set up snacks and dessert for Johnnie and his poker pals. She had fresh fruit and vegetables ready, a creamy potato soup, and even homemade ice cream. Since I had seen my friend back in London, Jane Lewis, bake in the kitchen several times, I volunteered to make the apple pie. It smelled strong and spicy coming out of the oven, and I secretly wanted to do a victory dance over this little triumph. At least I knew my future family could always count on me for dessert.

The doorbell rang, and Rachel steered me away from gloating over my pie sitting on the counter and nudged me toward the door. She opened the front door and a group of three men, shouting their salutations and giving Rachel a hug and a kiss on the cheek, walked in and greeted me.

Rachel introduced us. "Dillon, Frankie, and Jim, this is my sister-in-law, Isabella."

"Well, hello! I didn't know Dr. George had a sister." Dillon's compact frame carried him over, and he shook my hand. His golden yellow hair matched the pullover sweater he wore.

"And a beautiful one, at that," Frankie said as he adjusted his thick glasses.

Jim shook his head. "Don't mind them, they're a couple of graduate students who somehow found their way into Jonathan's good graces."

I shook Jim's hand and gave him a good lookover. He resembled the actor Vincent Price with his dominating eyes and thin mustache. "Well, it's nice to meet you. Do you work with my brother?"

"We're colleagues," Jim said. "I teach physics at the university."

"That sounds wonderful." It really didn't, but I just wanted an excuse to keep looking at Jim. Rachel ushered the guys into the dining room so they could have a seat at the table. She went into the kitchen to grab the food and drinks while I stayed in the dining room with them.

"Do you live around here?" Frankie took off his glasses and wiped the lenses with his shirt.

"No, I've actually been out of the country a few years. I just got back from London."

"Studying?" Dillon asked.

"No, working. I'm a clerk in the U.S. ambassador's office." It would have been infinitely more interesting to tell them I was a spy.

"Must be exciting," Jim said in an encouraging tone. "Did you go to Radcliffe?"

"Yes," I said with a grin.

Johnnie finally came in. "Are we ready, gentlemen?"

"You bet we are," Dillon said as he adjusted his yellow sweater. "Are you joining the game, Isabella? Maybe you can help out your brother."

Johnnie laughed and took his seat. "Actually, Dill, her fiancé will be."

Both Frankie's and Dillon's gazes seemed to go directly to my diamond ring. Dillon seemed not to be fazed and smirked. "Then we should grill him, right big brother?"

"I assure you, there's nothing to grill him about. Neal is a swell guy," Johnnie said.

Rachel had come in with the refreshments. "I love Neal!"

"You'll like him too," I said to the guys, though I laughed inside at the thought of Dillon trying to "grill" him.

"Isabella, go grab your pie and bring it over for the boys." She began pouring drinks.

I went into the kitchen and grabbed the pie from the counter. I thought about cutting a slice for Delana, who was staying in the other guestroom upstairs, but then decided that I'd just wait. My mother had retired to bed earlier, complaining of a headache.

Just as I made it back into the dining room, the doorbell rang. My heart jumped, and I set the pie in the center of the table before signaling to Rachel that I'd answer the door. I breathed a sigh of relief when I saw Neal. I quickly stepped outside and closed the door. It was still very warm outside, and the sun hadn't set yet. He stood there, in silence. Before even speaking, I lightly touched his cheek and sent a whisper of magical energy toward the part of his brain responsible for processing pain. A quick probe told me that he was fine. The only thing I could detect out of the ordinary was the amount of alcohol coursing through his system.

"Neal, what happened?"

"You were right about Hotaru."

"So you caught up with him?"

He nodded. "We got into a brawl, and I told him that if he ever came to this house or near your family, that I'd kill him."

"Well, that sounds productive. Any particular reason why you had more drinks than a sailor?"

"Did I mention we brawled in a bar? All that fighting can make a bloke thirsty."

"I see..." I could tell there was something else exchanged besides blows. What did they say to one another?

"Now, will you tell me about Robert Cambria and his

79

connection to your father?"

"Johnnie's friends are here. They're waiting for you so they can start the game."

"Of course, I haven't forgotten. Then later tonight?"

"I can tell them you're not feeling well. Do you want to go lie down?" I didn't know why he didn't bother to use any body magic to counteract the alcohol.

"I'm well enough."

"They're waiting for us," I said.

He gazed at me, his expression unreadable. "Very well, ladies first."

I sighed and opened the door. I led him into the dining room and had him sit across from Johnnie. I hoped that a carefree evening with my brother and his friends would help Neal relax, and maybe he'd go more into detail about what happened between him and Hotaru.

"Johnnie," I said, noticing that he hadn't tried my dessert, "do you want some pie?"

He smiled a little too hard. "Rachel said you made it. I...didn't know you cooked...food."

"I'm full of surprises, aren't I?" I cut him a slice and shoved the plate in front of him.

"Go ahead," I prompted, "try it and tell me what you think."

Johnnie looked to his right at Frankie, and then to his left at Jim. When no one said anything, he grabbed his fork and loosened his tie. "It does smell delicious--yes, a hint of cinnamon, right?"

His companions watched him with an odd fascination and gestured for him to take a bite. He shoveled a piece of pie into his mouth and squinted. He chewed slowly and paused to smile at me. "This is unbelievable," he said in a high-pitched voice.

"Really, Johnnie?"

"Thank you for the pie." He swallowed and smiled at me.

I smiled too, and cut another slice. All the guys looked at

each other, and when I set the next slice in front of Neal, the others spoke about how delicious it smelled and how they couldn't wait to try.

Neal shook his head. "I think we should heed poor Jonathan's silent warning."

Jerk. He was just mad that I didn't share about General Cambria. "You like my pie, Johnnie, right?"

He sucked in his lips and answered in a strangled voice, "Uh huh."

"It may taste a little different, I admit, but I thought it'd be interesting to be a little more creative with the mixture of spices."

I broke off a piece of pie with Neal's fork and offered it to him. He opened his mouth and let me feed it to him. Without a single expression of displeasure, he ate the pie. "Thank you, love."

"I need some beer or something," Johnnie mumbled.

Rachel had come in with a book in her hand and her purse hanging on her shoulder. "Isabella, are you ready for the book club?"

"Yes." I put down Neal's fork.

"I'll make sure to save you some pie," Neal said.

"I'll be back soon enough," I snapped in response to his cheeky tone. I headed out the door behind Rachel without looking back.

***

To my dismay, Delana had run out of the house and caught up with us just as we exited the front gate and turned onto the sidewalk.

"May I join you and Rachel?" She wrapped a blue shawl around herself--*my* blue shawl--and hung a shopping tote on her arm.

Rachel shrugged and smiled when she saw my annoyed expression. "Of course you can, Delana."

"Come on, then." I wished that Delana would just stay

81

holed up in her room for the night.

"We're not going in the car?" Delana asked, walking behind us.

"It's at my friend Roxanna's place, just a few houses down." Rachel looped her arm around mine so that we walked arm-in-arm down the street. There were a couple of kids out riding bikes, a few cars barreling down the street and turning into driveways, and the scent of food wafting throughout the neighborhood.

"Rachel, do you have any brothers or sisters?" I asked.

She shook her head. "I'm an only child."

"I'm sorry about what Mom said earlier. Sometimes she's a little more blunt than necessary."

"It's fine, really. Most of the time we get along well."

"Most of the time?"

She chuckled. "I hope you and Neal can stay. Have you made a decision yet?"

Neal was the last person I wanted to discuss right now. "No, but tell me, whatever happened with those McCall's stories? If Mom thinks you're good, then I'm sure the magazine should've been pounding on your door already."

"Do they have food at this...book club?" Delana caught up and sidled next to me.

"Certainly," Rachel said. "Did you bring a book that you'd like to discuss?"

"I borrowed one of Isabella's, and I'm halfway through." She opened the tote and started rummaging inside.

"It had better not be the one written in Turkish," I told her. Why did this woman invade my privacy like no other? Maybe she should start spying for SOE.

"No, it's a story book."

I decided to ignore her for the next ten minutes. "Rachel? What about the stories?"

"Oh, well...I did get a response from one of the editors, and he was actually down at the university for a visit, so I met up with him at a nearby café to discuss my prospective career." She stared at the ground.

82

"And?"

"Let's just say that he wanted to continue the discussion--" she peered at Delana and then whispered into my ear, "in his hotel room."

A wave of anger ran over me. "You refused, and so he destroyed any chance you had of getting published by the magazine."

She nodded. "I sent in at least one more since then, but of course he sent a letter in reply stating that my writing was...*the insipid musings of a puritanical housewife.*"

"What's this guy's name?"

"It's no use..."

"Just tell me."

"Philip Parrish."

"Well, Mr. Parrish is going to wish he had never done that."

She gave me an anxious look, but then paused in front of a hedge surrounding a large cottage. "We're here."

We passed beneath the arch, which I could sense was made of very old iron, and had the hint of an enchantment. Iron not only possessed the quality to deal corrosive damage to an enemy, but also to protect its user. The owner placed the arch here so that no one intending harm could comfortably enter the premises.

Interesting.

We made it up the porch steps and went straight inside since the door was already open. A woman wearing a small hat and business attire, Charlene, greeted us and had us sit in the living room. There were about seven other women sitting in a circle, some dressed casually while others still wearing their work attire. Rachel had taken the empty seat next to her friend, Roxanna, a tall woman with light brown hair and hazel eyes. Delana and I sat next to one another. Rachel introduced Delana and me, and recounted the old woman's tale of escaping Prague and finding her way here. If anyone should've gotten credit for saving her from the slaughters by the Nazis and Black Wolves in

83

Czechoslovakia, it should've been Brande and my friend Jasmine Léon. They were the ones collaborating and smuggling people into France and securing safe passage for them to other countries.

"Welcome, Isabella and Delana. It's an honor to have you here." Roxanna smoothed her deep blue dress, then approached and grabbed our hands and squeezed them. I could sense an aura of magic surrounding Roxanna, though it wasn't very strong. She gasped when she picked up on traces of magic emanating from Delana and me. Without another word, she reclaimed her seat, and the meeting began.

Charlene began describing her latest read, *Windswept*, and how she loved the chronicling of the Marston family's challenges and triumphs. Several of the other women wrote down the book title and author, thanking Charlene for the recommendation. Rachel went next and introduced *The Keys of the Kingdom*.

"Even though I was raised Methodist," she explained, "I found myself drawn into the story of Father Francis Chisholm. He endured much suffering and maltreatment as a child, yet became the most caring and humble man of all. It's a story about people, both good and bad, and the settings--well, the story will take you from Scotland to China. It's wonderful, really. You should all read it when you get a chance."

Everyone copied down the title and author once more. Roxanna suggested that Delana share. Unfortunately she had nodded off, but the girls were gracious about it and Charlene even went to grab a hot cup of tea for her. Delana rubbed her sleepy eyes and grabbed the tote, pulling out a red book that looked awfully familiar.

"Let's see," she said, blowing some of her hair out of her face with a huff. "This book is entitled...*Three Weeks*, by some woman named Elinor Glyn."

Oh God.

I blushed as I excused myself to the kitchen where I got

acquainted with a tall glass of wine. Within seconds, I heard a roar of raucous laughter mingled with shocked squeals. I hoped they wouldn't ask where Delana had gotten the book. It just so happened that I had received it at a pub from a barkeep who had a penchant for finding raunchy books.

Roxanna came in, still carrying a lilt of laughter from the living room. She spied me downing my drink and gave me a sympathetic squeeze on the shoulder. "I take it you're familiar with the book?"

I nodded. "But it sounds like Delana can explain the story much better than I could."

She went over to the cutting board and started slicing some bread and a block of cheese. "Well, let her know that she's welcome here any time, and so are you."

"Thank you." I studied her, trying to pinpoint her magical abilities. "I noticed the arch over the walkway and all the hedging. You've created a very balanced environment, Roxanna."

She began placing the bread and cheese on a platter. "Thank you. I left the Gray Tower ten years ago a Practitioner."

"Nature magic?"

"Yes. And you're an alchemist, right?"

"It looks like your senses are well-tuned."

I wasn't sure if I should ask her about why she may have left the Tower. For some people, it could be a touchy subject. Most Practitioners left because the Tower had judged them deficient, as people who could never rise to the ranks of Elite or Master. The Tower would train them of course, so that they wouldn't kill themselves or others by accident or misuse, but would quickly turn Practitioners back out into the world. On the other hand, some Practitioners were just happy with basic training, and left on their own to choose whatever vocation suited them. Of course if the Tower *really* wanted you to stay and continue training, it often had ways of making that happen.

"I have improved in some things over the years," she said, grabbing the platter. "I do healings, a bit of elementalism...that sort of thing."

A wizard trained in nature magic could restore or disrupt the natural flow of human and creature bodies, and even manipulate and transform them. They knew how to work the energy inherent in the forces of nature like elementals, and could break curses and lift enchantments.

"Could I ask you something?" I finished my drink and set the glass on the counter.

"What is it?"

"Could you...read me, and tell me what you sense?"

She looked at me with a puzzled expression. "Oh, then let me give this to the girls, and I'll be back."

I watched her leave with the platter, and then berated myself for having asked her to look inside me. But I needed to know *specifically* what other people saw when they looked at me--and better to ask Roxanna the Practitioiner than Neal Warren the Elite Philosopher. I knew that in general, other wizards could still read me as an alchemist, but how long would that last? Each time Neal looked at me and said nothing, I knew he sensed something that wasn't supposed to be there. He would slowly unravel the web until he'd finally unmask me--and then he would have to make a choice between our friendship and the Tower.

When Roxanna returned, she grabbed a clean cloth and wet it, then rubbed a little soap into it. She brought the cloth over and began rubbing my hands. "First, clean your hands. Then, clear your mind."

I took a deep breath as she soaked the cloth and placed it over my outstretched hands. Water dripped to the floor, but she paid it no attention as she took the cloth away and proceeded to dry my hands with a new one. She then grabbed my hands, holding them in hers, and just stood still for a good minute or two. When I was about to ask her if she sensed anything, her hold became a grip, and she mumbled something.

I got nervous and broke away. "What is it?"

"I'm not sure. Your body and magical aura seem balanced, but then at the same time I sense something else. I see you, but there's some type of mask too. But then again, I don't expect to read an Apprentice Wizard like I do normal people or other Practicioners. It's probably the protective spells you've set up around yourself to guard your psyche against attacks. If there was something you were looking for, I'm sorry I couldn't find it for you."

"Don't be," I said. "Thank you."

I would need to go to the Gray Tower and have this so-called mask fortified by the wizards who had placed it there to begin with. But until then, I'd have to be very careful. I already had Delana's cousin, Nena, seal my mind so that mentalists couldn't see into my thoughts or memories. But I couldn't control the fire that had erupted around me, and I needed my father's allies at the Tower to help with that. What if I had another crazy dream and woke up in flames like I did that time in France? How would I explain that to Neal if it happened again?

Roxanna gestured toward the living room. "Let's finish up. Whatever it is, I'm sure it will work out fine."

I put on a smile, even though I felt like I had been punched in the gut. "I'm sure it will."

CHAPTER EIGHT

Night had fallen when Rachel, Delana, and I said our goodbyes to the other women. We made our way down the passageway and beneath the iron arch. Though the street had grown solitary and silent, as soon as we left Roxanna's house, I felt a menacing presence behind us. It tried to cloak itself at first and blend in with the atmosphere, but I could still detect it. When I glanced at Delana and saw her expression, I knew she had felt it too. I gave her a silent nod, giving her permission to use any powers at her disposal.

"Rachel," I said in almost a whisper, "someone dangerous is following us. I want you to run as fast as you can down to the house. Don't try to stop for us or wait."

"I'm not leaving you." She grabbed my hand.

"Please." I squeezed her hand, using my body magic to impress upon her the urge to go home.

"All right." Her hand slipped from mine, and she sprinted down the street toward the house. We felt the presence still behind us.

"He's getting closer," Delana warned. "I think it's the wizard Ammon warned me about."

"The elemental wizard?" I tried to reach out with my senses for Hotaru, but all I got was a cold, brooding force of power waiting in the darkness and ready to unleash itself.

She shook her head. "You call them warlocks, no? This one's a warlock, not a Tower Slave."

"A warlock? Why would he be here?"

She smirked. "Ammon said because Octavian, the Cruenti Master, holds you responsible for the death of his brother."

Well, I couldn't say this was unexpected. "Delana, get a spell ready." I grabbed my golden alchemist's knife from my purse and laid it against my vitriol bracelet, using the power from the alchemical bracelet to charge the knife with magical energy.

"I'm ready when you are." Delana's eyes gleamed red.

"Now."

We both spun around to confront the presence behind us, but saw nothing, and only felt a shadow of what was there. A pair of headlights and the rumble of a car engine headed our way from the opposite end of the street, and we both tensed and readied our magic. The car slowly approached, and when I saw the driver and passenger, I relaxed. They pulled up to us and stopped.

"Lainey...Jameson, what are you doing here?" I motioned to Delana to go follow Rachel. She mumbled something to Ammon and then took off.

"We got word from SOE that there's a warlock named Ryker headed this way," Lainey said. He stopped the car and Jameson got out and steered me inside. Once Jameson got back in, Lainey resumed driving.

Jameson spoke up. "We don't know who sent the information from the London office, but it was passed from OSS in Washington and on to us. We've got a security detail on your family now."

"Thanks. I have a feeling he's here already, so be careful. Did SOE explain why Ryker was after me?"

Lainey parked the car in front of the house. I could see a couple of FBI agents in a car across the street. Delana and Rachel waited on the front porch.

"No, it didn't explain why," Lainey answered. "What did you do to piss off a warlock?"

"I killed some of them while on mission in Europe." Served them right, especially if the warlock was a Cruenti.

"Miss George," Lainey said with a nod of approval, "I finally got around to reading your report from SOE. I think I'm beginning to like you."

Jameson grinned and shook his head. "Just remember we'll be around to help. Each agent is carrying a gun with iron-tipped bullets and an imperium collar."

I made a move to get out of the car, but then paused when I remembered something. "This is something personal, but I was wondering if you could find any information you may have on a Philip Parrish. He's a McCall's magazine editor."

Lainey nodded. "I'll make a few phone calls."

Jameson gazed at me. "We haven't seen or heard from Hotaru Kimura. Do you think he left the area?"

"I don't know, but Neal is back. I don't think Hotaru will come around my family, but he may try to track me if I leave Cambridge. How's General Cambria holding up?"

"Cambria is starting to complain about the security detail, but other than that, he's fine." Jameson got out and came over to my side to open the door for me.

"Thanks," I said, as he offered his hand and helped me out. "Can you try to find out who sent that message from SOE?"

"We're already on it," Lainey said.

"Good luck." I crossed the street and headed toward Delana and Rachel who were still standing on the porch. When Jameson and Lainey saw me walk up the steps and go inside, they took off.

Delana yawned and then went straight upstairs. Rachel and I went through the living room and could hear Johnnie still in the dining room with Neal, Dillon, and Jim. Frankie had already departed. We came around to the dining room and saw that the playing cards had been shoved aside and several empty bottles of beer stood on the table. The guys sat around absorbed in some type of serious discussion and hadn't noticed us. Jim grew excited about something Neal wrote down on a napkin, and thanked him when he handed it to him.

"I'm in awe," he said, examining the napkin. "I never even thought to look at it from that perspective! I've spent the last two months trying to figure out that equation. And you say you just work in the embassy as a liaison?"

Neal downed another bottle of beer. "Wasted talent, I suppose."

Johnnie wore a huge grin. "This was the best poker night I've ever had. I can't believe I won five times!"

Jim chuckled. "Sheer luck, my friend. Next time I'll have the upper hand."

Dillon smirked. "I wish Dr. Grey could've come tonight. Wouldn't you like to see the look on his face after losing?"

"Oh, come on," Johnnie said. "Dr. Grey is not that bad once you get to know him. He's just...very dedicated."

"Yes, to himself!" Dillon laughed. "I swear if he weren't building a reputation off of that Suleiman project, he wouldn't even have bothered coming to Harvard. You know how snobbish some Brits can be." He stood and slapped Neal on the shoulder. "But not you, buddy. You're all right."

"Yes, thank you." Neal glanced in my direction and gave me a wry smile.

Jim looked at his wristwatch. "Dill, are you ready to go?"

Dillon looked up and smiled at us. He had taken off his yellow sweater and lounged comfortably in his white short-sleeved shirt. "Rachel, Isabella...how was your book club?"

Rachel sighed and shook her head. "Jonathan George, I hope you didn't spill any beer on that carpet."

Johnnie wisely said nothing and began collecting the bottles. Dillon and Jim said goodbye to us and then headed out. When Johnnie and Rachel hauled the empty beer bottles into the kitchen, I approached Neal and sat next to him.

"There's a warlock named Ryker tracking me. Octavian sent him because I got Marcellus decapitated."

91

Marcellus Eckhard, or "Marc," was a Cruenti warlock who ran a Nazi research laboratory in Reims, France. He believed my dad was the Drifter, and wanted to lay hold of my father so he could drink his blood and steal his powers. However when we raided Marc's lab a couple of months ago, the warlock was cut down by a sword-wielding Catholic priest.

"I sensed Ryker down the street as well." Neal opened one last beer bottle. How much was this man planning to drink tonight? "We'll set up an ambush and flush him out. He can't be allowed to make the first move."

"So, I promised to tell you about Robert Cambria..."

"Meet me at the guesthouse."

"Why?"

"The old woman," he simply said, as if that were reason enough. I didn't necessarily blame him.

"Okay."

Rachel came back in. "Did you enjoy the game, Neal?"

"Most certainly. Did Jonathan tell you that he won five times?"

"Really?" She gazed at my brother with suspicion as he came in from the kitchen with a grin across his face.

"Good job, Johnnie." I smirked and glanced at Neal.

"Well," Neal stood, "I'll be off to bed. Thank you for your hospitality."

"Oh, Neal," Rachel said as she wrapped her arms around him and gave him a kiss on the cheek. "We're practically family."

I cringed a little. "Goodnight, Neal."

As Neal left the dining room, Rachel grabbed the remaining beer bottles and took them away. The Turkish texts came to mind, and I pulled Johnnie aside. "Do you remember Veit Heilwig?"

"You mean Dad's old friend from Germany? Yes."

"I met him a couple of months ago."

"Where?"

"In France, but...he's dead now."

"What's going on?"

"He left me his diary, and some of it is in Turkish...just like some papers Dad left me."

"So you've been looking into his last trip to the Ottoman Empire as well."

I nodded and took a seat. "These are important, Johnnie. No one knows about these, not even Neal. I need to come with you tomorrow to meet Dr. Grey. I need him to tell me what the texts say. It has to do with our father and me."

His gaze grew tense. "Why was the FBI here?"

"They're here to protect you."

"Are you going to tell me what from? Is there anything else I should know?"

"Well," I said in a level voice, "don't trust anyone who may approach you claiming to be from the Gray Tower."

He frowned. "I'm not letting you anywhere near Dr. Grey unless you tell me everything."

I gritted my teeth. "I can't...not yet."

"It's not fair. You...you go off for all these years and just come back with secrets that could get us killed."

"Johnnie--"

"Yes it's all to protect us, I'm sure." He shook his head, probably thinking about that night my mother threw a vase at my father's head to try and keep him from taking me for testing with the Gray Tower. My father had told my mother what he did was for my benefit, while holding back so many crucial details. It never occurred to me Johnnie could feel helpless and frustrated like my mother once did.

"I'm sorry."

"Whatever it is," he said, "I hope you know what you're doing. I'll take you to Dr. Grey when you're ready to actually tell me what's going on."

Suddenly I had a mind to give him a good jab in his shoulder and let him know that this wasn't easy for me. If only he knew what I've been through, he'd understand. Whatever resentment or anger had been boiling beneath the surface, he could take it and direct it at our father or

93

whoever else--but not me.

Johnnie turned away and went to join Rachel in the kitchen. I waited for them to go upstairs, all the while still arguing against him in my head. Whether he liked it or not, I needed to see Dr. Grey in the morning about the Turkish texts. I finally stood and passed through the kitchen and out the back door.

I walked past the garden and down the cobblestone pathway, and was careful not to crush a single petunia. I went and knocked on the door, and at Neal's beckoning I entered. He sat on the floor with his back against the loveseat. He wore a white fleece undershirt and plaid pajama pants.

He made small movements with his index finger, creating tiny luminous words, phrases, numbers and questions in mid-air. I had seen Veit Heilwig do something similar, although Veit used the ability to cast alchemical spells without the use of an alchemist's knife. It seemed Neal was sorting out a picture in his mind; the gears were turning, his calculations running and re-running, and there were missing pieces. Did he want me to complete the puzzle?

"How are you feeling?" I slipped off my heels and winced. I should've worn more comfortable shoes today.

"I feel subdued, but it can't be helped after imbibing so many barbiturates."

I walked around his mid-air collage of facts and numbers. I settled on the floor next to him and spoke. "General Cambria was a close friend of my father's. Our families would spend vacations together, and Robert Jr. and I even went to the same schools. The general volunteered to come that day, when the Army needed to deliver the results of its investigation into my father's disappearance. I'd probably see him once a year after that, usually around Christmas, until I left for college. I hadn't seen him in ten years until this week. He had promised to keep something my father gave him--something meant for me. He left me

94

his wedding ring, and it's enchanted. He'll find me with it."

I also mentioned the cryptic note my father had left me while in France, but avoided the subject of Veit Heilwig, his diary, and the Turkish texts. I was certain Neal had read the report I submitted to MI6 before leaving London, and I hoped he wouldn't pry into what happened with Veit.

"Has your father tried to contact you since you've been here?" He began connecting names and phrases with a bright silvery line.

"No, I'm still waiting."

"You want to help him."

"He's my father. Why wouldn't I?"

"You want to help him even though it could destroy lives?"

I glared at him. "You don't know what he's capable of. You don't know what any Drifter is capable of. If the Masters stopped executing them and burying knowledge about them, then maybe they could actually learn something."

"It's in our best interest to safeguard our knowledge about a Drifter's abilities. If the previous three Drifters had known and understood the depth of their power, they would have been unstoppable. One of them has already done much harm to the world."

"Well let me ask you a question. Back in London you told me you weren't one of the seven trackers. I think you lied. Why haven't you admitted to being one of the trackers?"

"Would it make you feel better if I did? I think I've been fairly inactive as of late, in case you haven't noticed."

"I didn't mean it in that way." His comment stung me. He had been here protecting my family this whole time and has helped me on more than one occasion--his actions hadn't gone unnoticed. Brande was a tracker too, and he sided with me.

"May I ask how close you and Brande are?"

I wasn't going to share with him how I felt about

Brande, and the twinge of guilt I felt over it whenever I thought of Ken told me that I had better not. "We're good friends. We trust each other with our lives."

"You don't want to discuss Veit Heilwig...why?"

He was starting to do that Philosopher thing where he'd ask you a bunch of successive questions and then at the end--voilá! He's figured out everything and had you confessing to kidnapping the Lindbergh baby. It was definitely time to start wrapping up this Q&A. I would try deflecting his line of logic by turning the conversation toward feelings and emotion.

"Neal...I feel guilty about not being able to save Veit. I found out that he knew my father and remained a faithful friend, even though it resulted in him being expelled from the Order. Veit died helping me."

I lowered my gaze and blinked; I shed a few false tears. They've gotten me out of some tight spots while on assignment back in Europe. Neal brushed my left cheek with his thumb and then leaned in. He nestled his right cheek against mine, and though his lips brushed against my skin, he didn't kiss me. He framed the other side of my face with his hand.

He said in a gentle voice, "Your body temperature is too low, and your breathing hasn't quickened, which means these tears aren't the result of a saddened emotional state."

Damn it.

I broke away. "Fine, I know you read the report I gave to MI6. Everything you want to know about Veit Heilwig is in there. Case closed."

"Veit Heilwig stole several texts given to the Tower from Mehmed VI's personal collection. Did you know this?"

"Master Erin told me he stole something, but she didn't say what." I've made it through Nazi checkpoints and interrogations--but it looked like I would have to retreat from my tangle with a Philosopher.

"There are still unanswered questions, Isabella."

"You're telling me," I said, pretending to yawn. "I think

I need to get to bed. We'll figure out what to do about Ryker in the morning." I stood and went over to my heels, deciding to carry them instead of putting them on again.

As I stepped through the doorway and onto the deck, Neal asked me one final question: "Do you trust me?"

"Why would you need to ask that?"

"Because you're holding back."

"Maybe it's for a good reason," I said with a harsh edge. "Brande may have sent you here to help, but it doesn't mean I have to share everything with you."

I turned and walked off, once more stepping onto the pathway. The curved stones felt cool and hard beneath my feet, and I made sure to land my steps lightly. I was forced to halt when I felt a shiver run up and down my spine, and the subtle prying of someone's magic trying to force its way into my mind.

No. He wouldn't.

I spun around and saw Neal racing toward me, and my heart dropped as I turned back around and fled toward the main house. He caught up to me and tackled me from behind, and we tumbled down into the grass.

"What the hell are you doing?"

"Don't move."

"What--" I lost my train of thought when a twelve-inch dagger cut through the air and lodged itself in the ground just inches from my head.

"It's the warlock, Ryker." He grabbed the dagger and got up, facing the direction of the guesthouse.

I sunk my fingers into the earth and laid Fire and Air symbols, and charged them. I quickly stood, just in time to hear three more whizzes in the air and taste the essence of cold steel. Neal held the dagger upright and made a quick arch with it to deflect three knives that came hurtling toward him, though he had little light from the guesthouse deck and open doorway.

I felt the warlock to my left. He was almost a shadow, but I dodged a punch he threw and reciprocated with a jab to his face. He quickly recovered and pulled out another steel dagger, but I sent a gust of wind hitting him sideways and knocking him to the ground. He rolled into the fall and made it to his knees just in time to parry Neal's strike. They went back and forth, countering each other's strikes and thrusts, until I flicked my wrist and sent a thin stream of fire toward Ryker.

The warlock swung himself backward to avoid the fire, and Neal voiced an enchantment that called the fire to rebound and cling to the dagger. I rushed toward them as Neal thrust the fiery dagger at Ryker, who had activated a Circle of Protection. I knelt to the ground and began using the dagger to lay an Earth symbol--an upside down triangle with a vertical line running through the bottom--and an Air symbol. Combined, both symbols would hold Ryker in place, and he wouldn't be able to move. However, when the warlock saw what I intended to do, he made a quick motion with his hand and jumped into the air, disappearing as quickly as he had come.

Neal quenched the flame on the dagger's blade and drew in a deep breath. "This was a test. He wanted to gauge our skills and strength."

"You could've gotten him if you weren't drunk." I approached and grabbed the second dagger from him. I examined both of them, but there were no distinctive designs or markings on the hilts.

"I'll place a Circle of Protection around the property," he said, looking up into the night sky.

"If he comes back and breaks your Circle, you'd be alone over here. Why don't you stay in the main house?"

"I doubt he'll be back tonight, or that he could break my Circle...but I'll do as you say."

"Here you go." I handed him the daggers. I could taste the enchantment latent in the metal, meant to help Ryker track whoever possessed it. It would be best for Neal to keep them instead of me.

"I take it you're no longer displeased with me?" A faint

glow emanated from his hand as he focused on the daggers. I could feel his magic at work, unraveling the enchantment woven into them.

"Well, when a guy saves a girl from getting impaled by a dagger, she tends to warm up to him. You get to sleep on the couch tonight."

He broke the enchantment on the daggers, and the light from his hand subsided. "I'll be inside shortly. Let me cast the Circle."

I headed toward the veranda, stopping to pick up my shoes, but then turned to face Neal once more. "Can I ask you something about the Drifter?"

His expression was unreadable. "Yes."

"You said a Drifter already harmed the world. How?"

"How well do you remember your Tower history?"

I shrugged. "I know the basics."

"Are you sure? Or, like most Practitioners and Apprentices, were you busy sneaking into Prague for late night outings?"

I waved my hand through the air. "For your information, I followed the rules and passed all my courses." Okay, maybe I did sneak into a dance hall or bar a few times, but he didn't have to know that.

"Isabella, when was the Order of Wizards founded?"

"In the early Middle Ages."

"When did the Cruenti and Black Wolves arise?"

"At the same time as the Order."

"*Before*, the Order. Before."

A chill ran down my spine as I began to see where he was leading me. "What happened back then?"

"The first Drifter, Besart Frasheri, opened a rift between time and eternity back in 1265. This allowed demons in the spirit world to sense and be drawn to wizards."

Disgust took hold of me and I felt like I couldn't breathe. "I think I've heard enough."

He gazed at me as if saying that he wasn't finished, and I had better stick around to hear the rest. "Since then, more rifts have been opened by successive Drifters. As far as I'm concerned, the Drifter is responsible for the existence of Cruenti and Black Wolves, and for Octavian. Did you think the Order simply decided on a whim that it didn't like Drifters, or that the trackers acted out of envy or fear of the Drifter? We are the world's last line of defense against its total destruction."

"Okay, you've made your point."

The back of my throat ached, and my heart began racing. I knew that the type of magic a Drifter could do was forbidden, but I didn't know that the first one brought Cruenti into our world, and through them, the Black Wolves. It seemed the Order of Wizards had a dual purpose: to train wizards who would help guide the world, and to protect it from the Drifter. To protect it from me. I turned away, not even sure if I could offer any kind of argument or justification. I went inside the house and sensed the moment he cast his Circle of Protection. I felt it extend throughout the property. I stood in the darkness of the kitchen, watching him and expecting him to come inside immediately, but he didn't. He lingered, and still looked as though he were contemplating those pesky questions he couldn't find answers to.

***

An unnatural quiet and odd glow in the night sky clued me in to the fact that I was in a dream. I stood in the kitchen and gazed through the window that gave view to the garden and guesthouse. The stars in the sky seemed to fade, and I wondered what sort of dream this was.

Or was this another vision of the future?

My stomach churned, and I hoped that I could suppress these visions for as long as I could. They always portended something evil or tragic, never anything good. I feared the more I allowed this ability to emerge, the easier it would be for my mask to slip. One other time when I had a vision-dream, I had fallen asleep in a bathtub. I awoke in the flames of Zaman's Fire while still in the bath water, and Brande had to pull me out and absorb the fire. He said he almost couldn't handle it.

I cleared my mind and willed myself to wake up, but it didn't work. Instead, I felt a presence drawing me upstairs toward my bedroom. I walked through the hallway and headed upstairs, feeling the pull of some unseen force. When I reached my door, a familiar scent of cologne wafted toward me. As soon as I stepped inside, I saw Ken sitting on the floor with his back against the bed, with Veit's diary cradled in his lap, bundled along with the Turkish papers.

He had the diary open, and looked up at me with his warm brown eyes. He wore a black shirt and pants, and his blond hair was brushed into a side part. He smiled at me, and I smiled back at him. I didn't care if this was a dream--I was happy to see him the way I remembered him when he was alive. I walked over and eased onto the floor next to him, and he wrapped his left arm around me and pulled me in closer. His touch felt warm and comforting.

"I'm going to help you understand this, baby." He pointed with his right index finger to the page with the celestial symbols.

This was the oddest...well, one of the oddest dreams I've ever had. My gaze went from the diary to his face. "How do you know about this? Is this real or a dream?"

"I'm real. I'm standing over you right now in your bedroom."

Okay, maybe this was the oddest dream I've ever had. I was far from being a spiritual guru, but I assumed he would've already...moved on. I hid my discomfort and pointed to the page he had shown me earlier. "Ken...tell me what you know about this."

He withdrew his left arm from around my shoulder and pressed his hand against the text. "The Drifter is an instrument of chastisement. You're meant to punish an arrogant humanity and make war against people in all

101

times and in all places."

"And are Cruenti part of the punishment? They're helping Hitler slaughter people and take over entire countries. Who said I had to do this to people?" My heart fell in my chest, and despair clutched me.

"Baby, I know this is hard for you to accept because you have such a sensitive heart, but this is what you are--and I think it's beautiful."

I grew more disturbed. I remembered Neal's words about the first Drifter, but I didn't want to accept them. I couldn't. This description didn't fit who I was and it didn't reflect my life. I wanted to see the *end* of war, and I wanted to help people, not hurt them. Something was wrong here. He saw the worry and confusion on my face and tried to kiss me. I halted him.

"I believe you when you say you're real. You're projecting yourself into my mind as Ken, but tell me who you really are." I held my palm up, facing forward. The gesture invited him to share some of his magical energy with me so I could identify him. I knew he had some type of magic, otherwise he wouldn't have been able to project himself into my mind like this.

"Isabella, you know who I am." He mirrored my action and pressed his palm against mine. He sent a tendril of energy spinning through my arm and spreading throughout my body. I could taste it like metals, and its flavor was sweet at first but then turned bitter. It left my mouth dry and my stomach aching.

It was Ammon--and he sure as hell wasn't a humble spirit, but a demon.

In an unsteady voice, I told him, "You're not welcome in my home, and certainly not in my dreams. I want you to leave."

He stared at me, with Ken's face. "You don't have the authority to wield my name against me, so don't try it."

"Does Delana know what you are?" I tried every mental trick I could think of in order to pull myself out of the dream. I hoped he couldn't tell what I was doing.

Ammon sneered. "I'll kill her in her sleep one day, and repay her for what she did to me."

I slid to my left in order to create a gap between us, and thought he would have an angry outburst. Instead, he extended his hand and stroked my leg. It made me angry that he still looked like Ken.

I slid away again, out of his reach. "What do you want with the Drifter?"

I could now see impatience and anger in his eyes. He watched me with a cold look, and spoke. "I'm going to bend you to my will and use you as my instrument. We will do amazing...terrible things."

At that, I dropped all subtlety and jumped to my feet and ran for the door. I let out a strangled cry when I felt him right behind me. As soon as my hand touched the doorknob, everything became a blur, and I woke up in a sweat and with my heart racing. I nearly fell out of bed when I got out to check for the diary beneath. It was still there. I turned on the lamp and glanced around the room, trying to shake Ammon's creepy confession of standing over me. I grabbed the diary and took it with me as I headed to Delana's room, all the while reaffirming in my mind the decision to send her away. But then I doubted forcing her to pack and go would keep Ammon away.

My hand quivered as I delivered a few knocks on her door, loud enough to gain her attention but not anyone else's in the house. I heard her bed creak and her feet pad against the floor. She opened the door and wore a sleepy expression, but didn't seem surprised or angered at my late night intrusion. She motioned for me to come inside and turned on a lamp sitting on the nightstand. She sat on the bed and gestured for me to do the same.

"You know why I'm here," I said. My voice sounded shaky and weak.

"It was Ammon, wasn't it?"

I nodded. "Why are you here? Why did you want to

103

come with me?"

"Because I believe in Zaman. I believe you can help."

"Delana, I'm not even sure if I'll make it through the rest of this month with so many people wanting me either captured or dead. I'm trying to understand these powers, and I'm still not sure if I even want to use them. If I can remain an alchemist, then I think I'd choose that. It's a lot less complicated than being a Drifter."

"It won't last," she said. "You know it won't. And that frightens you."

"Well does your demon frighten you?" I gripped the diary, shuddering at the thought of Ammon using the appearance of someone I cared about, the man I could have married.

"I am sorry for bringing this on you, Isabella. I fought Ammon when I was younger, and used an old spell to bind him to me so that he would not go and harm anyone else."

"That was foolish," I told her. "You have a great deal of strength, but you can't just go around binding demons like that. He told me that he's going to kill you in your sleep."

She looked at me with a glimmer of hope in her eyes. "You can destroy him."

"Maybe you need an exorcist or something. Have you ever thought about going to the Church for that?"

"No, an exorcism will only break the binding and send him away. He'll only find me again, which is why I need him to be destroyed."

"Well, guess what, I don't know how to destroy a demon. Sorry."

"If you come into your full power, you will know how." She reached for the diary and opened it to the exact page Ammon had shown me.

"What do you know about this?" I asked.

"Have you interpreted it yet?"

"I will, in the morning. My brother has a colleague who reads and writes Turkish."

"Good. Again, I apologize. I thought that after all these

years that perhaps I finally had him under control. Ever since I saw you that day, he's grown more restless. You've changed."

"Just be careful, and don't provoke him. I'll see what I can do, but I can't promise anything. A Confrontation can be dangerous, which is why we usually left it to clergy to deal with."

"Thank you."

I closed the diary and stood, giving her one final glance. "How do you live with it? You've had him bound to you for years."

She frowned. "He drove my sister to suicide and terrorized my family. If you've seen everything I have, then you would want to protect others from it. I knew he might've killed me, but at the time I believed I had no other choice."

"I'm sorry about your family. I'll try to help in whatever way I can."

I cradled the diary in my arms and headed out. Instead of going to my bed, I went to my mother's room. I had no qualms about jumping into her bed like a scared little ten year old and curling up under her sheets. I refused to sleep alone tonight.

"What?" My mother said, turning toward me, "Did your fake fiancé call off the never-was-gonna-happen wedding and run off?"

"I had a nightmare."

"Must've been some nightmare."

More than a nightmare, it was a message. Ammon wanted me to know that he would find a way to kill Delana and break free so that he could pursue me. Not a very welcome message, if you asked me. I shook off his horrible words and consoled myself with the knowledge that he could never make me do anything against my will. The only question was, would I be strong enough when I had to Confront him, or would he use every half-truth, temptation and wile in order to weaken my resolve.

CHAPTER NINE

Johnnie looked like he wanted to throttle me when I showed up to his class. I didn't make a fuss and sat in the back as he lectured to his students. I wanted to feel indignant about his anger, but I knew that if I were in his position that I'd feel the same way. Actually, I had been in his position. I resented everyone who kept secrets that affected my life, even when it was to protect me. Now it seemed I did the same thing and tried to justify it. I could admit it wasn't fair, but what else was I supposed to do?

When he dismissed his students and they all shuffled out, I locked the door behind them and claimed his chair. "Sometimes the truth is dangerous, Johnnie."

"Let me decide what to do. Let me at least have the choice." He wore the same expression as that day our father whisked me away, when I was no older than ten.

"Then...for now at least, whatever I show you here...you can't tell anyone else." I pulled out the diary and loose papers.

He crossed his arms "I think the only reason you're doing this is because you need Dr. Grey."

"I need you too, Johnnie." His statement was hurtful, but I didn't blame him.

He turned and walked over to his chalkboard, his shoulders and back straightened. I couldn't tell what expression he wore on his face, but I could feel that what I said had affected him. All he truly wanted was my honesty, and my trust.

I spread the diary and loose pages across Johnnie's desk. He took a few seconds to view the diary pages, and then started nodding. "The first three pages are in Turkish."

"Astute observation, professor. What else can you tell me?"

"I can tell you that this double page here with the constellations and symbols isn't a map at all. It's a code."

I knew it. "Good...what else?"

"Now mind you, I'm not fluent, but the Turkish pages in this diary have nothing to do with the code."

"How much would you like to wager it goes with the loose papers I got from Robert Cambria?"

He took a look at the other texts lying next to the diary. "You're right, it does."

"What can you make out from the diary?"

"It speaks of a wizard named Zaman, but he may just be an archetype and not a real person."

"Why?"

"Well, Zaman is Turkish for *time*."

I perked up. "It's talking about a time wizard."

He gave me an odd look and then browsed the Turkish page again. "It says that...I don't even know if I'm reading this correctly...Zaman passes through fire."

I drew in a quick breath. "So whenever Zaman passes through fire, that's when he travels through time?"

Johnnie stuttered. "I-I really can't be completely sure about that. Maybe if this were in Persian or Arabic--"

"Does it say anything about how Zaman controls this?"

He paused. "I'm not sure what these other parts are saying. What does this have to do with you? Is Zaman real?"

His eyes told me that I had better not even think about lying or shying away from answering. "Yes."

He frowned. "How real?"

"If I tell you, then promise me you'll go see Roxanna..."

He let out an incredulous laugh. "Rachel's book club pal? I hardly think--"

"Promise me you'll see her and ask her to set up a protective barrier around today's memory."

"She's a wizard?"

I nodded. "I'm not spilling another word unless you promise to do it."

His expression grew serious. "I promise. Now tell me."

"What would you say if Zaman was someone you knew?"

He gazed at me. "But Zaman's a *he*. At least according to this text."

"What if...fate chose a female Zaman? I bet no one saw that coming."

He pulled back. "You can't be serious?"

I shook my head. "Johnnie, our father isn't dead. He's been fooling everyone, making them believe--"

"Why?" he asked in an angry tone that took me by surprise. "Why would he do that?"

He looked hurt, and he gazed at me as if I were part of the deception. "I didn't even know Dad was alive until earlier this year when I was in Paris. Believe me, I was just as shocked as you are now."

"So after all these years, he never once thought to contact us? Or Mom? Even if it's just to let us know he was alive?"

"He had his reasons."

His eyes narrowed. "When were you planning on telling us about him? Or was this something only you were supposed to know because you're a wizard?"

"Johnnie, it's not like that."

"Then explain it to me so I can understand."

This was just another reason for me to be angry with my father. He should be the one explaining all this to Johnnie and Mom. "The Gray Tower believes I'm dangerous." I reached for his hand and held it. "The Masters believe I shouldn't exist."

"No..." he shook his head. "They're wrong."

"I feel the same way, Johnnie. Luckily, they don't know that it's me they want. Our father made them believe he's Zaman--or as we call it in the West, the Drifter. He did it to save me."

He still looked like he didn't believe me. "Is he really alive?"

"Yes, and I wanted you and Mom to be able to see him. He's supposed to see me before the end of the year."

"And those texts he left you, why do you need them interpreted?"

"To understand what it means to be the Drifter. To understand how to control my powers so I can show them that I'm not some time bomb waiting to go off."

He started when we heard a knock. With a nervous expression, he went over to unlock the door and welcomed in a man who looked to be in his thirties. The man wore a crisp white shirt and gray tie, and had vibrant brown eyes. His dark wavy hair was as thick as Johnnie's.

My brother cleared his throat. "This is Dr. Michael Grey...and Michael, this is my sister, Isabella."

Dr. Grey approached and shook my hand. "A pleasure, Miss George. Jonathan has mentioned you before. He told me you've been in London."

"Yes, perhaps we've crossed paths there before?" His accent definitely made him a Londoner. Why did he seem so familiar to me?

"I'm afraid not, but I'll be returning there next year. If you're acquainted with Sir Edwin Grey, then you've met my father."

Everything suddenly connected. "Do you have a sister around my age? And she likes to spend a lot of time in France?"

He laughed. "Yes, that would be Nora."

So Adelaide was Nora Grey. I wondered if he knew his sister was an SOE agent. She helped me get safely back to London when I had finished my Paris job. "I'm very glad to meet you. Your sister is a friend of mine."

"Michael," Johnnie said as he handed the loose papers to him, "we would like you to take a look at these texts."

"Very well, then." He smiled and then examined the papers. "This...this is from Mehmed VI's private collection. Where did you get these?"

"A wizard of the Gray Tower gave them to me." I handed him the diary.

"This is amazing." He seemed to barely breathe as he read through the papers. "Most texts from the Ottoman Empire that I've read only dealt with law, history, and religion...but this is the first I've encountered where it discussed wizards."

"I managed to make out a few words and phrases about Zaman," Johnnie said. "Can you tell us anything more?"

"It says that Zaman is considered wise, a leader...someone who upholds righteousness. Did you see this part about passing through fire?"

"Yes," I answered. "How does Zaman control that?"

He took out his pen and began scribbling on a sheet of paper. "Well the real question, at least for me, is why are these symbols in here?"

As he began copying from Heilwig's celestial code and the papers, Johnnie asked, "Is there even an advantage to Zaman using his abilities?"

Dr. Grey turned the notepad toward us so we could see what he wrote. "I think you have more profound matters to consider. The thirteenth sign of the zodiac is Ophiuchus, the serpent. His position in the sky is between the tip of Scorpio's tail and Sagittarius's arrow."

Jonathan examined the symbols again. "The Dark Rift..."

"You mean the Milky Way, in the center of the universe?" I glared at them when they both gaped at me as if expecting anything else but that question to come from my mouth. "I do read, you know."

"Of course," Dr. Grey blustered, "yes, that's quite right."

"So how does the alignment of the stars relate to

Zaman?" I hoped no one expected me to start reading palms and consulting Hollywood types or the president.

Dr. Grey continued. "Zaman would probably have the ability to use the information, written in the heavens if you will, to predict and even guide future events. Think of the universe as an open book and the stars are part of its language."

"This is what the Masters call the Akashic Record," I said. "And what about that number?" I pointed to the "23.5" written near the center of the page.

"The Greek mathematician Eratosthenes was the first to discover that the earth is tilted at a 23.5 degree angle," Johnnie said. "No one really knows why the earth is tilted like this, but it's the reason why we have four seasons."

Dr. Grey nodded. "Some philosophers and astronomers believe that the earth once stood upright, no tilt whatsoever. Could you imagine what that would be like today?"

"Perpetual spring," I murmured.

Johnnie snapped his fingers." The Garden of Eden!"

"Except we're broken." Dr. Grey set aside his copy of the notes. "A 23.5 degree tilt to the earth's axis means we're existing in an unnatural and destructive state."

"So...is it up to Zaman to fix this unnatural state?" I asked.

"Who's to say a previous Zaman isn't the one who caused it to begin with?" Dr. Grey frowned.

"But we don't know that," I told him, though a small part of me feared the possibility of the Order being justified in putting the Drifter to death.

He began copying more notes. "Aside from the mystical meanings...just the real world ramifications of this are astounding. Isabella, have you thought about talking to Dr. Sheridan?"

When I looked askance at Johnnie, he whispered, "It's Jim...remember him from poker night?"

I nodded. The handsome Vincent Price look-alike. "Jim Sheridan? Of course."

Dr. Grey wore a huge grin and translated more of the texts for us. "Here are the Turkish meditative spells translated into English. I suspect you'd want to go the route of theurgy on this. Studying the translated spells will allow you to understand how Zaman controls his abilities."

I began collecting the loose papers and stuffing them back into the diary. "Thank you."

His smile faded, and he gave me a sidelong glance. "You're...not leaving the papers with me?"

I snorted. "No, why?"

"Just these few pages trump all the work I've been doing on Mehmed VI's collection this past year. It's no exaggeration when I say they pale in comparison. This could help us understand why war and destruction are raging through our world today, and it may even give us answers on everything from world peace to advances in technology and human enlightenment."

I shook my head. "Sorry, but this isn't necessarily something I want shouted from the mountaintops."

He gave me a knowing look. "Ah, I understand perfectly now. You want to keep this a family discovery--it's rather endearing actually."

"Excuse me?"

"I want you and Jonathan to know that I'm willing to incorporate this into my existing project and share the credit with you. And let's suppose any financial benefit proceeding from the lectures and tours can be split...fifty-fifty."

"You are nothing like your sister," I said. "You call yourself a scholar? It seems you're only interested in something if it has money attached to it or boosts your reputation."

He raised a finger. "If I didn't translate this for you and provide those explanations, you'd be lost right now." He faced Johnnie. "I'm sorry, Jonathan, but you would have had better luck explaining that *the dog chased the ball* in Turkish than interpreting the rest of the texts on your own."

"Go to hell," my brother retorted.

Dr. Grey tensed and then abruptly shoved the remaining papers toward us. "You're making a mistake, Jonathan. There's a missing page, which you'll undoubtedly return begging me to interpret."

"There is no missing page," I snapped back. He wanted to find any excuse to get his hands on the texts again.

He stood and stalked away, leaving the classroom door wide open. I reached for the remaining papers and suddenly realized that he still had those handwritten copies. For a moment, I was frozen in shock. Of all the powerful people who would've loved to get their hands on that text--and have tried--the one person to swipe it was a smug college professor with scrawny legs and a sense of entitlement.

"Johnnie--"

"He took his copies!" He dashed out of the classroom after him. I shoved everything else into my black handbag before joining the pursuit. They were already outside the building and heading north toward College Yard. I caught up to Johnnie and widened my distance from him so we could try to flank Michael near the Peabody House, but a group of gawking students got in our way and slowed us down. Johnnie saw him run in the direction of the physics labs, but when we got over there, Dr. Grey had vanished.

I ran my hands through my hair and growled. I shook my head and looked at Johnnie in disbelief. My brother had a pained look on his face, and I knew he felt horrible. Dr. Grey may not have intended to hand his copies over to our enemies, but his decision to keep them and do whatever he wanted with them would likely end up accomplishing the same end.

With heavy breaths, I pulled away from Johnnie when he tried to grab my hand and guide me back toward his classroom. In my head, I knew this wasn't his fault, but I was so angry that I didn't want him to touch me or talk to me right then.

"I'm sorry, Izzy," he whispered, walking alongside me and staring at the ground.

All I could think of was how this would be used against me. The moment Dr. Grey would speak to the wrong person or announce the existence of the pages, both the Gray Tower and Octavian's warlocks would seek to gain hold of them. They'd find out that he got the information from me, and then the question would arise as to why I would be in possession of these texts.

When I glanced at my brother and saw his heartbroken expression, I relented and grabbed his hand. "It's...not your fault, Johnnie."

"I'm actually supposed to work with him on the Suleiman project tomorrow. Maybe I could..."

"No, this was my responsibility. I'll have to deal with it." For a fleeting second I did think about Johnnie confronting Dr. Grey later, but seeing how the man operated, he would probably call for security and accuse my brother of harassment, or even try to harm his reputation.

As we passed College Yard and headed southward toward the classroom, we spotted Johnnie's poker pals, Frankie and Dillon. "Dr. George," Frankie said, "would you and Isabella like to join us for lunch?"

My subtle expression directed at Johnnie indicated my answer. "We were actually going to have lunch at home today. Perhaps tomorrow?"

He looked slightly disappointed. "We'll see you later, then."

They said goodbye to us and continued on their way. When we made it back to his classroom, I made sure to lock the door. I didn't want any further interruptions. Johnnie had reopened the diary and began looking through the translated spells.

He looked at me with a worried expression. "Are you sure you want to do this?"

"I have to be able to control this. I don't have a choice."

"Seems like you were doing just fine as an alchemist."

"I thought so too, but the truth is that I may not be one for long, not if the mask slips."

"All right, then. How about we start with this one?" He held up one of the translated notes. It was called Zaman's Fire, and explained how to detect the onset of the mysterious fire that periodically engulfed me since I was a child.

The instruction said that I could control the fire and use it either as a shield or a weapon. Brande had once absorbed the fire, but he claimed it was almost too powerful, even though elementals normally absorbed flames without harm. There was a simple meditative exercise I needed to do each morning so that the flames would be under my control. Johnnie also read through some spells with me that were meant to slow or speed up the flow of time around me, and how to access the Akashic Record.

"Don't you think it's odd that none of these instructions contain any warnings? Things you shouldn't do?"

"That sounds like something Mom would say."

"Really, have you even considered the effect something like this could have on other people around you? I want you to be able to control this, Izzy, but you have to make sure it's safe."

I snatched the papers from him. I placed them along with the diary into my handbag. "Thanks for the lecture. I'll see you later."

"So we're not having lunch?"

"Go have lunch with Frankie and Dillon. I'm not hungry."

Before he could say another word, I was out the door and made a point to slam it shut. Who did he think he was, telling me how to approach this? Didn't he think I already played these things out in my mind a million times? He wasn't even a wizard, so how could he possibly understand? No...let me not begin to think like that. It didn't matter whether or not he was a wizard. He knew this

115

was dangerous--and that with a serious misstep, it could very well be my undoing.

***

I felt guilty about storming out of Johnnie's classroom. I knew that he had only wanted to help and was just worried about me. Just because we translated those texts and learned a few things didn't mean that we knew everything, including consequences and pitfalls. I hadn't even voluntarily cast a single spell related to these powers, and the only reason why I was acquainted with Zaman's Fire was because it activated on its own.

When I arrived back at the house, I went straight upstairs and opened the diary along with the Turkish papers and Dr. Grey's translations. I sat on my bed and re-read the part that talked about Zaman being a wise leader, and someone good. It gave me hope, and reminded me that I could still prove the Tower wrong and show them that at least *this* Drifter would not summon demons or rain down destruction on people. But first, I needed to understand these powers and control them.

The translated instruction for slowing down time said to listen to my heart. I closed my eyes and slowed my breathing. I reached deep inside and thought of time as something fluid, moving slowly yet purposefully. I fed magical energy into my thoughts, and still allowed myself to remain in a meditative state. After a few minutes, I opened one eye to see if anything had changed--the clock on the wall opposite of me tick-tocked at its usual pace, and a trip to the window overlooking the backyard revealed the disappointing view of everyone else at the table enjoying lunch as normal.

I tried the meditation once more, and when nothing out of the ordinary occured, I grew frustrated and decided to head downstairs. I went straight to Neal, who was once again having lunch with my mother and Rachel. Delana sat

116

at the table as well, a little more quiet than usual. I wondered if Neal said anything to intimidate her. He barely tolerated her presence and probably would not stand for her to talk.

"Good afternoon, everyone." I took the empty seat next to Neal and absentmindedly squeezed his hand. Despite some of his contrary beliefs, he turned out to be a staunch ally. Perhaps if he spent a little more time around me, then maybe he would start to think differently about the Drifter.

"I thought Johnnie was coming back with you," my mother said.

"He's having lunch with the guys down at the university. How are you, Rachel?" She had dark circles beneath her eyes, and she wasn't her usual bubbly self. She seemed to barely touch her broccoli soup, and her water glass was half full.

"I haven't been sleeping well recently," she said, attempting to smile.

"Why don't you go lie down, Rachel. I'll clean up." My mother fixed a plate of food for me and filled my glass.

Delana took a few bread rolls and tossed them into her shopping tote. "Excuse me, I am done now." She left for her room.

"How long will you allow that woman to stay here?" Neal asked when she was out of earshot.

"She's odd," my mother commented as she cleared the table of empty plates and bowls. "I'll give you that."

I began playing with my food, wondering the same thing myself. Still, I told her that I would try to help. If all else failed, I'd just have to convince Delana to get an exorcism. "I'll...talk with her."

When my mother hauled the dishes away, Neal asked, "Was there any sign of Ryker while you were out?"

I shook my head. "How about you?"

"He hasn't returned."

I reached into my handbag and took out the loose papers, but not the diary. "This is why I went with Johnnie

117

today. We wanted to get these interpreted."

He examined the papers. "The stolen texts. How long have you had them?"

"Since I saw Cambria. He gave them to me."

"I see." He gave me a look as if silently scolding me for withholding information--again.

"Why do you think Veit stole them?" I wanted to see what theories he would come up with, but hopefully not the correct one.

He gazed into my eyes. "It's obvious Veit took these for your father in order for him to learn about the powers of Zaman, the Drifter. Your father must've intended to reclaim the papers through you, or if he perished, they would remain out of the Tower's hands."

My mother came out with a worried expression and approached. "Isabella, Rachel is asking for you to take her to the doctor. She won't say what's wrong."

Neal glanced at me and saw the concern on my face. "I'll drive."

"How strong is your Circle of Protection?" I asked.

"I've just fortified it. The old woman has strength. She can stay with your mother."

"All right."

I grabbed my handbag and we got up and went into the house. Rachel was in the living room reclining on the sofa. Delana sat next to her and touched her forehead.

"Rachel, you want to go to the doctor?" I asked, grabbing her hand and leading her from the couch. I used our physical contact to search for any signs of illness or injury. There were none.

"Yes, please."

"Delana--"

"Yes, I know. I'll stay."

I handed Neal the keys and we went out the front door. I helped Rachel ease into the car and got into the back seat with her.

"Where to?" Neal asked.

"Dr. Caine's," Rachel said, breathing deeply. "He owns the farm property just northwest of here."

As Neal pulled out and drove us down the street, I held Rachel's hand and looked into her eyes. "How do you feel?"

"I'm all right. It's not what you think."

"Really?"

"It's not Delana. I did speak with her though."

I let out a breath of frustration. What if Rachel's session with Delana had sparked the interest of Ammon? Could he have made her ill and I just couldn't detect it? We swayed as Neal made a left turn onto a long stretch of road. We passed a few equestrian properties, and Rachel pointed at the one toward the end.

"Well, what is it then?" I asked.

"You know that day I was sitting at the kitchen table speaking with her?"

"Yes."

"Well, she said that I was going to have a baby...and I think it's true."

"You're pregnant?"

Out of the corner of my eye, I saw Neal pull out a pistol. "Brace yourselves, there's a warlock standing in the middle of the road."

He rolled down the window just enough so that he could aim the pistol and start firing. I looked up just in time to see Ryker, with his golden hair cropped short and high-neck black sweater, pulling out two Cossack daggers and deflecting the bullets. My heart pounded in my chest as Neal accelerated the car and drove straight toward the man.

Rachel let out a terrified scream right before impact. We jerked forward as the car crashed--whether it was against Ryker, I didn't know--and suddenly the entire world spun around, and I went bouncing around in the back seat and hit the roof of the car. When all became still, I felt my face pressed against the rear window. The car was upside down, and when I realized that I was the only one in it, I panicked.

"Rachel!" I tried to ignore my body aching and my head

119

throbbing. I pulled my alchemist's knife from my handbag and grabbed the extra rings and put them on. I scraped my arms and legs as I crawled through the broken front window.

About a hundred yards away, I saw Neal fighting with Ryker. The warlock's face was bloodied and he had a look of rage in his eyes, probably because Neal had managed to co-opt one of his Cossack daggers. Ryker parried a few of Neal's thrusts but got sliced on his left arm. He quickly constructed a protective magical shield and then backed away so he could pull out a revolver and shoot at Neal. It seemed Ryker wanted to use his enchanted weapons before resorting to pure magic.

Neal had been anticipating Ryker's move and deflected the bullet. He struck the warlock's shield with the dagger and it shattered, sending an eerie blue flame leaping into the air. When I felt pain in my right shoulder and my head continued throbbing, my thoughts went back to Rachel. I scanned the area, and at first saw only the lonely stretch of road and a few horses grazing in the pastures behind white fenceposts. My heart almost stopped when I finally spotted Rachel, just to the west side of the road, lying unconscious beneath a tall tree.

I forced myself to my feet and stumbled in the opposite direction of Neal and Ryker's fight. I rushed toward Rachel, my chest tightening and my breaths stifling with each step. I was afraid to go to her, but I was more afraid not to. My senses went off, and I nearly choked on an evil presence that clouded around me like pitch-black smoke from a fire. It made me sick.

I fell to my knees beside Rachel and placed my hands on her head. As I sent a wave of healing energy throughout her body, mending the bruise on her face and the broken bones in her left hand, I felt a small tremor. She slipped in and out of consciousness, but I continued working on her, calling her name and talking to her, and afraid of what I would have to face with Johnnie and my own conscience if she never woke up.

Though it was dangerous, I had no choice but to pull back my energy and pray it was enough for her, because I would now need my magical strength for defense. I gripped my knife and quickly enclosed us in a loose circle of alchemical symbols: Earth, Air, Fire, and the symbol of decay--Putrefaction. Ryker had indeed been testing us last night, toying with us, even. Three Black Wolves, his reinforcements, had just landed in front of me, and they were ready for blood.

CHAPTER TEN

Out of the corner of my eye I could see Neal making his way toward us, but he had to pause every few seconds to fend off Ryker or deflect one of his attacks. The Black Wolves that landed in front of me could sense the spells I laid and stood outside the symbols encircling Rachel and me. They all wore their uniform black garbs and silver hoods, but each one had its unique deformity. I cringed at the tallest one, which had a greenish tint to its skin, and claws for hands and feet. The second looked like it had sockets but no eyes, and the third reminded me of a very hairy satyr. This was what became of wizards who consorted with demons and made pacts with them. They eventually devolved into these abominations.

The eyeless Wolf crouched to the ground and slithered like a snake toward Rachel. I released both Fire and Air at the same time so that a whirlwind of fire swirled and hit all three Black Wolves. The one with claws and the satyr backed off, but then reached out with their power and began breaking down my symbols so they could reach us unobstructed. The eyeless one shrieked in rage and said something in its infernal language.

"The next time Octavian wants to send his dogs after me, at least let him send the ones that can talk." I cast a Circle of Protection that spread and stopped just before the symbols that encircled Rachel and me. I glanced at her and saw her eyes flutter open.

"Isabella?" She took one look at the Black Wolves, with their maligned forms, and fainted.

My alchemical symbols shattered from the counterspells of the satyr and clawed Wolves, and they began snarling like a pack of hungry dogs. They latched onto my Circle of Protection and began drinking its energy like water--it wouldn't hold up another minute. A croak escaped my throat, and with tears stinging my eyes, I pressed the tip of my knife's blade into the palm of my right hand. I stood and ran outside of the weakened Circle of Protection, hoping that the scent of my blood would draw them toward me and away from Rachel. With shaking limbs, I picked up my pace and bolted toward the large tree to the right.

I looked back and saw the eyeless one tilting its chin upward and its nostrils flaring. It bared its teeth and flew toward me, and I took cover behind the wide tree trunk. I held my knife and readied to thrust it into the monster's face as soon as it showed, but suddenly the ground beneath me shifted, and the tree came plummeting onto me. I made a swift roll to avoid getting crushed, but the trunk caught my leg, and I fell onto my stomach. I pulled my leg free and shifted myself onto my back, but an invisible force hit me and pinned me against the ground.

I peered eastward and saw Neal battling with Ryker. Their feet moved quickly as they both tried to keep their balance while parrying each other's thrusts and strikes. Ryker spun and made a vertical cut with his dagger, and Neal deflected it and came in with a spell of ice on his blade. Ryker parried and commanded a burst of fire to erupt from his dagger, and slashed at Neal. He swerved and dodged Ryker's blade, and delivered a side kick to the warlock's stomach. Ryker stumbled, and Neal closed in and made a quick strike to the man's chest.

Ryker shouted something, and the satyr Black Wolf rushed in his and Neal's direction. Although I saw in the distance Ryker's arms and legs get slashed, and Neal finally making a killing strike, I didn't think he would be able to turn around and reach me quickly. Neal stood hunched over, exhausted, and had to defend himself against the satyr Black Wolf that charged with its mouth widened to an enormous size.

I screamed when the eyeless Black Wolf jumped on me and released the invisible force that had been holding me down. It pinned my arms down as it peered into my eyes, blocking my view of Neal. I struggled to break free and beat back the Wolf, dreading at any moment being ripped to shreds. The Black Wolf's nose flared again, and its gaze traveled down my arm until it reached my bloodied hand. I cried out in disgust as its black tongue shot out and burrowed itself into the wound and began making slow rhythmic swallows. The other Black Wolf, the green one with claws, came bounding from behind us and shoved the eyeless one aside. It didn't surprise me. I had seen Black Wolves turn on their Nazi masters and eat them, even the non-warlocks. The Wolves eventually got to a point where they would no longer recognize authority or any rational motive--if something had blood pumping through its veins and was edible, it was dinner--and unfortunately, I was on the menu. The only person I've seen completely control them was Marcellus, Octavian's brother, who could speak their strange language and had the strength to make the Wolves submit.

However the two Wolves over me didn't look ready to submit to anyone or anything. The one with claws tore at the eyeless Wolf's face and tried to seize me. The eyeless one opened its mouth and shot out a stream of fire, engulfing the other creature in flames. The clawed Wolf stood there shrieking until its face melted, and it collapsed to the ground. I stared in shock when I realized that the eyeless Wolf had just used Zaman's Fire to kill the other one.

I should have died in the car crash.

This monster should not have any of my powers, not

even a portion of them. As the eyeless Wolf jumped back onto me and bared its teeth, I swung my knife in an arc and stabbed it in the head. It roared, and I withdrew the knife and made another stab. It backed away, and I screamed for Neal. I glanced over in his direction and saw him with both of Ryker's enchanted daggers, making methodical stabs and cuts to the satyr Wolf's torso and tendons. An odd flash erupted from the satyr Wolf's mouth, and Neal went flying backward over the fencepost. The Wolf flew over to him and shapeshifted into Neal's double, and the two fought. The false Neal mimicked Neal's moves but moved a little slower because of its injuries. Neal spun and made downward strikes with both enchanted daggers into the false Neal's chest. It convulsed and bled a thick black substance before morphing back to its original form; it slumped to the ground dead.

I scrambled to my feet and turned toward the eyeless Wolf that had just regenerated from the stab wounds I gave it. The monster warily approached, sniffing in the direction of my hand again, looking for more blood and magic. It's tongue shot out and struck my knife-hand like a whip. My fingers spasmed, and the knife fell to the ground. As I swooped down to pick up the knife, the Black Wolf was on me in a flash. I sank to my knees as I dug my fingers into its pale face in order to keep it away, but its teeth grazed the side of my face, and I knew this time the Wolf was going to completely drain me of my blood and kill me.

Suddenly I felt my father's ring that hung around my neck warm up; it generated heat until it almost began to burn. An invisible force catapulted the Black Wolf into the air, and then it exploded in a ball of fire. I doubled over, still on my knees, gasping for breath. My heart leapt when I saw my father rushing toward me from the south. He finally returned, as he had promised.

"Dad!" I winced and sat with my legs folded beneath me. They felt like rubber, and my right hand throbbed and my ribs ached without mercy.

125

My father knelt down and touched my cheek. "Isabella, let's go--"

I recoiled when one of Ryker's daggers pierced my father from behind and the blade emerged from his chest. Neal twisted the dagger, and my father's face screwed up in pain. I let out a scream of shock, feeling as if I were the one being stabbed. Dread paralyzed my entire body as I watched my father clench his teeth. Why was Neal doing this?

"Your advanced age has become a liability, Carson. This was bound to happen." He pulled the blade back and released my father.

"That blade," my dad said as blood flowed down his shirt, "the enchantment on it..."

Neal tilted the blade and saw a faint green glow. The corner of his mouth twitched, and blood suddenly poured from the corners of Neal's eyes like tears. "Clever...you changed the enchantment."

I raised myself up on my knees and threw my arm around my father in a half-hug position. I kept him close to me, but also held my knife ready. I shot out a rush of energy to mend as much damage as I could, but it was no better than putting a band-aid on a gunshot wound. My father needed someone with stronger healing abilities to save him from bleeding to death, and he would need it fast.

"Whatever that enchantment did...I hope it kills you." The words spilled from my lips like venom as I watched Neal cough up blood.

Neal wiped his mouth with the back of his hand. "I'm very sorry, Isabella, but some things are worth a broken friendship."

"Dad," I whispered. His head slid onto my shoulder and he groaned in pain. I managed to stem the blood flow, but not by much. "We need to get out of here. You need a proper healer."

Neal drew a gun and pointed it at his own head. "The enchantment he placed on that dagger is called *Lex Talionis*.

What happens to Carson will also happen to me, and vice versa. He has anticipated that I would rather save my life and heal us both, but he is mistaken. I intend to save the world."

"Neal, don't do it!"

A shot rang out just as a blast of wind knocked the gun out of his hand. The green silhouette surrounding the dagger subsided, signaling that the enchantment had been broken. Brande rushed toward us and peered at both my father and Neal. He probably wanted to make sure he didn't have to break any other enchantments.

Neal turned and faced Brande. "Are you here to stand in my way, or are you here to do your job?"

Brande stared at him. "Go and signal the other trackers, Warren. That's an order."

Neal faltered as he rose to his feet, and he threw Brande a suspicious glance. He spoke a Word and disappeared in a flash. Brande started toward us; with his tall muscular build, he was dangerous even without using his magic. I gulped and laid a Circle of Protection. My fingers trembled as I brandished my knife.

"What are you doing? Why did you send Neal to get the other trackers?" As far as I was concerned, Brande should've killed Neal the moment he broke the enchantment that intertwined Neal's life with my father's. Of course that was assuming Brande was on my side to begin with. Did he truly stand with me?

Brande halted. "We don't have much time. All of the trackers are magically bound so that we could never kill each other. It would've been futile battling with Neal."

My father raised his head and rose to his feet. He almost collapsed, but made his best effort to stand and face Brande. "Are you also a true believer, Brande Drahomir?"

Brande eyed him with distaste and reached into his pocket. He tossed a familiar tiny pouch toward my father and he caught it. Brande always carried that pouch with him and had even given me a similar one before. My dad stepped outside of my Circle of Protection, and when I saw that he had no fear of Brande, I relinquished my hold on the Circle, but I still gripped my knife and readied a spell in my mind.

"Get out of here, Carson."

"Not without my daughter." My father swallowed the jade powder from the pouch. He would be fully healed within minutes.

"Isabella!" Rachel raced toward me from the direction my father had come in. Dirt caked her hair, and streaks of muddy tears ran down her face. She stumbled halfway but managed to regain her balance. When she reached me, she held onto me and seemed ready to pull me away.

My father glanced at Rachel and me. "We must go. Now."

"Carson," Brande growled, "Neal has already signaled the other five trackers. I can feel it. *You're* the one who needs to go."

My father glared at Brande. "I know why they chose you. Are you certain that I'm the one who can't be trusted?"

I gazed at Brande. He had disappointed me in the past. But then I thought of everything I had been through with him, how we even risked our lives for one another. Did that mean anything to him? Or did he want to play both sides?

I looked straight into Brande's eyes. "Are you here to help us? Because if you are, then you need to do something about those trackers." I prayed he didn't turn out to be like Neal.

"I'm helping you now. Tell your father to go, and I'll stay with you."

"No," my father said. "You know what's at stake, Isabella. Come with me."

"What about Rachel? I can't just take off and leave her." I held onto her, worried about what I could've missed when I hastily healed her, and hoping that nothing had happened to that budding life inside her.

"If you trust Brande," my father said, grabbing my arm

128

and pulling me toward him, "then he can take Rachel home where she'll be safe."

I shook my head. "Just go, before Master Priya gets here with the others. You'll have to meet up with me later. Just use the ring again."

My father let go of my arm. "Have you read Veit's diary? Do you understand the meditations?"

Before I could get in another word edgewise, Brande spoke up. "That's enough. They're near. If they see her fleeing with you, then they'll treat her no different than you."

Brande was right. Back in France when I had first reunited with my father, Master Priya had caught up with me and was ready to drag me to the Gray Tower for an interrogation. If Brande hadn't stepped in and blocked Priya from taking me, I would probably be rotting in the Tower dungeon--or dead.

My father gritted his teeth in frustration. He stared at the ground, and I imagined him reworking his calculations. He looked up at me. "Put your Fire into the water, and into your heart. Make the ripples and pulses burn."

"Go," Brande said. "I'll stay with her." He stepped back, but still eyed my father with wariness as if expecting an attack.

My dad faced Brande. "If anything happens to my daughter--"

"Then it means I'm dead," Brande said.

My father looked like he would rather have that happen, and then softened his expression when he gazed back at me. "Remember what I said--Fire, water, ripples, pulses."

"Okay," I said, nodding at his cryptic words.

Tiny wrinkles etched my father's face and his dark hair had become sprinkled with grays. His eyes betrayed his emotional exhaustion, though physically the jade powder returned him to his full strength. He lifted his hand and extended his fingers in a gesture, and the overturned car flipped right-side up. The broken parts reconnected and repaired. He formed another gesture, and a streak of lightning flashed across the sky, carrying the essence of his magical energy, which the trackers would sense and follow. I could already feel them coming in from the East, and the amount of raw power I felt from all six of them combined made me afraid for my father.

My dad started running north along the road with an agility and speed of someone half his age. He voiced an enchantment, and a gust of wind carried him away. Now I could both see and feel the presence of Neal and the other trackers--it was like watching smoke and lightning dance together in a storm. Brande gestured toward them, and they bypassed us and turned north. I hoped that my dad didn't have to stop to fight all six wizards.

"I'm sorry, Rachel." I half-expected her to draw away or flinch. She knew that I was associated with the Tower, but witnessing events like today probably made her want to have nothing to do with another wizard.

"That...that was your father," Rachel said with a look of confusion. It would probably take her a while to process it all. Her gaze went between Brande and me. "Who is this?"

"Let's go to the car," Brande said, gently taking Rachel's arm.

"Where's Neal? Is he hurt?" She looked ready to cry again.

I flanked Rachel and walked along with them toward the car. "Neal is alive. There are a few things I have to explain to you."

"Isabella," she said, opening the door and getting into the back seat with me. "Do you think I should still go to Dr. Caine?"

Brande shook his head and got into the driver seat, but I ignored him and said, "Yes, just to make sure everything's okay."

Brande started the car and then faced me. "This can't wait?"

"No, I need to talk to you before I let you near my home

or my father."

He opened his mouth to argue but then seemed to change his mind. He pulled off and began driving the last quarter mile toward Dr. Caine's farm property.

***

Brande and I waited in Dr. Caine's sitting room. The office was attached to his house and he had been practicing from there for some time. The doctor was pleasant enough when we met him, a cheerful and elderly man. We gave him a false story about a minor car accident, and he bandaged my hand and gave me a hot wet cloth to wipe my face with. I assured him I was fine and that Rachel was the one who needed the most attention. He ushered her into his exam room.

I wanted to start asking Brande questions, but an elderly woman in a floral dress sitting across from us made it a little difficult. When she left for the restroom, I laid a Circle of Silence around us. I decided that now would be the time for him to tell me everything he knew, and to reaffirm that he would side with my father and me. I bitterly thought about Neal and his betrayal, and wondered if I should just cut Brande out of my life altogether. The only reason why I even allowed him to come with us was because he had just saved my father's life...and mine too. The other trackers would not forget that Neal almost had my dad when Brande stepped in. They would lay the blame of my father's escape at Brande's feet.

"Why did you even send Neal to me?" I peered into his gray eyes, and watched for any signs of nervousness or untruthfulness.

"I didn't send Neal to you. He had stolen the Agate stone ring and replaced it with a fake. I can't taste metals like you, so I didn't know the difference until the fake stone was shattered in a fight yesterday."

I cursed at Neal in my head. He had lied to me and

131

made me believe he was my friend. I was just beginning to trust him, and now it's all been ruined. I saw the unease in Brande's expression and said, "Neal's been with me for days. At my home, with my family. He showed me the ring and said that you had sent him to look after me."

"What else did he tell you?"

I shook my head. "Let me ask the questions. Tell me about the spells that bind the seven trackers. You can't kill each other...what else is there?"

"We can't reveal another tracker's identity to outsiders. We also have two oaths to keep: we won't turn to forbidden magic to carry out our task, and we will not leave the group unless dismissed by one of The Three."

"Well, not all of you have been keeping your oaths. Hotaru went rogue and killed innocent people when he tried to track down my father in France. He killed Ken Aspen." My throat constricted and I felt my eyes brim with tears.

He lowered his gaze. "I...didn't know. If I had been there--"

"I know you wouldn't have stood by. I don't blame you for what happened to Ken."

"I'll make sure Hotaru regrets what he's done. I'll speak with the Masters myself."

That made me feel a little better, but he wasn't off the hook just yet. "And what about you? I don't need a partial ally--I need all of you."

"I meant everything I said, and nothing's changed."

"You'll continue helping me? And my father too, even though you apparently hate each other?"

"Yes."

"Why?"

"You know why," he said in his deep voice.

I most certainly did, and I felt something for him as well, but I needed to guard myself. And, even though it might've sounded crazy, part of me still felt like I was tied to Ken. Suddenly I was at war with myself, trying to make sense of why I couldn't just look Brande in the eye and tell him to leave me alone. That's what I should've done, but instead I raised my hand to his face and caressed his cheek. He reciprocated the gesture by pressing his warm lips against the palm of my hand in a slow kiss. I ignored the shiver of excitement that ran through me, and I withdrew my hand. I felt guilty again.

"My father said they chose you for a reason. I think I know why."

He tensed, as if already guessing what I was about to say. "Isabella--"

"Some of what you trackers do is not too far off from spying. If I had to guess your role, it would be to remain close to me because the trackers knew my father sought me. If Master Priya, Hotaru, and all the others failed, you would at least still be with me and able to make the final strike against my father. They didn't care if you befriended me or seduced me--just get the job done. Am I correct?"

His gaze held steady, though I could feel he was uncomfortable. "After I stopped Master Priya from apprehending you in France, I think he gave that task to Neal. He grew suspicious of me."

"They'll blame you for my father getting away today."

"It depends on the perspective. I saved another tracker's life and helped signal the others to Carson's trail."

"What about staying behind with me? What will Master Priya say about that?"

"Priya will know that you no longer trust Neal, so it would be useless to send him back to you."

I frowned. "Yes, and the one I do trust is sitting here with me. How convenient."

I wasn't going to deny that I learned new things about him, that I had gotten a glimpse of who he truly was when I last saw him in Paris, and he was a good man. I didn't know at what point he had developed feelings for me, but I knew they were genuine. However I still had a nagging feeling that Brande struggled with whether or not he'd fully side

133

with me or submit to whatever the Gray Tower wished. It was no secret he was a candidate to one day head the Order. For most people, that would be something difficult to walk away from.

"I understand why you feel that way, and I think this will be the only way to convince you otherwise." He unbuttoned the top of his shirt.

"Brande, this is neither the time nor the place..."

"If this won't convince you, then nothing will." He grabbed my right hand and guided it to his firm chest, right over his heart. The palm of my hand tingled as it rested against his skin. I realized what he wanted to do, and I tried to pull my hand back.

"Brande, you can't do that." I tried to wrest my hand away once more, but he held it in place.

A heart-bind was a spell rarely used nowadays. It had been done in the past by ancient communities to bind wizards to their oaths or as a good faith offer to ensure a certain task would be completed, and by foolish lovers who'd promise themselves to one another only for one of them to end up dead. If Brande did a heart-bind with me, he would be giving me the power to kill him with the force of my will. I didn't want that type of power over him.

"I promise I won't bring harm to you or your family, and I will not work against you."

"I don't think you should do this," I whispered, though I made no further attempt to break free. With each heartbeat I could feel tendrils of energy, as smooth as silk, sliding over my hand and sealing the bind.

He released my hand. "Now, are you convinced?"

I sighed and began buttoning up his shirt. "I've gotten angry with you over little things. What if you piss me off and you drop dead?"

He smiled. "Something tells me you'll be more forgiving from now on."

I released the Circle of Silence. I glanced over at the old woman sitting across from us who had returned; she was pretending to read a magazine. Although she couldn't hear the tail end of our conversation, our physical gestures and actions must've given her an eyeful.

Rachel and Dr. Caine emerged from the exam room. I immediately stood and approached her, noting the smile on her face. "Everything's fine, Isabella," she said.

"So far," Dr. Caine said. "I told her to phone me if she has any of the symptoms on this list. I'll come down to her house for a check up tomorrow." He handed me the sheet of paper.

"Thank you, doctor."

"You're welcome, and congratulations, Rachel."

"I'll drive," Brande said, heading for the exit.

I faced Rachel. "I'm sorry...about everything."

She grabbed my hands and squeezed them. "I think there are a few things you need to tell Mom and Jonathan. Don't you? You owe them the truth."

I nodded. "Yes."

We pulled into the driveway, and as soon as the car stopped, Rachel hopped out and ran inside. I grabbed my black handbag and walked inside with Brande. Instead of seeing Rachel making her announcement in excitement, she stood rather subdued and quiet. When I saw who sat on the couch next to my brother, I understood why.

"Ian. What are you doing here?"

My boss folded his hat in his hands and stood. He looked pale, and his eyes were red with fatigue. "Isabella, I'm very sorry to intrude like this. Is there somewhere we can talk privately?"

My heart froze in my chest. "Y-yes. Of course."

CHAPTER ELEVEN

My shoulders tightened, and I prayed he wasn't here to deliver news of someone's death. I thought of all my friends at SOE, and wondered what would prompt Ian to come all the way from London. I led him past the study and the kitchen, and out through the back. Brande followed in silence.

My mother sat at the veranda table, sharing a bottle of wine with Delana. "Isabella, I was wondering when you were coming back. Is Rachel all right?"

"She's fine, Mom." I forced myself to smile and gestured toward the two men. "This is Ian and Brande."

"Yes, Ian, from the ambassador's office." My mom shook his hand and then Brande's.

"A pleasure to meet you, Mrs. George." Ian inclined his head.

"Ian and I need to discuss some important matters...work matters. Excuse us." I gave Brande a sidelong glance when he continued following, but I didn't bother to send him away.

We went inside, and for a moment I tensed at the memory of Neal being here. If I saw him again, I swore I'd throttle him with my bare hands. Ian took a seat next to me on the loveseat, and Brande stood near the door like a sentinel. I eyed Ian with a worried expression, knowing that something huge must've happened for him to travel all the way from London and shirk his duties at SOE headquarters to speak with me.

"I was the one to warn the FBI about that warlock, Ryker," Ian said. He clasped his hands.

"Well, good. Thank you."

"Don't thank me just yet." He looked at Brande. "Can...you excuse us?"

"No." He stood near the door and gazed at us.

Ian groaned. "Isabella, the reason why I'm here is because Ryker's my fault."

"How is he your fault? Octavian sent him as retribution."

"That's only part of it. Do you recall how I only went to Finley's Pub once and then stopped?"

"What does that have to do with anything?"

"Well on my visit there I...I got entangled with that she-devil, Casandra, and ended up going home with her."

"Ian...you didn't."

Wonderful. He just had to choose to jump into bed with a Cruenti warlock--one I particularly didn't like. She always hung around the pub we frequented in London, claiming to be reformed, and spending her time dancing and drinking. Everyone at the pub, including the barkeep, treated Casandra with fascination, because most of them didn't know or experience what a Cruenti was really like. Cruenti often played up the romantic vampire myth when around normal people, but just let a tasty wizard walk by and a Cruenti would lose control, just like that creepy Morgan who attacked me back at Nena's house.

Ian shifted in his seat. "I didn't know she worked for Ryker. They took pictures and threatened to expose me--"

I buried my face in my hands and growled. "I don't believe this..."

"They said they would tell SOE that I was one of their sycophants. I may be many things, but I'd never want to try to be initiated and become a Cruenti."

I wanted to punch him. "So you let them blackmail you? *You're* the leak?" I saw Brande leave his post and approach. If I didn't say anything, he'd probably kill Ian.

"You have to believe that I'd never do anything to harm you," Ian said, watching Brande with wide and frightened eyes.

"Too late for that." I crossed my arms to keep myself from laying hands on him. "Do you know how many people are dead because of you?"

His lips trembled. "It started off with them asking for bits of information, nothing that seemed to connect to anything further. I never told them anything that could directly endanger you or give you away."

"They're smarter than that. They could've easily taken what you gave them and made use of it."

"I know that now, and when you came back from Paris and told me about your identity being discovered...that's when I realized the ramifications of what I've done...and that's when I tried to break away from them."

"How did you know Ryker was going after Isabella?" Brande asked.

Ian answered, "Ryker wanted me lure her back to London. I knew if I did, that she'd be walking into a trap. I put out the warning to the FBI immediately and came here as soon as possible. At this point, what happens to me is of no concern--my life is over. It's all over."

I stood so quickly that Ian instinctively flinched. He probably expected me to start blasting him with a spell. This could've all been avoided if he had just trusted me enough to help. Even if what he did was something so horrible and idiotic, we could've found a way to deal with it. "Why didn't you come to me, Ian? Why didn't you ask for help?"

He looked at me through watery eyes. "Haven't you ever done anything you were ashamed of?"

I tried to remain calm as I gazed at him. "Ian, how much information did you give them? What did you give them?"

"They know the codenames of five different agents,

mostly wizards. They know some of our code words and safe houses. When Ryker tried to give me this last assignment, he was particularly interested in you, and asked about Marcellus Eckhard and your father."

I stared at him, wishing that someone else sat in front of me spilling this confession. Ian was more than just my handler and my boss. He was a friend, a second brother to me. He may not have intentionally wanted to harm me, but he ended up doing so anyway. "It must've been good and well to slip Casandra and Ryker information as long as you didn't have to suffer the consequences."

Brande peered into Ian's eyes when he asked his next question. "You could've just put out the warning to the FBI and do nothing further. Why did you come here?"

"Ryker threatened to plant false letters identifying Isabella as the traitor," he answered. "He thinks I'm here under his orders, but I wanted to come and tell you the truth. If I'm going to be found out, then it might as well be like this. Forgive me, Isabella, for being a coward."

"Cowards get scared and run, Ian. You got people killed because you wanted to protect your reputation. Will you let me take you in?"

Ian ran his hands through his hair. "Can you take me in to Morton?"

I nodded. "That'll be the first step. Consider yourself under arrest."

"You know what this means for me," Ian said in a hoarse voice.

"Yeah, I think it's called justice." Though I said these words in anger, underneath it I felt hurt. Taking Ian in to MI6 as the traitor we've been searching for would carry the penalty that anyone else guilty of treason would have to face--death.

"Brande." I gestured in the direction of the main house. "There are FBI agents parked outside the house. Have them come and escort him out."

Brande gave Ian one last glare before walking out. I

turned away from Ian and brushed my tears away with the back of my hand. When I faced him again, he could no longer keep his composure and began weeping.

"I'm sorry, Isabella. Please, at least understand my situation."

"Don't talk to me."

Brande returned with the two FBI agents who had been part of the security detail for the house. I informed them about Ryker being dead, and one of the agents told me that the local police already received a phone call and were at the scene with a few other FBI agents near the equestrian properties.

I nodded and told them, "Mr. Pearce has just confessed to being an accomplice of Ryker's. Take him to Jeffery Field and hold him there. Call Special Agents Lainey and Jameson and tell them to meet me here."

They cuffed Ian and escorted him out. He slumped his shoulders and hung his head low. I didn't know whether I wanted to curse or cry. I started pacing back and forth, already fearing and imagining how it would all transpire once we reached London.

"I'll go catch up with the trackers," Brande said.

"Do you have to?"

"I'd prefer not to, but I will."

I nodded. "I can take care of Ian, and I think I'd rather do it by myself anyway. It looks like I'm going back to London."

"If I see Carson, I'll find a way let him know."

My mother and Delana came in. "What's going on with Ian? And where's Neal?"

Brande motioned for Delana to join him outside. He knew me well enough that I'd want to answer my mother without any eavesdropping or bystanders.

I took my mother's hands in mine, and told her that I didn't work in the U.S. ambassador's office in London, but with SOE as a spy. In a broken voice I told her of Ian's betrayal, and how it almost cost my life. I could see the worry in her eyes, and the wrinkles in her frown deepen as I explained all this. However, part of me still held back about Dad--I couldn't tell her he was alive.

"So you ran halfway around the world? For what?" she asked.

I shook my head. "Part of me felt like I did have to get away from you, but it became more than that. I wanted to do something...be a part of something important instead of just sitting at home worrying."

"Like me, right? Is that how you always saw me?"

"Yes," I replied in a low voice.

I wasn't going to lie to her about it, not now. She never liked the fact that my father got me involved with the Order of Wizards, and she especially hated when I went to train with the Tower after college. She probably wanted me to be like Johnnie, already married and sitting around smoking Mint Juleps with her. But that was never going to be my life, and I accepted that--I just wished she had the heart to do the same. Her eyes filled with tears, but she didn't let them fall. She crossed her arms and looked at me with that same disdain she held for my father all those years ago.

"You're going to end up the same way Carson did if you keep doing this. He thought he was protecting us, and he thought he was doing great things. But what's wrong with just coming home to your family? Carson missed out on us, and you're going down the same path and not even realizing it."

In a shaky voice I told her, "I will never end up like him."

"When I noticed that owl ring you're wearing, I asked Johnnie about Veit Heilwig. He's dead. How many more of your father's friends are dead? And damn it, I might be standing here but I feel like I died years ago too. So what are you protecting, Isabella?"

"You don't understand."

She sighed. "I understand enough to know that you can't come back to this house if you still have anything to

141

do with the Order, or getting into gunfights and betrayals, or whatever else it is you're doing."

I stood there and stared at her, wondering how this all fell apart. I was beginning to believe that I had a second chance to rebuild my relationship with my mother, but instead I felt like I had been stabbed in the heart. I felt the same rejection I had experienced when my mother asked my father why I couldn't be normal, right in front of me, when I was just a girl.

"So...you hate me that much?" I asked.

"If I hated you, I wouldn't have said a word. Sometimes it takes the people who love you to set you straight and let you know that you're not perfect and you do *not* have all the answers."

"Yeah, sure."

I shouldered my way past her and went into the front house. Johnnie sat in the living room with Rachel. She had apparently told him her good news, because he wore a huge smile and kept giving her kisses. I felt terrible having to leave, especially like this, but a small part of me couldn't deny the truth in my mother's words. I was about to take off again, like my father, and leave her with questions, doubts, and hurt. Rachel almost died today because of the danger I was involved in, and what about Henry Smith who blindly aided my father because he looked up to him as a hero? And there was Veit Heilwig, the alchemist, who had also cooperated with my dad. Too many people were paying too high of a price--which was exactly why I had to keep certain things from her. I didn't want her to end up being the next one who had to pay.

I hastily introduced Brande to my brother, and thankfully, Rachel put an end to any potential questions or slip ups from Johnnie about Neal. Johnnie asked me about our father, and I told him I wasn't sure when he'd see me again.

Johnnie pulled me aside. "I visited Roxanna after lunch today and had her fix my memory of what happened at the university."

"Good," I said. "And have Roxanna fix Rachel's memory of today as well. Stay safe."

"I'll take care of Mom and Rachel, and if you ever need anything, I'll help take care of you too."

A sad smile crossed my lips, and I wrapped my arms around him, resolved to never again ask for his help. It was better not to. It was safer. "Thank you, Johnnie."

"Let me know when you can come back home," he said.

"As soon as I can."

The doorbell rang, and Rachel went to answer. She came in with Jameson and Lainey. I turned to Delana and spoke to her in a low voice. "I have to leave for London. What do you want to do?"

She grumbled. "I have a niece there. I suppose I can stay with her for a while."

"Then you can fly out with me."

"Fine." She went upstairs to grab her belongings.

When Delana came back down, I gave my family a quick hug and said a final goodbye as Lainey and Jameson headed out to the car. Delana went with them, and I followed, with Brande at my side. When they got into the car, I paused and turned to face Brande.

"I'll see to your father," he said.

"Thank you, Brande."

He stepped in closer toward me, and I stood on the tips of my toes and wrapped my arms around his neck because of his height. That's how I'd always give him a hug. I could feel the warmth of his muscular body and the beating of his heart--I almost couldn't believe he had let me place a heart-bind on him. As I gazed into Brande's eyes, Lainey blared the horn--even though I was already next to the car.

"I'll...be going now," Brande said.

"Take care." I released him and let him open the door for me, and I slipped inside. Lainey started the car and took off.

Jameson sat in the passenger seat and turned to face me.

"We heard about Ryker. Good job."

"Well, Neal actually took care of him, but you ought to know that we had a falling out. He left."

"That's too bad," Jameson said. "I kind of liked him."

"I never liked him," Delana interjected.

"Meh," Lainey said. "So what's the story with you and that guy back there?"

"He's...someone close to me."

"Now *him*, I like," Delana said. "Nice strapping Czech man...maybe if more wizards looked like him, I would've joined the Gray Tower forty years ago."

"By the way," Jameson handed me an envelope, "we've got some dirt on that magazine guy, Philip Parrish."

I took the envelope from him and opened it. "Hmm, looks like Mr. Parrish has been laundering money."

Jameson explained, "He lost some money a year or two ago on an investment, and now it seems he's trying to recoup the loss. Why is it again that you wanted this information?"

"Justice. I promise. Will you have any time to pay him a visit?" I placed the sheet of paper back inside the envelope and put it into my handbag. I almost got angry again just thinking about how the slime bag treated Rachel and ruined her chance at a writing career.

"We're on it." Jameson said.

I glanced out the window and saw that we were approaching Jeffery Field, in Boston. The Army Air Corps mainly used it, though there were a few commercial flights available as well. My stomach ached with hunger, and I realized that I hadn't eaten since lunch. With a painful rumble in my belly, I thought about the conversation between my mother and me, and wanted to cry.

"Jameson, what time is it?"

"Five o' clock. Why?"

"I'm starving."

"Here--" Delana reached into her tote. "Eat this." She pulled out the wrapped up corn bread from the other day.

"Thank you." I tried to hide my grimace as I took the corn bread from her and nibbled at it.

Lainey pulled up to the checkpoint at the gate where a soldier sat at a booth. He stepped out and approached the driver side window. Jameson and Lainey presented their badges and then the soldier signaled the others at the gate to let us through. The closer we got to the air hangar, the tighter my stomach seemed to clench. It bothered me that I was taking Ian in like this, but what else could I do?

We exited the car and went inside the air hangar. There wasn't really a place to stash a prisoner, so they had Ian still cuffed, sitting in a chair near the storage compartments, with a guard posted on each side. His head hung low, and I couldn't tell if he was asleep or just too ashamed to raise his head. I didn't even want to think of what would await him once we returned to London, but it made me even more upset to think of how much damage his unscrupulous decision had dealt.

Lainey and Jameson went to speak with one of the captains and gave instructions for our flight. Delana hung close to me, probably thinking I'd ditch her at the last minute and leave her to the mercy of the Air Corps. I noted with irritation that she wore my blue shawl again, and that she still kept that shopping tote, but at least she wasn't going around offering to give anyone a reading. I thought I saw that weird gleam in her eye that she'd get when a spirit communicated with her, and I immediately tensed.

"That man over there," she nodded over toward Ian, "all I see is sadness and darkness."

"So do I," I whispered.

Jameson went over to Ian and instructed his guards to take him aboard the plane that had been readied for us. Lainey headed straight toward me with a somber expression and reached inside his jacket pocket. "The President and General Donovan decided to phase in the first cohort of agents. I believe someone recommended you...if you want it." He handed me a CIA badge.

145

In disbelief, I took the badge and examined it. It looked like they used an older picture from one of my files. "I'm not even done with SOE..."

"General Donovan said it doesn't matter. You've earned it." He winked, and I wanted to plant a kiss on his balding head.

Jameson approached with a grin on his face. "How do you like your badge, Agent George?"

"It's all right, I suppose." With a smile I closed it and slipped it into my handbag.

"Everything's ready," Jameson said. "You can board the plane now."

"Thank you." I gave them both a hug. "Be safe."

Delana followed me to the plane and we boarded. All I could think about was what I would tell our superior, Joshua Morton, once we reached MI6. I glanced in Ian's direction, and he just sat there wearing a blank expression. The captain had an officer accompanying Ian for the flight, but I didn't think it was of any use. He didn't have any fight in him, and he hadn't put up any resistance. This was a man who wasn't going anywhere, except to his own execution.

CHAPTER TWELVE

"Back so soon?" Lt. Richard Carr took off his headgear and unzipped the top of his jumpsuit. At first he didn't fly on missions as often as he used to, but it seemed after I returned from Paris, he began hopping into bombers and fighter planes as often as he could. He noticed my somber expression, which was out of the ordinary when we saw each other here at the Royal Air Force base.

"Hi Richard, I have pressing matters to attend to," I said, gesturing toward Ian and the U.S. soldier who escorted him. "Can you get a couple of your guys to come with us down to Morton's office?"

When Richard saw Ian shackled and looking disheveled, he snorted. "What is this?"

"Richard, it was Ian. He's the traitor. He confessed everything to me."

His face blanched and his jaw dropped. "No, it can't be..."

Before I could say anything else, Richard had stalked toward Ian and his guard. The soldier saluted him. "Lieutenant Carr, sir. I was instructed to give this to you." He handed Richard a file folder.

Richard took it but fixed his stare on Ian. "Is it true?"

He lifted his gaze for the first time, and looked Richard in the eyes. He licked his cracked lips and said in a low voice, "Yes."

"So...who was it?" Richard shoved the file into the hands of a nearby Royal Air Force officer.

Ian's lower lip trembled. "I don't..."

"Who was it? Who were you responsible for getting killed?" When Ian only lowered his gaze again, Richard prodded him. "Was Stella one of them? Did she die because of you?"

I felt a dull ache in my stomach at the mention of my friend. She had been missing for five months before I discovered that she had been caught by the Nazis and died at Dachau. "Richard," I said as I approached, wondering why I was trying to be the voice of reason, "we don't know the extent..."

He held his hand up in a gesture to silence me. "Bollocks, he should be able to recall if he gave them her information. You remember Stella, don't you, Ian? She...she had brown hair, and a lovely smile..."

Ian lowered his head. "Richard--"

"And her favorite color was yellow, she loved dancing, and she told me that when she came back from France that she'd let me take her to dance."

Ian raised his head and looked up at Richard again. "I--"

Richard decided not to let him finish his sentence and smashed his fist into Ian's face. A couple of officers had to rush over and pull Richard off of him. I didn't make a move to help Ian. I just felt numb.

"Max," I called to the pilot who had run over to us. "Help the officer get Ian into a car. We're going to MI6."

Richard seethed with rage. "That bastard!"

"I'll take care of it, Richard."

When Delana poked her head out of the plane, the last to exit, I gestured for her to come join me. "I'll get a cab for you. What's your niece's name?"

"Alina," she said, rummaging through the tote. "Take this with you. If it glows, then that means I am under attack by Ammon." She handed me a sapphire pendant.

148

"Take care, Delana."

She touched my cheek with the palm of her hand. "Thank you, Isabella. I pray you stay strong in the face of what's to come."

I frowned. "You mean Ian?"

She shook her head. "Hell is coming."

She headed out toward the exit with an escort and disappeared. I looked at the pendant once more before placing it on my silver chain. One of the mechanics passed by and I asked him for the time, and he told me it was past 3 a.m. When one of the officers, Max, came back in and signaled to me, I knew it was time to go.

Richard came up and grabbed me by the arm. "Don't pity him. Pity Stella, and everyone else who's dead or rotting in a Nazi prison because he exposed them."

"I know how to do my job." I pulled my arm free.

"I hope you do," he said in a broken voice. "I truly hope you do."

***

We reached the mansion at Bletchley Park that housed MI6 as well as teams of codemasters and naval officers working around the clock. We came in at sunrise, and the receptionist wore an expression of mild shock as the Air Force officer and I signed in with Ian in between us. We had called ahead and the agency knew to expect us, but it still must've been a heavy blow to many to see an SOE handler, who had previously been well liked and respected, hauled in like a criminal. An agent approached us and introduced himself as Bancroft. He had the build of a professional boxer and wore a scowl on his face. With a grunt, he came and took Ian into custody. I walked alongside them as we headed toward the lift that would take us to the interrogation room beneath the G-Block. As we went down to the basement level, I stole a few glimpses of Ian and noted that he seemed a little more focused and less weepy. I

149

turned away when he looked at me, but he spoke to me anyway.

"I'm very sorry, Isabella. Please...speak to me."

His eyes betrayed hope and despair at the same time. I opened my mouth to say something, but I didn't even know what I wanted to say to him. I finally stuttered, "It's best...it's better if you don't say anything to me."

"Could you forgive me?"

Bancroft punched him in the stomach and he doubled over. "If it was up to me, I would've asked the Air Force lieutenant to shoot you in the head. Feckin' traitor." He pulled Ian along when the doors opened and brought him down the hall to the interrogation room. Joshua Morton, the MI6 liaison who oversaw SOE operations, stood outside with his hands in his pockets, and for a fleeting second I wondered if they really were just going to shoot Ian.

"Mr. Morton, sir." Bancroft nodded toward Morton and walked Ian into the room. The door closed behind them, and Morton approached me.

"Why are you here, Isabella?"

I gave him a startled look. "Ian came to me...he confessed to me. I think it's only right that I be here."

"Is that so?" he asked with a frown beneath his dark beard.

Bancroft swung the door open with a frightened look on his face. "He's poisoned himself! He had an L-tablet lodged in his jaw."

"Go get a medic," Morton instructed him.

As Bancroft ran down the hall, Morton and I rushed into the interrogation room to find Ian slouched in his chair and his head against the table. My legs wobbled and my chest constricted. Morton reached Ian before I did and checked for a pulse. He looked at me and shook his head; the arsenic would kill Ian before the medic even got here.

"It's over, Isabella."

"No, it's not!" I screeched at him.

I placed my hands on Ian's head and neck. I could feel

the poison coursing through his system, and counteracted as much as I could with my body magic. Ian began convulsing, and then he vomited over the table. Bancroft rushed in with the medic who rolled a wheel chair in. The men hoisted Ian and set him into the chair, then the medic took him out.

"They'll get him to a hospital," Morton assured me when I tried to follow them. "Bancroft, escort Isabella upstairs to my office."

Bancroft nodded, and I looked askance. "Why do I have to go to your office?"

"Just do it." He left the interrogation room.

Bancroft reached for my left arm, but I batted his hand away. "I know how to get there."

All the same, he fell in step with me as I walked out, and I grew worried. We went up the lift in silence, and when I made it to Morton's office, Bancroft let me in and closed the door behind me. Morton sat at his desk, with a calm façade over a deep-seated unease. I walked toward his desk and paused just a few feet away.

"What is it, Morton?"

He flung a sheet of paper onto his desk and invited me to read it. "SOE sent this to me."

I read the letter in disbelief. It was the incriminating note that Ryker and Casandra had threatened Ian with if he didn't comply with their demands. Besides appearing to have been written by Ian and exposing him, it also indicated that I was an accomplice. This didn't look good at all.

"Morton," I said with a lump in my throat, "this is a false statement. Ian was being blackmailed--"

"Well I don't know that because he poisoned himself before I could speak with him."

"He was desperate, he said his life was over."

"So were you his accomplice? Did you expose other agents and give away SOE's secrets?"

"Of course not. You know me--"

"Apparently not that well." He shifted in his seat. "Why

151

did Ian go to America?"

"To warn me about the warlock, Ryker, the one who had been blackmailing him."

He paused and looked at me as if sizing me up. It made me angry because my loyalty should've never come into question so easily, even with these so-called incriminating letters. General Donovan was right; this war had everyone questioning their allies and people's loyalties.

"Isabella, I can't afford to pat you on the back and tell you everything is fine. I think you left some facts out of your last report when you came back from Paris. Now you're simply suffering the consequences."

I discarded decorum and addressed him by his first name. "Joshua, I understand you have doubts and you want answers. But don't you dare sit here in judgment over me, not without hearing the whole story."

The office door opened, and Jane Lewis barged in. she regarded her half brother with a warning look and rushed to my side. "Joshua, I just saw them take Ian to the hospital...why are you doing this to Isabella? You said you were just going to talk with her."

"I haven't done anything, and I *am* talking with her."

"Whatever it is you think she's done, it's not true. She's one of our best agents."

"Then how do you explain this?" Morton grabbed the letter and walked it over to Jane. "Her loyalty doesn't lie with us."

I clenched my fists and glared at him. "You don't know anything about my loyalties."

Jane folded the letter and gazed at her brother. "Let me tell you who she is to me. When Anna was killed--"

"Jane--" he protested.

"When they killed Anna, Isabella made certain that at least her burial site was marked, and then she hunted down the criminals who shot our sister. Now put *that* in one of your reports."

He wavered. "I've...been using all my resources to find

152

them. I couldn't understand why those men simply vanished off the face of the earth."

Jane's expression softened. "You never told me that. It felt like you never told me anything." She turned toward me and squeezed my hand. "Go, Isabella. Whoever made Ian write this letter is the one who needs to be brought in."

"Damn it, Jane!"

"No," I said, letting my hand slip from hers. "I haven't done anything wrong. If I run out of here like this, it'll only convince him that he's right--which he's not."

Morton grunted. "I'll call a car to take you home. You're suspended pending investigation. *And* I'm sending agents to watch your flat. I don't want to see you here at Bletchley Park or at the Baker Street office until this is over. Is that understood?"

I wanted to argue against him, but if I said another word he would fire me and throw me into jail. I turned and walked away with Jane down G-Block and through the front reception area. When we stepped outside, my eyes stung with tears of anger.

"I'm so sorry, Isabella." Jane crossed her arms and stared at the ground. "I feel terrible about Ian."

"So do I." I stood in silence in front of the mansion, and headed for the car as soon as I saw it pull up. The driver opened the door for us, and I shouldered my black handbag and got inside.

When we arrived at our building, I wanted to drag myself upstairs to my flat and crawl into bed, but Jane insisted that I stay with her. After a quick bath, I borrowed one of her nightgowns (one of the non-frilly ones) and devoured a plate of leftover woolton pie. I wrapped my hair in a towel and settled onto her sofa with a cup of hot coffee. She yawned and motioned to the clock to let me know it was almost 8 a.m., and I technically hadn't gotten any sleep, but I assured her I'd get some rest soon. When she retired to her bedroom, I reached into my black handbag and pulled out Veit's diary with the translated texts.

I pushed aside some of her magazines on the coffee table and laid out the papers. I secretly tried to do the meditations again during the plane ride over here, but I failed at it again. I began wondering if Dr. Grey was telling the truth about the missing page, and if it contained instructions that I needed. I thought about my father's words and the texts' instructions. I was listening to my heart, I cleared my thoughts and made sure nothing impeded me, so why wasn't I controlling time? The only thing I knew how to do so far was the Zaman's Fire meditation, and how to call forth the Fire as a shield or weapon.

Put your Fire into the water, and into your heart. Make the ripples and pulses burn. I still didn't know what my father's cryptic words meant. How was I supposed to put Zaman's fire into water and into my heart? I grabbed a pen and paper and wrote down his instruction. I wrote down all kinds of question marks and interpretations. After staring at the sentences for a few more minutes, I thought about approaching it not from a mystical perspective, but just one of plain old decoding. My father knew my occupation...it would be easier to just give me a code rather than some lofty spiritual insight.

Put your Fire into the water, and into your heart. Make the ripples and pulses burn. I underlined "water" and "ripples," and circled "heart" and "pulses." It dawned at me that the "heart" I was supposed to be listening to was my actual physical heart, not my emotional one. In a meditative state, these pulsations would be steady and slow. And water ripples would obviously be faster. The heart pulsations would help me to slow time, and the ripples would help me to quicken it. I slowly began to understand how this would work.

In normal human brain activity, we perceived and reacted to events surrounding us in terms of time. Think of enduring a boring presentation that's torturously slow though it's only been five or ten minutes. Imagine having talked on the phone with your sweetheart and discover that hours had passed. Our minds didn't measure time the way clocks did. Our minds interacted with time, but according to these texts, a Drifter's mind did so in a unique way. Instead of feeding these meditations with my magical energy, I needed to use Zaman's Fire.

I called forth a simple spark from the Fire, making it steady and quiet. Next, I envisioned a dark pool of water rippling. As the ripples traveled and spread, gray images moved about in my mind and I felt a pull right below my rib cage. I felt as if I had stepped into a dream or memory, and I stood in the Courtyard of Light at the Gray Tower. My stomach clenched with fear as I remembered the last time I had a vision about this place: I saw Beata, the Master Wizard who belonged to the Council and wore the White. She fell from on high and was impaled on the golden sword of a statue.

The word *war* impressed itself into my mind, and I let out a low groan. I could never let that happen at the Tower. I would have to avoid violence at the Tower at all costs. I drew in a deep breath and squinted my eyes, and willed myself to escape the vision. The room spun, and when I focused again, I was back where I started in the living room.

The vision of war in the Tower frightened me, and I wondered if it really was a good idea to go back to there. If anything happened and I entirely lost my mask, I wouldn't stand a chance against the trackers or any more assassins Octavian decided to send after me. Still, I needed to meet with my father's allies at the Gray Tower and solicit their help in demonstrating to the Masters why I was for the same cause they were and would never turn to the other side. I also wanted to make sure the Masters punished Hotaru for murdering Ken and those other men. I would need to be there to plead my case.

I turned my attention once more to the diary, and this time I used my spark of Fire to feed the pulsations of my heart. I closed my eyes and focused my burning heart on slowing time, and it surprisingly began to strain me. I felt like I was pushing a boulder up a hill. When my body began trembling, I commanded the slow strain to halt, and I opened my eyes.

Everything felt still and quiet, like in the vision-dream I had at my brother's house. I stood and went over to Jane's window and peeked through an opening in the curtain. Several cars in the street were frozen in mid-drive, and men and women walking down the street stood as still as statues though they were mid-stride. I looked across the street and saw the car Morton had sent over. Two MI6 agents sat inside, motionless. My heart dropped in my chest when I saw a shadow figure flit down the street from right to left. I stared through the window to see if it would return or come back down the street, but after a few minutes I focused on the pulsations once more and released them, willing time around me to resume its normal course. The cars in the street rumbled and moved at regular speed, and the people's footsteps pattered against the ground.

Though I was impressed with what I had been able to do with the meditations, I didn't know what to make of the shadow figure I just saw. I told myself that I'd be careful, especially if the shadow returned. I decided to move on to the numbers and entire part about Ophiucus, but my eyelids grew heavy and I kept yawning. After swaying a few times and reading the same line three times, I decided that I needed rest. I secured the papers inside the diary and placed them all back inside the bag. I pulled the blanket up to my chin and drifted away into a dreamless sleep.

***

I awoke in the late afternoon to a note left beside me from Jane explaining that she had gone down to SOE headquarters at 64 Baker Street. Her note also said that she had called to check on Ian. He was in a coma as a result of taking that L-tablet, and no one was sure he'd ever wake up. With a heavy heart, I hung around Jane's flat for a few more hours, mainly because I knew I had no food upstairs in mine, and finally when sunset came, I gathered my belongings and headed upstairs so I could grab a change of clothes.

What's the point of changing into clothes? I asked myself. I wasn't going anywhere at the moment, and if I did, I'd have MI6 agents tailing me. I used to make fun of some of the SOE agents who would retire from spying and stay at home in their pajamas. I swore it would never happen to me-- well, fate had a funny sense of humor. Now, the only things I lacked were a cigarette and a glass of Scotch.

I almost stumbled when I saw a strange man standing at my door. He wore a black fedora and trench coat, and carried a dark brown suitcase. He wore round spectacles, which emphasized his oval face and large dark eyes.

"Can I...help you?" I shifted the handbag in front of me. I still wore the nightgown I had borrowed from Jane.

"Miss George," he said in a German accent. "I'm Mr. Urbano. Your father sent me."

I let the slow burn of Zaman's Fire rise in me, and I kept it ready. "Urbano is...more Italian than German, don't you think?"

He smiled. "Let's step inside, and I'll explain to you why I'm here."

"Let's not," I said.

He nodded in understanding. "Trust is a precious commodity nowadays. I'll prove to you that Carson sent me."

I still held onto the Fire inside me and tensed. "Okay...Mr. Urbano. Go ahead."

"In your most recent meeting with your father, his last words to you were, *Put your Fire into the water, and into your heart. Make the ripples and pulses burn.*"

As he spoke to me, I reached out with my senses and inhaled the scent of an enchanter. He was not a mentalist. He couldn't have read my mind, especially with Nena's seal

157

still on it. "All right, what does my father want?"

"Please," he said, gesturing for us to step inside.

I pulled out my key and approached the door. Right before I unlocked it, I turned to face him. "One more question..."

"Yes?" he said.

"If you've been around my father long enough, then you ought to know what his favorite meal is."

He grunted, as if calling to mind an unpleasant experience. "Your mother's baked chicken. Impossible to get, though he always pines for it. I've smuggled many a chicken dish for him to no avail."

"Then I suppose if he really wants it, then he'll have to go home." I unlocked the door and he followed me in and sat down in my large cushioned chair. My cheeks stung with embarrassment when we both screwed our faces up at the stench of undone dishes assaulting our noses from the kitchen. "Sorry about that. I haven't been here in a while." I tossed the handbag onto a pile of newspapers sitting in a corner and opened my curtain to let some sunshine in. I ran into my room and threw on a robe and tied it. I came back into the living room.

He removed his hat to reveal a bald head, and he gazed at me with those large dark eyes. "I was with your father the night he faked his death in Rome sixteen years ago and began running. He wants you to know that he has constantly thought of you, and your mother and brother. At times, when he could, he has watched you all from afar without you even knowing."

I just stood there--mainly because all the clutter prevented me from finding a seat. I couldn't help but smile a little at his words. It comforted me to know that we weren't *completely* abandoned by my dad.

"Thank you...do you have a first name?"

"Urbano. Just, Urbano."

"Why did he send you tonight?"

"Your father intercepted a message from the U.S. Navy

on its way to Joshua Morton of MI6. The naval captain in the Shetland Islands has requested you specifically for a job which will benefit you greatly in regard to your relationship with the Gray Tower."

"I'm not sure if you're aware that I've been suspended."

"Which is why the message never reached Morton's desk, and why you will go meet with the naval captain and take the job he will propose."

I gestured toward the window that faced the street. I hadn't forgotten about the MI6 agents stationed outside. "Morton's men are watching me. If I leave like this, it will ruin me and I'll be blacklisted. Then I can just add the British government to the list of people who want to capture me."

He opened his briefcase and took out a vial filled with a bright red liquid. "May I have a strand of your hair?"

I didn't know how to answer that one. "Why?"

He removed his black gloves and gestured for me to come near. "Please, let's not waste time."

I walked over and twirled a strand of hair around my index finger and yanked it. I handed the strand to him and watched with fascination as he opened the vial and placed the hair inside. He corked the vial shut again and shook it until pink foam formed. He opened the vial and blew into it with a gentle breath. It was a subtle yet powerful whisper of magic. When the foam shimmered with brilliant colors, he flicked the vial in the direction opposite of him, toward the window, and let the foam fly out. I thought it would hit my cream-colored curtains with a splatter, but instead it landed on the floor and grew thicker, and rose in height. The pinkish color turned into a light peachy tone, and I began to make out the form of a body, of arms, legs, and a face--my face.

I gasped and stood to get a better view. I was looking at my double. "This is...very convincing."

"If anyone stops by to check on you, she will be here."

My double faced me and smiled. "I'm doing fine," she

said. "Thanks for stopping by."

I slowly approached and touched her shoulder, which felt real. "Hi, Isabella. Do you want to punch Morton in the face for thinking you're a traitor?"

She raised an eyebrow. "Very funny. Now, if you'll excuse me, I'm exhausted. I need to go lie down." With a flip of her hair, she walked into the bedroom.

I faced Urbano. "What if someone asks her a question she can't answer?"

"She will explode."

I frowned. "I don't want anyone to get hurt."

He stood. "Don't worry, she'll explode as foam and then dissolve. No one will be harmed."

"All right, so we're going up north to the Shetland Islands?"

He nodded. "You might want to change into something warm."

I went back into the bedroom and put on two shirts, a pair of trousers, along with boots and a sweater. My double lay in bed watching me. It was kind of creepy. When I finished dressing, I turned to her and said, "Goodbye, Isabella."

"Goodbye," she replied. "And good luck."

I went back out to meet Urbano. He peered out the window in silence. I went over to look out as well, and saw the lampposts below lighting the dark street, and a fresh pair of Morton's men sitting in an unmarked car across the street. Someone stood inside a red telephone box toward the left, just a few feet away from the MI6 agents, and two men in suits coming from the direction of the public gardens walked and talked together, coming from the right.

Urbano gestured for me to stand closer to him. "I've sealed your front door so that anyone wishing you harm would have a difficult time entering. It will last even when your double is gone. However if I go out the door with you, it will weaken the enchantment--so let's take the window, shall we?"

I let out a low breath. "My father has some interesting associates."

He adjusted his spectacles and pointed out the window. "That man over there in the red telephone box is a Cruenti, as well as the two men walking down the street who've now apparently stopped to smoke cigars. I doubt this is a coincidence."

I was impressed. He detected them before I did. The stench of their tainted magic began trickling through to me. "I don't think a wizard fight in the middle of the street is going to help us evade MI6."

"I'll take care of it. Now, hold onto me...tightly." He opened his trench coat and pulled out two black pistols.

"Okay..." I wrapped my arms around his neck and held on.

"Hold tightly," he said once more, prodding me closer to him.

The window opened and I felt the pull of gravity as he jumped out with me hanging onto him. I shivered as the cool night air brushed against us. Our trip down was quick, but it also felt as if we were floating. As soon as our feet touched the pavement, he extended his arms and pivoted to the right, shooting the two Cruenti who were smoking cigars and watching the building. The bullets must've been enchanted, because the warlocks went down quickly without regenerating.

I still held onto him, and turned to see the third Cruenti in the red telephone booth to our left run out and rush toward us. The two MI6 agents, one tall and the other short, jumped out of their car and called out to Urbano, referring to him as "Mr. Morton." An invisible force knocked Urbano's gun from his left hand, but he immediately drew a shimmering knife and threw it straight at the Cruenti's head. The blade pierced the Cruenti right between the eyes, and a pop and flash went off, and the warlock's head split and he collapsed to the ground.

"What's happening, Mr. Morton?" the taller agent asked

with his weapon drawn. He didn't even notice me standing there and holding on to Urbano like a needy child.

"How did you jump out of that window, sir?" the short agent queried, staring directly at Urbano and ignoring me. It seemed as long as I held on and stayed close to the wizard, I was invisible to the other men.

"I'm a *very* good jumper," Urbano replied. "It was a foiled attack. I'm sure you can clean up this mess."

"What about Agent George?" the tall one asked.

"You can go and check on her for yourselves. I must go now."

"Of course, sir." The short agent slipped his gun back into his holster and gestured to the tall one. They ran into my building.

"You're hurting my neck," Urbano said. "You can let go now."

I released him and flashed him an apologetic smile. "I think I'm beginning to like you."

"Thank you. Your father trained me." He motioned toward a black car parked down the street. "Shall we?"

I wasted no time in following him and jumping inside. He started the car and we took off into the night. I began wondering how meeting the naval captain and accepting his job proposal would help me with the Gray Tower--and if it was all worth it. If I failed at this, then I'd be worse off than I was before.

CHAPTER THIRTEEN

"I told you to wear something warm." Urbano grabbed an extra blanket from the fisherman and wrapped it around my shoulders.

"I didn't think it was going to be *this* cold!" My teeth chattered as the frosty wind whipped my hair in different directions and penetrated the miniscule holes in my thick sweater. Though I also wore socks and boots, my warmest trousers and two shirts, it seemed nothing short of an insulated suit would keep me warm.

We had been traveling by boat for the last hour, heading north to the island where SOE launched operations to aid Norway across the sea. As a salty spray of water splashed and threatened to hit me in the face, I threw myself in line to be the first one off the boat when we landed. I thanked the boat crew and stepped off. This was my first time in Scalloway harbor, and I felt a surge of pride run through me when I saw the three U.S. submarine chasers in the water. Most of the men running the Shetland Bus operation were fishermen who wanted to join the Resistance, much like the one who escorted Urbano and me here tonight. At least the aid of the naval vessels would ensure more chances of success.

"Are you going to tell me what the captain wants me

for?" I pulled the blanket around me even tighter as we headed toward a man with a flashlight. The darkness made us tread carefully over the uneven terrain.

"Everything will be explained inside." Urbano pulled out his own flashlight and clicked a signal toward the other man. We followed him past a few buildings before stopping at a warehouse beneath the ruins of Scalloway Castle.

"He's expecting you two inside," the man told Urbano.

"Of course," he shook the man's hand. "Thank you, William."

William acknowledged me with a smile and then went on his way. I hoped that wherever he was going that he'd remain safe. We stepped inside and it all looked plain enough. Crates that had been stacked up high stood in rows across the floor, and dusty workstations were lined up and waiting for engineers and mechanics.

Urbano led me to the farthest corner, where a set of false crates concealed a secret door. He guided us with his flashlight as we went inside and headed down an old stairwell. The stone walls and roof made me think of the castle, and I wondered if we were headed directly beneath it. At the bottom of the stairwell stood a reinforced iron door, one that had an enchantment placed on it. A translucent film of silvery-white covered the door, and oddly had been constructed to keep people *inside*. Urbano knocked twice and a man on the other side answered.

When he gave a codeword, the door opened and a young naval officer ushered us in. "Captain Skye is waiting for you."

"Where are we?" I whispered to Urbano. SOE and the U.S. Navy had set up an entire facility down here, but for what purpose?

"He's here, in his office." The young man rounded a corner and directed us to another iron door with an enchantment. Further down the hallway stood a rectangular gate made of steel bars. Beyond the gate were several doors along the corridor. It reminded me of a hospital--a mental one. Urbano opened the door to the captain's office and let me step inside first.

"Welcome to the Shetland Islands, Isabella George," Captain Skye belted out in a Cajun accent as he gestured for us to take our seats across from him. He smiled at me, but I immediately constructed a mental barrier as a precaution.

I cleared my throat. "It's nice to meet you, Captain Skye...or should I say, Master Skye?"

He folded his hands beneath his chin and stared at me. "While we're here, you may call me captain. I haven't been inside the Gray Tower for quite a while. Urbano, it's good to see you again."

Urbano inclined his head. "Likewise, captain. How long has it been?"

"Five long years," the captain said, before facing me again. "He's never told me how he avoided joining the Order but somehow managed to be a damned good enchanter. I think the only reason why I still speak with him is to get in on the secret."

Urbano smirked at the compliment. "On behalf of MI6, I've brought you Ms. George."

The captain continued holding my gaze, apparently sizing me up. I was doing the same, except it was more like a mouse analyzing a hungry lion. If Roxanna's powers as a nature wizard could be described as a flame, then Master Skye's was a roaring fire in comparison.

"Forgive me," I said, trying not to dwell on the man's breadth of magical strength, "but I haven't been told why I'm needed here."

Captain Skye shifted in his seat. "Many agents know about the Shetland Bus, but only a handful are aware of this facility here."

"You mean prison," I said.

He nodded. "And we only take in special prisoners, if you catch my meaning."

"Captain, is there someone--"

"It's Nikon Praskovya," Urbano said.

I faced the captain. "You brought me here because of Praskovya?"

"Not *just* because of her," Skye hastened to answer. "We're trying to find the location of the Den."

Just as the Gray Tower was the headquarters of the Order of Wizards, the Den was the center of operations for the coven of warlocks led by Octavian Eckhard. Octavian was a Cruenti warlock who led the Black Wolves and made an agreement to aid Hitler in the war. Many suspected that Octavian did this as a distraction, because his ultimate goal was to usurp the Gray Tower and eventually the world. I had fought his brother, Marcellus, during my Paris job, and I remembered how he claimed that he and Octavian were powerful enough to avoid the side effects associated with becoming a Cruenti. Usually after a few years of being turned into a Cruenti, a warlock would start to degenerate and lose his mental capacities. Physically, he'd turn into a monster, like the ones that fought alongside Ryker.

I gave Captain Skye a dubious glance. "I thought the Den was at Nuremberg Castle."

"That may be true," the captain said, "however, I happen to believe that while Hitler's occult items are there, Octavian is not. No, he's too smart for that."

Urbano spoke up. "Some sources claim otherwise. Nuremberg's guarded by enough Black Wolves to level a small country. If the place were only full of artifacts, then a small handful would've sufficed."

Skye leaned back, neither put off nor riled by our doubts. "Several Masters would agree with you, Urbano, but I happen to disagree with those Masters."

"Exactly," I said with just a little too much gratification in my tone. "They can be mistaken just like anyone else."

Captain Skye gazed into my eyes. "Isabella, I want you to help us with Praskovya because we believe she's been to the Den, that she has spoken with Octavian face-to-face."

I nodded. "Believe me, I'd love to crack her and find out where the Den is and get to Octavian. This war needs to end. But...I don't think it's going to work."

I wasn't trying to be a Doubting Thomas, but Skye probably chose me because I knew Praskovya's strengths and weaknesses better than anyone else. The problem was that she knew mine as well, and she had no conscience or morals holding her back.

"Isabella," Skye leaned forward, "I'm aware of your history with Praskovya and can understand why you're hesitant to speak with her. If you don't want to do this, then you are certainly free to go. But if you help us on this and we find the Den, then both the Gray Tower and the world will be in your debt."

The Gray Tower indebted to me--this was the benefit Urbano spoke about, and what my father wanted me to achieve. "I suppose I can go talk with her, but what if she doesn't want to speak with me?"

Skye smiled. "I don't think that's going to be a problem. Let's go and pay her a visit."

We rose from our seats, and I hid my shock when I noticed Skye reaching for a cane and using it to stand. Though the hair at his temples grayed, the rest was full and dark, and not a single wrinkle etched his face.

"You're probably wondering why I use this," he said, nodding at his cane and displaying its silver handle with a dragon engraved on it. "A lesson from my days of being young and foolish."

"We all have those days," I said, accepting his arm and carefully walking in step with him.

Urbano led the way as we exited the captain's office. We went down the hall, past a couple of naval officers on patrol, and toward the steel gate. Without a single gesture or utterance from the captain, the gate opened for us with a shriek of rusty iron. As we made our way down the dim hallway, I noticed an eerie quiet that fell over the area.

"Captain, how many prisoners do you have here?" I asked.

"Never more than fifteen."

167

"They're well-behaved," Urbano said.

"Half of these warlocks are psychotic," Skye said. "Some of the holding rooms are warded so we don't have to hear their god-forsaken blathering. Others have learned to hold their tongue."

We stopped at the twelfth holding room. Instead of using a key, Skye brushed his thumb against a few of the glowing symbols on the door's handle. The door clicked open, and he announced to Praskovya that I would be entering. He closed the door behind me and stood outside with Urbano, watching me through the small glass window in the middle. For some reason I thought the holding room would be like a psych ward, with white cushioned walls and Praskovya in a straight jacket. However it was as plain as any prison cell, with a bed, water closet, sink, and small table and chair.

Praskovya's eyes betrayed her amusement, though she didn't smile. She watched me take a seat at the little table across from the bed, and I felt awkward when I saw the golden imperium collar around her neck. She wore a white long-sleeved men's shirt and black trousers, and her blonde hair was pulled back into a low bun.

"You probably already know why I'm here, Praskovya."

She glanced in the direction of the door and peered at the men staring back at us through the small window. "They have tried, and they have failed. So will you."

"You seemed to have known Marcellus pretty well. I wouldn't be surprised if you did meet Octavian."

"Even if I did, you know how it goes. The same enchantment that would keep you from revealing the location of the Gray Tower would hang over those privileged enough to walk inside the Den."

She had a point. "Then let's talk about you."

Her eyes narrowed. "What about me?"

"How do you feel about a swift execution?"

She exhaled a low breath; she did that when something bothered her. "You're not here for that. You want to know where the Den is."

I had to make her believe that she needed us more than we needed her. "You're right, I'm not here for the execution. I'm just doing one last interrogation because Morton asked me to. You know how thorough he is."

Her jaw went slack. "Don't tell me Master Skye will be part of this interrogation."

I leaned in and said to her in Russian, "He might, but to be honest, he gives me the creeps."

That solicited a smile from her, and she switched over as well. "If you weren't such a Tower Slave, I'd ask you to free me."

I switched back to English. "Sorry, but that's not happening. You're going to be sorely disappointed, just like when you finally realized that the Russian government wasn't willing to pay your ransom. I'll just tell Morton that you had nothing to say and that you're ready to be hanged." I stood and turned toward the door, almost breaking into a sweat when she said nothing else. I thought she would call my bluff, but when I grabbed the doorknob, she finally spoke.

"I have a contact in Spain, by the name of Alban. He's my handler. He carries a talisman that can take him near the Den whenever Octavian summons him, or in an emergency. It works like a Transfer stone."

I turned back around and approached her. "And the talisman doesn't have any side effects?"

"Octavian is the most powerful Cruenti alive. You should see the things he is able to do." Her face contorted with disgust, and it caught me off guard. I never understood why she left us to work for that monster.

Captain Skye knocked on the door, and I saw him beckoning me to come out. I went and opened the door and closed it behind me. "What is it?"

"Don't fall for her mind games," he said. "You'd be walking into a trap trying to chase that lead in Spain. I just want you to try to get as much out of her as you can."

169

"I'm surprised you haven't done it already, captain. For some reason she's afraid of you."

"As she should be," he said with a predatory grin.

Urbano kept silent but gave me an encouraging nod. I said to Skye, "I know she wants any excuse to get out. She's hoping that I'll ask her to help me with meeting Alban. If she wears the imperium collar, then I'm willing to do it."

I wasn't going to let this opportunity pass me by. If I could uncover the Den's whereabouts and help lead to the fall of Octavian, then the Drifter would be a hero--not an outlaw. I turned and went back inside.

"Alban will not meet with a stranger," Praskovya continued, "and if I contact him and someone else shows up, he will only flee."

"Of course. You want to come with me."

"Not only that, I want this imperium collar off."

"How long has it been on? I would've thought it had drained your powers by now."

She glanced toward the glass window again. "Our dear captain replaces the collar every two days. He seems to believe that even people like me should not be robbed of their powers."

"That's rather generous of him," I said. "But if you're going to help me get Alban, you won't be taking that imperium collar off. It's my insurance." I'd feel uncomfortable controlling her through the device, but it was the only way I'd let her go with me.

"What if there was another way?" she asked.

"And what would that be?"

She grabbed the neck of her shirt and pulled it down to expose her chest. "Heart-bind."

I paused before letting out a low laugh of incredulity and looked in the direction of the glass window. Captain Skye and Urbano gazed back without saying a word. "You really want to leave this place, don't you, Praskovya?"

She stood and approached. "I get this collar off, and you get your insurance."

True, if Alban detected the collar, it would ruin everything. However, I knew Praskovya would never settle for going on this assignment only to return to the Shetland prison. At some point she'd try to escape while in Spain. I supposed I could do a temporary heart-bind, but it made me feel uneasy because the moment she'd make her move, I would have to act upon the bind and kill her.

"If you're serious about this," I told her as I stood to meet her gaze, "then I want you to repeat *exactly* what I'm about to say. If you hold up your end of the bargain, I promise that I'll bring you back safely."

"Agreed." She slowly exhaled another breath.

I placed my hand over her heart in the same way I had done Brande, and recited the words I wanted her to say. "*I vow to aid Isabella in her task and I will not betray her, or flee.*"

She repeated the phrase in a clear voice, and the tingling tendrils of energy spun forth and enveloped my hand. When the binding completed itself, my hand fell to my side, and I threw Praskovya a look to remind her of what would happen if she didn't fulfill her vow. Just one false move, and she'd be dead.

"Captain Skye," she said, already toying with the imperium collar, "get in here and take this damned thing off my neck. I'm going to Spain."

"Urbano," Skye said as he walked in with his cane. "Take Miss Praskovya down to room number one and have my Elite remove the collar."

Urbano came forward and pulled Praskovya with him out of the room. Skye studied me for a second before gripping his cane and holding out his hand. I reached out and took it, assuming he wanted me to walk arm-in-arm with him again.

"May I...read you?" he asked.

Suddenly the room grew colder than the windswept ocean. "Perhaps some other time, captain."

"No?" His hold became a grip.

"No." I snatched my hand away.

He stepped in closer. "Even without reading you I can tell something is wrong with you. You come in here and pretend there isn't, and you don't expect me to say anything about it?"

A chill ran down my spine, and I took a step back. "There's nothing wrong with me, Captain Skye."

His nostrils flared. "How do you know Jerome?"

I let out a startled breath. "Jerome? Who is he?"

I knew he was one of the original wizards who had helped my father, but I had never come across him while at the Gray Tower--at least I didn't think I did.

"Why don't you tell *me* who he is, since the imprint of his magic is on you." Skye had woven a paralysis spell around me, and I didn't even feel it until now. I hoped Urbano would return soon.

"Captain Skye, please release me. I don't know who Jerome is."

He peered into my eyes. "It looks like you're telling the truth about that. He doesn't go by that name anymore, and you're awfully young. It's Ekwueme, who wears the Yellow."

I didn't know whether to feel emboldened or shocked. Jerome, who had apparently changed his name to Ekwueme, was one of the Three Master Wizards who sat on the Council and helped run the Gray Tower. He was the most powerful Philosopher alive. When Captain Skye saw that I didn't give any further explanation as to why one of The Three had imprinted me with his magic, he grew incensed, and his pupils dilated until the whites of his eyes were swallowed in darkness.

"I ought to turn you inside out for your insolence, but if Ekwueme has gifted you in some way..."

If Skye hadn't paralyzed me with his spell, I would've been trembling. I saw my chance to escape and took it. "Ekwueme wouldn't be too pleased with you laying hands on me, now would he? So may I be excused, or did you want to sit here and harass me?"

He paused, as if weighing his options. "I swear if you're playing some kind of--"

"I need to get to Spain. If you have any questions, ask Ekwueme yourself." My muscles relaxed, and the paralysis he placed on me subsided.

"This conversation isn't over," he said, stepping aside.

"Goodbye, captain." I rushed past him but paused at the door when he called out to me.

"And just get rid of Praskovya when you're done in Spain."

"But I promised her--"

"You're not the one with the heart-bind on you, are you? Just do it, and save us all the trouble."

My stomach fluttered as I left the holding room and went down to number one. An Elite Alchemist, Wes, had already removed Praskovya's collar. With a satisfied grin, she donned a thick black coat and addressed me in a friendly tone. "I look forward to working with you again."

Urbano handed me his black pistol. "Be safe."

"Thank you," I said, eyeing Praskovya with distrust.

"Isabella, let's put the past behind us. Tomorrow we may be the best of friends." She chuckled.

"Wes," Urbano motioned to the wizard. "Take her toward the front and we'll meet you there."

"Yes, sir." He escorted her out.

Urbano turned to face me. "I must leave you now. I wish you success in your endeavor."

"Will I see you again?"

"I hope so, otherwise I shall always remember you as the girl who hurt my neck." He offered me his hand, and I shook it.

"Thank you, Mr. Urbano."

I went ahead and met up with Praskovya. I guided her back down the way I first came, past the castle ruins and buildings, and back to the harbor. As we boarded the boat, I saw something in the sky. It blotted out a few stars and moved swiftly. I rubbed my eyes and peered again up into the night, but nothing else stirred. I chalked it up to a lack of sleep and went aboard the boat, mentally preparing myself for what I would have to do.

It seemed no matter what choice I made, Praskovya was going to have to die.

CHAPTER FOURTEEN

"If you're thinking about trying to ditch me at La Cocina, then just remember what I told you last night. And, distance doesn't matter. I'll enact the heart-bind if I have to." Of course she knew that, which made my threat unnecessary, but it was somehow an assurance to myself that I wouldn't have to look over my shoulder every ten seconds wondering if her trip to the ladies' room was really a car ride across the Spanish border. If I were in Praskovya's position, I'd probably already have a plan as to how I would get out of this mess--so what was it?

"Slow down," she said in a sleepy voice. "There's a checkpoint ahead."

"I'm not blind."

I pulled to a stop and turned off my headlights as the officer requested. "Good evening, ladies," he said to us in Spanish.

"Good evening," I replied and smiled. "Did something happen here?"

"I apologize for the inconvenience." He grabbed the passports we handed him and examined them. "The general wants to make sure certain people aren't crossing our borders."

"I understand." Spain had declared itself neutral, but it

175

didn't stop either side in the war from running operations in the territory.

"You're headed into the city?" He half-smiled at Praskovya.

"Does it matter?" She raised an eyebrow.

I lightly touched the officer's hand, impressing upon him a friendlier disposition toward us. "Please excuse my friend. She's crazy."

"I don't mind." He winked at me. "Have you been to Madrid before? Perhaps I can show you around. I should be off duty within the hour, and the way you're dressed it looks like you're headed to one of the nightclubs."

I immediately pressed the palm of my hand against Praskovya's mouth to halt any further comments from escaping. "Thank you, but we're meeting a friend. Perhaps next time."

He handed us back our passports. "Then goodnight, ladies."

I adjusted my black wrap dress and then turned the headlights back on. I pulled off, barreling down the road and casting Praskovya a sidelong glance. "Sometimes I wonder..."

"What?"

"If I would've really turned into someone like you. Believe it or not, I used to actually respect you. You were one of our best."

She glared at me. "I *am* one of the best. Sometimes our circumstances don't allow us to live in a perfect world, Isabella."

I snorted. "Sister, my world is anything but perfect. At least I have people who care about me."

She frowned. "And that is what makes you weak."

"So how's being a traitor and murderer working out for you? It seems to me you just ended up alone in the end."

When she didn't retort, I thought that would be the end of our argument--until her fist came flying at me. The car swerved as I recoiled and flung my arm out to block another incoming punch. I hit the brakes before reciprocating with a swing of my fist. After parrying each other's blows a few more times, I gathered my willpower and put pressure on the heart-bind. She doubled over and clenched her chest as if suffering a heart attack.

"Would...you really do it?" She struggled to breathe normally, and had a touch of fear in her eyes.

"Don't test me, Praskovya." I rubbed my right arm and had to overcome the temptation to place even more pressure on the bind.

After regaining my composure, I drove toward the nightclub where we would find Alban. I wasn't surprised to see La Cocina crowded, and I smiled to myself when I saw Jasmine Léon's name on the marquee. When Praskovya and I went to sit at the bar, I made sure to use a hand signal to let Jasmine know that I was on assignment and that she should not come over to greet me.

Back in France, Jasmine was known as *La Dame Rouge*-- The Red Lady. She sang and danced in the Éclat nightclub and fell in love with the city of Paris--and Paris fell in love with her. As a black performer, she resented the unwelcoming environment of segregated nightclubs in the United States, yet ironically our government depended on her and paid her as an informant and unofficial spy. In addition to this, she took it upon herself to hide French Resistance fighters when the Nazis had put bounties on their heads, as well as victims fleeing the slaughters in Czechoslovakia.

"A martini, Vasco." Praskovya handed the bartender a few francs, and when he opened his mouth to object, she stared him down.

"Umm...of course. Right away."

I noted all the exits before placing some pesetas on the bar counter as payment. "I said to blend in." I tugged at the hem of her dark blue sheath dress. If it rode up any further, she'd have half the guys in the club staring at her.

She glared at me, probably wishing she could just slip

177

into a comfortable pair of pants. She turned her gaze back toward the stage and watched Jasmine singing and shimmying to an upbeat song. "I remember her, the Colored actress. Is it true she's in league with the French Resistance?"

It sounded like she was fishing for information. "Just keep an eye out for Alban."

The bartender handed her the martini and she slipped him a note. "For you-know-who," she said before taking a sip.

Though I doubted people around us could hear our exchange over the blaring music, I leaned into Praskovya and whispered, "So when does Alban usually come by?"

"No later than 10 p.m. If we don't see him, he may have already come. He'll know that the note I left was from me."

"Does he live nearby?" I asked.

"You ask too many questions. Have a drink. Or is that against your self-righteous code of ethics?"

"Go to hell, Praskovya."

I turned to catch a glimpse of Casandra heading toward us. She wore a fitted blood red dress and her hair, the same color as Praskovya's, fell in loose waves. A cold, numbing anger filled me, and my heart began pounding. Praskovya sensed the abrupt change in my mood and backed away.

"I'd never think to see you here, Isabella. How's...oh, what was his name again? Ian?" She smiled, and I had the sudden urge to slap the smirk off her face.

"You have a lot to answer for," I said. "You made a mistake coming in here tonight."

She looked unconcerned and turned her gaze toward Praskovya. "Nikon, when did you become bosom buddies with her?"

Praskovya drank down her Martini and gestured for Vasco to bring another. "Buddy...is too strong of a word. Why don't you tell me what you're doing here?"

A tall man with dark brown hair interrupted us to ask Casandra to dance with him. She glanced at us, and without answering Praskovya's question, hit the dance floor with her partner, all the while watching us with calculating eyes. I wanted to lunge at her and claw those eyes out. She had probably fled London to escape MI6 and SOE since they were investigating her involvement with Ian and Ryker. I couldn't believe Ian fell for her wiles, and it angered me to see her over here carefree, drinking and dancing, while Ian lay disgraced and in a coma.

Praskovya accepted her new drink and took a slow sip. "I'm going to cut her head off."

"Well get in line," I mumbled, confiscating her martini and downing the rest of it.

She wore a shocked expression. "What was that?"

"Maybe she deserves it." I kept thinking about Ian.

"Now this is the Isabella that I like." She eyed me with approval and then said in Russian, "*Killer.*"

All right, when Nikon Praskovya complimented you like that, then maybe your moral compass needed a little readjusting. I looked askance when she showed me a folded slip of paper. "What's that?"

She smoothed the note between her fingers. "A waiter handed this to me while you were busy threatening Casandra. Either Jasmine Léon is a friend of yours, or she likes women."

I glared at her and snatched the note from her grasp. I opened it and memorized the address written down, then shredded the paper. "What time is it?"

"It's too late. We've missed Alban."

I cursed. "And we lost Casandra. She's gone."

Praskovya scanned the dance floor. "I have a feeling that she will return."

I let out an exasperated breath. "I know that you're not supposed to be actively working against me, but I would like for you to actually help me on this. If you get a note that's meant for me, then *don't* read it. If Casandra is wandering off, then let me know. Got it?"

She rolled her eyes. "Got it."

***

Since there was no use staying at the club, I decided to take Jasmine up on her offer to meet her at her villa in the Pozuelo de Alarcón neighborhood just outside the city proper. I certainly wasn't going to take Praskovya along, so I decided I would slip her a sleeping potion made up of valerian and poppy herbs enhanced with an infusion of magical energy. We arrived at the little house I had rented for us through some old contacts, and after we slipped into more comfortable clothes, I immediately went to the kitchen to pour wine and whip up a quick meal. We had few groceries, but I was able to make a dish of scrambled eggs with chopped vegetables and slices of bread and cheese on the side. Not exactly gourmet, but it would do.

Praskovya had no interest in helping me with the food, and just sat on the red couch in the living room pretending to take an interest in the decor. I brought the glasses of wine over and set them on the coffee table in front of her. I went back for the plates, utensils, and napkins. I settled down on a cushion across from her because I wanted to put a little space between us just in case she took another swing at me or tried to use telekinesis to send something flying at my head. I prodded a glass of wine toward her.

She ignored the wine and bit into a slice of bread. "You've grown spoiled."

I dug into my eggs. "What are you talking about?"

She glanced around the room. "This nice house, with its expensive tile floors and view of the city...what happened to staying in a gritty hotel where no one knew your name?"

"Come on, Praskovya. You should know--one day you're in a nice room and the next you're in hell. It just depends on the assignment." I polished off my eggs and ate a couple of slices of cheese.

"How do you think this will end, Isabella?"

I grabbed my wineglass and took a sip. "For you, badly,

180

if you do anything to break your oath."

She shoveled some eggs onto her bread and ate. "You say that, but part of me believes you will not enact the bind."

"Well I'm not letting you go. That's for sure. How did you even get caught up with Octavian?"

"That's none of your concern."

"Okay, fine. You said Octavian could do powerful things. What sorts of things?"

Her finger traced the rim of her wineglass, but she didn't lift it to her lips. "I've seen him level buildings, cast curses on people who weren't even in his presence, and he has knowledge of things happening from hundreds of miles away. Add to that his speed, intelligence and strength, and you have someone who's very hard to kill."

I drank more wine. "Is he more powerful than the Master Wizards? Or The Three?"

She shrugged her shoulders. "I don't know."

"Why are you afraid of Master Skye, aside from the obvious?"

She finished her eggs then asked, "Did you see his cane?"

I nodded. "Don't tell me he beats you with it."

"That dragon emblem on there represents what he becomes when he transforms himself."

I stared at her and wanted to laugh. "He turns into a dragon? Are you serious?"

"You don't have to believe me, but he becomes a black dragon at night. I'm sure that's why he enjoys staying up in the Shetland Islands where there are hardly any residents other than a handful of fishermen."

"I know of nature wizards who are able to change their faces, or hair color and height. But I've never heard of a full transformation like that. No one's done that in a hundred years."

"Fine, don't believe me."

I shook my head. "You've had too much wine."

She smiled. "I haven't had any wine."

"Yes, that' right. Why don't you have some?"

"I know you put something in my drink." She leaned over and switched our glasses. "If you drink from my glass, then I'll have some."

"All right..." I cleared my throat and drank.

She stared at me for a few seconds before bypassing her glass and taking the one I had been using. She sipped from it. "You're going to leave me here while you go to Jasmine Léon's villa?"

"That's the plan. By the way, I've built up a tolerance to this valerian sleeping potion--both drinks were drugged."

"Alchemist *bitch*..." She lunged toward me, but stumbled and crashed to the floor, unconscious.

I pulled her onto the sofa and noted the time. She should be out for the night and I'd just have to make it back before she woke. I secured my golden knife then slung on a holster and slipped my pistol inside, concealing it with my jacket. As I stepped outside to hail a cab, I thought of Casandra once more, and wondered if I really had it in me to run her down and outright attack her. I felt queasy at the idea of having thoughts similar to Praskovya, but at the same time I refused to let what Casandra did to Ian go unpunished. When I tracked down the Nazis who had executed Morton's sister, Anna, I had captured them and planned to bring them in. They fought back and preferred death on their own terms. However with Casandra, I didn't want to just chase her down and arrest her so she could go to prison in the Shetland Islands--I wanted her to suffer before getting a stake through the heart.

The cab got me to Jasmine's in less than fifteen minutes. It pulled into the villa's long driveway, parking close to the main house. As I approached the front door and knocked, I tried dispelling all these bitter thoughts and feelings. For now, at least I would be among friends.

"Good evening," the maid said to me in French as she welcomed me in. Good, Jasmine knew to keep those in her regular employ with her when away from home.

"Good evening, Lydie." I smiled and stepped inside.

"Would you like me to take your jacket?" She gave me a timid smile in return.

"Thank you, but no." I looked ahead and saw Jasmine already rushing toward me.

"There you are! For a moment I didn't know if you'd show up." She ushered me into the living room and sat me on the couch. "So what's brought you to Spain? I thought you were off on vacation."

I gratefully accepted a glass of water from Lydie. "I was, but..." I lowered my gaze and thought about Ken.

Her smile faded. "I know about Kenneth...OSS told me right before I left Paris. I'm so sorry." She wrapped her arms around me and gave me a hug. "Call me what you want, but I wouldn't blame you one bit if you decided to quit."

"It's too late for that."

"You're still young, you have your whole life ahead of you." She ran her fingers through her dark waves and gave me a sad smile.

I finished my water and set the empty glass down. "I'm going to get the person who killed him, Jasmine."

"Is there anything I can do?"

I shook my head. "Just be careful. Rumors are spreading about you being involved with the French Resistance."

She shook her head and accepted a drink from the maid. "Look at you...all work. You need to go back to your vacation. You need one."

I smiled when I saw Penn come in from the hallway. He wore a burgundy silk robe over his pajamas and he had cut his hair even shorter since the last time I saw him. "Hey, Penn, what are you doing here?"

Jasmine told him in French, "Don't say anything."

He rumbled with laughter and approached me. "You know how Jasmine gets lonely and always wants company."

"It's good to see you." I wrapped my arms around his thick, stocky frame and gave a tight squeeze.

"By the way," he said as he took a seat across from us, "I have some jade powder you might be interested in."

"How much?"

"Three ounces...so, enough for few healings."

"I want it."

He pulled out a small velvet satchel and handed it to me. "For you, I'll cut the price down to two hundred."

"Give it to her," Jasmine said. "I'll pay you."

I tucked the satchel away in my coat pocket. "Are you on assignment, or just in Spain to perform?"

"OSS asked Jasmine to collect information about Nazi experimental programs that they think are being run here in Spain," Penn answered in a tone of disapproval.

"You mean the ones run by Dr. Meier?" I had heard my fill of horror stories about those programs. They especially liked using wizards they captured as test subjects.

"See, this is why I wanted to leave you in Paris," Jasmine said, wagging her finger at him. "I've been on assignment here before. I know how to handle myself."

Penn shook his head. "Let them get one of their professional spies to do it, and leave you out of it."

"Jasmine's right," I said. "We don't always need a guy running after us and trying to save us all the time." I leaned back and glared at him.

Penn ignored my comment. "And what are you doing in Spain? Getting into more trouble I suppose?"

"Do you know a warlock named Alban? He likes to spend his evenings at La Cocina."

He shook his head. "Never heard of him. Why are you after him?"

If I told him why, he'd probably try to throw me into a car and drive me out of Madrid. "SOE wants him. He's a criminal."

Penn gave me a look that told me that he wasn't satisfied with my answer. "I swear you women are going to give me a heart attack."

Jasmine went over to him and eased into his lap. "We'll be careful." She kissed him, and all the tension in his face melted away.

The doorbell rang. "Are you guys expecting anyone here at this hour? It's past midnight."

Lydie came rushing into the living room. "Miss Léon," she said in a harsh whisper, "it's the Spanish police."

Four uniformed policemen barged in. The one with the thick mustache, who introduced himself as officer Carmona, addressed us. "Miss Léon, we need you to come down to the station with us."

"For what reason?" Penn asked, shielding her.

"This is official police business," he said.

As soon as he said these words, I reached for my pistol beneath my jacket. "Carmona" had let his true accent slip through. These men were anything but Spanish policemen.

"Hand over your weapon," the second officer said, gripping Lydie's heart-shaped face with his hand, "or else your friends will die." He dug his fingers into the soft area just beneath her chin and made her sob.

I slowly pulled out my gun and handed it to the third officer who came around to grab it. He took the gun with his right hand and made a sudden movement with his left. It took me a second to realize that he had punctured me with a tiny needle attached to his ring.

Run! I screamed in my head, but my mouth felt numb and my jaws clenched. I dropped to my knees and pulled out my golden knife, flicking my wrist to create an Air symbol. The fake officer wrested my knife from my grasp, and my mind was too far-gone to activate the symbol.

I finally slumped to the floor, and as my vision blurred, I strained to hear what ensued: shrieks, furniture toppling amidst a physical fight...and gunshots. My eyelids drooped and my mind became befuddled from the drug. When I could only hear Jasmine weeping, I knew that the imposter officers had killed the others.

185

CHAPTER FIFTEEN

I awoke when I felt a sharp pain in my stomach. I tried to rise, but my head swam and my upper-body felt weak. A pair of cold cuffs clamped down around my wrists and chained me to a flimsy cot. I turned to my side as much as I could and scanned the large room. Long counters ran along the walls, and at the opposite end stood an upright platform with more chains and cuffs. A workstation island sat in the center. I felt nauseated when I noticed body parts stuffed inside glass jars. Fear crept upon me as I realized that the "tools" at the workstation were fortified with enchantments meant to tear, break, and destroy.

When I heard the lock on the lab door click open, I lowered my head and closed my eyes, pretending to be unconscious. I recognized the fake officer Carmona's voice as he came into the lab room with another man. Carmona came right over to my cot and spoke to me.

"Are you awake?"

I didn't respond, partly out of fear and also by chance if I could continue eavesdropping and learn anything of use.

"Perhaps it was too strong of a dosage. She's been out for nearly twenty hours," the second man said in a heavy German accent.

"Well, she's not dead," Carmona said. "She's breathing."

"She had better not be dead," the other man said. "I

need her for the next experiment."

My eyes involuntarily shot open, and my gaze fell on Carmona. He had ditched his Spanish police uniform and wore black fatigues. "Ah, there she is. Good evening, Isabella."

"Who are you?" I glanced at the door on the opposite side of the room--my only exit.

Carmona brushed his finger across his mustache, and the hairs crinkled and shrunk until they disappeared and left a clean-shaven face. His round face became more oval, and his jet-black hair turned a deep blond. He looked annoyed that his appearance had changed. "I believe you're looking for me. I'm Alban."

Odd, I would've been able to feel his magic by now. Even the strongest and most talented wizards couldn't mask themselves for too long from those who also had powers. We could always sense one another, as well as the tainted magic of warlocks and Cruenti. I reached out with my senses and tasted pure gold laced with the enchantment of an imperium collar. There were no imperium collars present though, but what did catch my attention were the metal linings along the ceiling--gold linings.

"And I am Dr. Falk Meier," the second man said, observing me through his spectacles. "I created this..." he pointed to the ceiling at the imperium gold. It certainly subdued the magic use of alchemists, elementals, and others--but what about the Drifter? Falk never had one to experiment on, and I needed to make sure it stayed that way.

I said in a level voice, "A lot of people are looking for you as well, Falk. What do you hope to gain by these experiments?"

"Progress. Governments may dislike that a man like me created imperium gold, but they still purchase the material so they can make their collars." He approached me and knelt to eye-level as if speaking to a child. "I'm not here to inflict mindless torture, but rather to study you."

187

"But not before I have my turn," Alban said. "She's a spy, and she has useful information." He shifted in his seat, visibly uncomfortable in a room lined with the warded gold that prevented him from using his powers--and me from using my alchemist abilities.

Falk stood. "At least let me run some preliminary tests, then you may interrogate her."

"What do you want to know, Alban?" I kept my expression calm and watched his reaction. I refused to let Falk anywhere near me for "preliminary tests."

Alban faced Falk. "Give me ten minutes."

Falk glared at him, but relented. "Very well. I suppose I can go check on the others. Just make sure you don't harm her too much."

My insides froze as I watched the doctor walk out. As soon as the door opened, I heard a cacophony of screams coming from down the hall. Alban pulled up a chair from the workstation and brought it toward me. He sat in the chair and leaned back as if engaging in casual conversation.

"I can take you out of here," he said. "You don't need to stay here and suffer. Just give me what I want."

"What about my friends you attacked back at the villa?"

"Everyone is dead, except Jasmine Léon. The only reason she's alive is because I'm going to make you watch her suffer if you don't tell me what I want to know. Nikon won't tell me why she's in Spain, but that's of little consequence."

My chest tightened, and I pulled at the chains that held me down. Penn was gone, and Jasmine might soon share his fate. So, he found our safe house and had gotten to Praskovya...she was probably chained up down the hall cursing me for dragging her into this. "Then you received the note from last night?"

He nodded. "And I would have met you at La Cocina, but Casandra warned me that you two were together. I heard that Nikon was arrested in London, but she's of no use to us if she's been compromised."

"If you want anything out of me," I said, "let Jasmine and Praskovya go." I never imagined I'd be asking for that woman's safety, but as long as she kept her end of the bargain, I would likewise keep mine.

"You're not in a position to make demands. Especially on Nikon's behalf." He leaned forward and I spotted a silver chain around his neck. A talisman, shaped as a miniature Asclepius wand, hung on the end. It was a winged rod wrought of silver, with a snake twirled around the length. This was the talisman Praskovya had spoken about that allowed Alban to teleport near the Den.

My gaze went from the talisman to his eyes, and I balled my fists. "Let them go."

Alban sneered and pulled me from the cot with a surprising amount of strength. The chains broke and he flung me toward the upright platform on the other side of the room. I shouted in pain as my back crashed against the cold hard slab. Alban raised my arms and wrapped the hanging chains around my wrists just below the cuffs. I winced when he gave the chain a final tug in order to tighten my wrists together.

"Let's start off with why Nikon's working with you and why SOE sent you after me, shall we?" He went over to the workstation, grabbed a scalpel, and began heating it over a bunsen burner. The scalpel glowed an eerie green color in reaction to the heat.

"Where's Jasmine?" I asked, but he ignored me and approached with the glowing scalpel. I grabbed the hanging chain and swung my feet up, kicking him in the stomach and making him stumble backward. When he approached again and swung the knife, I timed my kick so that I hit his chest and caught his silver neck chain with my foot. I used the weight of my foot to break the chain and send the talisman to the floor with a clatter.

Alban quickly retrieved the talisman and glared at me with murder in his eyes. I tensed and readied for another attack, but Falk came back into the room. "Why did you take her off the cot?"

"It doesn't matter," he replied. "Go ahead and start your test, then we'll see if she wants to cooperate."

Alban approached and I tried kicking again, but he grabbed my legs and made a flick with the scalpel on my thigh. I shrieked as the searing pain penetrated through my skin and into my bones. My eyes watered, and my limbs trembled as the agony began spreading through the rest of my body. Falk approached with a long needle, repeating to me that he only wanted to do preliminary tests.

And then everything went black.

***

I half-opened my eyes, and when I felt a cool liquid touch my lips, I instinctively backed away. I hadn't forgotten where I was.

"It's just water," Falk said, setting the glass aside. "I'm going to experiment on you today. Hopefully you'll survive."

My hands and feet were strapped down, and I sat in a sturdy large chair. I opened my eyes all the way and saw Falk dip a rag into water and ring it out. He held it against my temple, and I sucked in a quick breath at the sting. We sat in a smaller room that also had the imperium lining on the ceiling. There was a small bed in the far corner, and a table and extra chair behind Falk.

How long had I been out? What did they do to me?

"Are you going to test on me today?" Fear weighed down my body more than the straps did.

"You mean tonight," he said, grabbing a cotton swab and miming with his mouth so that I could open mine. "It's evening again."

I felt sick again when he swabbed the inside of my cheek. "What do you want with me?"

"Just from your blood samples I can tell that you're quite unique. I don't know how, but I suspect I'll soon find out."

190

"I'm sure you've tested on many other alchemists."

He chuckled to himself. "I have."

The door opened and Alban stepped in with Jasmine. A gun in a holster hung at his side. "Here's your friend." He shoved her into the room, and she stumbled toward me.

"Jasmine, are you okay?" A flash of anger ran through me when I noticed her bruised cheek.

She nodded and knelt next to me. "You?"

"I'll be back." Falk stood and took the swab and other utensils with him.

Alban closed the door after the scientist left and faced us with a grin. He took Falk's chair and sat across from us. "Are you ready to talk now, Isabella?"

Jasmine gripped my shoulder. "Don't tell him anything. He's just gonna kill us anyway."

"Or, I may not." He stood and approached Jasmine. "You may put on a brave face, Miss Léon, but I know your type."

"You don't know anything about me." She rose to her feet and met his gaze.

He inclined his head toward me. "She's used to this life. She knows how this game is played. But you...you like fine clothes, fine wine, and a life of glamour. Not this."

He went for a lever on the wall and pulled it. I let out a screech as I tasted and felt metal spikes from a contraption in the chair pierce my lower back. I clenched my teeth and forced myself not to scream again as I felt my flesh tear.

"Stop it!" Jasmine pulled at the straps in an attempt to loosen them, but she froze when Alban came back over to us.

"Another one of Falk's inventions. I can place you in a chair like this, and perhaps then Isabella will want to answer my questions."

Jasmine saw the pain and worry on my face, and she sneered at him. "You're a coward."

"Your employer is the coward," he said, reaching for her right arm and gripping it. "A cowardly country that wants

191

to stay out of this war, yet sends girls in to do its dirty work." He recoiled when she slapped him, and he drew his gun. He aimed straight at her.

It felt like fighting an uphill battle trying to slow my heart's pulsations during a moment when I felt it beat most frantically. I forced myself to focus on the Spark, and then the passage of time as slow as my steady heartbeat. I heard the gunshot, and everything slowed down. I felt something grow inside me. It started off as a burning sensation in my belly, then it extended throughout the rest of my body. A bright orange flame tinted my view of the room, and I could feel the chair straps loosen and stretch like old rubber.

I broke away and rushed toward Jasmine, who stood frozen in time. Her eyes stared right at the bullet that crept toward her through mid-air. I stood in front of her and used the palm of my hand to deflect it. When it started slowly flying toward the ceiling, I approached Alban with trembling hands. The fire surrounding me grew in intensity with my rage toward him, and I seized him by the shoulders.

Time went back into normal motion, and Alban howled in pain as the fire burned and ate into his clothes and skin. He dropped the gun and fell to the floor writhing. Just then, Falk returned carrying a vial of bright blue liquid. With a panicked expression, he ran toward one of the levers on the wall that activated the alarm. I was just about to whack him with Zaman's Fire when Jasmine stepped forward with Alban's gun and shot at Falk. The bullet pierced his hand and broke the vial he carried. Instead of pulling the lever, he fell against the wall shrieking. The blue substance had spilled onto his hand and wrist, and large pus-filled boils grew on his skin and travelled up his arm, neck, and face.

It sounded as if Falk was calling for help, but he could hardly form words as the boils now covered his entire face and began to burst. Both Jasmine and I cringed with disgust as the scientist painfully heaved and vomited before collapsing to the floor and straining to speak.

Jasmine's hand shook as she pointed the gun at Alban, who had quenched the flames but still suffered from their burns. "Some of the people I helped hide from the Nazis told me about these labs...about what that scientist did. This warlock is no better."

I nodded. "Well, we don't have to worry about them anymore."

She gazed at me as if that weren't enough, as if they both needed to suffer all over again. I couldn't say that I disagreed with her, because I feared what we would find once we went to open up those other rooms. To be honest, I didn't even know if there were any other survivors besides us.

Alban lay on the floor convulsing and fighting to hold on to the last wisps of life. The Fire had hungrily consumed his flesh, and he just lay there in agony. Jasmine seemed ready to shoot him, but then decided against it. I didn't say anything--he spent his last few moments writhing in agony as he had done to so many others. When he expired his last breath, I approached and confiscated the talisman from his pocket as well as my sheathed alchemist's knife. I went over to Falk, who lay on the floor disfigured and with his limbs making jerking motions. I searched his lab coat and grabbed my rings and the sapphire pendant Delana had given me. Falk also had a key on him, and so I swiped that too. When he tried to reach for me, I pulled away in disgust. *Let the monster rot.* It took me a moment to realize that Jasmine just stood there staring at me.

"What?" I asked.

"I didn't know you could do that." Jasmine's eyes widened at the sight of the flames surrounding me.

"It's...a rare ability."

She clutched the gun. "The wizards trapped here can't use their powers because of the imperium gold. It doesn't affect you?"

"Maybe it affects individual wizards differently," I said, hoping she wouldn't pry any further.

She nodded. "I don't know how many people are still alive. I heard them screaming."

"Then let's go help them."

I didn't know who else I'd encounter in this place, so I tempered the fire around me down to a soft glow that was invisible to the naked eye. However, I was ready to let the flames loose again if needed. I stepped into the hallway and braced myself to hear wailing and screaming like the ones from last night, but only silence greeted me. I motioned for Jasmine to follow, and with nervous breaths, she walked behind me carrying the gun.

We reached the end and spied around the corner. Two German guards dressed in fatigues were at a central desk chatting with each other. I noticed that there were two wide corridors behind the station and wondered which one led outside. One of the guards wore a key ring with several keys attached, and I thought about the other rooms in our corridor. How many people did these monsters kidnap and use as test subjects?

My tongue almost clung to the roof of my mouth because I was so dehydrated. I licked my lips and gestured to Jasmine as I mouthed an instruction. She nodded in understanding and readied herself. On my count, we both stepped out and each went after a guard. She fired at the guard on the left and missed but hit him in the torso with the second shot. I shielded myself from the other guard's gunfire with the glow of my Fire and fed energy into my pulsations. When his movements slowed down to a near halt, I rushed in his direction, with my palm ablaze, and hit him square in his face. I let go of the pulsations and time returned to normal; the guard lay on the ground motionless with his face charred and unrecognizable.

"Do you think there are more guards?" Jasmine asked.

"I don't know." I tossed her the key ring. "Let's go back down the hallway and open those doors."

We ran back in the direction we came from and opened the first door, but the room was empty. We opened the second door and saw a young woman with her head shaved bald sitting in a chair much like the one Alban had me in. The woman's empty dead stare met ours, and her bloated body was discolored like a drowned corpse. A terrible stench wafted toward us, and we both gagged.

"Those bastards." I doubled over and pressed my hand against my stomach, willing myself not to sick up.

"God Almighty," Jasmine said in a low voice as she shut the door. With trembling hands, she went and banged on the third door, and this time we heard someone call for help.

We unlocked the door and stepped inside. A man with pale skin sat in the center of the room. He was strapped to a chair and wore a metal helmet on his head. It reminded me of an electric chair.

"Help...help, please..."

I ran over to him and began cutting the leather straps loose. "Don't worry, we'll get you out of here."

He shrieked when I tried to pull the helmet off. "It's attached to my head," he gasped. "It's part of my head."

The sight of the bolted down helmet and the congealed blood that formed around his ears repulsed me, but I managed to support him as he stood. "What's your name?" We walked him into the hallway, and I let Jasmine take him. He quivered like a frightened animal.

"I'm Raymond. Thank you..."

"I'm Isabella. And this is Jasmine."

"Thank you, Isabella." He faced Jasmine. "You're...the singer. What are you doing down here?"

"Getting into trouble," she answered.

We freed two other men and a woman. All of them wore white hospital gowns and approached with relieved expressions when they saw us. However they kept looking over their shoulders as if expecting an ambush.

I heard a few moans and calls for help fill the hallway. "Are you able to help the others?"

The men nodded, and I handed them the corresponding

keys to the other rooms. The woman we freed, Mia, approached and spoke up. "We can escape through a set of double doors on the other side of the compound, but it's warded."

I nodded and motioned for her to wait with Jasmine and the others. I took the key to the last room and went to open the door. Praskovya was inside, strapped to one of those upright platforms. Her eyes were open, but she didn't blink or show awareness of anything. A breathing mask covered her nose and mouth, and fresh scars marred her arms. Did Alban show up at the house and just take her unawares? Guilt crept upon me; if I hadn't drugged her, she would have been able to escape Alban, even if it meant she'd be out of my physical reach.

For the first time ever, I felt pity for her.

I went to her and unhooked the mask. I cringed when I pulled it off and a long narrow tube slid from her mouth. As I unhooked the straps, she took a few deep breaths and started mumbling. "Nastya...Nastya..."

I loosed the last strap and eased her into my arms. "Hey, Praskovya. It's me."

She slumped in my arms and said in a hoarse voice, "Enact the heart-bind."

"What?" I tried to help her stand, but she refused.

"Kill me."

What did they do to her? "No, it's not going to be that easy."

She slapped me. "Do it."

"No." My eyes watered from the sting of the strike, and I gritted my teeth in frustration. I seized her by the shoulders and tried to pull her along, but she shoved me away.

"Do it! Kill me!"

"Why do you want to die? Why now?" I shouted back.

She leaned against the wall for support and gazed at me. "I asked you how you thought this would end. This is how it will end."

"Who's Nastya?"

Her face screwed up in pain. "Just leave me."

"Sorry, not doing it. No one deserves to rot in this hellhole except the people who built it." I grabbed her by the arm and expected her to punch me, but this time she moved her legs and came along.

We ran toward the midway point in the corridor where everyone else had congregated. When Jasmine confirmed that every room had been checked, I led the group back toward the central security desk. Mia, the woman who had told us of the warded double doors, said that the wide corridor to the left led to supply rooms and the operating room. The corridor to the right was the one that led to the warded doors--but then we'd have to fight our way through ten armed guards stationed near the exit.

I pulled Jasmine aside. "Get everyone into the other corridor, the one where the supply rooms are. I'll go and clear the way."

"Are you sure?"

"No one can use their powers while inside here, and they probably wouldn't have the strength to fight even if they could."

"I can back you up, Isabella."

I shook my head. "Save your bullets. We may need them once we get past the double doors."

"Okay." She ordered everyone toward the left corridor.

I turned and headed toward the corridor on the right, and Praskovya came up behind me. "You might want this..."

I took the dead guard's pistol from her. "Thanks. Now go with the others." She looked at me as if I were crazy, probably wondering what exactly I planned to do with no magic and a gun. She turned and followed the group.

I headed down the dimmed corridor past some research rooms and toward the second security desk. I paused and listened for any sounds, but the unnatural silence grew, and I got worried. Where did those ten men go? I heard footsteps coming from the other side of the double doors, the same ones we'd need to get through in order to reach the exit. As the doors opened, I positioned myself and aimed the gun at whoever was coming my way.

"I knew it was you causing that ruckus on the other side of the laboratory." Casandra wore dark pants and a white top, along with a holster. She didn't bother to pull out her gun.

I glanced around. "Don't tell me you got hungry and ate those guards."

"They're already waiting outside the exit with orders to shoot anyone who makes it out." She rolled her tongue across her front teeth and exposed her sharpened canines.

I fired a shot straight at her head, and she swerved and dodged the bullet. I shot twice more before taking a few steps backward, and there she stood, slowly making her way toward me with a smirk on her face. I got nervous and looked up at the ceiling. Imperium gold lined the area out here as well. I still couldn't use my alchemist abilities, so how the hell was she able to avoid getting hit? Were Cruenti immune to imperium gold?

"Looks like you're a hard woman to kill," I said, before pulling the trigger two more times.

"It seems you're quite special as well." She waved her fingers. "That...aura around you, what is that?"

"Why don't you come and find out?" Out of sheer desire to finish off the round, I fired the last bullet at her before dropping the gun.

Her eyes flickered with an unnatural light, and in an instant she closed the gap between us. She yanked my hair so that my head inclined at an angle, and when I felt her breath on my neck, I acted. The glow around me grew into an aura of heat, and I pulled her in. She let out a shriek when her skin began to shrivel and fold. I shoved her away and grimaced at the flesh hanging off the right side of her face. Her hand quivered as she reached for the injured side. I drew my golden knife and imbued it with searing heat from Zaman's Fire, and thought about Urbano and how he took out that Cruenti back in London. When Casandra rushed toward me, I threw the knife and nailed her right in her heart.

She stumbled and fell to her knees, her bones cracking against the solid floor. She shuddered and raised a trembling hand, and then I felt a searing pain hit me in the shoulder. I fell backward. I was just about to bring forth a protective shield, but she had finally succumbed and fell dead on the floor. I rose to my feet and stood silent for a few seconds before going over and prodding her with my foot. When I turned her over, I shivered at the wide-eyed look of shock on her disfigured face. I retrieved my knife and wiped the blade against her pants leg. I stood and hissed at the flash of pain that ran through my muscles and knew that I'd be too exhausted to use my Drifter abilities soon. My lower back also still throbbed with the wounds from the piercings of that torture chair.

I turned to head toward the corridor that would lead me to Jasmine and the others, but paused when I felt a dark presence. Though I scanned the area and saw nothing, I knew a pair of eyes watched me. Suddenly a dark figure emerged from the floor at the far left and glided toward Casandra's body. I backed away with sweaty palms, and my heart pumped faster with each second.

The shadow figure seized her by the torso and pulled her along the floor with impossible speed. It looked as if she were sliding across the ground. For whatever reason, the shadow figure wanted to go through the drain system in the far corner, but the body obviously couldn't fit through the metal grate. I heard a sickening crunch of bones as the dark figure crashed the body against the grate in an attempt to pull it through, causing the legs to fold backward in an unnatural position. All the while her eyes, with that same expression, still stared at me.

I made a move toward the corridor, and the shadow figure finally released the body and disappeared. I ran over toward Casandra's body, and though it disgusted me, I pulled the body over to the left and laid it parallel to the wall. I went back over to the grate and peered downward into its dark depths. Once again, the shadow figure was gone.

My legs felt like rubber as I ran back down the corridor, and I questioned whether or not using my Drifter abilities really did have its drawbacks. I suddenly felt tainted...dirty. Did my powers call that shadow figure? Or was it just drawn to Drifters? I thought about the one I saw outside of Jane's flat, and I didn't even want to entertain the possibility of there being more of these things lurking in the shadows. I rushed past the first security desk and wasted no time in regrouping with the others--and to also warn them about the guards waiting outside the warded double doors.

We went back to the other side and gathered at the warded doors, and I asked Raymond and Mia if they knew of any other possible exits. Raymond shook his head. I cleared my throat and tried to push away the pounding headache creeping upon me, and the frightening image of the shadow figure taking Casandra. "We need to get out of here now, so we're just going to have to make this our way out," I said.

The other survivors crowded around us. There were only eight of them. Raymond asked me, "You wouldn't happen to have Falk's key, would you?"

"Yes..." I pulled it out.

"It will open the double doors," he said, "though it won't do us any good if there's a small army out there."

"I'm willing to bet that the doors are warded because the imperium lining doesn't extend out there. This will give us our advantage." I slipped the key into the keyhole and turned it. The door opened with a groan, and a dark stairway leading upward awaited us.

"I can scout ahead," Raymond said.

I shook my head. "Praskovya and I will go."

"I'm coming too." Jasmine moved to join me.

"No," I told her.

Praskovya tossed Jasmine a revolver. "If she wants to come, then let her."

"Fine."

I signaled to Jasmine, and we headed up the dark stairway. It ended with a long iron gate that ran forty feet across, and I could sense that its corrosive properties had been activated. To touch the gate would literally decay human flesh. Parts of the gate were boarded up, but through missing pieces we saw an alleyway. I decided to hold back on any body magic just in case I needed my energy to do alchemical spells. I used my golden alchemist's knife to neutralize the iron in the gate and then picked the lock. I pushed it open just enough to slip through and carefully stepped into the alleyway.

I rushed to the other side of the alley and crouched behind a large crate. A couple of bullets whizzed past me from down the alley. I saw Jasmine and Praskovya across from me near the gate, and they fired shots from their positions and took cover behind some other crates adjacent to the gate. Flashlight beams hit the adjacent walls and the ground in search of us, but we remained hidden. When we heard the fall of footsteps coming down the alley toward us, we took more shots. Three guards dove behind a pile of boxes and reciprocated the gunfire.

I hit one of them in the chest, and he collapsed to the ground. Praskovya flicked her wrist and sent heavy boxes tumbling down onto the other two men. When they managed to climb from beneath the boxes, she and Jasmine were already on them and they surrendered.

Now where were the last five guards?

I felt a lump in my throat when a police vehicle drove up and blocked the end of the alleyway. It shined its headlights in our direction. Were these more imposters or real police? Did the last few guards call them in for backup? I signaled for the other women to keep their guns trained on the captured guards, and I approached the vehicle with slow steps and my arms raised. The driver stepped out of the car and approached, and to my surprise it was the checkpoint guard Praskovya and I had spoken to the other night.

"Hello," I said to him in Spanish. "Do you remember me?"

"I do. I have a couple of friends of yours with me." He nodded in the direction of the car.

I took a step back and was just about to order Jasmine and Praskovya to retreat when I heard a familiar voice. "Isabella, it's us!"

I gasped, and the tension in my shoulders and neck faded. Ernest Wilson and Lucien Laurent rushed toward me, and I embraced both of them. I hadn't seen them since they helped me raid a research laboratory in France a couple of months ago. Ernest was a black pilot for the Red Tails, and had run flight missions in addition to once posing as a Moroccan businessman in order to catch a Spanish assassin. I had met Lucien in Paris when Gestapo agents murdered his father, because he had aided the Resistance. The Gestapo had also killed my friend, Renée.

"What are you doing here?" Lucien took off his jacket and wrapped it around me.

"I was on assignment but got caught and ended up in that lab down there." I gestured toward the alleyway.

Ernest looked at Lucien and then faced me. "We've been purging the territory of these labs since we last saw you in Paris. Guillermo and some other officers have been helping. We've got twelve men with us."

I remembered the last five guards. "Did you see five men with guns, dressed in fatigues?"

"They ran when they saw us," Guillermo said.

I tightened Lucien's jacket around me when the cold night air sent a prickly cold breeze against my face. "There are about ten other survivors down there. I came out to clear the way for everyone else. Dr. Falk Meier is dead."

"Good," Ernest said in a bitter tone. When Ernest had agreed to help me back in Paris, he had told me of a previous mission where he and Lucien uncovered another experimental lab in Catalonia. He cursed and complained about it then, and he looked ready to do so again. He looked a little drained.

When the men started toward the alleyway, I halted them. "I'll go tell the others it's safe to come up. They're going to need medical attention and transportation."

I ran back toward Praskovya and Jasmine. The two captured guards were sitting on the ground with nervous expressions since the women still held them at gunpoint. "Jasmine, help's here. Get those men toward the front, and the *real* Spanish police will take care of them."

"All right," she said, motioning toward the men with her gun. They followed her instructions and headed toward the front with arms raised.

"And what about me?" Praskovya asked.

I thought of Captain Skye's order and cursed at the man in my mind. "You died in the lab, so make sure you're a ghost. No more working with Octavian's people, and no more spying."

She eyed me with suspicion. "You're going to let me go, just like that?"

"I didn't say we were best friends. I'm not releasing the heart-bind, not until Octavian is defeated and this war is over. Only then will I consider your vow fulfilled."

She nodded. "What about when they collect the bodies?"

"Casandra had your same hair color, height, and build...no one has to know she was here tonight." My stomach churned.

"How did you do it?"

"Do what?"

"Escape a warded room and kill all those people?"

"Just go, Praskovya."

She gave me a mysterious look. "Nastya...was my twin. When we were sixteen, our father became a sycophant and was initiated to become a Cruenti."

My jaw tightened. "He sacrificed her to a demon, didn't he?"

203

She clenched her teeth and nodded. "Then he put me into Octavian's service, and when he ordered me to infiltrate SOE, that is what I did."

She had done more than that. She played her role so well that when I first joined SOE, I asked Ian to pair me with her on a few assignments. I liked her efficiency and brains, and when we weren't arguing with each other, we actually got along well. I felt on some level she had enjoyed her time at SOE too, except when the time came to abandon the organization and return to Octavian, that's when we were on assignment in Belgium, and she asked me to join the other side. I refused, and she tried to throw me out of a window using telekinesis. Now, I held her life in my hands. It would be easy to just enact the bind--but it wouldn't be easy to watch her gasp her last breath of air and crash to the ground. I made a promise.

I stood there in silence for a few moments, and finally said, "For what it's worth...I'm sorry about your sister."

She inclined her head in acknowledgment of my comment, and then took off in the opposite direction. She disappeared in the darkness. I hoped she took my words seriously--I would not release her from the bind until this was all over, and if I caught her spying or working for the enemy, then I really would kill her.

I ran back toward the iron gate and called down to Raymond and the others. When they made it out and stepped into the alleyway, they seemed to breathe a collective sigh of relief and gathered around me. Some embraced me, while others thanked me and just squeezed my hand. I pointed them in the direction of the police vehicle and told them help had arrived, and they eagerly shuffled down the alley. Raymond was the only one to fall behind and walk with me.

"You saved our lives, Isabella."

"What Falk Meier did down there was wrong. I wasn't going to leave anyone behind."

He smiled at me. "Thank you."

I gazed at the metal helmet, and my heart sank. "Is there...any way to fix that?"

He shook his head. "Probably not without killing me."

A couple of ambulances pulled up, along with three more police cars and a fourth unmarked car. The medics came in and swooped everyone up, including Raymond. I went over to Jasmine, Ernest, and Lucien. "I need to rest. I feel like crap." I said.

"I'm so tired...but I won't sleep. I can't sleep." Jasmine wrapped her arms around Lucien and shook with sobs. She had probably just told him about Penn.

"I'm sorry we couldn't have found you sooner," Lucien said, holding Jasmine in his arms.

"You're here," I said. "And that's what matters."

***

Lucien and Ernest got Jasmine and me a hotel room back in Madrid. They wouldn't hear any different when we told them that they didn't need to stay a few doors down from us. Jasmine had already given her statement to the police and made arrangements for everyone who had perished at the villa. After an all too common restless sleep, I awoke in the morning and found her out on the balcony, sipping from a warm cup of coffee with one hand and holding a cigarette with the other. She was lost in thought, oblivious to the sunrise.

I joined her and at first stood there in silence, unsure if she wanted to hear my chattering. However she turned to me and regarded me with her deep-set eyes. "If I had made him stay in Paris, he'd be alive right now."

"I felt the same way about Ken," I said, grabbing the second cup of coffee sitting on the tiny table in between us. "I keep going over what I could've done differently, but the truth is that it's not our fault, even if we feel like it is. We can't change the past."

Or can we? A voice inside me questioned. What use were

205

these powers if I couldn't save the people I cared about the most? Even though that dream with Ammon was frightening, for the short time that I did believe it was Ken, it had felt comforting to see him and speak with him again. He shouldn't have died the way he did. He should still be here.

"I know," she said. "We're going to have to carry on for them. We can't do anything about yesterday, so we've got to focus on tomorrow."

I nodded in agreement, but felt conflicted over my hidden desire to use my powers to change the past. Could I really? I hadn't tried interacting with the past or future, but what would happen if I did? Still, there was that shadow figure. I didn't understand what it was or what it may have wanted. I knew that it wasn't Ammon, because I could sense his magic and identify him. I shuddered at the thought of Ammon masquerading as Ken and trying to get me to use my powers the way he wanted. Maybe Johnnie was right about me not fully understanding these powers. I must've made some type of misstep, and I had to figure out what it was.

"I have to get back to London," I said to Jasmine. "MI6 wants Alban's talisman that I took."

"What does it do?"

"Praskovya said the talisman could transport its user to the Den."

She let out a low breath. "You let that woman go?"

"Not completely. I did a heart-bind, so she's bound by oath to not work against me, or else she dies."

She finished her coffee and set it aside. "Well, I hope you guys do find the Den. I just know OSS is probably going to hound me about what went on here. Now I know why you went on leave. This life is torture."

There was a knock on the door, and we left the balcony and went inside. "Who is it?" I slipped my hand into my bathrobe's right pocket and held on to my golden knife.

"It's me and Luce," Ernest's voice said from the other

side.

I opened the door for them. "Come in."

"Are you ready?" Lucien asked as he entered with Ernest.

"Almost," Jasmine said, putting out her cigarette. "What time's my flight?"

"In thirty minutes," Ernest said.

"Thirty minutes? Why didn't you come earlier?" Jasmine crossed her arms.

"We thought you'd be ready by now," Lucien said.

"I just finished my coffee, and we're still in our bathrobes. I'm still deciding what I want to wear."

"Well we brought you those extra clothes from the villa earlier this morning. Just throw on something and let's go," Ernest said.

Jasmine shook her head and went back inside and opened the armoire. I followed, and she tossed me a clean blouse, skirt, and a light sweater with pockets. She pulled out a halter dress for herself and a matching velvet hat. She turned toward the guys. "Can you excuse us while we get dressed?"

"Finally," Lucien said in a low voice to Ernest.

"We'll be in the hallway." Ernest followed him out.

"I don't know how you do it," she told me as she changed into her dress. "I'd be the only spy with a suitcase full of clothes wherever I go."

I shed my bathrobe and stepped into my skirt. "I was once on assignment where five of us, men and women, were stuck in a safe house together. We literally ate, slept, and changed clothes in the same room. We definitely didn't have an opportunity to pick and choose what we wanted to wear."

She wore an amused expression. "I really wish you could come back to Paris when this is all over."

"You know I will." I threw on my blouse and sweater. I grabbed the talisman and slipped it into my front pocket, protecting its presence by casting the alchemical symbol of

Secrecy: an upside down triangle within a circle with a second circle and triangle within those. It wasn't something I'd necessarily want Spanish officers to see or handle at the airport.

We went out to meet the guys, but they had abandoned the hallway and were sitting downstairs at the bar having drinks. "Jasmine," Lucien said, downing the rest of his wine and offering his arm to her. "Let's get to the airport."

"I lost my fake passport," I said. I doubted that would go over well with airport security.

"I've already got clearance to fly you over myself," Ernest said. "I'm going to be running a few missions for the Red Tails next week."

"I'm glad, but for goodness sake I don't want to hear about you getting shot out of the sky again." I gave both Lucien and Jasmine a hug and said my goodbyes to them.

As I left with Ernest, I couldn't help but worry about the talisman. How was it supposed to be activated? I hoped it hadn't been damaged in the fire. Suddenly I felt the warmth of the sapphire pendant against my skin and noticed a faint glow. Delana was under attack by Ammon. For the first time ever, I seriously considered going back on a promise I had made. However, I needed the demon destroyed just as much as she did, and now she was calling for my help. If he drove her to suicide or somehow killed her in order to break away from their bind, then he'd come after me with his full power. Whether I liked it or not, I needed to prepare to Confront a demon.

CHAPTER SIXTEEN

Confrontations had originally developed out of necessity. After the Black Plague decimated much of the European population in the Middle Ages, there weren't always enough clergy around to help combat demons-- especially demons who preyed on wizards. A collective of brave souls decided to step in and fill the role of engaging in Confrontations, where they'd aid a harassed victim by challenging the demon and sending it away. Sometimes it could be through an exorcism if the person had great faith and skill, or it could be a matter of ritualistic magic coupled with a clear and unbending will. Sometimes the person doing the Confronting would simply lift a curse that the victim had been placed under.

Few wizards were skilled in Confrontations nowadays, and often such a task was once again left to clergy. I had read before how Confrontations would take place, and had even seen a few done--but observing it and doing it myself were two different things. If a Drifter did cause demons to be drawn to wizards, then it wasn't unreasonable to assume the Drifter could also send these evil beings back into the spirit world. Delana had said that Ammon needed to be destroyed, not simply cast out, and that my Drifter ability could accomplish it. I would probably have to attack Ammon with Zaman's Fire and destroy him in the

Confrontation.

However, if he still appeared to me as Ken, it would be much more difficult. Logically, I knew that it wasn't Ken, but my emotions refused to submit to reason. My heart had been weighed down with anxiety and grief, and I still didn't have any closure. The last time I saw Ken alive, we had argued with each other, and the man who murdered him was still running loose. I blamed myself for what happened, and kept thinking about what I could've done to make things turn out differently.

I knew this would be difficult, and so before leaving Spain, Ernest and I had stopped at a tiny church where I picked up a few items that I knew I'd need for the Confrontation with Ammon. Even when we arrived in London and recuperated for a few hours at a hotel, I still felt my shoulders tightening and my head throbbing in anticipation. I felt more confident walking into this Confrontation in the late afternoon when the sun still shined and with an arsenal of holy items and Ernest at my side. As we made our way through the daily bustle of London's East End, I gave him instructions. "Delana's staying with her niece, Alina, and she'll be there to assist us. Depending on how things go, I may need you to help Alina restrain Delana."

"Wait...restrain her? Don't we just say a few prayers and you throw some magic dust on her or something?"

"It's possible this may end in possession...if it hasn't happened to her already. This is my first time doing a Confrontation, but I've seen it done before. I've been told that I have an ability that can destroy demons."

"But this is your first time?" He gave me a sidelong glance.

"You're free to wait outside, or head back to the Royal Air Force base."

"Don't try that with me. I said I'd help, and here I am."

"Good, then you're stuck with me." I handed him a slip of paper. "If it looks like I'm in trouble, go to this address and bring this man to me."

He read the note. "Who's Maolán Martin?"

"Number 33. We're here."

We turned and entered into a brick housing building that was only two stories high. As the smell of midday meals being cooked in kitchens wafted toward us, we headed down the hall to the door with a number eight painted on it. Before I knocked, I turned toward Ernest and gazed straight into his eyes.

"How strong is your faith?"

He seemed a little taken aback. "I...I went to church when I was a kid. Probably not as often as I should've, but I believe in God."

"Evil spirits like this thrive off of despair, and they'll do anything to drive you toward it. Having some type of hope, or having faith is a safeguard--but you really shouldn't speak to him, even if he addresses you."

"Does he have a name?"

"Yes, but I'm not strong enough to use it to bind him." I turned and knocked on the door.

When I heard a woman query us from the other side, I announced Ernest and myself in a firm voice. The door unlocked, and a thin woman with dark hair answered. She greeted us and introduced herself as Alina, and guided us toward her living room sofa that creaked and groaned when we took a seat on it.

"Thank you for coming," she said, twisting the hem of her apron. "Do you want to see her now, or would you like something to drink before you start?"

"Got any Scotch?" Ernest asked.

"We'll see Delana now, thank you." I motioned to Ernest, and he opened his suit jacket. He placed several items on the coffee table: a flask of holy water, a vial filled with blessed oil (which I had taken it upon myself to infuse with specks of gold), and a white handkerchief. I tied the handkerchief around the palm of my right hand and gave Ernest the water and oil.

"What's the handkerchief for?" He doused himself with some of the holy water, and I gestured for him to stop.

"It's a relic," I said, forming a miniature Circle of Protection on my forehead with the oil and following up with the sign of the Cross. "Brande gave it to me a long time ago. He said it touched the remains of St. Margaret...the one whose voice guided Joan of Arc."

"I swear that man can find anything." He faced Alina. "How is your aunt?"

"She asked to be left alone in her room after breakfast. I heard a terrible noise and...voices, but when I tried to check on her, she had locked herself inside. That's when I knew to do the signal for the pendant charm. It's been quiet for a while now, but..."

I stood and pointed toward the narrow hallway. "Which room is she in?"

"The second one, on the left."

They silently elected me to lead the way. I headed into the hallway and stopped at Delana's door. I gestured for Ernest to hand me the oil and drew a Cross right at the door. Something that sounded like a wild animal crashed against the door from the other side, and I fell backward.

With a shaky voice, Alina spoke. "Dela...your friend is here to help you. Can you unlock the door?"

When we heard the door unlock, I stood and turned the doorknob with my right hand. I slowly pushed the door open with my foot and kept my hand held upright. I slightly lowered it when I saw Delana sitting in the far corner of her bedroom. She was below the windowsill, crouched in a fetal position, and muttering to herself. Her hair fell loose in wild white waves, and her eyes carried that unearthly glow she had when speaking to spirits. I erected the faint glow of Zaman's fire around me, and told myself that I wouldn't do the pulsations or ripples--only the fire.

"Delana, what's going on?"

She cried. "Forty years. It's been forty years, and now I finally feel my mind and will slipping away. I shouldn't have asked for your help...it's too late."

I shook my head and knelt in front of her, but was careful not to yet make contact. "It's not too late. You can still win. Did he harass you today? What did he do?"

Her eyes watered. "I haven't slept for the last three days. He said the moment I closed my eyes, he'd kill me and throw me into Darkness."

"He's just trying to scare you," I said with a frown. "You have more strength than you think."

"What the *hell* is that?" Ernest stared in horror at a black cat standing on the windowsill, observing us from outside. And it was literally standing. It stood upright on its hind legs, and as soon as I lifted my gaze and spotted it, the cat turned around and ran away--still using only its hind legs.

"Oh, God help us," Alina said as she held her hands to her stomach as if in pain.

Ernest began breathing heavily, and looked like he wanted to vomit. He started pacing back and forth, biting his lower lip and swatting away something that only he could see. I felt like something was on my back, and my muscles instinctively tightened. The back of my neck burned. I knew I had to act quickly, so I took my right hand, swathed in the relic cloth, and placed it on Delana's forehead. She convulsed and began crying again, and when I felt whatever it was that was on my back grow heavier and start to crush me, I commanded the flames of my fire to emerge and form a protective shield. I felt invisible claws tear into my back.

"Ernest, go now!" I shouted. I screamed in pain as my eyelids fluttered and the room spun in swirling colors. I heard Ernest's heavy footsteps fade, and I closed my eyes and hit the floor.

I no longer heard Delana weeping or Alina gasping prayers. When I opened my eyes, I lifted my head from the hard cold floor, and saw that I was in Delana's room, but I was alone. All color in the room, from floor to wallpaper, had been drained. A sickly gray tinge settled over

213

everything. There wasn't even any furniture, and though the same window still hung there, I could not see out of it--there was nothing but darkness.

I immediately ignited my fire, spreading it from the center of my being and extending it outward around me. I didn't know if I hung in between consciousness and unconsciousness, but I was determined to handle any threat that would come my way. I was lying on the floor, frozen in place, when I heard a loud crash against the walls. It seemed to originate from the left side and then the right...from the ceiling, and then against me beneath the floorboards.

"I want you to leave Delana alone. If you continue to harass her, then I'll destroy you." My voice almost jumped an octave at that last declaration.

I rolled onto my side when I heard a low cry behind me. I turned and then gasped, and covered my mouth with the palm of my hand so that I wouldn't scream. My friend, Renée, was on the floor across from me in a prone position. She looked just the way I remembered her, from the black hair with the gray streak, all the way down to the dress and shoes I had last seen her in. I could taste decay exuding from her, and she struggled to peer at me through injured eyes.

"Isabella," she said in a weak voice, raising her head. "Is that you?"

"Renée," I cried.

"I waited for you to come back to the safe house that night, but you never returned."

"I did come back." I trembled as I tried to remind myself that this wasn't her.

"Agent Karsten returned, and he knew I had helped you. He hurt me, and I died alone."

"I...I wanted to come for you, but they were chasing us. I couldn't go to you."

"Where am I, Isabella?" She pulled herself toward me with her arms.

My limbs felt like rubber as I crawled backward on my hands and knees to keep our distance. Bile rose in my throat when I noticed that both of Renée's legs were broken. Was this how she died? Is this what she looked like after they murdered her? Ernest was the only one to see her body; he had gone into her house to check on her when we had also found Lucien's father, Otto, dead.

"You can save her." Ammon, still under the guise of Ken, suddenly appeared at my side and pulled me to my feet. He framed my face with his hands so that I gazed straight into his eyes. "I can show you how to use your powers to go back and fix the past."

I placed my hands over his. They felt warm and vibrant. "I can't go back. I can't change anything."

"I see something differently in your heart. I see doubt."

My stomach burned, and dread overcame me, because he was right. I couldn't lie, at least not to myself. The thought had occurred to me that these powers would be useless if I couldn't save those I cared about. And what was ignoble or corrupt about that? Renée was a beautiful, strong woman who sacrificed herself for her cause. And then Ken...

"You're not even really him," I said, backing away. I knew it in my mind, but the way he looked, smelled, talked and felt, was exactly the same.

"Then go back and save him too." He slipped his arms around my waist and pulled me into an embrace. "You can save me, Renée, and anyone else you desire. If you wanted, you could go and raze your enemies' fortresses to the ground this very moment. Before their tongues could cry out a warning, you would break the Gray Tower, and make Octavian bend his knee to you. This will be my gift to you."

"How...could I go back?" I asked the question before I even realized what I had said. My head began swimming, and I swayed a little.

He smiled. "I can't show you if you don't let me take over first."

"No," I said, shaking my head.

215

He frowned. "I understand now. You're glad Ken's dead because you're ready to move on to Brande."

A flash of anger ran through me and I struck him in the face with my right hand, which still had the relic cloth wrapped around it. He recoiled and snarled at me. I could see the imprint of my strike on the side of his face, and my mind suddenly grew clearer. I summoned Zaman's Fire, and layered it around me in a protective shield. Ammon stopped at the edge of the fire that surrounded me, and gazed into my eyes. When I saw a dark but frightened look in his expression, I seized on it. "So...you're afraid of the fire."

He gathered his composure and stepped aside to let me view Renée. She still lay on the floor, blind and broken. "Don't you want to know what happened to me that night, Isabella? How they tortured me and made me suffer? But worst of all was when you left me there...alone in the dark."

"No!" I shrieked. The fire rose and burned a bright white before diminishing and retreating back into my center. When I tried to ignite it again, I could only obtain that faint glow, as if my emotional outburst had somehow made me blow a fuse.

Now that I didn't have the full effect of my protective fire around me, Ammon approached. The gleam of desire was the only thing recognizable in his eyes. When I held up my right palm, with the relic cloth wrapped around it, he hissed, and an invisible force threw me back against the wall. I landed on the floor with a thud, but stood back up and managed to hold my protective hand out to keep him at bay. Renée had disappeared, and Ammon now assumed the form of Ian.

"Go on," he said, walking toward me and offering his right cheek. "Hit me again. Show me how much you hate me and want me to die."

"I don't hate Ian, and I *don't* want him to die." I held my right hand up protectively, but didn't strike at him.

In a flash, he grabbed my right wrist so that I couldn't

swing at him with the relic cloth, and he began pulling me toward the other side of the room where the bedroom door stood. As we got closer, the door swung open and revealed a gaping Darkness. "It'll be easier if you just let go," he said, pulling me toward the howling black hole. "I'll still help you save them, but then you must give me whatever I ask from you."

I knew that if he got me through that dark doorway, I'd be lost, gone. I couldn't let it happen. However I felt so weak, and didn't even understand why my fire had fizzled, that I couldn't break away. All I could do was call out for help--either that, or immediate death. I refused to go past that threshold and experience what he had planned for me. Just as we made it to the door, a rush of energy swept the room, and Ammon backed away. He still held onto me, but his grip loosened.

"She's not going anywhere with you," a familiar voice said. I turned my gaze toward the speaker, and my heart leapt in my chest--Ken. In my heart I felt it was truly him. He stood in front of the dark doorway.

Ammon released me and flew away as soon as Ken approached. I heard crashes, screams, and several voices, though they all seemed to come from somewhere outside the room. My throat constricted and I tried to speak to Ken, to tell him I was sorry and a million other things, but he held onto me with an urgent look in his eyes.

"Don't let him take you through that doorway," he said. "Keep fighting."

"Ken, I--"

"I know." He gave me a kiss on the forehead, the same way he did when I had last seen him alive. A sense of peace washed over me. "Help's here."

He disappeared in a flash, and Ammon immediately returned from wherever he had flown off to. This time he was a dark figure with wings, taller than a human being, with broad shoulders and red eyes. He came at me again, and I held up my protective hand and charged him. We met with a crash, and he screeched when the relic cloth hit the side of his face. His mouth widened and revealed rows of shattered teeth that gleamed, and the stench of death came from the back of his throat.

Though my legs shook and every instinct told me to break away and run, I kept the relic against his face as it tore through his skin like burning acid. I got worried when his gaping mouth became the size of my entire head and he tried to seize me between his teeth, but a strong hand on my shoulder grabbed hold of me and pulled me away, and I felt like I was swimming through water. Darkness clouded my vision, and I began to wonder if I had fallen through the doorway.

The hand on my shoulder jerked me backward again, and then I felt like I was flying. The darkness around me faded to gray, and then became light. I opened my eyes, and I was awake again in Delana's room. I felt the poor woman lying unconscious beneath me. My back was to her as I lay against her motionless body, though I could feel her chest rise and fall in laborious breaths. My eyes widened when I saw all the furniture broken and upturned, the bedroom door hanging on a single hinge, and Delana's tiny bed against the opposite wall and turned on its side. Alina was on her knees shaking and reciting a prayer. Ernest sat on the floor with a gash in his right thigh and a swollen cheek.

Directly in front of me stood Father Maolán Martin, with white hair so frazzled that it almost stood upright. Bloody lacerations marred his wrinkled face, and his limbs trembled. Despite his physical injuries, he still spoke with iron resolve in his voice and emanated power through his aged eyes. He had his palm open toward me, and I saw a white light glowing with a golden crucifix in the middle. I couldn't understand anything he said because he spoke Words, like a Philosopher. He spoke a long string of phrases, and at the end, he finally lowered the crucifix and said, "*Tu ergo arctius et conlabefactus, Ammon! In nomine Patris, et Filii, et Spiritus Sancti...Amen.*"

CHAPTER SEVENTEEN

Maolán finally released the Circle of Silence he had cast around the entire place, and I knelt by Ernest's side in the living room and cast a Circle of Healing. I concentrated on mending the wounds in his leg, and his puffy cheek that made it difficult to open his left eye. I also extended the Circle to Maolán, so that the cuts and bruises on his face would also close up and heal.

When I finished, he cast a greater Circle of Protection around us and then took a seat on the couch. He thanked Alina as she handed him a bottle of whiskey. He poured a glass for Ernest and himself while she headed toward her bedroom to check on Delana. I rose to my feet and sat in an uncomfortable wooden chair across from the men, taking in a deep breath and clasping my hands together.

"Maolán, thank you for coming."

He finished his whiskey and refilled his small glass. "Hmph. I never thought I'd hear those words coming from you...I never thought I'd come to your aid."

"Thank you," Ernest repeated for me. "You, ah, have powers like Isabella?"

"Aye, and I met her at the Gray Tower when I worked as an ambassador for the Holy See."

When Ernest gave a confused look at our apparent tension, I spoke up. "Our grumpy old Irish friend here got caught spying for the Church while at the Tower."

"And guess who blew my cover?" He wagged a finger in my direction.

I shrugged my shoulders. "How would you feel if you uncovered a Tower spy in the Vatican?"

"Amused." He smirked.

Alina returned. "She's still asleep, but her breathing is better now, like you said." She stared at the floor and smoothed her apron. "I'm sorry...I would offer you something to eat, but--"

Maolán stood and took a few notes from his pocket. He placed them in her hand. "I believe there's a market around the corner. Get what you need."

She wore a shocked expression, but quickly placed the money into her apron pocket. "Thank you."

"If you don't mind," Ernest said, standing, "I'd like to come along. Gotta get your fresh air after an exorcism."

Alina nodded and they headed out the door. When they were gone, Maolán's expression became grave, and he looked at me with a disapproving eye. "Why on God's green earth did you believe you could handle a Confrontation with that demon?"

"So you're here to lecture me?" I crossed my arms.

"We both know only certain wizards do that, and you aren't one of them. You have no faith--it's like going into a battlefield naked and weaponless."

"I have faith in magic," I retorted. "And I have a strong mind."

"Vapors in the wind," he said, observing me with a stern look. "Stop sipping gruel and start chewing the meat, child."

I sighed, not at all in the mood for a sermon. "I promised to help Delana. I just couldn't abandon her."

"And we all saw how well that was turning out for you. When I arrived, your friend was possessed and on a rampage. And you--you were out cold. It was the first time I had ever seen someone completely unconscious cry tears."

I stared at the old man. "She's going to be upset once she finds out you did an exorcism. She needed him destroyed." *I* needed him destroyed.

He sat back and gazed at me with his bright eyes. "And you were going to do it?"

My shoulders tightened. "Would he ever come back?"

He shook his head. "If the demon returns for her, I made sure that the first person he'd have to go through is me."

I admired his courage, but he looked like my grandfather's grandfather. "Please, be careful."

"I know what I'm doing." He poured another glass of whiskey. "Unlike some people."

I sighed and decided to change the subject. "You know, when he had me in that state of mind...he did everything he could to break down my defenses, and for a moment I thought I was going to fail."

He lifted the drink to his lips, and the whiskey was gone. "Sometimes the worst weapons are used against here--" he placed his hand against his heart, "--and here." He tapped the temple of his forehead with a finger.

I nodded in understanding. "Someone came to help me just before I crossed the threshold, someone I care about but who had died. After I spoke with him, I felt relieved. All the guilt and hurt I've been carrying around...they're not an unbearable burden anymore. Do you think it was really him?"

"Why wouldn't it be him?" He smiled. He looked friendlier when he smiled at you.

"Well," I said, "I guess I wasn't a complete moron. At least I knew to call you for help."

"Indeed, you did." He stood and grabbed his hat from off the table.

"You're leaving?"

He put his hat on. "Perhaps our paths will cross again. Hopefully, not too soon."

"Goodbye. I appreciate what you did."

He went over to the door and opened it, but paused and tightened his shoulders. He shut the door and slowly turned to face me. "I...suppose a sense of honor and Christian charity compel me to tell you this, but did you know that you're the Drifter?"

I sucked in a quick breath. I jumped from my seat and rushed over to him. "You knew?"

"Not before today," he said. "But I think your Confrontation with the demon left you as bare as a newborn babe."

"I was planning on going to the Gray Tower. I have allies there who can help me."

"I am not using any special sight, Isabella. If you walk outside of my Circle of Protection, any wizard in the immediate area would be able to detect you. And if that wizard understands what he's sensing--then God help you."

"I've been shielded with an enchantment most of my life..."

"Whatever was done, I can't duplicate it, my dear."

"Then how am I supposed to make it into the Tower to get this fixed if I can already be detected?"

He took the sapphire pendant between his thumb and forefinger, and uttered a Word. "Don't take off the pendant. If anyone senses anything odd and asks you about it, tell him that you recently experienced a Confrontation. This will obscure others' senses just enough."

I breathed a sigh of relief. "How much time do I have?"

"Five days. And *don't* use any of your Drifter abilities, or it'll nullify the enchantment."

"Thank you, and please, be safe."

"And the same to you." He tilted his hat forward and headed down the hallway toward the exit.

I closed the door and went to Alina's room where Delana slept. I sat in the chair next to the head of the bed and reached over to place my hand on her forehead. Her skin was cool to the touch, but her breathing remained normal. I smiled when her eyes fluttered open.

"Welcome back," I said. "How are you?"

She faced me with a remorseful expression. "You didn't have to do this. He almost destroyed you because of me."

"It's over now. We had help. Alina even went to get food."

She nodded and closed her eyes. I stood and walked out, heading back into the living room. This time I took a seat on the more comfortable sofa. When I heard rustling and voices at the door, I went to open it and let Alina and Ernest inside.

"One of these days," Ernest said as he placed the groceries in the kitchen, "I'm going to find a way to make a hamburger over here."

"Welcome to my world," I said, closing the door after them.

"How's Delana?" Alina asked.

"She just needs to rest."

"Will you be staying for a while?"

I shook my head. "Unfortunately, it seems I have to leave London."

Ernest grabbed an apple and bit into it. "Where are you going?"

I looked down and felt slightly anxious. "I'm going back to the Gray Tower."

***

Ernest was due back at the Air Force base, and I needed to prepare to leave. After saying our goodbyes, I caught a cab to Rose Garden, a corner café less than a quarter mile away from my building. While there, I called Jane Lewis and asked her to join me for lunch. I also called Bianca, my officemate, and asked her to meet me at my place because I knew she was headed to the Gray Tower as well. After a twenty-minute wait, Jane finally showed up and joined me at my table. I sipped on a cup of coffee and didn't even look at our food when the waiter set down our plates. I thought of how this would be our last meal together for a while. Who knew when or if I'd return?

"Don't look so sad," she said, reading my face. "The investigation will prove that you're innocent. I'm sure of it."

"Have you noticed anyone of interest entering or leaving the building?" I hadn't forgotten about my double that still walked around flipping her hair and vaguely answering questions.

"No," she said, shaking her head. "I've only seen the agents my brother sent. They're still parked across the street."

I smiled a little. "Thank you Jane, for everything."

She dug into her fish and vegetables. "Well, are you going to eat?"

I lifted my fork and took a bite. I wasn't hungry. "Listen...I have something I need you to deliver to the occult experts down at the laboratory. They're mostly Tower-trained, and you can tell them that I found it." I took out the talisman and handed it to her.

"What's this?"

"Something that could help us end this god-awful war. A warlock named Alban owned it, and it's supposed to lead to the Den."

She nodded. "I'll take it down later tonight."

"And there's one more thing," I said.

"As long as you don't ask me to watch you in that mad memory Circle again."

I shook my head. "Never again, I promise. I need you to tell Morton that I'm heading to the Gray Tower, but I don't want him to assume I'm going because of the investigation. If you asked your brother to let me leave for the Tower without incurring any penalty from MI6 or SOE, I know he'd agree to it. I'm not planning on going anywhere else, and I'm willing to accept the outcome of the investigation."

"I'll tell him, but I want you to promise me something."

"What is it?"

"That you'll be careful, and that you'll make it to my wedding in March. *And*, you're going to be one of my bridesmaids. You were always a second sister to me." She frowned again and looked ready to cry.

"Jane...don't cry. You know I'll be there. Just don't put me into an ugly bridesmaid dress."

She snorted. "I have better sense than that."

We ate and talked for a while longer, and then left for our building. When we passed through the public gardens and spotted the parked car on our street, Jane ran over to the two men sitting inside and began speaking to them as a distraction. As I ran inside the building and made my way upstairs to my flat, I felt a lump in the pit of my stomach. Going back to the Gray Tower was necessary, but it also had its dangers. While the Tower made it illegal to probe a person's mind, or would never pursue an accusation without evidence, I was more worried about how many Master Wizards would pick up on my odd magical aura and begin to ask questions. I feared whether or not Master Priya would come barging in with his trackers and demand my arrest as an accomplice to my father--and then I'd be a prisoner, and then I'd be unmasked.

However, I believed there was an answer to all this, one that didn't have to result in me fighting people and running for the rest of my life like my father did. I would gain as many allies as possible and prove that the Tower's law about Drifters didn't apply to me, and that we were fighting for the same cause. This was the key to winning all this. If Ekwueme, one of The Three, was one of the original wizards aiding my father along with Master Serafino Pedraic, then that was a very welcome start. Perhaps if we could sway the rest of the Council, and even the Head of the Order, then the law regarding the Drifter could be changed.

I unlocked my door and stepped inside my flat, but immediately froze when I felt a wizard's presence in my bedroom. I glanced around the living room and saw pink residue over the floor and my cushioned chair. Alas, the other Isabella had exploded. I readied some of the alchemical symbols that lay hidden throughout the place and crept toward my room where I felt the intruder. When I opened my bedroom door and saw who stood there, I scowled, and began feeding more energy into my symbols.

"I heard about your situation with Ian and Ryker," Neal said, closing my top dresser drawer. "I've submitted a statement to Morton about what happened in Cambridge."

I doubted he had included in his report the part where he stabbed my father. I crossed my arms so that he'd see I had no weapons. The last thing I needed was for him to hit me with an enchantment.

"You know, there's a name for guys who go through a girl's underwear drawer."

He ignored my comment. "Your doppelganger was quite interesting to speak with. Where have you been?"

"Out."

A flicker of a smile crossed his lips. "The ring you said your father gave you...I'd like to take it off your hands."

"Sure, why not." I leaned against the doorframe. "At least this time you asked for something directly instead of deceiving me."

He approached. "We are getting closer each day. Your father is old...tired. It's only a matter of time, and it's better if you accept his fate now."

I gritted my teeth. "Well have fun searching my flat. If you'll excuse me, I have to pack."

"Yes," he said, scanning the room and then heading over to my closet. "Where were you going?"

"The Gray Tower," I said. He was probably glad to hear that.

"If you still needed help regarding Hotaru--"

"I don't want your help, and I don't need it." I opened the closet door before he could, and I pulled out some clothes. I wouldn't need much since Tower law required me to be in an Apprentice's uniform while there.

"There's something different about you. What happened?" He walked over to my bed and sat on the edge. I pretended I was annoyed and sighed, but I quickly added more energy to the hidden symbols I had charged.

"You remember the woman, Delana." I went over to my dresser and collected undergarments. "That demon that you sensed tethered to her...well, we had our big showdown."

He scanned the room again, probably reaching out with his senses for the ring, but he seemed distracted by the different aura of energy around me--or maybe he felt my charged symbols. "Impressive. Sometimes I think you're far more than what you lead others to believe." He reached under the bed and pulled out my suitcase. He stood and laid it out for me.

"Are you done looking for the ring, or did Master Priya send you to stalk me as well?" I began throwing in my clothes. All of a sudden I tensed when I felt him directly behind me.

"You're wearing the ring on the chain around your neck, beneath your high collar. It's next to another enchanted item."

I charged every single hidden symbol throughout the flat and turned to face him. "You know I'm not going to give it to you."

He unraveled twenty of my sixty-four symbols. They felt like pin pricks to me as they broke down under his meticulous counterspells. "There's a high probability you will give it to me."

If I gave him the ring, it would be no different than walking him over to wherever my father was hiding. I saw what he did to my dad back in Cambridge, and I wasn't going to let that happen again. Besides, I couldn't take the ring off the chain without removing the sapphire pendant that was also on there--which would break Maolán's enchantment and expose *me* as the Drifter.

"Then you're going to have to fight me for it. And I'm not going to stop fighting, Neal. Is that what you want?"

227

He unraveled another twenty symbols. "Do you remember what I told you the last time I saw you in London?"

I frowned. "You told me to be careful, and that it would pain you if I were killed."

My fingers began shaking from the adrenaline rushing through me. I focused on a Putrefaction symbol, a spell of poison and decay, just beneath his feet. It may pain him if I were killed, but it didn't mean it wouldn't be by his hand.

He peered into my eyes, but then lifted his gaze as if listening to someone speak to him. "They've found Carson in Cairo. Master Priya is asking me to join them."

"Neal, don't..."

"Goodbye, Isabella." He spoke a Word and reconstructed all the symbols he had broken down. He turned and then left.

My heart sank, and my head began throbbing as I pulled my energy from the Putrefaction symbol I almost activated. I wondered if it would've been better to join my father when he had asked. Or would I have been holed up with him in Cairo fighting wizards? Maybe they were right about my father finally getting tired, because I already felt exhausted and I hadn't even started running.

There was a loud knock on my front door, and my heart leapt into my throat. When I didn't immediately answer, the visitor came in. I heard footsteps in the living room and was relieved to see Bianca walk in.

"There you are," I said, walking over to my nightstand and collecting alchemical tools and powders. I put on a false smile.

"Sorry I'm a little late," she said, lugging in her own suitcase. "I just came from the pub."

Bianca was my officemate back at SOE, and a friend. She was a Practitioner adept at body magic, but left the Gray Tower in frustration when her brother, a naval officer, was killed in battle. She had felt stuck in the Tower while others put themselves in harm's way, and so she left and joined

SOE. However the Tower decided it wasn't done with her, and the Masters wanted to pull her in for further training. Like I said, if they really wanted you to continue with them, they found ways to make it happen.

"SOE will be calling me back once the investigation's over." I closed my suitcase. Deep down though, a part of me feared that they'd never call, even if the investigation concluded in my favor. In any case, I had already decided what I needed to do. First, I would make Hotaru pay for what he did, and then I'd find every Master, Elite, and Apprentice at the Tower who was sympathetic to my cause, or would at least be open to some type of change. There just had to be another way, because it seemed the only other option was a full-on war. It would be those who stood with my father and me, and those who would oppose us. If my nightmarish vision that I had in France ever came true, then it looked like this would be a war that would destroy us all.

CHAPTER EIGHTEEN

The solitary lamp hanging from the window of the watchtower, the old Gray Tower, burned with intensity from its perch above the brick ramparts lining the wall. I felt a knot in my stomach as Bianca and I approached the Main Gate with Matthew, the Gatekeeper, and kept averting my gaze from his whenever he looked at me. I knew it was because my shield had been shattered, and only Maolán's enchantment protected me--for now. Tonight would conclude the third day of protection from the sapphire pendant, and when I'd awake in the morning, it would be the fourth. Maolán made it clear that I only had five days to get my Veil, otherwise I'd be exposed as the Drifter right in the middle of the Gray Tower itself.

Matthew pulled our luggage along on a cart and attempted to make small talk. He looked like a soldier who had abandoned rank and decided to get in touch with nature by living in the wilderness. He wore mismatched pants and shirt with a thick wool overcoat. His hair was just past his ears, and he wore a mechanical monocular over his right eye. When he saw that his small talk wasn't working, he decided to tell a few jokes. Unfortunately, I wasn't in the mood for humor, and when he found me less than forthcoming, he began wooing Bianca.

"I remember you," he drawled in his Australian accent. "You're back for training then?"

She shivered and glanced around. "I don't know how you can stand being out here at night all the time."

He checked his watch and snorted. "Just wait until midnight, lovely. It gets colder than the ninth circle of Hell!"

"Why don't you ask Master Bazyli to get someone to lay a spell to warm up the Stromovka pathway?" Bianca turned up her jacket collar and her movement stiffened. Rows of trees stood along the dirt road, coaxed by magic into a long archway that nearly obscured our view of the night sky.

I wrapped my arms around myself to stay warm. "This area doesn't need anymore magic. That's why it's so cold to begin with."

Bianca shook her head. "I don't remember it being like this when I first came. For goodness sake, it's the middle of August!"

Matthew gestured toward our right, where on the other side of the protective trees we spotted a trio of men gathered around a small fire, completely oblivious to us. "Since the invasion, we've had more traffic around Stromovka forest than usual."

When the Nazis invaded Czechoslovakia, they had taken Prague, unaware that the Gray Tower stood within their reach. Several enchanted entranceways throughout the country led to the Stromovka pathway and the Main Gate. Guests who had stayed here would swear that the Gray Tower was located in Bohemia, or Hungary or Poland, because the protective spells enveloping the Tower distorted their brains' sense of direction. Those of us who were initiated as members of the Order knew its exact location and each entrance.

I faced Matthew. "Have you spotted a Black Wolf yet?"

He looked taken aback, and pushed some of his shaggy brown hair out of his eyes. "No, but last week we had a few SS officers snooping around. They usually turn back within minutes."

231

I nodded. "You can have the porter take our luggage to our rooms once we're in."

We stopped at the massive double doors of the Main Gate, accented with iron and engraved with ancient symbols. A network of silver gears, both large and small, ran vertically down the center where the double doors met. Matthew rotated the eyepiece of his monocular, and the gears in the Gate shimmered and began to move. The Gate groaned as the cogs in the center turned and meshed, and the double doors opened to us.

"We've got some new rules," he said, jerking his head in the direction of the guard post past the gate. "Security will take you from here--and all your effects."

Bianca gave me a worried look. "We're safe here...right?"

I didn't know how to answer that, but at least I hadn't been daft enough to place the diary and papers in with my luggage. I had concealed them in a large pocket inside my coat, and sealed it with the alchemical symbol for Secrecy.

"Don't worry," he said, signaling the Elite wizard who approached us. "The only thing that could break our protection is an *Anomos* spell. The only advice I'd give is to not use the St. Martin Rotunda again to get here. The nearby area has been compromised, so someone could see you enter or leave the Rotunda."

We stepped into the light beneath a lamppost and glanced at the nearby guard post. It looked like a security booth you'd see at a military checkpoint except it was twice as large. Three Elites sat inside receiving radio transmissions and giving instructions to other security personnel scattered throughout Tower grounds. One of them turned toward us and came over. He wore the black double-breasted coat and black pants that all Elites wore while at the Gray Tower.

When he lifted his optical goggles, I recognized him and gave a tentative smile. "Anastasio, good evening. It's a little odd for Order members to go through security checks, don't you think?"

He didn't smile back, but his voice was warm. "We're just following orders, Isabella." He signaled to another wizard who came and carted our luggage toward the guard post. "I'll make sure your things get to your rooms. At sunrise you'll need to report to the infirmary."

Bianca frowned. "Does it look like we're sick?"

"Not you," Anastasio said. "You've been here within the last six months."

His gaze fell on me, and I stiffened. "I'll go see the Master Physician first thing in the morning."

"Make sure that you do," he said.

"G'night, ladies." Matthew rotated his monocular and stared at me for what seemed an eternity before turning and heading back toward the Main Gate.

Bianca and I continued down the cobblestone walkway that led to our palatial manor house. Since everyone ate in the kitchens down near the Grand Hall, the three large manor houses on the property divided into dozens of rooms with private baths. One manor hosted Elites, the other Practitioners and Apprentices, and the third manor served as the residence for guests of the Gray Tower.

When we made it to our rooms (Bianca's was next door to mine) and settled in, one of the security personnel dropped by and returned our luggage. I changed into a sleeping gown, yawned and stretched out on my bed, feeling both excited and anxious about meeting the wizards who had helped my father--and me--all those years ago. Would they be relieved to see me? Did they have a plan to move us forward? A million other questions raced through my mind, but fatigue drowned them out. I fell asleep with my lamp on, not because I forgot to turn it off, but rather because I didn't want to be alone in the dark.

***

"You might feel a slight shock..." Dr. Jian Lan pressed

233

the final electrode to my left wrist and then went over to turn on the EKG machine. I nearly jumped at the jolt of energy that ran through me as the machine monitored my heart--and probed for any enchantments or curses.

The Master Physician monitored the output on a long sheet of paper. He turned a knob on the EKG, and I could see wiring and some of the gears turning through one of the glass panels on the side of the machine. The inner-gears gave off an iridescent glow, and the machine made a beeping noise.

The doctor held up his left hand but still had his eyes on the output. "Is that pendant you're wearing enchanted?"

"Yes..." I prayed he wouldn't ask me to take it off. Maolán told me not to do it before Serafino and Ekwueme fortified my mask. They would have to do it for me tonight.

I glanced in the direction of the door and wondered how fast I'd be able to run. I never bothered to ask Dr. Lan's age, but he looked to be in his sixties. However, if I jumped off the exam table and fled, I supposed the Master Wizard wouldn't have to chase me--he'd just shut down my brain or stop my heart from beating.

I blew out a low breath and glanced around the exam room. A supply cabinet stood in the far corner with a vase of flowers on top. A storage shelf that ran along the wall held utensils and medical kits, and I could taste each and every metal present. And of course, the room had no window. However, the room did have a current of magical energy running through it. Subtle spells had been placed to promote clarity of mind and physical healing, but I also detected some type of magical alarm system.

"Isabella..." he finally lowered his hand. "Never mind. It's finished."

After writing down a few notes on the chart attached to his clipboard, he detached the electrodes from my wrists, ankles, and chest. I instinctively brushed my finger against the pendant, and I readied my tongue to launch into a longwinded explanation about Confrontations with demons.

"It's good you're back for more training," he said. "We haven't had as many alchemists admitted this year."

I clasped my hands. "Can I go now?"

A flicker of a smile crossed his lips. "We're almost done."

He instructed me to bare my neck. I gathered my hair into a pile and leaned forward, trying to block out the nightmarish image of Henry Smith. The doctor wanted to see if I had been hit with an *In Mente* spell.

"A lot has changed," I murmured. When he tapped me on the shoulder, I lifted my gaze to his and let my dark hair fall.

He exhaled a long breath. "We've had too many wizards return ill or cursed. The longer you're outside the Gray Tower, it seems the worse condition you return in."

I watched him jot down a few more notes on his chart and decided to change the subject. "Has Master Erin had any luck with hunting those Black Wolves?"

"Some," he said, placing his chart aside. "I noticed an aura--"

"I recently had a Confrontation with a demon."

He looked at me as if I told him I had gone playing in traffic. "Well, you don't need me to tell you how terribly--"

"I know, Dr. Lan. I've already gotten a few verbal lashings over it, but it couldn't be helped."

He sighed and took out a cigarette and lit it. "I'm going to send you down to one of my Elite Nature Wizards who can do a cleansing for you. Physically, you're fine, but...something's still off. If the cleansing doesn't work, then I'll have to treat you myself."

"I'm already on it. Thanks." I flashed him a smile and reached for my Apprentice uniform. He took the hint and left, closing the door behind him.

I took off my exam gown and slipped into the knee-length black tunic. I arranged the hood attached; it always reminded me of a veil. I hid my father's ring in my room,

235

but wore Veit's talisman ring on my left hand. I fitted my handguard on my right hand. The bracelet chain wrapped around my wrist and made a second loop around my thumb. A golden emblem hung from the chain: a circle within a square, within a triangle and greater circle: the alchemical symbol of the Philosopher's Stone. Since Apprentices of all the disciplines wore the same clothing, my handguard would identify me to others as a student of alchemy. Each school of discipline had its own emblems.

After arranging my uniform and putting on my black pants and shoes, I headed out of the infirmary and inhaled a deep breath. I had never thought I'd return here, and certainly not under these circumstances. With a nervous grin, I greeted a few Elites in passing and made my way toward the Grand Hall. It was the largest building on Tower grounds and hosted learning rooms and a Grand Room on the first floor, and the Masters' offices and residences on the second.

I cut across to the Grand Hall and went into the lobby where I'd receive my training schedule. The lobby always reminded me of a hotel's, with its damask rugs, wood rafters, and lounge furniture. Apprentices sat at tables having drinks and playing chess while a group of Practitioners headed toward the learning rooms. I spotted some guests who were mainly ambassadors from different countries, and a few people who were probably academic instructors for the Order's youngest members.

I went over to the wall where the schedule information had been posted. I ran my finger down the list of Apprentices names and found mine, but then frowned when I saw that I was supposed to report to room number three with the Boetheos.

This was the equivalent of sending me back to kindergarten. I could think of only one person who would send a seasoned Apprentice to be with Boetheos...Master Priya. I wasn't necessarily respectful toward the man when we had first met, but then I couldn't have imagined any

236

other way I would've reacted toward the chief tracker of my father.

I walked down the east wing of the Hall and went inside my designated room. My stomach tightened and my cheeks burned when everyone's eyes followed me. To add insult to injury, I was apparently the last to arrive. Master Faron Bazyli stood at the front of the room and stopped mid-lecture to grunt at me. Laughter escaped from a few of the Boetheos as I gritted my teeth and quickly sat in the only available seat. As Bazyli started up again, the Boetheo to my right caught my eye.

"What did they send *you* in here for?" he whispered.

The kid looked to be around seventeen, if that. "It's a long story."

Master Bazyli, hands clasped behind his back and pacing down the aisle, approached with a furrowed brow and slight haunch. "Isabella here will help me supervise you since the Master Alchemist is away and our illustrious Apprentice here has nothing better to do."

And he couldn't have told me this a minute ago? "I'm happy to help with supervision, Master."

"No you're not," he replied. "Thomas, Lily, and Chanda--report to Professor Luka for academic studies..."

He continued rattling off names and directing the Boetheos to other rooms down the hall, to serve in the kitchens, or to assist Elite wizards. He gave the remaining five to me and instructed us to head down to the training grounds. I rose from my seat and gestured for them to follow me out, but paused when I noticed Bazyli retiring to his chair and taking up a newspaper.

"Master, you're not coming?" I asked.

"Why should I? I'm sure you'll take care of my Boetheos. You can have them disperse for lunch after training."

I held back any further objections and walked the Boetheos out--two boys who spoke excitedly about the prospect of combat training, another boy and a girl who looked like they wanted to run back home to their parents, and the young man I had spoken with earlier in class. He caught up and walked along with me, and looked rather amused that he was taller than me. He had curly dark hair and red-brown skin.

"So...are you going to be helping us every day?" He wore the plain white shirt, dark pants and sweater all Practitioners wore.

I sized him up. "If you're going to start flirting with me, I'll have you know that I like guys who don't have curfews and can drive."

He smiled. "Most of the Apprentices don't even want Boetheos talking to them unless we're bringing them coffee or a letter."

"Wait...you guys bring coffee? I've got to start putting that to use."

"Might as well, Apprentice."

"Just call me Isabella."

He looked at me as if I had cursed in front of him. "Uh, yeah. I'm Cliff Wright. I'm from Brooklyn, by the way."

I shook his hand when he offered it. Though members of the Order came from all over the world, it was still nice to meet someone from the same country as you. "Welcome to the Gray Tower."

As we walked through the Courtyard of Light, my shoulders tightened at the sight of the statue of Divine Wisdom standing with her golden sword held high. I willed my mind to remain blank so that I wouldn't have to see that bizarre dream of one of the Master Wizards being impaled on the sword. I pushed it out of my mind as we passed the tailor shop and post office, and believe it or not, the Gray Tower also had a general store, a theatre, and a bank. It was as if a tiny city had merged itself with a European university and built an enchanted wall around it. Technically, the only tower we had was the old Tower near the Main Gate, but through the centuries, the entire grounds came to be called the Gray Tower.

When we made it to the training grounds, we saw

another group of Boetheos already sparring with Hotaru. Some of the teenagers looked like they had gotten a good beating, while others sweated profusely and tried to keep up with Hotaru's forms. A staunch and well-built Drago Moretti stood just feet away and watched them all from his one good eye. A black eye patch covered the other, and it made me think of the many arrogant trainees who'd try to point out the inadequacy only to have Drago whip them into submission without even using his magic.

Drago turned toward me and gave a nod of acknowledgement, and though I was sure Hotaru spotted me, he continued sparring with a terrified Boetheo. They both used practice swords, and the young man parried the Elite's incoming thrusts with a grimace on his face. Hotaru disarmed the Boetheo, who promptly yielded, but it didn't stop the jerk from pushing him to the ground.

A quiet anger built up inside me as I watched his Boetheos laugh in mockery. My Boetheos either shook their heads or tried to ignore the embarrassed young man. I approached him and offered my hand, but he appeared afraid to take it.

"You do him no favors by coddling him." Hotaru gestured for the young man to get up and stand aside.

"Silly me," I said, grabbing the abandoned sword. "I thought that in training, when someone yielded, that was the end of it. Apparently you like to watch people suffer."

His lips curved into a smile. "I just like to watch people squirm."

I answered with a thrust of my sword, and he parried. The Boetheos gasped and then gathered around in a semi-circle, while Drago just watched us. "Today my Boetheos are going to learn how to beat a coward," I said.

He snorted. "I'm not going to spar with you."

I smacked him on the side of his face with the flat side of the practice sword. "Afraid you'll lose?"

He positioned his athletic body in a defensive stance, holding his sword vertically. I made a downward swinging cut to his right leg and he parried. When he countered with a vertical strike, I blocked it and targeted his left leg. After a few more exchanges, I feinted another leg strike but then rotated the blade and struck him in his side. He made a low hiss, but didn't lose his composure. I breathed heavily through clenched teeth as I thought about Ken and those other people he had murdered. I positioned myself and watched him, hoping he'd make another move so I could have an excuse to beat him to a pulp.

He came in with a few aggressive strikes, but I had let my anger overcome me, and he easily closed in and disarmed me. I retaliated by kicking him in the groin and striking his wrist with the blade of my left hand, sending his practice sword clattering to the ground. He made a quick jab and I swerved to evade it, almost losing my balance. He lurched forward and tackled me, and I sank my fingernails into his face with enough ferocity to make him cry out in pain.

"Enough!" Drago didn't approach, and he didn't have to. His voice boomed toward us and demanded immediate obedience.

Drawing in deep breaths, I got to my feet and stepped away from Hotaru, and approached the Tower Armsman. "Drago, I wanted--"

"Don't care. We *train* on this field. Take your outside spats where they belong. Is that understood, Apprentice?"

"Yes, sir." I knew better than to press the issue with Drago.

"Hotaru is right," he said aloud to the Boetheos. "Will a warlock ask you if his spell has hit you too hard and apologize? A Cruenti will drink your blood and tear your head off before you can cry for your mama. And have you even seen a Black Wolf? Those sons of bitches are ugly!"

Both my and Hotaru's Boetheos stood there in stunned silence. One of the girls gathered her courage and asked, "Then...why haven't we trained with our magic here in the training grounds? We've just been doing swordplay without any magic use."

Drago motioned southward. "If I asked you to run all the way over to the old Gray Tower and back here to the fencepost, would you be out of breath? Tired?"

She gulped. "Yes, Mr. Moretti."

"Well your magic use requires energy, and just as you can strain yourself physically, you can strain yourself magically." He faced me. "Apprentice, how many times have you suffered exhaustion or skull-splitting headaches because you pushed yourself doing too many spells or very powerful ones?"

I cleared my throat. "More than I care to count."

"And how did you defend yourself when your hands were shaking and you couldn't cast a spell?"

"I've used weapons and hand-to-hand combat. Most of all, I used my brains."

Drago gave a satisfied nod. "The biggest mistake young wizards make is that they jump into trouble thinking they can throw around a few spells and emerge victorious. It's my job to teach you otherwise, and hopefully how to not get yourselves killed so easily." He turned to face me. "Isabella, this is your first time supervising Boetheos and you've already managed to irritate me. Go take a break, and dismiss your Boetheos for lunch."

I gave him a stiff nod and then motioned for my group to follow me. "Let's go eat." I turned one last time to see Hotaru, despite the red welts on his face, flash a smug smile in my direction. All I could think of was how very soon I'd wipe that smirk right off his face.

***

My mood lightened somewhat when I joined Bianca at a corner table in the eating area at the kitchens. I tuned out the hustle and bustle of clattering plates and silverware, of the chorus of voices, and just focused on my beef stew and Bianca's chatter.

"Kiaran walked me down to the garden today," she said with a grin. She wore her black hair in deep waves and had a glittering red brooch attached to her shirt collar to add flair to her Practitioner's uniform.

"Who's Kiaran?" I took a sip from my glass of water.

"Kiaran Luka...the English professor. The one they brought in from the University of Prague."

I half-smiled. "You like normal guys. Good for you."

"Oh, I think he was just being nice." Even as she said this, she wore a pleased expression.

"How are your studies?" I asked.

"Anastasio is training me. I guess when he's not doing security checks, he works under Dr. Lan."

When Bianca first tested at the Tower, she showed the most strength with body magic, though they told her she had some abilities of a Philosopher. I supposed my deep-seated dislike of Philosophers had rubbed off on her, because she abruptly turned away from anything having to do with Philosopher training and ended up cultivating her nature magic. I tried assuring her that I wouldn't like her any less if she chose to be a Philosopher, and that there were several Philosophers I did like and respect, but she detected my underlying bitterness and steered clear of it. I had shared with her about my family's difficulties with my father, a Philosopher, and I trusted her enough to tell her about him being tracked and hunted--but of course I held back the fact that he was merely a decoy and took the fall to protect me.

Cliff Wright and another Boetheo approached our table. "They ran out of coffee." He handed me a cold beer.

"Thanks." I motioned for them to join us.

"Looks like leading a group of Boetheos has its perks," Bianca said.

Cliff spoke up. "All of us were talking about how you went up against Elite Kimura today. Now those are the kinds of moves I want to learn. You should've hit him with a spell!"

242

"I doubt that would've gone over well with Drago," I said. "Besides, what's the first thing he teaches you about combat?"

Cliff sighed. "Rely on yourself."

I nodded. Drago always made sure we understood that having magical abilities didn't make us better fighters or any less vulnerable. Even though I hated how he had sided with Hotaru, everything he said was true. There had been many times when fighting with magic drained me physically, or wasn't worth a damn against a more powerful warlock. And, there were always imperium collars.

"Your friend doesn't speak much." Bianca swept her long dark bang to the side and glanced at the young man sitting with Cliff. He regarded her with a neutral look.

"His name's Sadik, and he said he's from Turkey. He's a mute."

"Then how do you know his name and where he's from?" I asked.

"He's a mentalist...and I'm a Philosopher. Well, at least we're going to be one day."

"You don't speak at all, Sadik?" Bianca eyed him with concern, probably wondering why the Gray Tower bothered with a mute.

Cliff answered, "Where he came from, his family didn't like the idea of a wizard in their house. They didn't treat him right. Now you know it's bad when your own family just sends you off to a Tower recruiter. Maybe he'll speak when he's ready."

"Sorry to hear that." I gave Sadik a sympathetic glance, especially when I noticed some scarring on his left ear and the left side of his neck.

A loud voice rang across the spacious eating area. "Kitchen Boetheos, you're done serving! Go to the training grounds, before Drago drags you out there. The rest of you lot, report to your Elites." Joran Macaskill watched the Boetheos clear the floor and exit.

243

Joran had on his Elite uniform coat, but the buttons were undone. He must've thrown on the coat on his way over from the dungeon and would probably slide out of it once he went back. He looked like he could be Drago's son with his stern face, barrel chest, and brawny build. Cliff and Sadik almost ducked beneath the table when Joran spotted them and headed toward us.

"Hi, Joran." Bianca rose from her seat. "I was just on my way out with these two."

Cliff and Sadik stood to join her. "See you around, Isabella--" he glanced at Joran and corrected himself "I mean, Apprentice."

"Bye, Cliff."

When the three left the eating area, Joran stared at me, and I could tell that he sensed something was off. "Master Pedraic wants to see you. Now."

I knew he'd contact me. I hoped that Serafino was already aware of the failing enchantment and that I needed it fortified as soon as possible. "Okay."

I stood and was just about to head for the exit when I saw the Master Alchemist approach. Her red hair hung in a side braid and she wore a black sheath dress. She must've come directly to us from the outside if she weren't yet in uniform. She walked with stiffness in her step, and her eyes betrayed exhaustion. I hoped that she had destroyed as many Black Wolves as possible while on assignment for the Tower. Joran tore his inquisitive gaze from me to see Cathana Erin approach. When Joran saw her face strained with fatigue, he frowned and stepped toward her--but then remembered that I still stood there watching them and instead folded his hands behind his back.

"Master Erin," he said with a slight bow.

She acknowledged him with a quick nod and then faced me. "It's good to see you again, Isabella," she said in her Irish accent. "I apologize for being away, and hope you were of use to Master Bazyli and the Boetheos. We will begin your advanced alchemy lessons soon."

"Take your time, Master Erin." My gaze went between her and Joran.

When Joran saw that I wasn't moving, he jabbed his thumb in the direction of the exit. "Master Pedraic. Now."

***

Master Serafino Pedraic sat behind his desk signing letters and talking with the Vatican ambassador, Father Gabriel di Crocifissa. A Boetheo sat in the far corner at a table with a large book open and standing upright in front of him. The book shielded him from the view of the two men. From my vantage point, I could see the young man nestling his head in his folded arms and sleeping. The hardwood floor creaked beneath my feet and caught the attention of Serafino and Father Gabriel, and the Master Wizard gestured for me to come and take a seat.

Like the other Masters who had permanent lodgings at the Tower, a door connected his study to his personal apartments. The office space alone spanned larger than my flat back in London, and years of occupation, visitors, and travels evidenced themselves on the walls as objects from tribal masks to prized artifacts were on display on shelves. A large window stood behind Serafino's desk, and the curtains were drawn to let the sunshine in.

I took my seat and said hello to Serafino, and then faced Father Gabriel. "Hi, Father. How has your stay at the Tower been?"

"Very hospitable, Isabella." Father Gabriel wore his black cassock and Roman collar. I wondered if the Tower allowed him to carry around his silver sword.

"You two are acquainted with each other?" Serafino asked as he sealed his letters. His clear blue eyes watched me.

"I met Father Gabriel in Paris back in June. He actually helped me bring down the laboratory that created the alchemical Plague."

245

"Imagine that," Serafino said. "The Vatican sends a warrior priest in to destroy Octavian's brother, and now he's here at the Gray Tower. What *will* they think of next?"

Father Gabriel smiled. "I look forward to learning more about the Gray Tower, Master Pedraic."

Serafino rapped his knuckles on his desk to grab the attention of his Boetheo in the corner, but the young man didn't respond. "Indeed, Father Gabriel. I for one have always appreciated the relationship between the Church and the Order of Wizards. Did you know that we honor your Albertus Magnus as a great medieval wizard?"

Gabriel arched an eyebrow. "Do you mean *Saint* Albert the Great?"

Serafino faced me. "They want to own everything, don't they? Albert the Great was a fine alchemist."

Father Gabriel had the abilities of an elemental wizard, but the Tower had never trained him. He believed that his powers were a gift from God, and he only used them for a specific purpose. Although the Tower contained members and visitors from various cultural and philosophical backgrounds, including religious, the Order of Wizards took a pluralistic approach to the question of religion and forbade proselytization on Tower grounds.

I turned and grinned at Father Gabriel. "I hope you continue to enjoy your stay."

"Thank you," he said with a wry smile.

Serafino threw a paperweight toward the corner with the sleeping Boetheo. There was a thud, and the young man's head popped up. "Yes, Master Pedraic?"

Serafino beckoned him forward. "Boetheo means *someone running to help* in Greek--behold what King Christian of Denmark sends me."

The young man smoothed his sweater and approached Serafino. "I apologize, Master."

Serafino presented him the sealed letters. "Two hundred years ago, you would've been strung up in the dungeon for such dereliction."

"We use the term 'holding cells' now," I whispered to Father Gabriel with a smirk.

"Take these letters to the post office, Theodore." The young man bowed and scurried toward the door. "And, this is for His Holiness, the pope." He handed the final letter to the priest.

"It will reach his hands as soon as possible." Gabriel inclined his head and then turned to face me. He shook my hand and gave a warm smile before heading out with the letter.

I stared at Serafino and said, "You...look just the way I remember you. I used Veit Heilwig's diary to unlock those buried memories."

He smiled, but it faded. "Yes, I'm all gray now and my wrinkles have deepened, and my heart is heavy, my dear. Needless to say, we need to fortify the enchantment tonight. It was dangerous for you to come here with it so weakened."

"I really didn't have a choice. How are you going to help my father? The trackers are gaining on him each day."

"Your father charged us with protecting you, not him. He made that very clear."

I bit my lower lip and thought about Neal and the others probably cornering him in Cairo. "So you're just going to let the trackers hunt him down and kill him?"

"I'd prefer not, but then we both know who they're truly after."

"How many of you are there?"

"Us?"

"Who actually don't want to see my head on a platter?"

"Not enough to turn the tide."

"Then maybe that's what we need to work on."

He paused, and then appraised me. "The other Master Wizards--"

"Many of them will stay with what they know. I understand. But what about the Elites and Apprentices? Maybe we can start with them."

247

"If we had time, then yes. For now..." he shook his head. "Let's take care of the enchantment. Meet me in the top room of the old Tower tonight at midnight."

"Fine. And there's one more thing."

"Yes?"

"Hotaru Kimura. He murdered U.S. servicemen while tracking my father. He also attacked me. He needs to be held accountable for what he's done."

He grimaced. "I told Master Priya to be mindful of who he chose to work with. Brande Drahomir has alerted me to the situation, and I've restricted Elite Kimura from leaving Tower grounds before our inquiry is complete. Was there anything else you needed?"

I shook my head. "I'll be at the Tower tonight. Thanks."

"Then I'll see you at midnight, Isabella."

CHAPTER NINETEEN

I supervised my Boetheos as they continued training throughout the afternoon, and felt more comfortable in their presence since as Practitioners they couldn't sense anything out of the ordinary about me. However when I handed them over to the Elites who'd be teaching the Boetheos in their particular disciplines, that's when I received raised eyebrows and inquiries about my odd magical aura. I gave a quick explanation about the Confrontation and gladly accepted the task of escorting Cliff back to Master Bazyli, who'd be training him as a Philosopher. If fewer alchemists had been admitted this year, as Dr. Lan said, then the number of Philosopher recruits had gone down even moreso.

When we made it back to room number three in the Grand Hall, Bazyli sat at his desk in the corner sipping from a hot mug of tea brought from the kitchens. He peered at us through his gray bushy brows and greeted us when we entered. I braced myself for his prying questions, but they never came. I began to wonder why.

"Today we'll work on our Words, Cliff." Bazyli drained his cup further before abandoning it.

I remained quiet and hovered near the doorway, as if keeping my distance would somehow lessen the impact of my aura. I wanted to see for a few moments what it was like to start at the beginning when learning to speak Words. Serafino said that the Order honored Albertus Magnus for his alchemy, and it also venerated Plato for his contribution of *Huperouranios Topos*--the Place Beyond Heaven. This was where the Philosophers believed the incorrupt essence of everything in existence dwelled, and because of the existence of these *True Forms*, everything (and everyone) thus had a True Name. When Philosophers spoke Words, they were invoking the True Name of persons, actions, objects and ideas.

Bazyli had Cliff sit at one of the desks toward the front facing him. He stood across from the young man and motioned toward his half-empty cup of tea. "I'd like to finish my drink, so why don't you command it to come to my hand through your Words."

Cliff stared at Bazyli and then turned his gaze to the right where the cup sat on the desk in the far corner. He spoke Words, and the cup jerked and nearly teetered off the desk. Cliff drummed his fingers on his table and sighed. "I can do this...I know it."

"I have no doubt you can," Bazyli said. "When you voice Words, let them flow smoothly and take your time. There's no need to be terse or rough."

I held my breath in anticipation as Cliff cleared his throat and tried again. The Words rolled from his tongue fluidly, and the cup flew off the table and nearly crashed at Bazyli's feet, but the man caught it. Though I couldn't see Cliff's face because his back was turned toward me, I knew he must've worn a pleased expression. I whispered a goodbye to them both, and as I headed down the corridor, I turned my thoughts back toward the next Master Wizard on my list who I needed to speak with--the mysterious Jerome, or as I knew him, Ekwueme.

When a Master Wizard ascended to the Council of The Three, he would choose a new name to signify that his mind, will, and entire identity was meant for the service and prosperity of the Gray Tower. The Three served as advisers to the Head of the Order of Wizards, they made decisions and decrees relating to Tower law, and they approved or rejected candidates for Master Wizard status. In fact, they would be bestowing the honor on a group of wizards tomorrow evening.

Each of The Three wore a color representing their magic, and their duty. Master Edom wore the Red, and he was the Master Enchanter who helped maintain and strengthen the Gray Tower's physical and magical boundaries. Edom was responsible for imparting us with the knowledge of the Gray Tower's whereabouts, and he could also rescind this gift from a member who had been expelled. Any outsider coming near the Tower would be deflected by Edom's protective spells, and the only thing that could ever unravel this protection was an *Anomos* spell, the most powerful enchantment breaker in existence.

Ekwueme wore the Yellow, and his color signified intellect and the power of thought. He was the Master Philosopher, and would use his projections and calculations to help forecast and guide world events, and those of the Gray Tower. The third member of the Council, Beata, wore the White and represented purification and energy. She was a Master Nature Wizard, and could feel and read the shifts in magical energy around the world. This was how the Order knew which territories to visit and gain new recruits to the Tower. This also helped when it came to hunting down Black Wolves, because of the particular negative energy that groups of them would give off.

I went straight across the lawn to the Council Hall, where The Three had their council rooms. A few Boetheos I had supervised earlier passed me and gave a quick hello as they went back to the kitchens for food and drink, or back to their residences. I walked up the front steps of the Council Hall and entered the arch-shaped building. The walls and dark marble floors inside reminded me of a mausoleum. I bowed when I saw Master Beata. She dressed in the same garnache as the other Master Wizards, except hers was white and she wore a matching long cape. I supposed wearing garnaches--which conjured images of monastery monks--was the preferred uniform for the Medieval Master Wizards, and no one ever bothered to update the attire.

I couldn't help but tense a little as we crossed paths, but she seemed to be in a rush and greeted me in a low voice before moving on. I felt uneasy about the fact that I was running out of time. I needed my mask fortified no later than tonight, and I doubted Serafino had done this on his own. I continued on toward the front desk. An Elite sat at the desk at the end of the long hall, and behind him stood a large door shaped as an arch. I was just about to announce myself and ask for Ekwueme, but the Elite spoke first.

"Isabella?" He pressed a button at the desk, and the large door opened. "Ekwueme is waiting for you."

"Thank you."

I stepped through, and the door closed behind me. This was my first time visiting Ekwueme's council room. There were three of them altogether, one for each Master Council Member to work on his projects for the Tower. Edom, the one who wore the Red, stood in the first council room with his door open. He was speaking with the Head of the Order, Kostek Ovidio. I rushed past to get to Ekwueme's room, and I entered with a sense of uncertainty. I remembered how Veit Heilwig once told my father that he helped us because they were friends--but why did Ekwueme want to help? Or Serafino? What did they hope to gain?

"Welcome, Isabella." Ekwueme gazed at a large mechanical globe suspended by an iron rod in the middle of the room. It slowly rotated and even responded to Ekwueme's promptings. An Elite Philosopher with dark red hair and unusual amber eyes, stood next to the globe with a clipboard and pen, jotting down Ekwueme's prognostications.

"Good afternoon, Master Ekwueme." I bowed.

Ekwueme turned and regarded me with warm eyes as he swept his golden yellow cape aside. He wore a dark gray garnache with black pants and long-sleeved shirt underneath. His swarthy face looked aged, though he had no wrinkles, and he was as tall as Brande. "The sporadic battles in the Pacific will continue," Ekwueme said, as the mechanical bronze globe rotated to display the Pacific Ocean. A throbbing red color beamed in the area to indicate conflict or war. "Japan continues to play this cat and mouse game, and if the United States continues to hold back, there is a ninety-eight percent chance of a strike from Japan by the end of this year."

The Elite quickly wrote down the information. "Have you calculated the likely target, Master?"

Ekwueme gestured for me to stand near him and get a closer look at the globe. "Pearl Harbor."

The Elite copied down the answer. "Should we inform the U.S. ambassador?"

Ekwueme gazed at me. "Yes."

I thought about Hotaru and how he murdered Ken, Henry Smith, and those other men. The U.S. would not be in the mood to hear anything from the Gray Tower at this moment, even if the Tower claimed it was trying to help.

I opened my mouth to speak. "Master--"

"I know what you're going to ask," he said. "I'll answer you."

Was it possible to be impressed and scared at the same time? "All right, then."

Ekwueme motioned for me to walk with him and circle the globe. The Elite ignored us and waited only for the Master Wizard's projections for world events.

"Philosophers can project events and people's actions based on logic, knowledge of human nature, and mathematical calculations. Strong Philosophers can project ahead a few hours, and the best can calculate the coming days."

"And you, Master?" I watched the globe rotate again,

and Ekwueme signaled to the Elite to let him know that he was dismissed.

When the other wizard left, Ekwueme said, "Your father can project by weeks, and I am the only person alive who can do so by months."

But it didn't mean Philosophers were perfect in their calculations, and their minds grew old and tired like everyone else's, sometimes moreso. Sixteen years ago he decided to aid my father in shielding me when I was just a child. He did this knowing it was treason to the Tower. Why?

"Why are you hel--"

"Bring that black book sitting on the table over there."

I followed his instruction and brought the book over. I opened it to the page he indicated. "What is this?"

"Your father brought that to me on January 10, 1925. He had discovered it in France."

The aged and worn page had an image of a gray tower filled with fire, and the very top burning like a bright torch. At the bottom of the page, a familiar signature had been written: Michel de Nostradame, or Nostradamus.

The room suddenly chilled, and I recalled my ominous dream. "The Broken Tower. You believe this will happen?"

"Believe?" He flipped the pages forward. "I work with numbers, facts, patterns and probabilities."

"Believed...calculated...whatever. My father took it seriously, and he brought it to you because he thought you would too."

He walked over to the door and opened it. He called the Elite back in. "Elias, please share with Miss George last week's projection for the Gray Tower."

Elias glanced down with his amber eyes and consulted one of the pages on his clipboard. "Nothing, Master."

The globe began rotating, and Ekwueme gestured toward Elias. "Three days ago, my projection for the Gray Tower."

"Nothing, Master."

"And...today's projections."

"Master, there are none."

"This has happened to me only one other time...in June of 1915." Ekwueme turned to watch the globe. "Elias, go to the Grand Hall and inform the U.S. ambassador that I wish to meet with him today. If he refuses, tell him that I'm aware of the atomic bomb project, and I have information that will be of use to him."

Elias bowed and left the room again. I watched Ekwueme give an anxious expression--June 1915--the month and year of my birth. I spoke up. "You're afraid. Something horrible is coming, but you don't know what it is. I'm supposed to help, right? I have to fix it."

He stared into my eyes. "I could have ordered your father's death that day. I knew exactly what he was asking of me. However, he made a compelling case as to why a little girl who burned with the Fire of Time should be allowed to live. Each of us involved in concealing you has had a hand in guiding you, and in molding you. You will be the only Drifter we allow to live. You are *most likely* the key to nullifying the prophecy of the Broken Tower, and succeeding where the other Drifters have failed."

I felt a lump in my throat, and anger arose in me. Once again, the Philosophers have reduced me to a calculation...a *probability*. "There's going to be a war here at the Tower, and it's your fault. I've seen it, in a vision."

He began circling the globe. "Explain."

"If the Masters hadn't indoctrinated people like Neal Warren, Hotaru Kimura, and all the others into thinking they're saving the world by killing the Drifter, then members of the Order wouldn't choose sides and fight one another. We're going to destroy ourselves, and *then* who's going to be here to stand against Octavian, his Cruenti warlocks, and Black Wolves?"

He shook his head. "You are incorrect. I've never made a projection that suggests a civil war would occur here. You should reassess your vision."

"How do you know? I thought you couldn't project anything recently for the Gray Tower anyway."

"There is an old saying back home in Nigeria. *A chuo aja ma a hughi udele, a mara na ihe mere be ndimmuo.* If the vulture fails to hover at the end of a sacrifice, then you know that something happened in the land of spirits."

"What does that mean?"

A firm knock at the door interrupted us. Kostek Ovidio, the Head of the Order, stepped in. His pure white hair fell to his shoulders, and coupled with his pale skin, it emphasized the severity of his all-black uniform. He greeted Ekwueme and then addressed me. "Come, walk with me."

A neutral expression fell over my face, though my shoulders tightened and the back of my neck burned. Ekwueme faced the globe once more, and it resumed its rotation.

"Master Ovidio, was there something you needed from me?" I followed him down the hall into a small private library. Most of the books were locked away in long glass cases that were protected by an enchantment.

"Isabella, I understand that you've been informed of...matters regarding your father." He gazed at me, and I knew he had detected my odd magical aura.

My throat felt dry. "Yes, and you probably know how I feel about it."

His deep brown eyes observed me. "I...wish to show you something."

"Ekwueme already showed me his projections."

"These are not projections." He pulled out a key and unlocked the nearest case. He grabbed a dark red book with its title in gold engraving.

I took the book from him and handled it carefully. I skimmed its pages. "This is two hundred years old."

"There are twenty more books like this one, some even older, which describe what I'm about to tell you."

I closed the book and set it aside. "Master, I'm not sure

what you're getting at."

"Some people who disagree with us about the Drifter say we are envious of his gifts, or we are cowards, or that we simply would never allow anyone to rival our power or position in the world. These are all false accusations."

"Then why?"

They didn't even want to judge Drifters on a case-by-case basis. I had risked my life many times fighting warlocks and Black Wolves, and sabotaging the Nazis. Why would someone like *me* be such a threat?

"Are you aware of the First Drifter, Besart Frasheri? His history is in that book you hold."

I nodded. "Yes, but I don't believe all Drifters should have to carry his guilt."

"Would you take that chance?"

"Why not?"

"Beata, who wears the White, has the unique ability to sense the rifts that Drifters create. A few days ago she felt a demon, or shadow being, enter our world. The Drifter has done this. Your father is growing in his powers, and now he willingly brings monsters to our doorstep."

I wanted to groan. Beata must've felt the shadow figure that showed up in Spain. It wasn't my father's fault, but mine. I thought maybe the dark being had just gone away, but who knew what it was up to right now? I thought about my brother and when he told me I shouldn't move forward until I understood more about Zaman, and in my desperation to quickly control my powers, I refused to listen. I didn't even want to look into whether or not Dr. Grey was correct about a missing page from the texts. I did all those meditations, and even used my powers to escape that laboratory, and now frightening shadow figures have stepped into the world. If anything ever happened to the exorcist, Father Maolán Martin, I'd also have an angry demon attempting to possess me body and soul, and use me as his tool.

I felt like a monster. Even if I weren't one, I'd be made

into one.

I bit my lip and decided not to argue any further against him. Could I even justify myself? I had already made one of the mistakes they feared the Drifter would make, even if it was unintentional. "If you want me to leave the Tower--"

"I don't want you to leave, but you ought to understand what kind of abomination you're protecting when you aid your father. Yes, I have heard of some of your exploits on your father's behalf. The only reason I have not thrown you into the dungeon is because Ekwueme asked for leniency."

I felt like withering like a dried up flower and sinking into the ground. This was how he would feel about *me* as the Drifter. Ovidio opened his mouth to speak, but then turned his gaze toward Master Bazyli who had ambled his way into the little library. I didn't even realize I had started trembling, and Ovidio gazed at me with a stern expression as if telling me that I would find no compassion or pity with him.

"Bazyli," he said, acknowledging the elderly wizard, "what do you say to Ms. George, who believes her father will not cause the world trouble?"

The old man slightly bowed. "The last time I answered that question, you placed me into early retirement."

Ovidio's jaw tightened. "I have an appointment to keep with The Three, Bazyli, but there is something we must discuss later. Isabella, you may not leave the Gray Tower without my permission. If you so much as walk by the Main Gate, I'll see to your punishment myself--and even Ekwueme will not be able to save you."

"Yes, Master." I bowed so that he wouldn't see the wounded look in my eyes.

"And I want you to go to the Master Physician for a cleansing. Now." Ovidio turned and headed for the door.

Bazyli stepped aside to let Ovidio pass, and then sighed in my direction. "The Master Alchemist asked me to take you down to the garden. I figured we'd gather ingredients for a new batch of rose pills since two Boetheos found the

Sherry in the kitchens and drank themselves sick."

I buried my anger and hurt, and responded, "Shouldn't they have been sent to the infirmary?"

Bazyli coughed--or chuckled, I couldn't tell. "They'll wait for the rose pills, and God willing, by then they'll have learned their lesson."

We left the private library and exited the Council Hall. We cut across the lawn and stepped onto the pathway that led to the garden. We passed a few ambassadors and they noted our uniforms, and greeted us according to our rank. I walked next to Bazyli, matching my pace with his and dying to ask him what he knew about my father. However every time it even looked as if I'd open my mouth, he began grumbling and shaking his head.

At his instruction, I picked up one of the wicker baskets sitting on a stand and began cutting roses by the stems. Once again I decided to broach the subject of my father in a roundabout way. "Master Bazyli, don't you think it's kind of ironic?"

He glared at me, his face darkening with the oncoming sunset. "What's ironic?"

I dropped another rose into the basket; the flower smelled sweeter to me than perfume. "That we're going to make a potion handed down to us from a Drifter."

"Hmph. Doesn't mean Nostradamus wasn't good at potions."

"Don't tell me you're that old," I quipped.

"I see you have your father's charm."

A flicker of a smile crossed my lips. "Isn't there anything that could be done?"

He squinted his eyes as the sky grew dark orange and daylight faded. "If I were you...I'd be careful about who I chose to speak with about this matter."

"Sorry, Master Bazyli."

He waved his hand. "I need to get to the old Tower to keep watch. Take the roses to the apothecary and follow the instructions from the potions book. And don't deviate from the rose pill formula."

"Of course."

I watched him leave, and I wondered what he had said in defense of my father all those years ago. It gave me hope that he could be an ally, but then I could also tell that he was bitter--Bazyli, the Philosopher, thrown into the old Tower and made to babysit Boetheos. I put a few more roses into my basket when I heard the padding of footsteps come in my direction. It was almost dark, but I could still make out the face of the man approaching.

He wore a suit and tie, and had mahogany colored hair and a large nose. He waved at me while walking and nearly tripped. He quickly gathered his composure and closed in. "Isabella...you're Bianca's friend, are you not?"

"Yes. Is there anything I could help you with?"

He gulped and pushed up the bridge of his eyeglasses with his index finger. "Well...I'm Professor Kiaran Luka, and you see, I've discovered that her birthday is next week...and you know..."

For an English professor, he was sure at a loss for words. "Are you asking me to tell you what kind of gift she would like?"

"Yes...and it would be convenient...yes."

A smidgen of jealousy sparked in me. I couldn't even remember the last time a guy was speechless over me like that. "Well, I have it on good authority that she loves anything with flowers. Good luck, professor."

He said something else, but I couldn't hear him because the dinner bell rang and crescendoed across Tower grounds. I pretended that I heard him and nodded. With a goofy smile, he waved goodbye and headed off to the kitchens. I turned just in time to see the Master Mentalist, Leto Priya, along with his tracker, Mehara, drag in a man with a black hood over his head. I felt my heart clench as they took their prisoner toward the dungeon.

Please...don't let it be him, I pleaded in my mind.

CHAPTER TWENTY

I quickly reached out with my senses, sending a tendril of energy shooting toward them like an arrow. I felt around for any connection to the prisoner, for any identifying mark of his magic. What if this was my father being brought back from Cairo, the "abomination," so they could execute him here before the entire Order of Wizards?

As soon as I formed the question in my mind, my vision went red and black as a searing headache gripped me. I dropped my wicker basket and buried my hands in my face to keep from screaming out.

Back off, warned Master Priya's voice in my head.

I slowly pulled my magic away from the trio, angry and frustrated that Priya had used his mental powers to swat my probe away like an annoying fly. As if he were still reading my thoughts, he shot a glance at me and furrowed his brow. It made me shiver. I turned away and thought about one thing I did finally ascertain about the prisoner-- he wasn't a wizard. Whoever he was, he had probably spoken with or helped my father in some kind of way, which meant that I needed to find out what he knew, and how I could help him escape.

But first, I needed to meet with Serafino at midnight so he could reinforce my enchantment. I clung to the sapphire pendant, and with a queasy stomach, headed for the kitchens.

***

I tucked myself away at a table in the patio area where I could breathe the fresh air and ignore the cacophony of the rest of the eating area. When I saw Bianca enter, I waved her over. With a cola in one hand and a few pages of notes in the other, she came over with a smile and sat across from my seat.

"What's this?" I dipped my spoon into my bowl of soup and ate.

"You need the Tower to hear you, to at least give you a chance, right?" She slid the notes over to me.

I read through the first page, which explained how Tower law was formed and the process of instituting, changing, or even abolishing certain laws. "Thank you."

She pulled one of the roses from my wicker basket and smelled it. "Have you ever heard of a High Council meeting?"

"No."

"That's because it hasn't been used in six hundred years."

I scanned the second page. "So it looks like whenever they needed to make an important decision or decree, they convened a High Council."

"And the issue with your dad counts as important, don't you think?"

"This could work," I said, though a part of me said that if they knew the truth about me, and the mistakes I've already made, that no one would even want to "hear" anything from me and just call for my head.

Bianca continued. "They don't even need all Masters present, just those who are on Tower grounds at the time. If a little over half side with your cause, then you're in a very good position."

"I'll still need more information on how this works."

Maybe she'd get tired of doing the research or forget about this. I felt terrible accepting her help when part of me didn't feel worthy of it. I wondered if the shadow figure would come back and if it could harm people around me. If it tried to take Casandra's dead body, then what could it do to people who were alive?

From the corner of my eye I saw a lean man in a white shirt and blue tie approach. His dark hair had been neatly brushed, and I could already smell his cologne. With a grin he pulled up a chair and sat at our table. "Ladies, I apologize for interrupting, but I just wanted to introduce myself." He held out his hand, and only Bianca shook it as she told him her name.

"We were having a private conversation," I said.

His smile never faltered. "My name is Paul Casey, and I'm the U.S. Ambassador to the Tower. You're Isabella, right?"

I wondered if he knew one of my connections back home and had recognized me. "What can we do for you, Mr. Casey?"

"I know about the murders in France, and I appreciate the help you gave the FBI. I want you to know that I've already filed a formal complaint with the Tower."

"But what do you need from us?" I asked.

He leaned in. "Isabella, you've confronted the culprit, and you were one of the last people to speak with Henry Smith. I need you, and a few friendly Tower wizards ready to dig their feet in and back me up. Master Pedraic has been the most helpful, but Master Priya hasn't even responded to my complaint."

A flash of anger ran through me at hearing Priya's name. "I'll help."

"Thank you. If there's anything I can do for you in return--"

"I think the Tower frowns on ambassadors wheeling and dealing like this," I said in a warmer tone.

263

He chuckled. "I've only been here three years, but I already know there's nothing *but* wheeling and dealing. They do us favors, and we return them by making phone calls to our presidents and heads of state, or whatever else they ask. Half the ambassadors here have a sister, a cousin or distant uncle that was trained here."

Yeah, and we were just one big happy family. "Well, I've got some work to finish at the apothecary, but rest assured you can count on me, Mr. Casey."

Bianca squealed. "I almost forgot to pick up my dress for the installment ceremony! Do you want me to grab yours from the tailor shop?"

I shook my head. "I'll do it. See you later."

"Okay, bye." She waved goodbye to Paul and rushed toward the exit.

"Goodnight, Isabella." He held out his hand, and I finally shook it.

"Goodnight, Mr. Casey."

"Please, call me Paul." He stood and excused himself before joining some other ambassadors at another table.

I grabbed the wicker basket and headed toward the exit. I rushed across to the apothecary. It stood next to the bank that had already closed for the evening. The apothecary lights were already on, and the door was unlocked. I stepped inside and saw Cliff and Sadik mopping the floor.

I closed the door behind me and locked it. "What are you two doing here? Shouldn't you be in bed or something?"

Cliff spoke up. "We...we got caught drinking the Sherry in the kitchens."

Sadik shot Cliff an accusatory glance as if blaming him as the mastermind behind the whole fiasco. I went over to the stove in the back and put on a pot of water to boil. I turned to face the boys and observed them. They seemed sober enough to me.

"So, do you still need the rose pills? Master Bazyli sent me to make some."

264

Sadik hiccupped, and Cliff placed his right hand over his stomach. "Yes, please."

I grimaced. "I don't think I've ever annoyed Bazyli half as much as you two did."

Sadik set his mop aside and grabbed a pen and paper. He scribbled something down and handed it to me. I read the note and sucked in a quick breath. "How did you know I was planning on seeing the prisoner in the dungeon? Do you know who he is?"

He may have been a mute, but it didn't mean he lacked intelligence. I searched his eyes for any telling signs, and all I saw was fear.

Cliff put on a pair of five-lens goggles and opened the formula book. He began plucking the petals from the roses and dropping them into a large bowl. "I can finish this, if you want."

"That's a complex formula"

"And I'm a Philosopher."

"In-training," I added. "You've both got a long way to go, kiddo."

Sadik tapped my arm and handed me another note. He apologized.

"It's...all right. How are you even able to probe someone's mind without them feeling it, and especially since my mind's sealed? I've only seen Elite and Master Mentalists do it that well. And don't you know it's against Tower law to read other people's minds like that?"

He glanced in Cliff's direction and wrung his hands. He probably thought he'd be punished with a beating or something. I wondered who gave him those scars on his neck and ear.

Cliff spoke again. "I think sometimes he doesn't understand how strong he is. You won't tell Master Bazyli, will you?"

Far be it from me to be the one ratting people out based on Tower law. "I won't say anything, but don't do it anymore, Sadik. It's dangerous."

The young man let out a grateful sigh as he took up his mop and continued his chore. Cliff sifted the jade powder, which imparted healing, and added it to the boiling pot. He then poured in an amber liquid from a vial, and he finally added the rose petals. He worked with such meticulous efficiency that I wondered if he had a secondary talent for alchemy. In any case, my thoughts turned toward the appointment I had to keep. I wasn't sure if the sapphire enchantment would wear off as soon as midnight came around or if I'd have the entire fifth day at my disposal.

"I'll see you tomorrow. Just take two pills each and bring the rest to me at breakfast tomorrow."

Cliff broke out into a wide grin. "So you want to have breakfast with us?"

I chuckled. "I'll see you two in the morning. Goodnight, Sadik."

With that same worried look in his eye, he waved goodbye.

I shrugged off the unease I felt at Sadik so easily reading my mind and left the apothecary. To my surprise, I spotted Father Gabriel engaged in conversation with the Master Alchemist. When Cathana saw me, she seemed a little caught off guard. She shook Father Gabriel's hand and mouthed a "goodnight" to me as she began walking toward the Grand Hall.

Gabriel turned toward me and approached. "Isabella, how are you?"

"I'm well, Father. So how's being a Vatican ambassador working out for you?"

He wore an amused expression, apparently detecting the hidden accusation. "I think the Holy Father has more important matters to attend to than spying on the Order of Wizards."

"Yeah? We'll see."

He shook his head. "It's almost midnight. I'll escort you to where you need to go."

"I'm perfectly safe on Tower grounds." At least for the

time being. I turned and headed toward the old Tower. I could see the top window illumined by candlelight and wondered if Serafino had sent Bazyli away.

"Nevertheless, I'll walk you," he affirmed.

I let him fall in step with me and studied his features. I still couldn't believe he was twice my age yet looked like a twenty year-old. I had once asked him if looking so young was a gift or ability of his. With my luck, I'd be dipping myself in youth creams and powders in twenty years.

"Father, since you're here, I might as well ask you something."

"What is it?"

"You specialize in fighting Cruenti, but what about demons?"

He gave me a bewildered look. "Are you having problems with one?"

"I've had a run-in with one. His name is Ammon."

The priest grabbed my arm so quickly and with such a painful grip that I immediately reacted by pressing my other hand against his chest and wresting myself free. I positioned myself in a defensive stance, my heart pounding at high speed. "What the hell is your problem?"

"What do you know about Ammon?" He looked just as troubled as I was.

"I don't know! That's why I asked you. If I knew you'd go psycho over it, I wouldn't have mentioned it."

"You're in danger--"

"Hey!" I backed away when he extended his hand toward me. "It's taken care of. Father Maolán Martin did an exorcism."

"On you?" His eyes widened.

"No! God, no. A woman...an acquaintance. I kind of stepped into the middle of it. I just wanted to know if Ammon ever came back, how to destroy him." I still kept my distance; I hadn't forgotten that Father Gabriel carried a sword--and was damned good at using it.

He averted his gaze and folded his hands behind his

267

back. When I heard the footsteps of several people approaching, I realized that our conversation had gotten out of hand. Three Elites, the same who had conducted security checks when I arrived, closed in on us.

Anastasio didn't bother to remove his optical goggles this time and spoke. "It's too late for such commotion." His gaze went between Father Gabriel and me. "Is he harassing you?"

I shook my head. "No, we just...had a misunderstanding. It's nothing."

"My apologies," Gabriel added.

"What are you two doing out here at midnight?" Anastasio asked.

Midnight? I should've been at the Tower by now! I felt a tingling sensation in my chest, and I knew it was the sapphire pendant losing its potency. If I didn't get out of here, I'd have the entire security team on me.

"Is...there some kind of curfew?" I asked.

Anastasio let out an irritated breath. "No, there's no curfew except for Boetheos, but I wanted to know what you are doing out here with him this late at night."

"Hey buddy, he was out here with the Master Alchemist. Ask her. I have to go." The tingling in my chest increased, and my heart began racing. I wondered how much of Maolán's enchantment had broken down.

"Anastasio," a familiar Australian accent rang out in a clear voice. The Gatekeeper, Matthew, stalked toward us. "There's something at the Gate that I want you to see."

Anastasio waved him off. "I'll be with you shortly."

"Let me clarify my statement, mate. I want you to see it...now."

Anastasio cursed under his breath in Spanish. "Just go," he said to Gabriel and me.

As Anastasio and his men followed Matthew toward the Main Gate, I threw Father Gabriel one last glare before running like hell down the pathway to the Tower.

"So," Master Bazyli said as he shut the curtain to the Tower window, "when they execute us all for treachery...what would you like the epithet on your headstone to say?"

"He was a man of progress, and of learning. He was a smart man...but not smart enough." Serafino Pedraic shut his spell book with an ominous thump, and his lips curled into a half-smile.

I sat on the floor with my legs folded beneath me. I pulled down my Apprentice's hood and had already removed my jewelry. Ekwueme skirted the edge of the Transformation Circle that surrounded me. He prodded and fine-tuned the spell that would be the building block for the others.

"Master," I said to Ekwueme, "were you the third man who came that night when my father took me away?"

His eyes caught the glow of the Transformation Circle and lit up like flames. "Yes, but you were a child then. You were more impressionable to the Veil."

He left the rest of his thoughts unsaid, though I had a pretty good idea of what they were. I was older, had already tasted my power as a Drifter, and with knowledge and memory I knew how to pull the Veil off.

"How did you convince the other Master Wizards that my father was the Drifter?"

Ekwueme stopped pacing. "We manipulated certain projections so it seemed your father knew the future, even ahead of me. We were able to cast a Veil on you and enhance your secondary abilities as an alchemist, and we worked together to impart your father with superficial abilities mimicking a Drifter."

Bazyli grabbed a worn wooden cane by the door. He mumbled a few names and what sounded like a mathematical equation. He struck the floor with the tip of the cane five times and then a blast of wind, loaded with a spell, filled the room and penetrated the walls. I could feel it extending throughout Tower grounds.

My expression fell, and my chest tightened. "Every wizard in the area must've felt that! Are you sure you aren't trying to get me killed?"

"Hmph." Bazyli tossed the cane into a corner. "For your information, I set up a Circle of Protection and a web of deflections throughout the entire area, so the Circle can't be detected. Only those stronger than me, of which there are only five, will be able to tell something's off."

I let out a low breath. "Great, so at any moment five Master Wizards could come barging in here?"

"I threw a little something in there to confuse their senses. They'll unwind the web and find each other at the end of it. And hopefully before they track me, we'll all be tucked into our beds. Now, are we ready to lay the Veil?"

"Let's begin." Serafino rose from his seat. He stood in front of me at the head of the Circle, while Ekwueme and Bazyli stood behind me, forming a triangle outside the Circle. I closed my eyes, and the memory of myself as a ten year-old girl flashed in my mind. The last time they had done this, my father was present, and his friend Veit Heilwig was alive and well.

I heard Serafino blow out a low breath, and a cool burst of air caressed my face and washed over me like water. The magic they worked felt harmonious and sounded like the whispering waves of the ocean. From Ekwueme's direction I could feel warmth creep toward me and latch onto my feet. It began to spread through my legs, past my belly, and burned my heart. I squinted as my eyes began to water from the pain, but froze in my position, determined not to throw the spell off balance.

When I felt something like silk fall over my face and arms, I knew it was Bazyli completing the Veil. It dawned on me that my father must've been the Philosopher who did this part of the spell.

I bit my tongue and held back a shriek when the burning

270

sensation left my chest area and blazed in my throat. My arms shook, and I arched my back. I held on at least until I felt the Veil finally enclose me like a cocoon. They stood around me, silent, and watching.

"Are we done?" I asked in a raspy voice. Tears streaked my cheeks.

"We are done, Isabella." Ekwueme broke the Transformation Circle and offered me his hand.

I held on with an unsteady arm and sweaty palm. I rose to my feet with caution. This Veiling was painful to endure as an adult. Had they really done this to me as a child? And my father let them? That gnawing doubt came back to me just then, posing the question of whether I was something to be manipulated and used as a weapon against others in the Tower. But I didn't want to be anyone's weapon. I would rather stop this war before it started.

"I...I want you to call a High Council." My tongue felt dry and swollen in my mouth, but I kept my gaze on Serafino.

"It would do no good," he shook his head. "And it's unfortunate that the Head of the Order has grounded you here."

"Just give me the names of other Masters who would side with us or at least be open to a High Council."

Bazyli dissolved his Circle of Protection with a single gesture. "I see what you're getting at. This whole time we've been in a defensive position, whether it was your father hiding and running, or us Veiling you. Maybe it is time to step forward and show the others what we believe and why. I would be in favor of a High Council."

I nodded. "If they want to go by the books and by the law, then so be it. It's time we started using those same things to our advantage, don't you think?"

Ekwueme spoke. "There are too many uncertain variables in convening a High Council when I cannot project for the Gray Tower."

"I don't know about you, but I'm tired of hiding, and I

am *not* going to be anyone's pawn. What do you think I am, that little girl who's not going say a damned word because you old men all know best?"

They had let me train at the Gray Tower, and they hid and protected me until I came into my power, but I doubted they expected only a hug and a Thank You card. Everything they did prepared me to be a warrior. This was why my father told me back in France that I needed to continue training. I never thought I could feel both admiration and repugnance at the same time. My father had to choose between his daughter and loyalty to the Tower, and he chose his daughter, knowing he would have to fight the Tower because of it. I didn't agree with Ekwueme about the Broken Tower being an external threat--the Broken Tower would occur if we kept tearing at each other and picking sides over the issue of the Drifter.

But I didn't want a war. I had seen its ugly side. Anything the Order of Wizards had built would be in ruins, and innocent people would get killed. I couldn't imagine having to fight against someone like Bianca or Cliff because they decided to go one way and me another. Though I was still angry with Neal, I didn't want to see him putting another gun to his head thinking he was dying for a noble cause.

"Then what would you have us do, Isabella?" Serafino asked. "Your father made us promise not to deviate from his plan."

"Well...if my father were in this room with us right now, he'd be open to listening to an alternative. Ekwueme, he brought you the Broken Tower prophecy because he believed it would come to pass unless you did something to make it turn out differently--isn't that the point of having me here? You all saved me hoping that I could change this."

Ekwueme nodded, and I saw that I had the other men's attention as well. They were finally starting to open their ears and eyes to me. "Explain further," Ekwueme prompted me.

"Okay...all the Masters who are on the outside are coming in tomorrow evening for the installment ceremony, right? I'm willing to bet--"

Ekwueme finished my thought. "That the Masters who've been outside the Tower, especially for many years, would be more accepting of a High Council and re-examining the Tower's law on Drifters. We have not seen a Drifter in a hundred years, and the world is a different place now since the Middle Ages."

I nodded. "This could work, especially if we emphasize an outside threat and the only one who could save them is the Drifter. My father sent me on a task that allowed me to find a special talisman that could locate the Black Wolves' headquarters. I've entrusted it to Order members working with the British government. If we work with them to bring down Octavian, then Hitler won't have his occult army backing him, and the rest of what he's gained will crumble. The Drifter can help save the world, instead of destroying it like they've claimed."

They all fell silent. Serafino finally said, "Leto Priya or one of the other mentalists would strip the truth from you. They'll see through it."

"Just let me work on that part, but what do you think?" I started to sweat, and I crossed my fingers in the hope that they'd agree.

Ekwueme bowed his head. "If the High Council is agreed upon, then you have a week to establish and complete it. If you can't get the results you're looking for, then we must get you out of here."

"Fair enough," I said. "Now please, tell me we can do something about my father. The trackers have caught up with him in Cairo, and he needs help."

Ekwueme spoke in a low voice. "I received a coded letter from him just a few hours ago through one of the ambassadors."

I perked up. "Good, what did he say? What does he want us to do next?"

Ekwueme lowered his head. "Isabella...Carson has projected his own death. He has little time left."

"What? No...you can't let that happen."

"I'm sorry," he said.

My stomach tightened, and I could hardly breathe. I looked at the other men to see if they'd say anything, but their expressions indicated that they had already accepted my father's words. I felt like I was experiencing the deaths of my fallen friends all over again, except it was worse because this was my father. Well, I didn't care what my dad had said would occur--he couldn't leave me, not like this. Though I felt like a hypocrite for thinking it, a small part of myself said that if the trackers killed my father, if they took him away from me...then I would rain hell upon them, and destroy them all.

CHAPTER TWENTY ONE

I woke up with a headache but managed to shower quickly and head over to breakfast. I stood in line and poured myself a cup of coffee, and the queasiness in my stomach warned me to hold off on eating anything heavy. I scanned the large eating area and looked for an empty spot. Most of the tables were filled with Practitioners and Apprentices eating and chatting, and I spotted a few Elites and Masters as well. The U.S. ambassador, Paul Casey, caught my eye and waved me over. He sat at a round table with three other men who wore suits. I really didn't want to sit with them, so I came over and stood, making it seem as if I were in a hurry to do something else.

"Isabella," Paul smiled. "I wanted to introduce you to a few of the other ambassadors."

I forced a smile. "Good morning."

The man closest to me, with dark hair and olive skin, shook my hand. "Achilles Gravari, from Greece."

"A pleasure," I said.

Paul spoke up for the other two. "My buddy here with the glasses is Svendsen from Denmark, and Rousseau is the French ambassador."

Svendsen peered at me through his glasses and gestured for me to take a seat, but I declined. "I'm sorry, I was in a bit of a rush, and I'm sure you wouldn't want me in the middle of your conversation anyway."

"On the contrary," Rousseau said through his thick mustache. "I've been telling the other men about the work you've done with the Special Operations Executive. On behalf of my country, I thank you."

I decided to sit after all. "Thank you for the compliment, but there were many other women who unfortunately aren't here to tell their stories."

"Humble *and* heroic. What did I tell you?" Paul nodded in Achilles' direction.

"Is this some kind of job interview?" I threw Paul a suspicious glance.

"Careful," Svendsen said, "or we just might turn it into one and steal you away."

"I've worked for the U.S. ambassador to London. I don't think I can abide another clerk job." I drank more coffee.

"Then how about adviser?" Rousseau extinguished his cigar and brushed his mustache with his fingers.

I lowered my voice. "And what would you want me to advise you on?"

Paul leaned in and whispered in my ear. "Give 'em your honest opinion."

Achilles cleared his throat. "Some of us feel the Gray Tower...isn't necessarily using its full strength to aid the Allies in this war. True, some wizards have beaten back the Black Wolves, but several of our requests for specific aid in our territories have been denied."

Rousseau toyed with his extinguished cigar. "Intelligence reports have indicated that Hitler and the Black Wolves have been gaining the advantage. Another ambassador said he was approached on the outside last month by an agent of the enemy, assuring peace and safety if his country abandoned the Allies."

This could be useful information. In a level voice I asked, "Why did you choose to tell me this?"

Paul said, "Kenneth Aspen was a friend of mine, and

that's how I recognized you yesterday. Seeing Hotaru Kimura rot in prison for those murders is something I personally want to see happen--and, it's clear you won't let the Tower get away with whatever it wants, or let it feed you deceptive crap. Some of our countries are unhappy with the Tower, and some of us are worried. I want you to honestly tell us, are we going to need to jump off the Titanic? Or can we still stay with it?"

Once again, this war had people questioning their alliances...questioning themselves. So, the Tower had dwindled somewhat. I recalled Dr. Lan's statement about there being fewer alchemists admitted to the Tower this year. Whether it was a lack of recruits or wizards being hunted down and eaten by Cruenti and Black Wolves, the Masters had to pick and choose where they would utilize their resources throughout the world, much to the chagrin of several countries. Hitler's alliance with Octavian's coven was a powerful one, no doubt. I had seen wizards turn traitor and side with them because they feared being on the losing side. If I could convene the High Council, convince them that the Drifter was not their enemy and was the key to bringing down Octavian and the Black Wolves, then they could lift the automatic death sentence hanging over my head. Only then would I unmask myself--on my own terms.

"Stay vigilant," I told Paul. "I think I'll have your answer by tonight. Are you attending the installment ceremony? They're promoting some wizards to higher rank." Paul and the other men answered in the affirmative. "Good, then I'll see you this evening."

I grabbed my coffee and rose from my seat. I gave Paul a quick squeeze on the shoulder as a gesture of thanks. When I turned and saw Cliff and Sadik seated at a corner table with a box in front of them, I remembered about the rose pills and headed over.

"Hey," Cliff said, pushing his bowl of oatmeal aside. "I packed up the rose pills for you. They work fine."

"Thanks. Good morning, Sadik." The young man

acknowledged me with a nod and then gazed down at his breakfast. I grabbed the box and finished my coffee.

"Can I ask you a question, Isabella?"

"Sure."

"I...heard about your father. Was he really a--"

"So they say," I said with an edge of bitterness. I almost wanted to launch into a tirade about the Gray Tower and how it treated my father--and how it would treat *me*--but held back my invective.

Sadik jumped in his seat, sending his plate of scrambled eggs tumbling onto the floor. His face turned red, and he gestured for us to remain seated when we moved to help. When I remembered how he was able to easily penetrate my mind, I quickly constructed a mental block.

I faced Cliff again. "Are you available for a research assignment? I'll let Master Bazyli know that you're doing it for me."

"Yeah. What is it?"

"I need you to go to the library and find out everything you can about the High Councils from the Middle Ages. Drop your notes off with Paul Casey. Do you know who he is?"

"Yep. I'll get started on it."

Sadik finished cleaning up the last of his mess. With an apologetic face, he pointed toward the clock on the wall.

"We've got to go," Cliff said, stuffing his mouth with his last spoonful of oatmeal. "Drago will kill us if we're late."

"I'm glad I don't have to go to the training grounds anymore." I smiled at them and stood as well. I had to drop the rose pills off with the Master Physician. While I didn't have to go sparring today, I did have an appointment to train with Cathana Erin, the Master Alchemist.

***

"Iron...Silver...Gold." I grimaced and licked my lips. "And Cadmium." I pulled the blindfold off and glanced at

Master Erin with a bored expression. She had opened four wooden boxes in front of me that revealed chunks of each metal.

She sat across from me, patient yet unreadable. "I understand you may find this tedious," she said. "However, you need to go beyond merely detecting and tasting metals. You must actually feel them. Once you can do that, then you can command them and rearrange them."

I rubbed my right temple, cursing at my headache for making a comeback. A piece of silver broke off and lifted into the air. The piece began to disassemble itself until all I could see with the naked eye were tiny shavings reflecting the light like sparkles. Without a word, Cathana commanded the shavings to fly toward me and up my nose. The metal's healing properties caused my throbbing headache to subside.

With a satisfied grin, she stood and began pacing. "Now that I have your interest, let me tell you that this isn't easy. This takes much practice, and if you don't exercise this ability each morning, the more energy it will drain from you when you use it."

I nodded in understanding, though deep inside I questioned the use of it all. My talents as an alchemist were borrowed, a superbly constructed facade. I felt like a fraud wasting Cathana's time when she could be training a real alchemist who needed this. Technically, she wasn't even supposed to train me since I was an Apprentice and not an Elite. However when I saw Cathana back in London, when she had captured Praskovya, the Master Alchemist had offered to train me directly, and said that she had known my father when he was at the Gray Tower.

"Master Erin, Elite Alchemists use gestures. How do you go from using a ritual knife to using your hands?" Now *that,* I would've liked to know.

"You must first feel and command, and then you won't have need of a ritual knife to conduct your magical energy. You'll be able to act upon any metal, including those in the human body."

"Really?"

"Seventy-five percent of the iron in your body is in your blood. And if you can manipulate iron, increase its temperature, or make it go where you want--imagine the possibilities in a battle."

"So what you're saying is that you're pretty lethal."

"I fight because I must."

I shut the box with the Cadmium; the toxic metal was starting to nauseate me. "Father Gabriel told me something similar before. Are you Catholic?"

She nodded. "He says he prays for you every day."

"That's nice to hear, though I'm a little shocked. Sometimes we're at odds."

"I think we all need a little faith, don't you?"

"I won't argue with that."

She walked over to a tall cabinet with glass doors, which stood in the far left corner of the training room. She opened one of the doors of the cabinet and retrieved two small wooden boxes. When she brought them over to the table, she gestured for me to close my eyes.

When I heard the first box open, I drew in a slow breath and inhaled the scent. "Silver...again."

"Now, this one, Isabella." She opened the second small box.

I snorted. "Plain old silver, Master Erin."

"Open your eyes."

My eyelids fluttered open, and I saw that both of the little boxes displayed sleek silver triangles, about an inch in height. They could easily be looped onto a chain. Cathana grabbed them with one hand each and held them apart. A low hum resonated between the two silver triangles, and an invisible force drew them together until they met. As soon as the two triangles united, I could taste a shielding enchantment mingled within the essence of the silver. Whoever possessed the two united pieces could construct a very strong magical shield and deflect attacks.

"That's amazing," I said. "I couldn't sense any enchantment until the two pieces met."

She nodded. "I confiscated these from a Cruenti warlock I defeated while on assignment for the Tower. After I run a few more tests, I'll deconstruct them and deliver samples to Joshua Morton at MI6."

When I saw her anxious expression, I voiced her unspoken thoughts. "Octavian probably created these. Not even you have seen an enchantment like this. If he's powerful and innovative enough to do this, then he's going to be one hell of an enemy to bring down."

"Exactly."

We both turned toward the doorway when we saw Hotaru enter. I immediately went cold and glared at him. He seemed to ignore me and spoke directly to Cathana.

"I apologize for interrupting, but Master Priya wishes to speak with you."

"Of course," she said. "Isabella, let's meet again after lunch." She rose from her seat and exited the training room.

When she was out of earshot, Hotaru closed the door and stood in front of it. He glared at me. "How I wish I would've strangled you when I had you under me in the general's house."

My heart thumped in my chest, and I prepared a spell in my mind. "I see that your murder spree wasn't taken too well by the Masters. For how long, exactly, are you stuck on Tower grounds?"

He crossed his arms and smirked. "Don't flatter yourself. I only received an admonishment from Master Priya, and only Serafino moved to discipline me, but that's inconsequential. I'm still designated to be installed as a Master Wizard at the ceremony tonight, unlike your beloved Brande Drahomir."

He caught me off guard, and I stammered. "Wh-what are you talking about?"

"His name has been struck from the list, and he will remain an Elite, for now. There are very serious consequences for aiding the Drifter, even indirectly."

For a moment, I thought he was referring to me, but then if he was, he'd probably be trying to kill me right now. I shook my head. "Brande and my father hate each other. I doubt they're partners in crime."

"But when it comes to you and Brande, it's a different story, isn't it? I've been waiting for Master Priya to finally pull him away from the task of remaining close to you. Priya has been so blinded by grooming Brande to become the next Head of the Order, that he's missed the man's double-dealing ways. I think those times when Brande could've helped us kill your father...he held back because of you." He slipped his hands into his uniform's coat pockets and came forward. When he saw I had no response, he continued. "I've known Brande since he was sixteen. We both arrived here as Boetheos in the same year. He wanted to become a Master Wizard more than anything, but thanks to a selfish little girl whose only concern is her abomination of a father, Brande will lose his place here."

Why the hell should I care what this guy said? He was here to intimidate me, and he knew he could use Brande to do it. However, I did worry sometimes when I enlisted someone's help, even if he didn't know the full truth about me, that it would end up costing that person far more than what he bargained for. Was it really selfish to get other people involved in protecting my father, and ultimately me? Good wizards were putting themselves in harm's way to Veil me, to obstruct the trackers...and to research about High Councils in the library. Damn. Cliff and Sadik--I shouldn't have asked them to do that for me. I hoped that Hotaru didn't know what the two boys were up to.

"Well," I said, rising from my seat, "thanks for the lecture. Maybe once the investigation's over and they see what you've done, you'll find yourself worse off than Brande."

If that put any fear in him, he didn't show it. I walked around the table and shouldered my way past him to get to the door. I had a spell ready in my mind just in case he wanted to try something. Even when I made it halfway down the hall, I turned to look back once more. He had disappeared.

I made my way to the general library and found Cliff in one of the smaller study rooms. Instead of Sadik sitting across from him reading ancient tomes, Kiaran Luka accompanied him and had several books spread across their table. I grimaced and thought about how even worse it would be for the professor to find himself in trouble because of me. He was a guest of the Gray Tower, not even a wizard but just an English professor whose job it was to educate the youngest members of the Order. I stood behind a bookshelf just outside the study room, with sweaty palms and thinking of a way to dismiss them from their research. I paused to eavesdrop on their conversation.

"...and my mom made me swear on the Bible that I didn't help set up a Ringer for the horse race. My dad's bet won us a hundred dollars."

Kiaran laughed. "At that point, I'm sure they suspected it was more than mere luck."

"Yeah, my dad's uncle was an Apprentice with the Tower, so he understood. My mom still told us it was cheating, so she said if she ever caught us at the bookie joint again, that we'd get a frying pan to the head!"

Kiaran wore an amused expression and wrote something into his notebook. "Sometimes I wonder what my life would have been like if I were born a wizard. Your world must be wondrous and beautiful, yet utterly powerful and terrifying at the same time."

Cliff sighed. "It's not all people make it out to be. It didn't keep my dad from dying. My mom's barely making ends meet. Maybe if I didn't come here, I'd be working in a factory right now and helping her out. I woke up this morning wishing I was normal."

"What is normal?" Kiaran closed the book and pulled another toward him.

Cliff gestured toward Kiaran's neck. "So why do you wear that silver ring on that chain around your neck?"

Kiaran's eyebrows shot upward and he pulled out the chain. "I didn't think anyone noticed."

"Are you married or something?"

He shook his head. "A long time ago someone important left this with me. I suppose one day...I'm going to give it to someone special."

I stepped away from my hiding spot and joined them. They both greeted me warmly, which made me feel even guiltier. I would have to finish up whatever research I needed done and tell them to just forget about it.

"It looks like you two are having a good time." I opened one of the books.

"Professor Luka's helping me." Cliff scribbled down some notes. "I hope you don't mind."

Actually, I did. The poor guy had almost fallen on his face in the garden the other day. I doubted he could survive an interrogation. "Thank you for your help. I can finish this myself...I know you both have other things to do."

"Don't be ridiculous," Kiaran said. "A friend of Bianca's is a friend of mine."

I smiled. "Did you find her a birthday gift?"

He closed yet another book. "I did. I hope she'll appreciate it."

"Well, it looks like you've collected more than enough information. I can do the rest."

Cliff yawned and pushed his book aside. "Did you still want me to take the notes to Mr. Casey?"

"Yes, and then after that, consider yourself relieved of your duties." Such a shame, these books were boring.

"You got it, boss." Cliff mimed a salute.

"Am I being fired as well?" Kiaran began collecting the books so he could return them to the shelves.

"Tell Bianca I'll see her tonight at the installment ceremony," I said. When Kiaran took the books toward the back, I asked Cliff, "Did Sadik communicate anything to you about the prisoner?"

"No. Why do you need to see that prisoner?"

"Whoever it is, he's not a wizard. He may be a friend."

"Be careful, then."

"You too, and keep an eye on the professor and make sure he doesn't get into trouble."

***

I shielded my eyes from the noonday sun as I walked past the training grounds and made a left at the building that housed staff workers and servants. Just beyond that stood a tiny office that led to the basement-like "holding cells." When we weren't in front of guests, we just called them the dungeon, because that's what they were. A staircase hewn of stone lead downward to a fortified door beneath ground level. Behind the door was a large dungeon area divided by walls in order to make several cells and two large rooms. I was certain such a place wouldn't pass a safety inspection; it was as old as the Tower. The dungeon held wizards who committed serious infractions or crimes on Tower grounds, and apparently non-wizards who they thought deserved it.

I drew in a deep breath and knocked on the office door, but no one answered. Joran must've been downstairs in the cell area. I stepped inside the office and passed Joran's desk that had a half-eaten meal sitting on top, and went over to the downward-leading staircase. I thought I heard a muffled voice, and I carefully went down the steps to the fortified door and pulled it open, hoping it wouldn't squeak.

I entered the tiny hall area of the dim dungeon. I clearly heard a man's voice coming from the next room. I knew I couldn't just open the door to the next room and walk through, so I went over to the left wall that ran all the way through the dungeon. We called it the "bone wall" because it was a hollow wall wide enough to fit a person in, and at one time human bones were actually found inside. We figured the medieval wizards had been serious about their disciplines and punishments. The bone wall stood in disrepair, and had several holes, but it ran across the entire area and would give me just enough cover to see what went on in the first two large rooms and the actual holding cell area.

I slipped through and felt a lump in my throat. I steadied my breathing and followed the male voice I heard. When I came upon the first room, I peeped through a hole and finally matched a face with the voice. Father Gabriel stood about fifty feet away at a granite slab covered with a white cloth, making an offering with his chalice in hand, and speaking in Latin. Cathana Erin knelt just a few feet away, attentively praying. I saw Joran in the corner furthest from them, pacing back and forth and turning his wrist to keep time with his watch. A communion service was the last thing I expected to see in the Tower dungeon, but as long as they were in the first room, it meant that they weren't with the prisoner.

I continued through the bone wall and took a quick look at the second room. A bunch of crates and supplies filled up a third of the room, and to the right stood a chair and table. A large black bag lay on the floor near the crates, and a pungent smell hit my nose. I quickened my steps and passed over to where I could see the cells. I peeped through another small hole and saw the prisoner. His clothes were dirty, and the collar of his shirt was soiled with blood. He had dark circles under his eyes and he looked pale and haggard. As if the silence of the holding area had been too much to bear, he made a loud cry and rattled his cell bars.

"Hey, let me out of here! I'm not a wizard...I'm an American. I know you bastards have ambassadors here, so let me speak to mine!"

I waited to see if anyone would come. It didn't seem as if anyone heard him. I raised my head and blew a whistle through the hole. At first he jolted and glanced around, but then he calmed down and spoke.

"H-hello? Hello?"

"Hey, why did they bring you here?" I asked.

He backed away from the bars and looked right and left. "Who's there?"

I cleared my voice. "I'm over here, behind the wall."

He stared right at the peephole. "My name's Gordon. Geez, don't tell me they stuck you in there."

"Hardly. Why did they drag you in here?"

"I'm just a private investigator."

"Is Gordon your real name?"

He snorted. "Excuse me if I'm not exactly the sharing type since you psycho wizards have me locked up in here."

"Listen buddy, I may be your only chance to get out of here. What's your connection to Major Carson George of the U.S. Army?"

"I'm one of General Cambria's guys. I delivered messages. Sometimes I kept an eye on the trackers--looks like they were also keeping an eye on me."

I thought of Henry Smith, who was also one of Cambria's operatives. I didn't know what the trackers planned to do with Gordon, but I didn't want to see him end up like Henry. "Gordon, tell me your real name. If I'm going to help you, I need to know who you are."

"Aw, hell..." He backed away from the bars. "This is a trap, isn't it? Listen lady, I just delivered messages, I never read them, and it was just a way to earn a few hundred dollars on the side. You don't have to do anything for me, just make sure the U.S. ambassador knows I'm down here."

He started ranting again and pulling at the bars. I was about to tell him to put a sock in it, but Joran came stalking into the holding area with a metal rod in his hand. He swung the rod and cracked Gordon's knuckles. The man grunted and pulled his hands away from the bars.

"What did I tell you about all that whining and moaning? Shut up!"

Gordon nursed his swollen right hand. "Is this the way

you treat guests? I need food and water--ever hear of those?"

"You'll get my hands around your throat if I hear another word out of you."

Suddenly, Joran froze. He inclined his head in my direction. I swore he could see through the bone wall and detect exactly where I was hiding. I slowly crouched, but the wall crumbled and dust went flying in my face and up my nostrils. I rose to my feet as fast as I could when I saw Joran closing in. He grabbed me by the arm, but I kicked him in the groin and broke free.

He made a jab with his right arm and I blocked it, reciprocating with a right hook. He pulled back to avoid the punch and then used telekinesis to send me flying backward. I hit the bone wall with a thud, and my head and back throbbed with burning pain. Before I could stand or even make another move, darkness fell over my eyes as he blinded me with a spell. If that weren't enough, he caused my stomach to involuntarily clench and rumble, and I vomited.

I coughed and wiped my mouth with the back of my hand. "I yield, Joran."

He lifted the blinding spell and then glared at me. I had learned a long time ago that if I ever fought anyone trained by Dr. Lan, and if I weren't coming out on the winning side, to immediately yield. The Master Wizard always instilled in his Apprentices and Elites a type of honor system where dealing critical or lethal blows were the absolute last resort. I was neither trained in nor abided by such a system, but I was glad Joran did.

"What do you think you're doing down here?" Joran asked.

I stood, my legs almost collapsing beneath me. "I needed to speak with him." I jabbed a finger in Gordon's direction. Gordon's gaze went between Joran and me, and he probably wondered if we were going to fight again.

Joran said in his gruff voice, "Let the interrogator speak

with him. You have no business down here."

"I just needed to know if he knew anything...about my father."

Joran's eyes narrowed. "That's none of my concern. Now get out of here, before I tell Master Ovidio what you're up to."

Just then, Cathana and Father Gabriel entered from the adjacent room. They both seemed surprised to see me. Gordon took it as another opportunity to solicit help.

"Hey...are you a priest? I went to Catholic school for a few years. Padre, help me."

Father Gabriel gave Joran a critical eye when he saw the pitiful state Gordon was in. "I thought I heard a voice back here. Who is he, that you would lock him up like this?"

"Master Priya brought him in," Joran said. "Someone put a seal on his mind, which means he's got something to hide."

Gabriel reached through the bars and held out his hand. When Gordon touched him, the dark circles beneath his eyes faded and returned to a healthy color. His skin took on a fresh and supple look.

"This man is not a wizard. Certainly such harsh conditions are uncalled for." Gabriel glanced at Joran again, the disapproval apparent in his eyes.

Joran sneered and faced Cathana. "Cat, I've tolerated your priest doing his church ceremony down here. Now he's going to tell me how to do my job?"

"Can I get some water?" Gordon asked Father Gabriel.

Joran looked ready to pounce on Gordon, but Cathana gazed at him with a silent plea, and he retracted. "There's a pitcher of water and a tin cup over at that table in the corner," he said.

I pushed my hair out of my eyes and wiped my face with my sleeve. "You guys have...church down here often?"

Father Gabriel brought the cup of water over and lifted it to Gordon's lips. The man clung to the cup with his good hand. Gabriel faced me. "The Tower respects religion, but

289

would not approve of any church establishing itself here."

"So *that's* why the Vatican sent you," I said in a triumphant tone.

Gabriel answered, "In a sense...yes."

"Well *I'm* not converting," Joran grumbled.

Cathana spoke up. "If anything, the destruction and evil we see in this world today only confirms that we need something greater to strive toward. Father Gabriel is not here to force anyone to believe as we do, but to those who wish to listen, we offer a light in the darkness."

In other words, Father Gabriel was a missionary to the Gray Tower, and if anyone outside the dungeon knew, he'd probably be sharing a cell with Gordon. "Well, I've got to hand it to you Catholics--you really take being universal seriously. Good luck with that."

I limped toward the door with a sigh, but Joran placed his hand on my shoulder. "Before you leave, I want to make it clear that anything you've seen here today is between us and no one else. I'm doing this for Cathana, because it's better than leaving Tower grounds trying to find a church or chapel."

I shoved his hand away. "Fine, as long as you don't tell Master Ovidio I came down here to speak with Gordon."

He nodded in agreement. "Then good day, Apprentice."

"Go to hell," I said. I stumbled through the doorway before he decided to smack me for being insolent. When I exited the room, I turned and pressed myself against the wall, spying on them once more through a hole. I really wanted to work some body magic to heal my aching limbs, but I didn't want the other wizards' senses to go off.

"I should go," Father Gabriel said. "I will speak with you later, Cathana. Goodbye, Joran."

The other man grunted in response, and Gabriel came my way. I swiveled and hid behind a large supply crate and waited until he left through the next room and up the stairwell. I was right next to that large black bag, and the pungent smell that hit me earlier became even stronger. I bent over and carefully opened the bag, and nearly cried from shock.

A dead Black Wolf.

It had three eyes and a long oval head. The skin looked dark and scaly as if it had been burned. This must've been what the Gatekeeper asked Anastasio and his security team to come and see last night. I closed the bag with shaking hands and went back over to the peephole.

"What are they going to do with him?" Cathana asked, gesturing toward Gordon.

"It's not our concern, Cat. If he's clean, then they'll drop him off back in America. If he's hiding something..."

"I'd appreciate it if you kept me updated."

"I'll see what I can do."

"Thank you, Joran." She leaned in and framed his face with her hands, and he gazed at her with a tender look that I would've thought impossible for him to pull off.

He leaned down to kiss her, but she turned her head so that his lips pressed against her cheek. "Uh...more...church tomorrow?"

She smiled. "If you wish."

Gordon slammed his empty tin cup against his cell bars. "How sweet. I guess you do have a heart. Now can I get a sandwich or something?"

Joran's expression darkened, but he held back any threats. "I'll call the kitchens and have someone bring food over."

Cathana whispered goodbye and left the same way Gabriel had. I didn't want to push my luck, so I ran toward the staircase and went up to the tiny office. When I stepped outside, I focused my energy on my left leg, my back, and my neck. Like a fresh cold glass of water, I sent a rush of healing energy through my body. When I was able to walk without limping, I dusted off my long black tunic and crossed my arms because there was a tear in the rib area.

I had to pass the tailor shop on my way back to my room, and decided to pick up my dress for tonight's ceremony. It was one of the few times we were allowed to dress in regular clothing while at the Tower. I thanked the dressmaker who handed me my dress. It had an off-shoulder neckline and was powder blue, my favorite color. It looked almost ethereal because of the chiffon and lace. I frowned when I noticed the hemline was shorter than what it should've been, but then a lot of dresses were made this way because of rationing and the war.

I held it in front of me, still concealing the rips and tears in my uniform, and headed for the Apprentice residences. My heart almost stopped in my chest when I saw Brande approach. He wore his Elite uniform, which fit quite nicely on his tall, muscular build.

However my thoughts turned toward Hotaru's words, and I couldn't shake the accusation he had made toward me earlier. When I looked into Brande's eyes, I saw strength, but also sadness. It made me feel horrible. No matter how much he wanted to put on a strong face for the world, I knew that it disappointed and hurt him to not be rewarded with something he worked nearly half his life for. And what if the Masters wanted to do more than just demote him?

I slowed my pace as he closed the gap between us. He spoke first. "How are you?"

"I'm...okay. We should talk tonight. I'll probably see you at the..." I lifted my dress as if that said it all.

He nodded. "Your father escaped in Cairo."

I sighed with relief. "Good, thank you."

I felt like an idiot. What else could I say to him? Thank you for throwing away your dreams, your destiny, maybe even your life? It must've taken a lot out of him to be alongside Master Priya, and Neal and the others, and appear to be working with them while subtly sabotaging them for my father's sake. For mine.

"You're upset." He raised his hand and brushed my cheek, sending my heart racing as his touch lingered.

"I'm tired..." I reluctantly pulled back and glanced around. Why did he have to do that? Did he want other people to see? Despite the way it made me feel when he touched me, any affection witnessed between us would just be used against him.

"I'll let you get some rest then." He gave me a confused look before continuing on his way toward the Grand Hall.

With a groan, I walked toward my room, all the while wondering if I were worth all this trouble. The only way I could make it up to Brande would be to successfully convene the High Council, win my case, and then get his name cleared. I remembered when I had first met Cathana and she told me that sometimes when a wizard disgraced himself, that his name would be struck from Tower records and those who knew him were forbidden to speak of him. It happened to my father and his deceased friend Veit Heilwig, but I promised myself that it wouldn't happen to Brande.

CHAPTER TWENTY TWO

"Hold still." Bianca furrowed her brows in concentration as she carefully applied a crimson lipstick to my lips with precise strokes.

"I know how to apply makeup," I told her as I shifted in my seat.

"Stop talking, will you? And besides, it's fun to let other people do your makeup. This is how they do the actresses in Hollywood."

"Sister, this is nowhere near Hollywood."

She laughed. "There. I'm done."

I grabbed the hand mirror and looked. I smiled a little. "Thanks."

"You look beautiful." She began taking out her pin curls and letting her long dark hair fall. She wore a silver dress with a jewel neckline.

"You look gorgeous, and I'm sure Kiaran will agree when he sees you."

"I hope so." She beamed.

When we were finally dolled up, we left the manor house and stepped out into the cool night air. A few other attendees walked along the same pathway. When we made it to the entrance of the Grand Hall, I greeted Paul Casey who stood out front. He smoked a cigar with the ambassadors Svendsen and Rousseau. The three men waved hello, and we greeted them.

"Ladies, you look lovely tonight." Paul grinned.

"Thank you, Mr. Casey." Bianca scanned the area. When she saw Kiaran approaching, she excused herself and went to join him.

Paul put out his cigar. "I'm not sure if you have an escort for tonight, Isabella..."

"You're it," I said, taking his arm.

"If you tire of him, we're also available." Svendsen adjusted his glasses.

Rousseau laughed and stroked his mustache. "We'll see you inside."

When the other two men left, I leaned toward Paul and whispered in his ear. "Did you get the notes?"

"I sure did. Looks like I'll do more than just ride the Titanic...I'll help steer it."

"I'll keep my word to stand with you over the complaint you filed, if you back us up tonight when we request the High Council."

"You've got it."

We walked arm-in-arm through the lobby and into the Grand Room that had been converted into a ballroom. Thirty large round tables were arranged throughout the room, and there was a dance floor in the middle. A band of musicians had set up, and toward the back stood a stage with a table reserved for the Head of the Order and The Three.

Paul and I sat at our table, and one of the servers brought us some drinks. I faced the ambassador and said, "By the way, they've got an American in the holding cells. He says his name is Gordon and that he works for General Robert Cambria. When you get the chance, you might want to speak with him."

Casey downed his drink and called for a whiskey. "Gordon...all right, then."

I also told him about the dead Black Wolf in the dungeon and how it could be used to our advantage. The fact that it got this close to the Tower, even if it didn't survive, was a huge problem--a problem the Masters apparently didn't want broadcasted.

I turned and saw Brande enter, wearing a black suit and tie. He looked good. Just when he turned and noticed me, Casey put his arm around me and whispered into my ear. "Leto Priya's headed our way at three o'clock."

I turned my head and glanced to the right. Cathana Erin accompanied Master Priya, and she wore a beautiful white dress. When I turned back around to find Brande, he had disappeared. My heart sank.

"Ah, Master Erin," Priya said as he came to our table and pulled out a seat for Cathana. "Two of our favorite Americans. Good evening, Ambassador Casey...good evening, Isabella."

I wanted to grimace when he sat next to me, and addressed him in a stiff voice. "Master Priya, congratulations on the elevation of your Elites--well, most of them."

He turned toward me, with his penetrating eyes and wrinkled round face. "Yes, Brande Drahomir unfortunately will not be among them tonight."

His comment felt like a stab. "And, how do you feel about Hotaru Kimura being a cold-blooded murderer?"

Paul chimed in. "I'm sure you received a copy of my formal complaint on behalf of the United States."

Cathana looked troubled. "I understand that Master Pedraic has disciplined Hotaru, and the investigation is ongoing. We never take these things lightly."

Master Priya faced Paul. "Mr. Casey, I have received your report, and I'm treating it as a priority. I simply ask for your patience."

Paul nodded. "Thank you."

"Leto," Cathana said, "when I agreed to accompany you for tonight, I expected gaiety, not politicking."

Master Priya smiled at her. "Forgive me, Master Erin. I shall speak no more of it."

The room erupted into applause, and everyone stood to

welcome Masters Ovidio, Ekwueme, Beata, and Edom. They shook hands and smiled at familiar faces as they made their way down the middle and to their seats at the table on stage.

Your father has injuries to his right hand and abdomen, Priya's voice told me in my mind. *He's getting old and tired; prepare for the day he must leave you forever.*

I clenched my jaw, trying to suppress the surge of anger and fear I felt. I shot back at him telepathically. *You've all been chasing him for sixteen years. What has he done to earn the death penalty from you?* I closed my mind off to the mental connection.

The applause ceased, and we sat. Priya forged another telepathic connection. *Carson spoke with me yesterday for the first time in ten years. He knew that by allowing me to telepathically communicate, that I could more easily track him. It's as if he's starting to give up and wants to be caught. Despite what you may think of me...Your father was my best friend.*

I crossed my arms and looked Priya up and down. I began wondering why he was keen on speaking with me about this. *Is this a roundabout way for you to try and read my mind?*

He cast me a glance. *Of course not, though I can already tell that you had a gypsy seal it. Let me be clear, Isabella: if I catch you anywhere near your father after tonight, then I will drag you down to the dungeon and deconstruct your mind so that when I am through with you, you will not even know your own name.*

Stop it. I cut the connection once more. He didn't try to mentally communicate after that.

The ceremony commenced first with the elevation of a handful of Practitioners to Apprentice, and then three Apprentices to Elites. Hotaru, along with Neal Warren and two others were elevated to Master Wizards. I noted that one of the other trackers, Mehara, had not been elevated. She sat in a corner to the far left, tapping her finger on her table and starting on her third glass of wine.

When the promotions were over, some of the men went

to the lobby to smoke, while others congregated around the newly installed Masters and offered congratulations. Half of the women went to go powder their noses, while some of the others took to the dance floor with partners as the band began playing *In The Mood*.

"Master Erin," Priya said in his baritone voice, "would you care to dance?"

"Of course, Leto." She took his hand and they left the table.

Paul tapped my shoulder and pointed toward Serafino and Bazyli. "Looks like they're going to Ovidio to make their request. I'll go with them."

"I'll come too." I made a move to stand, but he halted me.

"No, it can't look like you had anything to do with it. Let us take care of it and set it up. When they agree to the High Council, you can march in there and clobber the hell out of them."

"Fine, but make sure to follow the others' lead," I warned. "Ovidio doesn't like outside interference. Use the dead Black Wolf if you have to."

"Got it." He drew in a deep breath and met Serafino and Bazyli mid-way. After exchanging a few words, they approached the table with Ovidio and The Three.

As I sat and watched Bianca and Kiaran foxtrot to the upbeat song, and the throng of dancers enjoying the evening, I thought about Brande once more and how I wished he would've stayed. But why would he? To show up here, even for a few minutes, must have been painful. And it didn't help that Paul leaned in and whispered to me right when Brande spotted me. From his vantage point it must've looked like Paul and I were very cozy with each other.

"It's a shame to see such a beautiful lady sitting here all alone. Dance with me." Master Allan Skye, the alleged Black Dragon, extended his hand. He had brushed back his dark hair with its gray temples, and wore a single breasted tuxedo with a satin collar. When I refused to take his hand, he sent a jolt of energy up my spine so I would stand.

"So, is this how you usually get women to pay attention to you?"

He leaned his cane against the table and guided me to the dance floor. "I don't take kindly to backtalk, Ms. George," he said in his Cajun accent. He smiled in the direction of a couple of Elites who shouted his name and waved at him.

Everyone still danced the foxtrot, and though I moved stiffly, he glided gracefully with me across the floor. I glanced down at his leg. "I thought you had a bad leg, Master Skye."

"Sometimes it works, sometimes it doesn't...tonight it works." He smiled, but it didn't reach his light brown eyes.

"I don't want to dance," I said. "Especially with you."

His smile faded. "I see you went and got some work done. You're different from the last time we talked."

"What can I say? People change."

"Or maybe they just stay the same, and they wear masks to fool everyone else."

My stomach tensed, and I wondered if he suspected anything. When he saw that I was bothered, he smirked. "I told you our conversation wasn't over, Isabella."

The song ended, and the singer queued the music and began singing *Blue Moon*. I thought Master Skye would turn me loose, but he didn't. The lights dimmed and he led me in a slow waltz. As a nature wizard with an apparent disdain for personal space, Skye used our physical contact to read me. He sent a cool caress of energy from the top of my head all the way down to my toes. My breathing became shallow, and I tried to keep my face unreadable, hoping that the recent Veil was resilient enough to withstand it. His expression indicated that he was disappointed with whatever revelation he got from the reading, and for a moment I thought I had passed his inspection. However, his pupils dilated and blackness swallowed them. He leaned in and pressed his face into my hair and inhaled. I heard a low rumble that didn't sound like it could come from a human throat or lungs.

Black Dragon, I thought, as my heart froze in my chest.

At this point I was ready to break away, even if it meant drawing attention to us and causing a scene. Out of nowhere, Brande blind-sided Skye and enveloped me in his arms, all in a smooth motion. Skye narrowed his eyes, which had returned to their normal color, but one dark look from Brande told him that he had better back off. Skye retreated and disappeared into the crowd of dancers, and I continued swaying with Brande. My heart leapt with excitement as I wrapped my arms around his neck and leaned my cheek on his chest--right over his heart.

"What took you so long?" I asked.

"They asked me to interrogate the prisoner in the dungeon later tonight."

"Gordon..."

"Whoever placed that seal on his mind is a powerful wizard. Is he one of your father's friends?"

"Just shut up, Brande." I breathed in his scent and wanted to melt in the warmth of his arms. After a few moments of silence, I said, "Listen...I feel horrible about this. You should've been elevated as a Master tonight. You're better than all of them put together, in every way."

"Don't feel that way. I refused the elevation...I've made my choice."

"What?" I lifted my head and faced him. "But you wanted this more than anything."

"There's something else that I want more than anything." He gazed right into my eyes when he said this.

I stood on the tips of my toes and pulled him toward me until our lips met in a warm caress that tasted sweet and made me hungry for more. I felt myself bound up in him, mind, heart and soul. In that moment, I knew that I wanted to be with him always, but if that were to happen, I needed to be fully honest so he could choose all of me--not just the parts I chose to reveal. He needed to know who I really was.

I pulled back so I could speak, though my head spun and my entire being ached to be wrapped up in him again. "There's something I need to tell you in private. Can you meet me upstairs, in Serafino's study? I'll be up there in a minute."

He nodded. "I have to do the interrogation soon."

"All right. I won't be long."

The song ended and the room brightened. Brande turned and headed for the exit. Everyone cheered the band, and the lead singer, with a flourish of her hand, gave a deep bow. The master of ceremonies came up and spoke on the microphone, and said that an announcement was forthcoming. Ekwueme stood with Serafino and Ovido, while Paul made his way toward me with a smile.

As Ovidio spoke to the audience, Paul reached me and said in a low voice, "They've agreed to it, now it's up to you to get ready for this."

I squeezed Paul's hand and grinned. "Thank you, Mr. Casey."

He straightened his tie. "What do you think, Isabella? One day it just might be President Casey."

"If you do run for president, I promise I'll vote for you."

I said goodbye and headed toward the exit that led to the hallway. I didn't want to sit around and have Priya question me about my connection to the High Council decision--and I certainly didn't want to run into Master Skye again. Just as I reached the door, Neal came alongside my right and placed his hand on my shoulder.

"May I speak with you in private?" he asked.

I turned to face him. "No, Master Warren, you may not. Enjoy your new status--I'm sure you've earned it."

"Isabella...it's about the Turkish texts from Mehmed VI's collection."

I didn't want to hear any lies, and I didn't want him to try and manipulate me. Tonight was my victory. "I have nothing to discuss with you."

I turned away and exited the ballroom before he could say another word. The lights in the hallway had been dimmed almost to the point of near darkness, and I yawned, thinking of how late it must've been. Part of me felt queasy about talking to Brande and telling him who I was, but another part of me felt free. To one of the people who mattered to me most, I could finally stop hiding behind my mask.

I turned a corner in order to reach the staircase that led to the Masters' studies but paused when I heard Hotaru's voice. "You didn't want to stay for the rest of the ceremony?"

He hadn't yet turned the corner like I had, but I pressed my back against the wall and remained silent. As soon as he'd come around the corner, I would hit him with a spell.

"Why should I stay?" Mehara's regal voice retorted.

I breathed a sigh of relief--Hotaru probably didn't even see me. I peeked around the corner.

"You should stay and celebrate with me," he said.

Mehara carried a glass full of wine. I wondered if this was her fifth or sixth drink. She may have been inebriated and bitter, but her statuesque figure in her gold dress made her look like a goddess. "You told Master Priya and Master Ovidio that I was responsible for the Drifter escaping in Cairo...that I had failed."

"It's true." His face was emotionless. "If you had struck that bus when Carson was injured and jumped onto it, you could've had him."

Her eyes watered. "There were twelve people in there--some of them children. They had nothing to do with him. I should have killed them all?"

"You should've done what was necessary."

She sniffed. "Necessary. Was it necessary when you butchered those people in that safe house in France?"

His expression darkened. "Now we're even. I know you sided against me when the other Masters asked you about it."

She glared at him. "If I were you, *Master* Kimura, I'd be careful about the enemies I make."

He waved dismissively. "You women are always complaining about something, especially when you've had too much to drink. Come back into the ballroom."

"No."

"So, you're not going to...congratulate me?"

She swatted his hand away from her dress and turned away, and began walking in my direction. "You can congratulate yourself. I'm sure you're good at it."

He sneered. "This is exactly why you'll never become a Master Wizard. I'll see to it."

She took another sip of wine and continued walking away from him. She raised her left hand and snapped her fingers, and Hotaru fell face-first onto the floor. He rolled onto his back, and began swinging his arms at an invisible enemy. She let out a chuckle as he writhed on the floor.

"Mehara!"

She walked by me, and for a moment I thought she wouldn't notice me because of the dim light and the way I stood against the wall. However she turned and looked straight at me, her laugh of vengeance cut short. She quickly turned away and continued down the hallway toward the exit.

I turned and continued toward the staircase, and with slow steps I made it to the second floor. I felt like I could hardly contain my growing excitement as I headed toward Serafino's study to meet Brande. I passed Cathana Erin's room, and Leto Priya's as well. Suddenly a pair of arms wrapped themselves around me, and for a moment I was nearly blinded by an explosion of pain that traveled from my head all the way down to my knees. My assailant covered my mouth with his right hand so that my voice couldn't be heard.

I started kicking and flailing my legs when the memory of any magically defensive move I had ever learned was severed from my mind, like cutting a string. I bit his hand

and he grunted, keeping it pressed over my mouth. He pulled me into Priya's study, where a Circle of Silence had been set up. A whoosh of wind shut the door, and an electric shock ran through me, making me sink to my knees in agony. I went limp, and as soon as his hold loosened, I swung my fist at his head. He may have blocked my mind from fighting him with magic, but I could still at least physically defend myself.

"Be still," Hotaru said.

When I felt his mind try to connect with mine, I constructed a mental block and pushed him out. I elbowed him in the rib and rolled onto my side. He lunged toward me, and I kicked him in the stomach and sent him stumbling backward. I jumped to my feet, and when he rushed in again, I delivered a high kick to his head.

He hit me with a blast of wind, and I went flying into a bookcase with a crash. My muscles spasmed and burned, but I rose to my feet again. He closed in and grabbed my arm, and flung me to the right. I slid across Priya's desk and landed on the floor, my legs almost getting entangled with the chair. When I spotted a letter opener on the floor, I grabbed it and concealed it in my hand. Hotaru jumped across the table with ease and landed on me, and I thrust the sharp end straight into his face and pierced the roof of his mouth.

He gasped and backed off, withdrawing the letter opener lodged in his mouth and quickly working to repair the wound. I wasn't going to stick around to see if he succeeded, and I ran across the room, making it halfway to the door when I got caught up in a whirlwind that pulled me away and tore the air from my lungs. When I landed on the floor with a crash and gasped for air, he grabbed a fistful of my hair and pulled me to my feet. He shoved me face-first against the wall and sent another shot of burning pain flaring up in the back of my head. I felt blood trickle down my nose. I could see the door just a few feet away to my right. If only I could...

He pinned me against the bookcase and pressed something cold against my neck. An imperium collar. He placed it on me and clamped it shut and bound me. He immediately gave me an order: "Be still."

My limbs relaxed and any desire to kick or punch drained away. I stood there, my back still to him, and I was seething. "I'm going to kill you, Hotaru."

"It's Master Kimura. Now, I want you to open your mind to me."

He was a trained elemental wizard, and wasn't strong enough in mental magic to access my sealed mind without the aid of something like the imperium collar. He smoothed over the pain in my head so I could think clearly. When I tried to construct another mental block, he communicated his will to the imperium collar, and my defense crumbled. His mind forged a connection with mine, and he fumbled through my thoughts and memories, lacking the skill and finesse of a true mentalist--which meant all his mental rummaging hurt like hell.

He clearly saw tonight: my kiss with Brande, my conversation with Priya, and my alliance with Paul Casey. He dove deeper, skipping over entire days, and then came to a halt and hovered over the memory of Madrid, Spain-- my time at La Cocina with Praskovya, the ambush at Jasmine's house...and the Nazi experimental laboratory with Dr. Meier. I shrieked when he reached that part, and I drew in a sharp breath, because I felt like I couldn't breathe. I tried reaching again for my magic, but my mind drew a blank; the memory and knowledge of it were still severed. He finally released me and I sank to the floor, aching...exhausted...defeated. There was nothing else I could do or say.

I had been unmasked.

He stood next to me, leaning against the wall for support and breathing heavily. He looked like he was still in pain from being stabbed with the letter opener. Despite his physical discomfort, he looked down at me with a fleeting smile. "I must admit that your father is a genius. All this time you were within arm's reach...in plain sight, and no one saw it."

I felt ill to my stomach because I knew what this would mean. If it were only my life hanging in the balance, then I'd accept the burden--but Brande, and the other people who helped me...who believed in me...what about them? I tried to say something to Hotaru, anything I could think of that would at least have him and the other Masters consider leniency toward the others, but my words caught in my throat.

He bent over and pulled me up by the arm. I stood and watched his face.

"It's over, Isabella."

"The others," I finally managed to spill out, "they were only--"

"As guilty as you. Now, sleep."

My throat constricted and I wanted to challenge him with another argument, but the imperium collar once again curbed my will. My eyelids grew heavy, and I felt lightheaded. I didn't even feel myself sway and slump into his arms. I gasped, and darkness enveloped me.

CHAPTER TWENTY THREE

For a moment I thought everything that had happened was a nightmare. I wrinkled my nose at the smell of the soiled mattress beneath me, and it took a second for my eyes to adjust. No, it wasn't a nightmare, but a living hell. I touched my neck and drew back my hand in revulsion at the cold sensation of the imperium collar. I scanned the familiar brick walls of the dungeon and shivered at the cold breeze that came through. I could see Gordon asleep in his cell across from me.

I half expected alarms to be sounding, for people to come parading down here and gawking at me, the Drifter, a real one caught and imprisoned here at the Tower, and on her way to her death. However only silence greeted me, and that somehow felt more worrisome than anything else.

Had Brande, Serafino, Ekwueme and Bazyli taken up my defense and fought to the death? Or were they down here with me, imprisoned and incapacitated? I knew I could break the collar and use my Drifter powers--the mental severance that Hotaru had placed on me had subsided. And, I remembered that no one had ever fine-tuned this thing to work with Drifters. But what would be the point? Fight my way out so I could have that bloody vision of war in the Tower come to fruition? Escape and be on the run, alone, for the rest of my life? As much as it galled me to admit it, my mother was right. I was ending up like my father. And the worst part for me was that if something has happened to Brande...I didn't think I'd have the will to fight. I'd just rather die.

I heard footsteps, and I saw Joran approach with Cliff and Sadik. The young men stopped in front of my cell and pushed a sack they were carrying through an opening in the bars. Cliff spoke. "Master Warren asked us to bring this down to you."

I opened the sack and found a plain white blouse, dark brown pants, a belt, and slippers (I supposed when you were on your way to your execution, the style of shoe didn't matter). "Neal sent this to me?" A fleeting desperation took hold of me, and I felt around in the sack for a cell key, a gun...anything. When I found nothing, I sighed.

Joran pointed toward the left corner of the cell. "There's a bucket of fresh water, if you need it. I'll order something from the kitchens."

"I'm not hungry," I said in a flat voice. "Cliff, tell Master Warren...I said thanks." Okay, so he wasn't going to spring me, but this small gesture was...something.

Hotaru came in with Master Priya, and a sickening dread filled me. Joran greeted them with a curt bow, and the boys stepped aside.

"You've done well." Hotaru patted Cliff on his shoulder. "Your mother will be well taken care of, Clifford. You've proven yourself a faithful son of the Gray Tower. Now, go on to your lessons for today."

Cliff gave me an apologetic look, and he slumped as he headed toward the exit. Sadik followed him, not even able to look at me.

I'm sorry, Sadik said to me in my mind as he lingered near the exit. *Master Kimura told us to befriend you when you got here. The other day...I saw some of your thoughts, and I told Master Kimura what I saw.*

It would've been easy to blame Sadik and be angry with

308

him and Cliff, but they were just kids who had been manipulated. *Everything's going to be okay, Sadik,* I told him as he left.

Nothing would be okay, but I'd rather repeat that than to start screaming and raving like a lunatic. I gazed at Master Priya, not wanting to give Hotaru the satisfaction of acknowledging him, especially since the jerk made it a point to wear his newly made Master's uniform. "Master Priya, why...am I down here?" He knew that I was asking why I hadn't been killed once they captured me--unless they just wanted me awake when they did it.

"Isabella, it appears the discovery of you being the Drifter has caused quite a commotion. Ambassador Casey is requesting your release to U.S. custody and is threatening us with retribution, and Father Gabriel and a few other ambassadors are attempting to intervene as well. Some of the Masters have compunctions about executing a young woman--*and besides*, they say, *we've never seen a female Drifter*--and they believe perhaps it signifies something. However, a handful of Masters want to study you and *then* execute you. Ekwueme is asking us to wait for his next projection, while Brande Drahomir has suddenly picked up a newfound talent as a lawyer and is requesting for the High Council to convene today--and, you'll love this part, I do believe that Master Allan Skye is on the verge of proposing marriage. It appears you've made quite an impression on him. Frankly, all of this is giving me a headache. Once we have calmed the waters, we will proceed as we have always proceeded in regard to the Drifter. *Someone* must speak and act on behalf of the Tower, even when all others have gone astray. However, despite you being our most fascinating prisoner, I've actually come this morning to speak to the man in the cell across from you."

Joran walked over to Gordon's cell and glared at him. "You can stop pretending to be asleep."

"Okay...I'm up," Gordon said in a lazy voice. "Are you

going to keep asking me the same questions?"

Priya faced him. "Good morning, Gordon. I'm one of the wizards who brought you in. I am Leto Priya, the Master Mentalist, and I specialize in breaking seals. Whether or not you're aware of it, a wizard has placed a very strong seal on your mind. I wish to know why."

"He's one of Carson's men," Hotaru said. "It doesn't matter anymore, we have the true Drifter."

"Nevertheless," Priya said with an air of irritation, "we must be thorough."

"Thorough? That sounds like torture to me," Gordon said in a broken voice.

"Isabella, is he a friend of yours?" Priya stared at the man.

"Nope," I said as I went over to the bucket of water and splashed my face.

Priya said, "Masters Serafino Pedraic and Faron Bazyli are doomed with you--they've already confessed to shielding you all these years, along with Veit Heilwig and your father. It's all over, so why are you protecting Gordon?"

It seemed no matter how many times I denied it, they still thought Gordon worked for me or with me. Honestly, I didn't care--I was just relieved to hear that Brande was okay. However my heart sank at the thought of Serafino and Bazyli publicly confessing and taking all the blame. They probably did it in order to spare Brande and Ekwueme from suspicion and arrest.

I turned to face Priya. "Regardless of what you may think of me...I never wanted to hurt anyone. I was trying to help avoid the Broken Tower."

He gazed at me and didn't answer. There was a touch of confusion mingled with fear in his eyes. When he finally spoke, he said, "Come, Hotaru. I must speak with The Three. Joran, no one is allowed to visit these two prisoners. No one."

"Yes, Master." Joran followed Priya and Hotaru back out

the door.

I turned again toward my bucket and found a sponge, and dipped it in the water. I scrubbed my hands and arms, and removed the torn chiffon dress so I could put on the clothes Neal had sent me. My heart grew heavy at the thought of what was to come, and the only thing I had to be thankful for was that Brande never got to meet with me last night, and so wasn't condemned along with Serafino and Bazyli. The fact that the two men hadn't even been brought down to the dungeon must've meant that they were being held by The Three. It seemed their confession protected the knowledge of Ekwueme's involvement, and I wondered if the Master Philosopher could find a way amidst the commotion to whisk them away. And where was my father? Did all this fit into his calculations, or was he betting on me using my powers to escape? A part of me wanted to do it. In my anger and hurt I wanted to punish the Tower and unleash my powers, but then I knew I wasn't willing to pay the price for such a decision. If that were the case, I would have already accepted Ammon's offer.

"Hey...Isabella, right?" Gordon gave a sad smile.

"Yes, what is it?"

"Please tell me you have some kind of plan, because they're going to kill us."

I slipped my feet into the slippers and approached the bars. I looked into his worried eyes. "I'm sorry, but I can't help you. I can't help anyone..." Well, at least not without killing a lot of people, destroying the Gray Tower, and opening up a rift that would allow demons and frightening beings into the world.

I wiggled my right foot and took it out of its slipper when I felt something inside. I bent down and took out a folded note--I opened it and saw that it was written in Neal's hand:

Isabella,

311

In Cairo an associate of your father's handed me what appears to be the missing page from Mehmed VI's collection. You no doubt, like I did, questioned why the Turkish papers praised Zaman as a hero and leader despite the dangerous powers he possessed. According to this text, Besart Frasheri traveled extensively throughout Europe and Asia, and came to be known as "Zaman" in the Turkish Empire when he alleviated Sultan Osman's kingdom from a demonic attack. Frasheri found a way to close his rift--he had atoned for his sin. Rest assured that I have entrusted the page with Master Priya, in the hopes that this may be of use during the High Council.

I growled and crumpled the note. I should've given Neal the opportunity to speak with me last night. Priya was the last person I'd want entrusted with that page. He didn't even mention the text just now, which proved that he wasn't interested in the truth. He wanted to execute the Drifter and keep things the way they had always been. I wouldn't be surprised if he had already destroyed the text and would forbid Neal to speak of it.

I glanced at Gordon. He gazed at me in silence and gripped the bars, and for the first time I noticed he wore a silver wedding ring. "Don't you have something to live for, Isabella? I know I do. I want to get out of here."

"It's complicated, Gordon. I'm not sure you'd understand..." I lost my train of thought. I paused when I felt the air surrounding me grow dense, and the tips of my fingers tingle. In the tiny office above us, an elemental wizard was doing magic. What was going on out there?

An explosion erupted in the adjacent room, and Joran came flying backward, surrounded in flames. He landed on the floor right in front of us. He sprung to his feet and quenched the fire around him, but an invisible force lifted him in mid-air, and his throat constricted as he lost his breath. He tore at his collar as his face turned red and he struggled to breathe. Brande stepped through the doorway and wore an expression of rage. Joran still fought for air, and his eyes rolled to the back of his head.

"Don't kill him!" I screeched.

Brande released him, and Joran fell to the floor in a slump. He stepped over the unconscious man and yanked the key ring from his belt. Brande opened the cell door and I flew into his arms. I pressed my lips against his and took hold of his hand, trying to ignore the grim odds of a successful escape.

"Are you hurt?" He pressed the hilt of my golden knife into my hand.

"I'm okay." I slipped the knife into my belt.

Brande quickly broke the enchantment on the imperium collar and freed me. "Ekwueme told me that Master Priya convinced the Head of the Order to revoke the High Council meeting two hours ago. Master Bazyli left me instructions to an exitway in the old Tower. We're leaving."

"What about me?" Gordon screamed. "Help!"

I paused when Brande tried to pull me along. "Free him."

Brande hesitated at first, but then went over and unlocked his cell. "If you can't keep up with us," he warned Gordon, "then we'll leave you behind."

"You don't have to tell me twice, mister."

We ran up the stairway and through the tiny office, and onto Tower grounds. When a few Elites and Apprentices saw us, they immediately launched into action. Fire rained down on us, but I enclosed Brande, Gordon and myself in a Circle of Protection. Brande caused the earth to cave beneath their feet, and they plummeted down into a dark gaping hole.

We ran south, past the bank and tailor shop, and made it to the Courtyard of Light. We only needed to make it past the guests' residences and manor house before reaching the old Tower. We heard a few people yelling behind us, and someone calling for the alarm to be sounded. To our left we saw the Master Physician, Dr. Lan, coming out of the general store with a box of medical supplies. As soon as he spotted us, he gazed at us with a look of horror, and he shouted at us.

313

"Stop! Stop! What are you doing?" His supplies tumbled out of his arms and he ran straight toward us.

Brande sent a razor sharp line of fire blazing toward Lan as a distraction, and when the Master Wizard pivoted in order to evade it, Brande struck him with a blast of wind and sent him flying backward. However Lan caught hold of a lamppost mid-flight, swung around, and propelled himself forward, and landed on his feet.

"Take Gordon to the Tower," Brande told me. "I'll meet you there."

"No, Brande."

"Come on!" Gordon said as he pulled me along.

I looked back to see Brande intercept Lan. They shifted their feet quickly, parrying each other's strikes and trying to land blows. Lan shouted for Brande to yield, and when he refused, Lan paralyzed him with a spell, and Brande collapsed to his knees. The alarm sounded, and Lan sped toward Gordon and me. I pulled away from Gordon's grasp, gathered my will, and called forth Zaman's Fire. Gordon hid behind me, breathing heavily, and reminding me that we needed to get to the Tower.

"Not without Brande," I said.

Lan slowed his pace and wearily approached when he saw the Fire surrounding me. I really didn't want to use it, but I wasn't going to lie down and let him capture me. Suddenly the cobblestone pathway beneath Lan shifted, and the ground opened like a hungry mouth. Lan rose into the air to avoid sinking into the earth, and flipped into a roll. The doctor must've lost his concentration on the paralyzing spell, because Brande was on him again.

Cathana and Master Ovidio came from the south, the direction we were supposed to be headed in. The two closed in on us, though they kept a gap between themselves and us as a precaution. I turned to see how Brande was doing, and my heart nearly stopped in my chest. He was unconscious on the ground, and Dr. Lan stood over him, breathing heavily. I couldn't tell if Brande was dead or alive. A cry of frustration escaped my lips as I fed the blazing fire around me. I couldn't unleash it against Lan without hitting Brande.

"It's getting kind of tight here," Gordon said, as I hastily cast a Circle of Protection. With a single gesture, Master Ovidio broke my Circle, and it dissipated like hot steam.

Father Garbriel rushed toward me from Ovidio's direction, and to my surprise Kiaran Luka, the English professor, came running behind him. Father Gabriel gestured for Cathana to halt and not cast any spells, and he approached Ovidio and spoke with him, their voices barely audible over the blaring alarm system that still resonated throughout Tower grounds.

Ovidio and the priest exchanged a few heated words, and Kiaran slipped through and approached Gordon and me. I wanted to yell to the professor and turn him away before he got caught in the middle of our fight and got himself killed. However before I could say anything, Gordon slipped off his wedding ring and held it in the air. A high-pitched noise engulfed the entire Tower grounds, and everyone paused and covered their ears.

"Hi," Gordon said to Kiaran, once the screeching noise ceased. "Hey there. I think you have the other half of this."

Kiaran pulled the chain from around his neck and held up his ring. "Yes, it appears I do. You're the special person I'm supposed to give this to."

They were drawn to each other like magnets. Kiaran closed in and stood in front of Gordon, and handed him his ring, then took off running. Gordon snapped the two pieces together, and they made an almost musical sound. I immediately thought of the two silver triangles Cathana had shown me during training. The two rings activated some type of spell or enchantment.

A flash of light nearly blinded us.

The sky above us began swirling with colors, and a sound that reminded me of falling trees engulfed the entire area.

An *Anomos* spell, the most powerful enchantment breaker, unraveled the spells protecting the Gray Tower.

Suddenly the old Tower, along with the Elite residences and the Main Gate, erupted into explosions as if bombs had been dropped on them. People began scrambling out of the other buildings, and chaos ensued. Men and women from the Grand Hall and eating area ran for cover, a group of ambassadors followed Practitioners through emergency exitways that would lead into Stromovka forest. Several Elites, Apprentices, and Masters joined up to meet whatever force was launching the attack--some went north toward the dungeon area and others headed south toward the Main Gate.

When the sky folded and tore above us, a ball of fire came hurtling into the Courtyard of Light. Master Ovidio and Father Gabriel ran toward it and braced themselves to absorb the flames. I trembled, and my thoughts turned toward Brande, and I ran over to him. I knelt down and pulled him into my arms, checking for a pulse. He was alive.

I kissed him and sent a tendril of energy through his body, and he jolted awake. He stared into my eyes, and then turned his gaze to the right, toward the center of the Courtyard, where the statue of Sophia--Divine Wisdom--stood with a golden sword held high. I looked up, and witnessed the sight that I've been dreading.

Beata, the Master Wizard who wore the White, plummeted from the second story window of the Grand Hall and landed on the golden sword of the Sophia statue. The broken body just lay there, impaled, and the pristine white clothes quickly became drenched with blood.

"This isn't what I wanted," I said in almost a whisper. How could this have happened?

Brande grunted and sat up. I helped him rise to his feet, and then I saw Gordon walking toward us with a smirk.

My lips quivered. "What did you do, Gordon? Did my father give you that ring?"

Gordon paused and grimaced as if in pain, and his face changed. His teeth became more pronounced, especially his canines, and his skin took on a pale tinge. His facial features became more chiseled, and his shaggy hair receded to a cropped cut. He shed his Veil and uncloaked his true self. It was Octavian.

"Go, Isabella. Now!" Brande shoved me behind him.

Dr. Lan, Cathana, Ovidio, Father Gabriel, and Brande stepped toward Octavian and unleashed attacks. Sparks of fire crackled in the air around Octavian, and even I could feel the heat radiating toward me like a hot furnace. The flames rushed toward Octavian like missiles, and he rotated his upper-body with inhuman speed, and produced a misty aura of ice to nullify the fire that did manage to hit him. The left side of Octavian's head fractured into a thousand pieces, and the particles floated in the air like a dandelion seed head. I knew it was Cathana working with Lan to deconstruct his body. The Cruenti Master quickly enacted a counterspell and the fractured pieces began flowing in reverse until his head became whole again.

Octavian spoke in a grating voice using the language of the Black Wolves. In response to his call, ten Black Wolves swooped in toward Brande and the other wizards. A blur of magic, earth and fire, whooshed in front of me as they all launched into action with their spells. I caught a glimpse of Father Gabriel calmly drawing his sword, and he struck down a Black Wolf and parried an attack from another.

If there was ever a time for me to prove to the Tower that I wanted to fight against Octavian and not the Order, then this would be it. I gathered Zaman's Fire and gazed at Octavian who stood across from me. He began walking toward me again without impediment, since the other wizards who were near me were now fighting Black Wolves. I sent a halo of fire into the sky, with red-orange tendrils of flames hanging down. It looked like a lightning sprite, and I commanded it to hang right above me.

Octavian halted just a few feet away, staring into my

317

eyes as if it would tell him what move I'd make next. I commanded one of the fire-halo's tendrils hanging above me to shoot toward him, and he dove to the right. It hit him in the shoulder, and he fell into a roll. He got to his feet and rushed toward me with such speed that when I called down more fire tendrils to shield me, he was just inches away from my face. He fell back with a roar as his skin burned and sizzled from hitting my shield. He began regenerating.

I wanted to seize on the opportunity and continue weakening him, so I tried hitting him again with more tendrils, but he sped out of each tendril's reach, almost literally dancing circles around me. I sent a blaze of fire toward him like a streak of lightning, and he moved so quickly out of the way that I didn't even see him when he reached me again. I immediately took a step back and steadied my mind and focused on the pulsations. If I could slow Octavian down, then it'd be easier to kill him. However when I did begin the pulsations and time started to slow, I saw a dark hole in the air; it looked like a horizontal rip in the sky, and the dark hole formed an oval shape which then pulled itself upward to reveal a large iris. It was a dark gold color with red flecks, and a pitch-black pupil. A chill ran down my spine, and I knew I had to release the pulsations or risk another dark creature entering into the world. I let go of the pulsations, and gritted my teeth when Octavian pulled me into his grasp.

I called my entire halo of lightning and fire to crash down on us both. I knew I'd survive it, but I doubted he would. I pulled the halo down toward us with the power of my will, and closed my eyes in anticipation of the explosion engulfing us, but suddenly I felt an odd pull in my stomach area, and the entire world seemed to spin. I opened my eyes and saw that Octavian flew with me in his grasp to the roof of the Grand Hall. My halo with its tendrils had crashed and burned into the ground below.

I let out a low cry when I saw that a few men and women, non-wizards, had been caught in the halo crash,

318

and their scorched bodies lay on the ground. I felt ill to my stomach, and as Octavian's toxic power radiated toward me, my neck and shoulders stiffened with fear. He stood behind me and gripped my right arm with his right hand, and had his left hand on the back of my neck. When I tried to break free, he squeezed down hard and made me grunt in pain.

"I could kill you for what happened to my brother in France," he said in a dark, full-toned voice. He had discarded his false American accent and spoke with an Austrian one. "But Marcellus had grown reckless and arrogant. He did not want to listen to me."

In a quivering voice I asked, "Are you any better?"

"Didn't you play a role in all this, Drifter? In seeking to save the Tower, you instead guided its demise."

He motioned for me to take in the horrific view below. I twisted and flailed again, but he pressed down on my neck once more as if warning me that he'd snap it if I continued fighting. I glanced down below at the Tower grounds. I could no longer see Brande, or the others who were with me when the attack began, and I could only hope that they were still alive. I saw the bodies of over twenty Practitioners in their simple sweaters, strewn across the lawns and walkways. They never had a chance. I almost fainted when I saw some of them were half-eaten. Staff workers and teachers who hadn't the opportunity to escape through the exitways were running in every direction, some of them getting caught in the crossfire of magical battle and a few even getting seized by Black Wolves. Apprentices and Elites fought for their lives against warlocks who had now joined the fray, and I saw a dozen Cruenti corner two Master Wizards who were bloodied and exhausted.

"Okay, you have the Tower now, like you always wanted." My voice was unsteady and hoarse with grief. "So call off your warlocks."

Octavian said nothing, and still gripped my right arm with one hand and the back of my neck with his other as he

319

stood behind me. I almost jumped when I felt his hot breath just beneath my right ear, and I used my left hand to grab my golden knife. As he drew in a deep breath, I slid the knife from my belt. When he parted his lips and pressed his open mouth against my neck, I swung and thrust the blade into his chest.

He gasped and released me, then drew back. He dislodged the knife, and blood flowed down his shirt, but he didn't collapse. I must've missed his heart by a centimeter. I backed away when he glared at me, but froze in place when I saw him slit his left wrist. Why would he do such a bizarre action?

"Stop!" I screeched when he grabbed me and tried to press his wounded wrist to my lips. This disturbed me more than him trying to bite me or drink my blood--why would he want me to drink his?

I would've screamed again except I didn't want to open my mouth. I sank to my knees in an effort to keep my distance, but he pulled me in. I sent a shield of fire bursting forth and he recoiled. I rolled to the right and off the roof of the Grand Hall, and fell and crashed into a ledge just above the first floor. My right shoulder burned with pain and my hand shook as I held on. My Fire burned through my center and I brought it out, and used it to break the window in front of me. I propelled myself forward and rolled inside.

Another earthquake shook the Tower grounds, and two more explosions sent fire and black smoke leaping into the air. I hissed in pain as I forced myself to stand, and I could feel fatigue and soreness tear through my body. I glanced around the dim room and immediately recognized it; I was in Master Serafino Pedraic's study, with its tribal masks and artistic displays. I started toward the exit when Octavian came crashing through the same way I had, but he landed on his feet. I called forth my Fire again, but the building shook and a large black creature with wings glided down from above and seized Octavian from behind with its black talons. It pulled him outside.

Black Dragon, I thought. I hoped that Master Skye would eviscerate Octavian.

I stumbled out the door and into the hallway, which was hollow and silent, and I kept telling myself that it was best that everyone inside the Grand Hall had already vacated. A part of me wished however that at least *someone* ran at my side. My heart pace quickened and my body began trembling, but I pushed myself forward, because I knew I had to reach Brande, though I didn't know what happened to him or where he was. When I reached the first floor, I walked past a few learning rooms and almost slumped to the floor with exhaustion. I pressed my right palm against the wall for support, and made a right turn into the lobby and out of the building.

I glanced around as I made my way toward the Courtyard of Light. Smoke still billowed everywhere, a few voices could be heard, and the hairs on the back of my neck stood as currents of dark magic broke down any last magical defense latent in Tower grounds. I had to pass over the bodies of several more Order members, some of them unrecognizable. I sprinted past the Courtyard when I thought of Octavian and whether or not he had escaped the Black Dragon's grasp.

I felt the faint whisper of elemental magic being let loose, and my chest tightened as I thought of Brande. The magic I detected seemed to be coming from behind the general store, where an emergency exitway stood. I made a right turn and ran toward the building, and when I made another right and went behind the store, I froze in my tracks. Though I could see the weakened, faint glow of the enchanted exitway emanating from the brick wall just across, Hotaru stood there blocking my path. I wasn't going to leave without Brande anyway, but nothing good would come of Hotaru standing sentinel at one of the last exitways.

His arms and face were bruised and bloodied, but he otherwise looked intact. He narrowed his eyes as he gazed at me, and positioned himself directly in front of the

321

exitway. "Trying to escape after you've brought ruin upon us?" he asked.

"Master Priya brought Octavian into the Tower, not me." I brought forth my Fire and concentrated it in my hands.

Hotaru charged and made a strike with his left hand, but I blocked it and reciprocated with a strike of my own. My hand lit up with a flame from my Fire and I spun and landed a blow on his shoulder. He fell back and grimaced from the pain, then wore a shocked expression. As an elemental he had been used to absorbing and creating fire, not being harmed by it. He could've easily buried me in an earthquake or commanded the air to leave my lungs, but it looked like he had already exhausted himself in battle. He gritted his teeth and rotated his shoulder, then drew a knife.

He gripped the weapon and spoke. "I'm not letting you through the exitway. You should die here with all the other abominations."

"You idiot," I said. "You spent all your magical energy and now you want to stand here fighting me instead of going through the exitway."

He sneered. "That man that I killed at the safe house..."

Heat rose in my face and I shouted, "He wasn't just some man. His name was Kenneth!" I swerved and avoided the slash of his knife, and reciprocated with a hard jab to his nose. I made a quick dip and swung my leg, knocking him off his feet and sending the knife falling to the ground.

We both rushed for the weapon, but I reached it first. He threw himself forward with a savage shout and knocked me onto my back. Both of our arms shook as I held the blade upward, attempting to drive it into his chest, while he halted me and crushed my hands in his to try and make me drop the knife.

"You're weak and pathetic," he said. "Just like that man. He said he wasn't going to let me hurt you or your family-- now we both know he was wrong."

I felt a surge of strength, fueled by rage, race through

my limbs. I jerked the knife sideways, to the left, which caught him off guard. With a quick flick of my wrist, I sliced the skin on his hand, and he jumped back. He quickly stood and frowned when he realized that it was an alchemical symbol, an upside down five-point star--reverse Fixation. I erected a shield with Zaman's Fire, and he looked ready to charge me again as his mouth frothed with saliva and blood. But it was too late. His skin grew ash gray and rippled like water. He opened his mouth to scream, but instead his entire body exploded.

The last time I had done such a spell, I looked away. This time, I didn't.

My body still trembled with adrenaline as I lowered my magical shield, and I rose to my feet. With a startled breath, I saw Neal approach with a shimmering pistol in hand. He had discarded most of his Master's uniform, but still wore a black long-sleeved shirt and pants. I could see blood streaming down from his left temple and bloodstains on the left side of his neck. He glanced at the mess that used to be Hotaru; with all the carnage around the entire grounds, he probably assumed it was the work of a Black Wolf. I froze in place, partly out of caution, and also because my limbs were burning with pain. I opened my mouth to speak, but he spoke first.

"Ekwueme and the other Philosophers are sweeping the entire area. We've ordered all Order members to retreat and leave the Gray Tower. If we find any other survivors, we'll take them with us."

"How many Black Wolves and Cruenti are still out there?" I asked.

"Quite a few. They've killed many of us, and we've killed many of them."

"And Octavian?"

"He's still on Tower grounds. You must leave."

I wanted to sick up at the image of him trying to force me to drink his blood. "The last time I saw Octavian, Master Skye came as a black dragon and seized him. If he's still alive after that, then maybe you and the other Philosophers need to get out of here."

"I'll leave, when it's time. I must stay with the Philosophers for now and clear the area. There may be more survivors."

When I saw the grief in his eyes, I almost wanted to cry. I had never seen Neal or any other Philosopher, not even my father, display such sorrow in a single expression. Watching the Gray Tower fall must've been like experiencing the end of the world for him. It hurt me too to see this all laid waste, especially since I had friends here, but it must've been much more painful of a sight for him to endure. I slowly approached and wrapped my arms around him.

"I'm sorry, Neal. I wanted to prevent this...I wish I could've."

He paused for a few moments before speaking. "You received my note?"

"Yes. Sorry about not listening to you earlier, but you deserved it."

He gave a smile that didn't reach his sad eyes. "I'll seal the exitway once you're through."

I released him and shook my head. "I need to find Brande."

Another earthquake hit us and an explosion erupted on the west side. A frightful roar in the sky made us both look up into the air, but we saw nothing. He squeezed my hand in a parting gesture. "If Brande is here, he'll go with us. Goodbye, Isabella."

"Don't say it like that, and *don't* get yourself killed. I'm staying too."

Serafino rounded the corner with Cliff and Sadik, and Brande came behind them, cradling a half-conscious Mehara in his arms. She still wore the gold evening gown from the ceremony last night, and I wondered if she had woken up late from her drunken slumber to see hell loosed all around her.

Serafino shouted to us. "Get through the exitway, I have to seal it now! The Black Wolves have brought in reinforcements. I'm staying with the Philosophers."

I motioned for Brande to go through first with Mehara, and he passed into the luminous exitway. Sadik went next, and Cliff was behind him but paused right before going through and said, "Isabella...I saw Professor Luka. He took Bianca."

My heart sank. "Go and follow the others." He did as I said and slipped into the light in the wall.

"Go, Isabella." Serafino had an urgent look in his eyes.

"I'm coming with you," I said. "I need to save Bianca."

Professor Kiaran Luka was a sycophant. I thought his praise and affection for wizards came from the experience of being among them and appreciating them--apparently he wanted to become one, and Octavian must've offered it to the English professor. I was willing to wager that he had agreed to hold on to that silver ring and help enact the *Anomos* enchantment breaker in exchange for initiation to the coven of Cruenti warlocks. If I didn't find Bianca...he would sacrifice her to a demon.

"I'm sorry, Isabella, but there's no time." Serafino formed a gesture with his right hand and I went flying back toward the light in the wall.

Neal gazed at me, then turned to join Serafino. Ten Cruenti warlocks turned the corner and rushed toward them. I called out to them, but I kept falling back as if through a tunnel, and a burst of light blinded me. I hit the ground and turned my head to wipe the grass and dirt from my mouth. I stood and saw that I was in Stromovka forest.

It felt like I had woken up from a nightmare. The branches of the tall trees swayed in the breeze and shielded me from the noonday sun. The grass stood firm yet plush beneath my feet, and the only sounds I heard were birds chirping. Whoever else made it through this exitway before us were now long gone, though I did see a few lifeless bodies near the pathway that led to the gardens. Making it out of the Gray Tower didn't guarantee our safety, especially since the city of Prague was currently under Nazi occupation. We were still in enemy territory.

"Isabella," Brande said, approaching from behind.

I turned to face him and ran into his arms. "Thank goodness you're okay."

He let out a low sigh. "Father Gabriel and Cathana Erin escaped, but I don't know if Dr. Lan made it. They captured Master Ovidio, Edom, and a few others. Everyone else is either scattered or dead."

I frowned. "Neal said all the Philosophers were still there. They'll bring out anyone else they find."

"Then they need to do it quickly," he said. "There are Nazis patrolling the forest."

"Where are the others?"

"Over here." He led me away from the pathway to a small copse where Sadik and Cliff sat on the grass in silence. Mehara lay sprawled on a bench behind them, weeping.

"We need to leave this area," I told Brande. "Hell, we need to leave the country."

He nodded in agreement. "Our first step is to get into neutral territory. We can try for Sweden up north, or go west to Switzerland."

"We might have to do that, unless you think it'll be easier to just head east into Russian territory and then make our way up north."

Mehara let out a mocking laugh that almost ended in a cry. "Why don't we just go through Poland while we're at it, or head straight into Germany. I'm sure our enemies will love that. And, if that weren't enough, we're stuck with the Drifter?"

"Thanks for joining the conversation," I said.

She sat up. "The Germans have cut us off from the rest of the world. We can't go anywhere unless we're willing to cross their territory or their allies' territories. Everyone who escaped into Prague, where are they? Where did they go?

326

They'll have to sneak past the borders or risk capture here in Czechoslovakia."

"If we stick together, we can do this," I said.

Brande spoke. "We can go south into Hungary. I have some contacts there who can help get us across the north of Italy and into Switzerland."

"We're going to die," she said, looking straight at Cliff and Sadik. "I'm the only one brave enough to tell you the truth."

Brande glared at her. "I didn't save your life so you can throw it away, or endanger ours. None of us would survive long on our own with the Nazis and Black Wolves prowling the forest."

Mehara's jaw tightened. "Then...Switzerland it is."

We all froze when we heard voices and the rumble of an engine nearby. Brande motioned for us all to stay in place while he scouted ahead. He left for a few moments and returned to report back: two armed trekkers had pulled up along the pathway carrying two SS officers each.

Mehara stood. "Get out of my way."

We all eyed each other and followed her out of the copse, and made sure to take cover behind some trees. We heard a buzzing in our ears and much of the surrounding sound had been blocked out as if we'd put on earplugs. Mehara had lain the groundwork for mind control, and shielded us from it while directing it toward the officers. When the SS officers spotted Mehara across from them, two of them jumped out of their trekker while the other two remained in theirs with the machine gun trained on her. The officer closest to her approached with caution and asked if she had any weapons on her.

In answer to his question, Mehara gazed at him and his partner, who stood just feet from her with weapons drawn, and in a low voice commanded them to turn around and shoot the other two officers sitting in the trekker. They spun around and shot the two men in the vehicle with deadly accuracy. With a glazed look in his eyes, the officer on the

327

right then stepped forward and handed her his gun. He then began shedding his uniform and leaving the garments on the ground in front of her.

When he had stripped down to his underwear, she told him, "Get back into your trekker and go kill as many SS officers as you can."

He immediately obeyed and went over to the vehicle, jumped inside, and took off.

"And what about me?" the officer to her left asked.

She held up her left hand and a grenade from the remaining trekker flew toward her. She caught it and presented it to him. "Your checkpoint is near, yes?"

"Yes."

"Then go blow it to Hell, and you can go along with it."

"Of course." He grabbed the grenade, turned on his heel, and went into the parked trekker. He shoved the two dead bodies from the vehicle, and the engine rumbled and he drove in the direction he had come from.

The buzzing ceased and our ears opened fully. We finally came forward, and Mehara handed Cliff the SS officer's gun. "You've never killed anyone," she said. "Get used to doing it."

"Okay..." Cliff gave me an anxious look. I quickly showed him how to handle the weapon. I didn't think Drago had gotten to this part yet with the Boetheos.

Brande faced Sadik. "Do you know how to do a sight deflection?"

Sadik's eyebrows shot up and he faced me. *I don't know what that is! What should I tell him?*

Brande gestured toward Mehara. "Show him." He took off toward the pathway that we'd have to travel down in order to leave the forest and the city.

Mehara faced the mute young man. "It's like creating a mirage so that when people look at your friend Cliff, they will see something else. In case you haven't noticed, we're going to be traveling through German-friendly Hungary, and he'll be very conspicuous."

Cliff crossed his arms. "Just say it, it's because I'm black."

Mehara grabbed the trousers from the SS officer's discarded pile of clothes. "Sadik, stay with your friend. If you're more than ten feet apart, the deflection won't work. Read my mind and see how to do it."

Sadik gazed at her as if reading a book. She slipped into the black trousers, put on the officer's boots, and pulled the gold dress over her head. She threw the white shirt on, over her strapless black brassiere, and glared at Cliff and Sadik when they pretended to stare at the ground.

"Oh *please*," she said. "I've had to endure your thoughts ever since I've been on that bench back there."

They looked embarrassed and then ran to join Brande. I could feel his magic subtly working as he laid hidden traps for SS officers who may try to follow us or come down the pathway from the north. I cleared my voice. "Do you know if...Master Priya survived?"

Her eyes watered and her voice grew hoarse. "Octavian drained him."

"No..." I gasped and almost doubled over.

I wasn't particularly fond of Master Priya, but he had that final page that vindicated the Drifter and spoke about closing the rifts. If Octavian destroyed him, then I didn't know how I'd be able to recover the information I so desperately needed. This also meant that Octavian now possessed the powers of a Master Mentalist in addition to all the other ones he already had. I could only imagine what the Cruenti Master had planned for the wizards who were taken prisoner--and then, there was Bianca. I didn't even want to think of what she'd have to endure if we couldn't reach her in time. We needed to find the Den, not only to save the others, but also to pay them back for what they've done to us and to the entire world.

Mehara wiped her teary eyes with the back of her hand. "I...wanted to tell you that I'm sorry about Kenneth Aspen. I've never agreed with what Hotaru did at that safe house. I

329

can also see in your mind the truth about that missing page, and who you truly are."

I gave her a nod of acknowledgement. "Thank you."

She sniffed. "What do you want to do when we make it to Switzerland?"

"Contact the British government. They have a talisman that can lead to the Den. We'll regroup and gather everyone willing to join us, and then we go and take back the people they've kidnapped, and destroy Octavian and the Black Wolves once and for all."

A large explosion boomed west of us, and smoke rose into the sky. The burst of gunfire drowned out the birds chirping, and faint shouts could be heard in the distance. Brande motioned for us to join him and Cliff and Sadik. We ran over to them, and Brande took my hand in his.

"Are you ready?" he asked.

"I don't really have a choice. I have to be."

We took off parallel to the cobblestone pathway. The forest's beauty had been marred by the smoke, fire, and blood. We stopped only once near the gardens for a quick rest, to drink water, and collect edible plants and wild berries. Then it was time to run again. I caught a glimpse of the old Tower that stood just above the tree line. Most of it was gone, and only a burned shell remained. The image of the Broken Tower impressed itself on my mind, and I pondered if this would've happened no matter what.

My thoughts turned to Neal, and I offered up a quick prayer for his safety. I felt an odd sense of calm, knowing that both he and Mehara had once sought to hunt me down, but were now willing to help. They gave me a chance. I was also glad to have Brande at my side, and the knowledge that I could close the rifts. Now all I had to do was learn *how*. Despite what had happened today, I believed there was hope for me...and there was still hope for the entire world.

***

About The Author

Alesha Escobar is the author of *The Tower's Alchemist (The Gray Tower Trilogy, #1)* and is currently working on the final book of the Trilogy. If you've enjoyed this read, please share your review online and recommend it to others!

Made in the USA
Lexington, KY
03 January 2015